Carol Shields

was born and raised in Chicago and has lived in Canada since 1957. She studied at Hanover College and the University of Ottawa. Author of six novels, including *The Republic of Love*, which was shortlisted for the 1992 *Guardian* Fiction Prize, and *The Stone Diaries*, which was shortlisted for the 1993 Booker Prize, Carol Shields has also written three volumes of poetry and numerous short stories. She now lives in Winnipeg and spends each summer in France.

CAROL SHIELDS

Mary Swann

Flamingo
An Imprint of HarperCollins*Publishers*

Flamingo
An Imprint of HarperCollins *Publishers*
77–85 Fulham Palace Road,
Hammersmith, London W6 8JB

Published by Flamingo 1993
9 8 7 6 5 4

Previously published in Paladin 1992

First published in Great Britain by
Fourth Estate Limited 1990

Author photograph by Gerry Kopelow

ISBN 0 586 09151 3

Set in Garamond

Printed and bound in Great Britain by
Caledonian International Book Manufacturing Ltd, Glasgow, G64

For Sara Ellisyn Shields

Swann

The rivers of this country
Shrink and crack and kill
And the waters of my body
Grow invisible.

Mary Swann

Sarah Maloney

1

As recently as two years ago, when I was twenty-six, I dressed in ratty jeans and a sweatshirt with lettering across the chest. That's where I was. Now I own six pairs of beautiful shoes, which I keep, when I'm not wearing them, swathed in tissue paper in their original boxes. Not one of these pairs of shoes costs less than a hundred dollars.

Hanging in my closet are three dresses (dry clean only), two expensive suits and eight silk blouses in such colours as hyacinth and brandy. Not a large wardrobe, perhaps, but richly satisfying. I've read my Thoreau, I know real wealth lies in the realm of the spirit, but still I'm a person who can, in the midst of depression, be roused by the rub of a cashmere scarf in my fingers.

My name is Sarah Maloney and I live alone. Professionally — this is something people like to know these days — I'm a feminist writer and teacher who's having second thoughts about the direction of feminist writing in America. For twenty-five years we've been crying: *My life is my own.* A moving cry, a resounding cry, but what does it *mean*? (Once I knew exactly what freedom meant and now I have no idea. Naturally I resent this loss of knowledge.)

Last night Brownie, who was sharing my bed as he does most Tuesday nights, accused me of having a classic case of burn-out, an accusation I resist. Oh, I can be restless and difficult! Some days Virginia Woolf is the only person in the universe I want to talk to; but she's dead, of course, and wouldn't like me anyway. Too flip. And Mary Swann. Also dead. Exceedingly dead.

These moods come and go. Mostly Ms. Maloney is a cheerful woman, ah indeed, indeed! And very busy. Up at seven, a three-kilometre run in Washington Park — see her yupping along in even metric strides — then home to wheat toast and pure orange juice. Next a shower, and then she gets dressed in her beautiful, shameful clothes.

I check myself in the mirror: *Hello there*, waving long, clean, unpolished nails. I'll never require make-up. At least not for another ten years. Then I pick up my purse-cum-briefcase, Italian, $300, and sally forth. *Sally forth*, the phrase fills up my mouth like a bubble of foam. I'm attentive to such phrases. Needful of them, I should say.

I don't have a car. Off I go on foot, out into a slice of thick, golden October haze, down Sixty-second to Cottage Grove, along Cottage Grove, swinging my bag from my shoulder to give myself courage. Daylight muggings are common in my neighbourhood, and I make it a point to carry only five dollars, a fake watch, and a dummy set of keys. As I walk along, I keep my Walkman turned up high. No Mozart now, just a little cushion of soft rock to help launch the day with hope and maybe protect me from evil. I wear a miraculous broad-brimmed hat. The silky hem of my excellent English raincoat hisses just at knee length. I have wonderful stockings and have learned to match them with whatever I'm wearing.

"Good morning, Dr. Maloney," cries the department secretary when I arrive at the university. "Good morning, Ms. Lundigan," I sing back. This formal greeting is a ritual only. The rest of the time I call her Lois, or Lo, and she calls me Sarah or Sare. She's the age of my mother and has blood-red nails and hair so twirled and compact it looks straight from the wig factory. Her typing is nothing less than magnificent. Clean, sharp, uniform, with margins that *zing*. She hands me the mail and a copy of my revised lecture notes.

Today, in ten minutes, Lord help me, I'll be addressing one hundred students, ninety of them women, on the subject of "Amy Lowell: An American Enigma." At two o'clock, after a quick cheese on pita, I'll conduct my weekly seminar on "Women in Midwestern Fiction." Around me at the table will be seven bright postgraduate faces, each of them throwing off kilowatts of womanly brilliance, so that the whole room becomes charged and expectant and nippy with intelligence.

Usually, afterwards, the whole bunch of us goes off for a beer. In the taproom on Sixty-second we create a painterly scene, an oil portrait — women sitting in a circle, dark coats thrown over the backs of chairs, earrings swinging, elbows and shoulders keeping the composition lively, glasses held thoughtfully to thoughtful lips, rolling eyes, bawdiness, erudition.

They forget what time it is. They forget where they are — that they're sitting in a taproom on Sixty-second in the city of Chicago in the fall of the year in the twentieth century. They're too busy talking, thinking, defining terms, revising history, plotting their term papers, their theses, and their lives so that no matter what happens they'll keep barrelling along that lucent dotted line they've decided must lead to the future.

2

Last night my good friend Brownie — Sam Brown, actually — aged thirty, earning his living as a dealer in rare books, living in an Old Town apartment decorated in mission-revival fashion, son of a State of Maine farm labourer, dropped in to chat about the theme of castration in women's books. While I was demurring a little about the way in which he arrives at his critical judgements — like a noisy carpet-sweeper darting under obscure chairs and tables — he dropped the golden name of Mary Swann. "Your Mary," he announced, "is a prime example of the female castrator."

That surprised me, though I knew Brownie had been reading Mary Swann's book, since I had lent him my only copy; and I demanded proof for his conclusion. He was prepared for this — he knows me well, too well after all these months — and he pulled from his jacket pocket a piece of folded paper. Clearing his throat and holding his head to one side, he read:

A simple tree may tell
The truth — but
Not until
Its root is cut.

The bitter leaf
Attacks the stem,
Demands a brief
Delirium.

"Preposterous," I said. "She's talking about societal and family connections and you're thinking about crude anatomy. Roots! Stems!"

He smiled, refolded his piece of paper, and invited me for a walk in the park. We set off into the cold, I in my winter things — knitted scarf, woolly hat — and with my collar turned up to my ears. I slipped my arm through Brownie's. Cordially. Affectionately.

I am fond of him, *too* fond, too fond by far, and he may well love me, but with an ardour sunk under a drift of vagueness, as though he's playing through that crinkled head of his scenes of former conversations and encounters. He's too lazy, too preoccupied, too much a man who dallies and dreams and too given to humming under his breath that insouciant little tune that declares that nothing really *matters*. That is why I'm drawn to him, of course, seeing him as an antidote to my own passionate seizures. For Brownie, today's castration theory will be tomorrow's soap bubbles. His mind, like a little wooden shuttle, is forever thinking up theories to keep himself amused. Being amused is his chief ambition. And getting rich. Dear Brownie.

We walked along in silence for a few minutes, watchful for muggers, kicking the piles of fallen leaves. The cold was intense for so early in October. Brownie gave me a quick hug and, putting on his fake cockney accent, said, "I thought you'd be chuffed that I gave your bird a turn."

I am, *I am*, I told him. I'd been urging him for two years to read Mary Swann, ever since I wandered into his store on Madison Street, The Brown Study, and found no more than half a shelf of poetry. Inferior poetry. We had an argument that first day. Real money, he told me, big money, was in vintage comic books. He was depending on his Plastic Man collection to keep him in his old age. Poetry gave him pyloric spasms, economically speaking, and he only carried the biggies, Carl Sandburg and Robert Frost and that ilk. Volumes of poetry didn't sell, didn't move. Whereas a first edition of *The Sun Also Rises*. . . . And Updike. And lately, Ivy Compton-Burnett. I like to argue with Brownie about such things. He shouts. I shout back. An extra piquancy settles on us, a round little umbrella of heat. Still, one can't count on Brownie.

I like to think that my view of him is detached.

This man has serious limitations, I tell myself. I should overlook the cynical addiction to comic books. I should discount that smile, which flashes too readily, too indiscriminately. What is the value of a smile anyway?

Still he has a certain erudition, an appealing, splintery intelligence that, like the holes in his sweaters, conceals a painstaking grasp on the business of reality. Yes, but he is a lightweight; though he denies it, he thinks of a book as a commodity. Yet, a lightweight can be good company at times, especially when that lightweightedness is so arduously cultivated and so obviously a defence. Or is it? That shunting breath and laughter of his ripples with energy. But can he be trusted, a man whose brain dances and performs and hoists itself on market trends and whimsical twenty-four-hour theories? No. Yes. Possibly.

I keep my objectivity about Brownie polished and at the ready, yet again and again it yields to wild unaccountable happiness when in his company. Yes, but he is indolent. Ah, but under the indolence he has ambition. That may be, but it's a scheming ambition. Remember what he once said, that he'd cheat his own granny to make a buck. He cares for nothing. But why should he? Why should anyone? I don't altogether understand him, but what does understanding between people really mean — only that we like them or don't like them. I adore Brownie. But with reservations. Last night I was close to loving him, even though he dumped my Mary Swann into the same bathtub with Sigmund Freud. He didn't mean a word of it though; I could almost bet on it.

3

For a number of years, for a number of reasons, I had a good many friends I didn't really like. One of them was a fellow graduate student, a downy-cheeked boy-man called Olaf Thorkelson who kept hounding me to marry him. He was young, wise, opinionated, good, and joyful, but weak at the centre. What I wanted was a man of oak. My mother had one, my grandmother had one, but at that time I had only Olaf.

I told him that I was afraid of marriage, that it could only lead to a house in Oak Park and the tennis club and twin beds and growing deaf. He said he could see my point, but that at least we could live as lovers. No, I said, that wouldn't be fair to him. He said he didn't care a fuck for fairness. I said that fairness was the rule I lived by. (A fugitive conscience is better than no conscience at all.) This went on all one spring and left me so exhausted that by June I had to go to bed for a week. Oh yes, the indomitable Sarah, slain by indecision.

The sight of me spread weakly in bed moved Olaf at last to guilt, and he urged me to go away for a bit and "think things through." His sister had a friend who owned a cottage on a lake in Wisconsin, and since it was empty for the summer he would get me the key and put me on a Greyhound bus.

Two days later I was there, walking on a pebbly strip of beach and admiring the cleanliness of cirrus clouds and bright air. The cabin was a flimsy, friendly affair with wood floors that sloped and creaked and a fireplace so smoky and foul that on chilly nights I lit the cookstove instead for warmth.

I particularly loved that cookstove, the prepossessing way it stood away from the wall, all bulging girth and black radiance. The wondrous word *negritude* formed on my tongue as I opened its door and poked in newspaper and kindling and lit a match. At the top of its heat it shuddered and hissed like a human presence, and I thought how fortunate a woman I was to have such a good, natural, uncritical companion at this time in my life. All month I amused myself by making sweet soufflés — rum and apricot and lemon — and in that black hole of an oven they rose to perfection.

When I wasn't making soufflés I plunged into the singular pleasure of cottage housekeeping. There are rewards in cleaning things — everyone should know this — the corners of rooms, dresser drawers, and such. I concocted a primitive twig broom and bashed joyfully at cobwebs and dustballs. A clothesline that I found stretched between two trees seemed to say to me: *Isn't life simple when pared down to its purities?* In the cabin, resting on an open shelf, were an eggbeater, a wooden spoon, an iron frying pan, four bowls, four cups, and a plastic dishpan, which I emptied out the door on to a patch of weeds. Swish, and it was gone.

The cabin had a screened porch where I took to sitting in the hottest part of the afternoon, attentive to the quality of filtered light and to the precarious new anchoring of my life plan. Serenity descended as the days wore on. I absorbed the sunny, freckled world around me. Olaf could be dealt with. His supple sexual bulk faded, giving way to a simple checklist. My thesis revision could also be managed, and so could the next two years of my life; that was as wide a span of time as I cared to think about. In the distance was the heaving, spewing lake, broad as a small sea and impossible to see across. The long afternoons dipped and shimmered. Flies grazed stupidly against the screen. "Hello, fellow creatures," I said, suspecting I was going blobby in the head but welcoming the sensation.

Seated in a wicker chair on that dim porch I seemed to inhabit an earlier, pre-grad-school, pre-Olaf self. My thesis, *The Female Prism*, and the chapter that had to be rewritten were forgotten, swirled away like the dishwater. Instead there were trashy old magazines to read, piles of them in a mildewed wicker basket, and a shelf full of cottage novels with greenish, fly-spotted pages. I read my way through most of them, feeling winsomely trivial, feeling redemptively ordinary, and, toward the end of the month, at the end of the shelf, I discovered an odd little book of poems written by a woman named Mary Swann. The title of the book was *Swann's Songs*.

4

At that time Mary Swann had been dead for more than fifteen years. Her only book was this stapled pamphlet printed in Kingston, Ontario, in 1966.

There are exactly one hundred pages in the book and the pages contain one hundred and twenty-five poems. The cover design is a single musical note stamped on rather cheap grey paper. Only about twenty copies of *Swann's Songs* are known to have survived out of the original printing of two hundred and fifty — a sad commentary on literary values, Brownie says, but not surprising in the case of an unknown poet. How Mary Swann's book found its way down from Canada to a cottage on a lonely Wisconsin lake was a mystery, *is* a mystery. A case of obscurity seeking obscurity.

Even today Swann's work is known only to a handful of scholars, some of whom dismiss her as a *poète naïve*. Her rhythms are awkward. Clunky rhymes, even her half-rhymes, tie her lines to the commonplace, and her water poems, which are considered to be her best work, have a prickly roughness that exposes the ordinariness of the woman behind them, a woman people claim had difficulty with actual speech. She was a farmer's wife, uneducated. It's said in the Nadeau area of Ontario that she spoke haltingly, shyly, and about such trivial matters as the weather, laying hens, and recipes for jams and jellies. She also crocheted doilies. I want to weep when I think of those hundreds of circular yellowing doilies Mary Swann made over the years, the pathetic gentility they represented and the desperation they hint at.

Her context, a word Willard Lang adores, was narrowly rural. A few of her poems, in fact, were originally published in the back pages of local newspapers: "A Line a Day," "Rimes for Our Times," and so on. It was only after she was killed that someone, an odd-ball newspaper editor named Frederic Cruzzi, put together and printed her little book, *Swann's Songs*.

Poor Mary Swann. That's how I think of her, *poor* Mary Swann, with her mystical ear for the tune of words, cheated of life, cheated of recognition. In spite of the fact that there's growing interest in her work — already thirty applications are in for the symposium in January — she's still relatively unknown.

Willard Lang, the swine, believes absolutely that Swann will never be classed as a major poet. He made this pronouncement at the MLA meeting last spring, speaking with a little ping of sorrow and a sideways tug at his ear. Rusticity, he claimed, kept a poet minor and, sadly, there seemed to be no exceptions to this rule, Burns being a different breed of dog. My Mary's unearthly insights and spare musicality appear to certain swinish critics (Willard is not the only one) to be accidental and, therefore, no more than quaint. And no modern academic knows what to do with her rhymes, her awful moon/June/September/remember. It gives them a headache, makes them snort through their noses. What can be done, they say, with this rustic milkmaid in her Victorian velours!

I tend to get unruly and defensive when it comes to those bloody rhymes. Except for the worst clinkers (giver/liver) they seem to me no more obtrusive than a foot tapped to music or a bell ringing in the distance. Besides, the lines trot along too fast to allow weight or breath to adhere to their endings. There's a busy breedingness about them. "A Swannian urgency" was how I put it in my first article on Mary.

Pompous phrase! I could kick myself when I think about it.

5

I live in someone else's whimsy, a Hansel and Gretel house on a seventeen-foot lot on the south side of Chicago. Little paned casement windows, a fairy-tale door, a sweet round chimney and, on the roof, cedar shakes pretending to be thatch. It's a wonderful roof, a roof that gladdens the eye, peaky and steep and coming down in soft waves over the windows with fake Anne Hathaway fullness. The house was built in 1930 by an eccentric professor of Elizabethan literature, a bachelor with severe scoliosis and a club foot, and after his death it was, briefly, a restaurant and then a Democratic precinct office. Now it's back to being a house. At the rear is an iron balcony (loosely attached, but I intend to have it seen to) where I stand on fine days and gaze out over a small salvage yard crowded with scrap iron and a massive public housing project full of brawling families and broken glass.

I bought my freak of a house when the first royalties started coming in for *The Female Prism*. I had to live somewhere, and my lawyer, a truly brilliant woman named Virginia Goodchild, said it could only happen to a person once, turning a Ph.D. thesis into a bestseller, and that I'd better sink my cash fast into a chunk of real estate. She'd found me just the place, she said, the cutest house in all Chicagoland.

This house has been sweet to me, and in return I've kept it chaste; that is, I haven't punished it with gaiety. No posters or prayer rugs or art deco glass here, and no humanoid shapes draped in Indonesian cotton. I've got tables; I've got a more than decent Oriental rug; I've got lamps. (Lord, make me Spartan, but not yet.) In my kitchen cupboards I've got plates and cups that *match*. In the dining-room, admittedly only nine feet by nine feet, I've got — now this is possibly a *little* outré — a piano that used to sit in a bar at the

Drake Hotel, and after I finish my paper on Swann for the symposium in January, I intend to take a few piano lessons. Brownie says playing the piano is as calming as meditation and less damaging to the brain cells.

I hope so, because I've never been able to see the point of emptying one's mind of thought. Our thoughts are all we have. I love my thoughts, even when they take me up and down sour-smelling byways where I'd rather not venture. Whatever flickers on in my head is mine and I want it, all the blinking impulses and inclinations and connections and weirdness, and especially those bright purple flares that come streaming out of nowhere, announcing that you're at some mystic juncture or turning point and that you'd better pay attention.

Luckily for me, there have been several such indelible moments, moments that have pressed hard on that quirkly narrative I like to think of as the story of my life. For example: at age eight, reading *The Wind in the Willows*. Then saying goodbye to my blameless father (bone cancer). At age fourteen, reading Charlotte Brontë — Charlotte, not Emily. Then saying goodbye, but only tentatively as it turned out, to my mother, a woman called Gladys Shockley Maloney. Next, reading Germaine Greer. Then saying goodbye to my virginity. (Goodbye and goodbye and goodbye.) Then reading Mary Swann and discovering how a human life can be silently snuffed out. Next saying goodbye to Olaf and Oak Park and three months of marriage, and then buying my queer toy house downtown, which I fully intended to sell when the market turned. But unsignalled, along came one of those brilliant purple turning points.

It came because of my fame. My mother has never understood the fame that overtook me in my early twenties. She never believed it was really me, that mouth on the book jacket, yammering away. Neither, for that matter, did I. It was like going through an epidemic of measles, except that I was the only one who got sick.

Six months after *The Female Prism* appeared in the bookstores someone decided I should go on a book-promotion tour — as though a book that was number six on the nonfiction bestseller list needed further pumping up. I started out in Boston, then went to New York, Philadelphia, Pittsburgh, and Cleveland, then hopped to Louisville, skipped to Denver and Houston, and ended up one overcast afternoon on a TV talk show in L.A. The woman who interviewed me was lanky and menacing, wore a fur vest and was dangerously framed by lengths of iodine-glazed hair. To quell her I talked about the surrealism of scholarship. The pretensions. The false systems. The arcane lingo. The macho domination. The garrison mentality. The inbred arrogance.

She leaned across and patted me on the knee and said, "You're not coming from arrogance, sweetie; you're coming from naked need."

Ping! My brain shuddered purple. I was revealed, uncloaked, and as soon as possible I crept back to Chicago, back to my ginger-cookie house on the south side, and made up my mind about one thing: that as long as I lived I would stay in this house. (At least for the next five years.) I felt like kissing the walls and throwing my arms around the punky little newel post and burying my face in its vulva-like carving. This was home. And it seemed I was someone who needed a home. I could go into my little house, my awful neediness and I, and close the doors and shut the curtains and stare at my enduring clutter and be absolutely *still*. Like the theoreticians who currently give me a bad case of frenzies, I'd made a discovery: my life was my own, but I needed a place where I could get away from it.

6

God is dead, peace is dead, the sixties are dead, John Lennon and Simone de Beauvoir are dead, the women's movement is dozing — checking its inventory, let's say — so what's left?

The quotidian is what's left. Mary Swann understood that, if nothing else.

A morning and an afternoon and
Night's queer knuckled hand
Hold me separate and whole
Stitching tight my daily soul.

She spelled it out. The mythic heavings of the universe, so baffling, so incomprehensible, but when squeezed into digestible day-shaped bytes, made swimmingly transparent. Dailiness. The diurnal unit, cloudless and soluble. No wonder the first people on earth worshipped heavenly bodies; between the rising and the setting of the sun their little lives sprouted all manner of shadows and possibilities. Whenever I meet anyone new, I don't say, "Tell me about your belief system." I say, "Tell me about your average day."

Dailiness to be sure has its hard deposits of ennui, but it is also, as Mary Swann suggests, redemptive. I busy my brain with examples.

Every day of his short life, for instance, my father pulled on a pair of cotton socks, and almost every day he turned to my mother and said, "Cotton lets the skin breathe." He also made daily pronouncements on meat that had been frozen: "Breaks down the cell structure," he liked to say. "Destroys the nutrients." In the same way he objected to butter, white bread, sugar — "attacks the blood cells" — garlic (same reason), and anything that had green pepper in it.

He was otherwise a mild man, a math teacher in a west-side high school. His pale red hair, the drift of it over his small ears, his freckled neck and the greenish suits he wore in the classroom — all these things kept him humble. His small recurring judgements on garlic and green pepper were, I've come to see, a kind of vanity for him, an appetite that had to be satisfied, but especially the innocent means by which he was able to root himself in the largeness of time. Always begin a newspaper on the editorial page, he said. Never trust a man who wears sandals or diamond jewellery. These small choices and strictures kept him occupied and anchored while the cancer inched its way along his skeleton.

My mother, too, sighing over her morning cup of coffee and lighting a cigarette, is simply digging in for the short run. And so is my sister, Lena, with her iron pills and coke and nightly shot of Brahms; and Olaf with his shaving ritual, and Brownie with his daily ingestion of flattery and cash. Who can blame them? Who wants to? Habit is the flywheel of society, conserving and preserving and dishing up tidy, edible slices of the cosmos. And there's much to be said for a steady diet. Those newspaper advice-givers who urge you to put a little vinegar in your life are toying, believe me, with your sanity.

Every day, for instance, I eat a cheese on pita for lunch, then an apple. I see no reason to apologize for this habit. Around two-thirty in the afternoon Lois Lundigan and I share a pot of tea, alternating Prince of Wales, Queen Mary, and Earl Grey. She pours. I wash the cups. Sisterhood. Between three and five, unless it's my seminar day, I sit in my office at my desk and work on articles or plan my lectures. At five-thirty I stretch, pack up my beautiful briefcase, say good night to Lois and hit the pavement. The sun's still keyed up, hot and yellow. Every day I walk along the same route, past grimy shrubs and run-down stores and apartment buildings and trees that become leafier as I approach Fifty-seventh Street. About this time I start to feel a small but measurable buzzing in the brain that makes my legs move along in double time. There I am, a determined piece of human matter, but adrift on a busy street that has suddenly become a conduit — a pipeline possessing the power of suction. Something, a force more than weariness, is drawing me home.

There's no mystery about this; I know precisely what pulls me along. Not food or sex or rest or succour but the thought of the heap of mail that's waiting for me just inside my front door.

Among my friends I'm known as the Queen of Correspondence, maintaining, in this day of long-distance phone calls and even longer silences, what is considered to be a *vast* network. This is my corner on quaintness. My crochet work. My apple sauce. Mail comes pouring in, national and international, postcards and air letters and queer stamps crowded together in the corners of bulging envelopes. Letters from old school friends await me or letters from sisters in the movement. Perhaps a scrawl from my six-year-old nephew, Franklin, and my real sister, Lena, in London. My editor in New York is forever showering me with witty, beseeching notes. Virginia Goodchild, my former lawyer, writes frequently from New Orleans where she now has her practice. Olaf, in Tübingen, keeps in touch. So do last year's batch of graduate students and the year before's, a sinuous trail of faces and words. There are always, always, letters waiting. A nineteenth-century plenitude. I tear them open, I burn and freeze, I consume them with heathenish joy, smiling as I read, tapping my foot, and planning what I'll write back, what epics out of my ongoing life I'll select, touch up, and entrust to the international mails.

Mailless weekends are hell, but Monday's bounty partially compensates. Every evening I write a letter, sometimes two, while the rest of the world plays Scrabble or watches TV or files its nails or whatever the rest of the world does. I write letters that are graceful and agreeable, far more graceful and agreeable than I am in my face-to-face encounters. My concern, my well-governed wit, my closet kindness all crowd to the fore, revealing that rouged, wrinkled,

Russian-like persona that I like to think is my true self. (Pick up a pen and a second self squirms out.) The maintenance of my persona and the whole getting and sending of letters provide necessary traction to my quotidian existence, give me a kick, a lift, a jolt, a fix, a high, a way of seizing time and keeping it in order.

Today there's a thick letter from Morton Jimroy in California. A four-pager or I'm an elephant's eyebrow. I can't get it open fast enough. There I stand, reading it, still in my coat and hat with my beautiful briefcase thrown down on the floor along with the mutilated envelope.

I read it once, twice, then put it aside. While eating dinner — a boned chicken breast steamed in grapefruit juice and a branch of broccoli *al dente* — I read it a third time. I've been writing to Morton Jimroy for almost a year now and find him a teasing correspondent.

Today's letter is particularly problematic, containing as it does one of Jimroy's ambushing suggestions. I'll wait exactly one week before I reply and then — now I'm eating dessert, which is a slice of hazelnut torte from the local bakery — I'll send him one of my two-draft specials.

It's a guilty secret of mine that I write two kinds of letters, one-drafters and two-drafters. For old friends I bang out exuberant single-spaced typewritten letters, all the grammar jangled loose with dashes and exclamation points and reckless transitions. Naturally, I trust these old friends to read my letters charitably and overlook the awful girlish breathlessness and say to themselves, "Well, Sarah leads such a busy life, we're lucky to get *any* kind of letter out of her."

But in my two-draft letters I mind my manners, sometimes even forsaking my word processor for the pen. Only yesterday I wrote a double-drafter to Syd Buswell in Ottawa. "Dear Professor Buswell," I wrote. "On behalf of the Steering Committee of the Swann Symposium, may I say how much we regret that you will not be presenting your paper in January. Nevertheless, we hope you will attend and participate in discussions." I keep myself humble, am mindful of paragraph coherence, and try for a tincture of charm.

For Morton Jimroy, *the* Morton Jimroy, biographer of Ezra Pound, John Starman, and now Mary Swann, I get out my best letter paper and linger over my longhand, my lovely springy l's and e's, aglide on their invisible blue wires. And I always do a second draft.

Once again — now I'm having coffee, feet up on the coffee table —I read Jimroy's letter. Though his home is in Winnipeg, Canada, this letter is from California where he's spending a year putting together his notes on Mary Swann. Today's letter, like his others, is imbued with a sense of pleading, but for what? — who can tell? His are letters from which the voice has been drained off, and instead there's a strenuous concentration, each casual phrase propped up by rhetoric and positioned so as to signal candour — but a candour undercut by the pain of deliberate placement. Ring around the rosy. How am I supposed to interpret all this? Painstaking letters are born of pain; I must be generous, I must overlook transparent strategy, stop sniffing for a covert agenda. But there's something unsettling in the way he's always wringing a response from me. I am summoned, commanded to comment and comfort and offer gifts of flattery.

He has one rare quality that I suspect is genuine: an urge for confession, or at least intimacy. We've never met and have no claims on each other, and there's no real reason for him to tell me about the depression he suffered after his book on Starman was published, a long painful depression, which — he told me all this in a previous letter — neither medication nor analysis was able to heal.

My dear Sarah,

I am someone who can understand how Flaubert must have felt when seized with doubt about the validity of art, his terrifying perception — false, thank God — that art was nothing but a foolish and childish plaything. This was exactly the state of my mind when Oxford Press sent me my advance copy of the Starman biography some years back. It arrived, I remember, at breakfast time — forgive me if I've written this before — swathed in a padded envelope. I opened it at once, regarded its gleaming cover and experienced — nothing. The granola and milk in my bowl had more reality than this pound and a half of text with its appendices, its execrable, sprawling annotation, and, worst of all, its footnotes. These footnotes, I realized at that moment, were footnotes on Starman's footnotes. And I could imagine what would occur in the future, as surely as day must follow night: a graduate student would one day construct footnotes on *my* footnotes to *Starman's* footnotes. The thought brought a physical sense of shame. I felt not only self-disgust but the fierce sadness of a wasted life, the conviction that I had done nothing but dally with the dallyings of other human beings. Such a feeling of depression — perhaps you know, though I hope you don't — can be swift and overwhelming. It seemed to me at that moment that not a single man on earth had ever spoken the truth. We were all, every last one of us, liars and poseurs.

Ah, but on that same morning, in the same lot of mail, came the latest issue of *PMLA* (a periodical, by the way, that I often feel contributes to the gastritis of the lit business). On this particular morning I opened the journal to your article on Swann. Who is this Mary Swann? I wondered. And who is this Sarah Maloney? I read quickly through your introduction to *our* poet. And then came to those eight quoted lines from "March Morning." (By coincidence, it *was* a March morning, a murky, tenebrous Winnipeg morning.) Reading, I felt a oneness with this Mary Swann. (I never think of her by her Christian name alone, do you?) I felt that same "Iron flower of my hand/Cheated by captured ice and/Earth and sand." (I have little patience with those who consider Swann a primitive because she didn't use four-syllable words. She was — is — a poet of great sophistication of mind.) But it was the vigour of the lines that struck me at first, the way they shifted and worked together, cross-bonded like plywood sheets. (You see how she infects me with her colloquial images.) My only disappointment was in finding she had written so little, though one is grateful for what does exist, and there are the love poems to come — *if* they come, I've never trusted Lang — and, of course, the notebook.

About Swann's notebook, I am wondering once again if I can persuade you to change your mind about sharing its contents, at least partially. My research here has gone extremely well, but I've been frustrated by having to rely on secondary and tertiary sources almost exclusively. (Swann's daughter, whom I've been interviewing, is a woman of opaque memory and curious insensitivity — she has, for instance, saved only the most cursory notes from her mother, not the confiding letters that I am sure must have existed.) It seems to me that a page or two from the notebook — I would of course pay for photocopying and so on — would bring our graceful Swann out of the jungle of conjecture and, as she herself would say —

Into the carpeted clearing
Into the curtained light
Behind the sun's loud staring
Away from the sky's hard bite.

Do, Sarah, let me know if this request from a fellow scholar
is impertinent. I feel, and I am sure you will agree with me, that
Mary Swann belongs to all of us, to the world, that is — her
poems, her scraps and ciphers, her poor paltry remains.

It now looks as though I will be able to come to the symposium
after all, and I will be happy to deliver a few remarks, as you
suggest, on the progress of the Life. I am sorry to hear that Buswell
has cancelled, though it seems a trifle paranoid of him to think
his notes were stolen. Mislaid, perhaps; but — stolen!

I so look forward to meeting you in person, though I know
you already as a dear friend. Such is the power and warmth of
your letters.

With affection,

Morton Jimroy

He's ingenious, Morton Jimroy. But worrying. Every sentence,
the way it shapes itself around a tiny, tucked grimace — I feel the
weight of it all. (Lifting the paper to my face I inhale the faint smell
of cigarettes.) I will have to write him a careful letter. (Now I'm
dressed in the old sweatshirt I wear to bed, part of my dark ritual.
I've already phoned Brownie to whisper good night, and I've
propped myself up in bed with my reading light shining over my
shoulder.) I will have to tell the good persevering Morton Jimroy
how pleased I was to hear from him, how warmed I was to hear
him assert, once again, that it was I who introduced him to the work
of Mary Swann. All of this is true. It will flow out of my pen
untroubled.

But I will have to say *no* to him about the notebook. Politely.
Correctly. But conceding nothing. *No*, Morton. I cannot. I am sorry,
Morton. I regret. I wish. I understand your position. But no, no,
no, no, no. I am not yet ready to publish the contents of Mary
Swann's notebook.

Dear Morton. (I'm sliding into sleep, adrift between layers of consciousness.) Dear Morton. Soon the prima facie evidence will be in
the public domain, available to all, et cetera, et cetera, but now,

for a few months longer, until January, please forgive me (yawn), Mary Swann's notebook is mine.

7

Happiness is not my greatest need. My greatest need is to feel that every part of me is fully in use, or *engagé* as people used to say a mere ten years ago, and that all my sensory equipment is stretched as nervously as possible between a state of apprehension and a posture of pounce. I want my brain to be all sinew and thrum, chime and clerestory, crouch and attack.

Which more or less describes my condition on Saturday, a gilded October afternoon, when I attended a new exhibition of pencil drawings executed by my extraordinary friend and sometime mentor, Peggy O'Reggis.

I had spent a frivolous morning in bed with Virginia Woolf, lunched on herrings in sour cream, and then taken the bus down to the Dearborn Gallery. By the time I got there the room was filled with a zesty mix of friends and strangers, mostly between the ages of twenty and forty, all of them chatting, nodding their heads, embracing, drinking wine and peering with squinty eyes into Peggy's tiny crowded drawings, which always remind me of snapshots of the brain's prescient vibrations. The colours she favours include a lollipop pink and a rich oily green, and what she draws are ideas. With resolute angular turnings, each pencil line duplicates the way that precious commodity *thought* is launched and transformed. Here there was a calculated mimetic thrust, there a microscopic explosion of reason, here an intellectual equation of great tenderness and, next to it, a begging void exerting its airy magnetism.

As in her previous exhibitions, the drawings were all titled — for which, being part of the word culture, I thanked God. Images can speak, yes, but some of us need to be directed toward the port of entry. Yet there's never anything authoritarian about Peggy's titles, just a nudging, helpful "Untroubled Night" or "Open Heart" or, the one I most admired yesterday, "Vision Intercepted."

Standing before "Vision Intercepted" with my glass of red wine in hand, I experienced that sharp electrical fusing that sometimes occurs when art meets the mind head-on. Beside me, sharing my brief flight of transcendence, were a yellow-haired woman in a rawhide jacket and my old friend Stephen Stanhope, the juggler. We didn't speak, not even to exchange greetings, but instead continued to gaze. The moment stretched and stretched, the kind of phenomenon that happens so rarely that the experience of it must be cherished in silence and persuaded to linger as long as possible.

And so, riding home on the bus, I gave myself over to the closed eye's bright penetration, trying to call back the image of Peggy O'Reggis's circling, colliding lines and colours. A pattern or perhaps a sensual vibration began to dance across my retina and grope toward form. I summoned it, let it emerge, luxuriously let it have its way. But something kept spoiling my satisfaction, some nagging thought or worrying speck at the periphery of vision. I opened my eyes. The sun poured in the dirty wondows, warming my arm. A woman with a blanket-wrapped baby on her lap sat across from me, a slender, long-necked black woman with amber eyes, clearly infatuated with her child's beauty. With a free hand she stroked its knitted blanket. The baby made cooing sounds like a little fish and stared dreamily up into an advertisement for men's jockey shorts. In the ad, a man with a bulging crotch was leaping over a bonfire, an expression of rapture on his daft face. He and the small baby and the baby's mother and I seemed suddenly to form one of those random, hastily assembled families that are hatched in the small spaces of large cities and come riding atop a compendium of small pleasures. But today's pleasures, pungent though they were, made me less willing than usual to surrender my earlier perception.

What was it that was getting in the way? I poked part way into my subconscious, imagining a pencil in my hand. There was my usual catalogue of shame. Wasted time? Careless work? Had I forgotten to phone my mother? — no. Shopping to be done? Someone's feelings hurt?

Guilt has the power to extract merciless sacrifices, but it was not guilt that was interfering with my attempt to bring back the voluptuous sensation that briefly enclosed me in the Dearborn Gallery. It was something smaller and less formed, an act of neglect or loss that scuttled like an insect across my consciousness and that, because of the wine or the wooziness of the sunshine, I was unable to remember.

Later it came to me. It was midnight of the same day. I was ready to go to bed, but first I was locking the doors, checking the windows, turning out the lights, listening to the silence and darkness that blew through the house. My thoughts were of Mary Swann, how she must also have performed night rituals, though not the same ones as mine. I tried to imagine what these rituals might be. Might she have looked out the kitchen window into the windy, starry night, trying to guess at the next day's weather? Would she hook a screen door or perhaps set a kettle of soup or oats on the back of the woodstove? Perhaps there was a cat or dog that had to be let out, though she had never in her poems or in her notebook mentioned such a cat or dog.

And then I remembered — Lord! — what had been begging all day to be remembered. It was Mary Swann's notebook, which I keep on a bookshelf over my bed. I had not seen it there for several days.

8

In a sense I invented Mary Swann and am responsible for her.

No, too literary that. Better just say I discovered Mary Swann. Even Willard Lang admits (officially, too) that I am more or less — he is endlessly equivocal in the best scholarly tradition — *more or less* the discoverer of Swann's work. He has even committed this fact to print in a short footnote on page six of his 1983 paper "Swann's Synthesis," naming me, Sarah Maloney of Chicago, the one "most responsible for bringing the poet Mary Swann to public attention." This mention on Willard's part is an academic courtesy and no more.

Ah, but Willard's kind of courtesy amounts to a professional sawing off, a token coin dropped in a bank to permit future withdrawals. Willard Lang's nod in my direction — "S. Maloney must be cited as the one who" — is a simple declaration of frontier between authority and discovery, Willard being the authority, while S. Maloney (me) is given the smaller, slightly less distinguished role of discoverer.

In truth, no one really discovers anyone; it's the stickiest kind of arrogance even to think in such terms. Mary Swann discovered herself, and therein, suspended on tissues of implausibility, like a hammock without strings, hangs the central mystery: how did she do it? Where in those bleak Ontario acres, that littered farmyard, did she find the sparks that converted emblematic substance into rolling poetry? Chickens, outhouses, wash-day, woodpiles, porch, husband, work-boots, overalls, bedstead, filth. That's the stuff this woman had to work with.

On the other hand, it's a legacy from the patriarchy, a concomitant of conquest, the belief that poets shape their art from materials that are mysterious and inaccessible. Women have been knitting socks for centuries, and probably they've been constructing, in their heads, lines of poetry that never got written down. Mary Swann happened to have a pen, a Parker 51 as a matter of fact, as well as an eye for the surface of things. Plus the kind of heart-cracking persistence that made her sit down at the end of a tired day and box up her thoughts into quirky parcels of rhymed verse.

It was an incredible thing for a woman in her circumstances to do, and in the face of so much implausibility I sometimes chant to myself the simple list that braces and contains her. Girlhood in Belleville, Ontario; schooling limited; nothing known about mother; or father; worked for a year in a local bakery; married a farmer and moved to the Nadeau district, where she bore a daughter, wrote poems, and got herself killed at the age of fifty. That's all. How Jimroy intends to boil up a book out of this thin stuff is a mystery.

My own responsibility toward Mary Swann, as I see it, is custodial. If Olaf Thorkelson hadn't badgered me into near breakdown and driven me into the refuge of northern Wisconsin where Mary Swann's neglected book of poems fell like a bouquet into my hands, I would never have become Swann's watchwoman, her literary executor, her defender and loving caretaker. But, like it or not, that's what I am. Let others promote her and do their social and psychoanalytical sugar-jobs on her; but does anyone else — besides me that is — detect the little smiles breaking around her most dolorous lines? Willard Lang, swine incarnate, is capable of violating her for his own gain, and so is the absent-minded, paranoid, and feckless Buswell in Ottawa. Morton Jimroy means well, poor sap, but he'll try to catch her out or bend her into God's messenger or the handmaiden of Emily Dickinson; or else he'll stick her into a three-cornered constellation along with poor impotent Pound and that prating, penis-dragging Starman. Someone has to make sure she's looked after. Because her day is coming. Never mind what Willard Lang thinks. Mary Swann is going to be big, big, big. She's the right person at the right time for one thing: a woman, a survivor, self-created. A man like Morton Jimroy wouldn't be bothering with her if he didn't think she was going to take off. Willard wouldn't be wasting his time organizing a symposium if he didn't believe her reputation was ripe for the picking. These guys are greedy. They would eat her up, inch by inch. Scavengers. Brutes. This is a wicked world, and the innocent need protection.

Which is why I find it impossible to forgive myself for losing her notebook.

9

It's been lost for several days. Since Monday probably, maybe Tuesday.

I'm not willing yet to admit that it is *irretrievably* lost; it is just — what? — misplaced. Any day now, tomorrow maybe, I'll find it under a pile of letters in my desk drawer. It might have got slipped into a bookcase, it's so small, one of those little spiral notebooks the colour of cheap chocolate. It's just waiting, perversely, to surprise me one day when I least expect it. It might be under a corner of a rug. Or right out in plain sight somewhere, only my eyes are too frantic to focus on the spot.

I'm not a careless person, though I remind myself a dozen times a day, as a kind of palliating commentary, that this is not the first thing I've lost. Once, when I was married to Olaf, I lost my wedding ring. I was devastated, almost sick, and hadn't been able to tell Olaf about it because I knew he would see it as a portent; and there it was, two weeks later, in a little ceramic dish where I kept my paper-clips. Another time I lost my first-edition copy of *The Second Sex*, which I'd bought at Stanton's for ten bucks back in the good old days. For months I'd wandered around like a mad woman, wrenching cushions off chairs and wailing to the walls, "Books don't just get up and walk away." In the spring a dear friend,

Lorenzo Drouin, the medievalist, found it wedged behind a radiator in my living-room.

About the lost notebook my mother is sympathetic but vague. She asks if I've checked the pockets of my raincoat or lent it to a friend or thrown it out with the newspapers — preposterous suggestions all, the utterance of which points to her essential helplessness and to how little she understands my life. "It'll turn up," she murmurs and murmurs, my comforting plump spaniel of a mother. But helpless, helpless.

I visit my mother every Sunday. On Sunday morning in the city of Chicago other people wake up thinking: How will this day be spent? What surprises will it bring? Sunday is a day with a certain lustre on it, a certain hum. The unscheduled hours seduce or threaten, depending on circumstances, on money or friends or on health or weather; but there is always, I'm convinced, an anticipatory rustle, a curtain sliding open onto possibility.

Not for me, though. You might say I'm a professional daughter, or at least a serious hobbyist. On Sundays I get on the L and go to see my mother, who lives in a third-floor apartment on the west side. She expects me at 1:00 P.M. give or take five minutes. She watches from the window as I come trotting down the tree-lined street, slips the brass chain off the lock, and enfolds me in her heated feathery arms, saying, "Hi there, sweetie pie."

Immediately the two of us sit down in the dinette to a full dinner, roast chicken or ham with mashed potatoes, frozen peas or string beans, and for dessert ice cream in a cereal bowl. My mother and I talk and talk, and if I stop now to think of those scattered others outside in the streets or parks of Chicago who are freely disposing of the day, it's with scornful pity. The beckoning Sunday spaces are revealed in all their dinginess. Whatever possibilities had winked and chittered in the morning have by this time dried up, and here sit I, the luckiest of women, brimming with home-cooked food and my mother's steady, unfocused love.

Nevertheless, I'm full of jumps and twitches today.

"Something's bothering you," she divines.

"That idiotic notebook," I rage. "I still can't find the damn thing."

"Oh, dear." The mildest profanity confuses her. "Let me give you some more coffee. It'll calm you down."

My mother's the only person I know who believes coffee possesses tranquillizing properties. She lifts the coffee pot, holds on to the lid, and pours. Light filters through the Venetian blind. Above her head, on a small shelf, is her row of Hummel figurines and Delft plates. Also a small Virgin Mary, rather crowded to one side, which she was given as a young girl. (I'd be a better woman if I didn't notice such things.) My mother's dressed today in a pantsuit, her new coral double-knit, which is generously cut and comfortable around the hips. She never wore pants until she was in her late fifties; then her legs lost their shapeliness, overnight becoming straight and thick as water pipes. Her grey hair is always combed and pinned in place to form a roll at the back of her head; if this roll of hair were pinned a mere eighth of an inch higher, it would be stylish instead of matronly. Still, she takes pains with her appearance. Even when she's home alone in her apartment, she wears lipstick, a bright pink shade, and a touch of blue eye shadow. She also wears large button earrings; she likes silver; not real silver, of course — she's never been able to see the sense of expensive jewellery. She owns about twenty pairs of these large round earrings, which she keeps on a clear plastic earring rack on her bureau.

All that stands between my mother and me are trivial preferences of diet and reading matter and decor. I don't own an earring rack like the one on her bureau, and she has never heard of Muriel Rukeyser. And what else? Not much. A scholarship, a few exams, some letters after my name instead of before. (*Mrs.* — she would like me to be a Mrs.)

"How's that pain in your side?" I ask, to change the subject. "What did LeBlanc have to say about that?"

"Dr. LeBlanc?" Her sly courtesy. "He just said we'd have to keep an eye on it." She shakes her head, trying hard to look merry. "But you know, I think it's going away, the pain."

"That's good."

"Yes, I've got a feeling —"

"It's not keeping you awake then?"

"Heavens no, you know me, I sleep like a log."

"Last Sunday you said —"

"Nothing wrong with my sleep. I've always been a good sleeper."

"Hmmmm," I say, knowing my mother's habits, how she stays up until two every morning watching TV talk shows, and then is wide awake by six-thirty, sitting at the table, her heavy shoulders erect over a bowl of All-Bran, a cup of coffee before her, alert for the seven o'clock news coming out of her kitchen radio, ready to reach for her first cigarette of the day.

My mother has weathered life reasonably well, upheld, my sister and I believe, by her natural inclination toward sadness and turned by it into a kind of postulant, fumbling her way through small, meaningless acts of contrition. She always seems fresh from the country of tears, though I haven't seen her cry openly since Olaf and I announced our divorce. The divorce cast her down, perhaps because she perceived some motive unconfessed. My sister's divorce caused similar alarm and confusion but, except for my father's death and the two divorces, her sadness seems starved of particulars. Like a spider who eats her mate, she has absorbed the sadness of the world into her heavy bones and bloodstream. It's always there, like a low-grade fever.

I'm amazed by how, despite it, she manages. She reads the newspapers, goes to mass, plays canasta. Today she's leaning on the table and talking calmly about the price of baby-beef liver. After that she tells me about an article in the back of the leisure section of the newspaper: how to remove thrips from gladiolus bulbs.

I know what she suffers from: she suffers from "it." The nameless disease. An autumnal temperament. Constitutional melancholy. *Ennui. Angst* is close, the word I'd use if it weren't such a cheap scrubbing-brush of a word. I once tried to explain *Angst* to my mother, who said she found the idea of it incomprehensible. But existential anxiety is what she has, a bad case, a suspicion — she would never acknowledge it — of emptiness at the heart of life.

I imagine that my father watched with bewilderment the spectre of this large, perpetually grieving woman. My coked-up sister, Lena, has been driven by it to fits of self-indulgence, new cities, new lovers, and a series of bizarre jobs. And I've been forced into a kind of reckless ebullience; my mother's malaise, or whatever it is, has declared that the regions of despair must be forever closed to me, and that the old Sarah Maloney, dimly remembered even by me, is far behind — that mild Catholic daughter, that reader of Thomas Hardy, with shoulder-length hair and wide pleated skirts. Another Sarah has taken over, twenty-eight, sanguine, expectant, jaunty, bluffing her way. Her awful sprightly irrepressible self appals me.

How does it happen that this giddy girl and tenacious scholar inhabit the same small swervy body? A good question. A *meaty* question. Unanswerable.

I kiss my mother goodbye energetically, praise her cooking, tell her to look after herself, remind her of her doctor's appointment, and then go swinging off down the street. The light, so lurid and promising earlier in the day, is feeble now, and the trees look misshapen, as though they've been recycled from dead brush. Autumn. This is a time of day I particularly like and feel attuned to. A narrow passageway, dilated just for me. The word *crepuscular* pops into my head, then disintegrates, too queenly a word for a patchy night like this. And here comes a gust of wind, knocking the leaves off the branches and leading me back to reality.

Ah, but what is reality? In a fit of self-mockery, thinking of Brownie, I ask myself this question, and an answer comes dancing in front of my lips. Reality is no more than a word that begins with *r* and ends with *y*.

Exactly. Oh, Lord!

10

Most of the men I know are defective. Most of them are vain. My good friend and mentor Peggy O'Reggis lives in a universe in which men are only marginally visible. Ditto my lawyer, Virginia Goodchild, a committed citizen of Lesbos. At least half of my graduate students are determined to carry their own tent pegs, to hell with the male power structure and to hell with penetration as sexual expression. They've bailed out. All these women send me invitations, literal and subliminal, but something in me resists.

Genes probably, or maybe conditioning. At least once a month, ever since my divorce, my mother inquires, shyly, stumblingly, fingering her St. Agatha's medal, whether I've "found someone." A man, she means. She looks at me sideways, her large round earrings at attention. Am I still seeing that nice . . . Stephen Stanhope? Only occasionally, I tell her, not having the heart to explain that Stephen and I ended our love affair months ago. I'm not sure what happened.

Maybe just that his identity was threatened because I wouldn't move in with him — as though anyone in her right mind would abandon the uniqueness of a fantasy house on the south side for a brick duplex out in Maywood. He also accused me, gently, of being ashamed of his profession, which is juggling, an accusation with not a shred of truth to it. Didn't I once live (briefly) with a tree surgeon? Didn't I make a trip to the Everglades with a man who repaired pianos?

I don't like to raise my mother's hopes, and so it wasn't until last week that I admitted to her that I was "seeing" a man called Brownie.

The minute I made this statement, over roasted turkey breast and mashed turnips, it all seemed ludicrously untrue, a story I'd invented in order to please her.

It happens fairly often, this sensation of being a captive of fiction, a sheepish player in my own *roman-à-clef*. My dwarfish house is the setting. The stacked events of the day form the plot, and Brownie and I are the chief characters, sometimes larger than life, but just as often smaller. Tonight, Tuesday, we are shrunken and stagey, a pair of fretting silhouettes lolling on a sofa in front of my fireplace.

The first time I saw this fireplace I thought it was hideous, a wavy opening in the wall, framed all around by shiny, ginger-coloured tile that in the daylight always looks faintly dusty. It has turned out to be surprisingly efficient, as fireplaces go, deep and with a strong draft. Once lit, the fire burns cleanly, a wide brush of calm, bright, yellow-centred flames that are reflected all around the tile edges and transformed into something cool and marble-toned. I burn good, dry, sweet-smelling logs, which cost me exactly one buck apiece, but I save on kindling, making do with my students' old term papers and exam booklets.

"Try to be calm," Brownie, just back from California, is saying about Mary Swann's lost notebook. "You're overreacting. You're —"

"If you're going to suggest I'm ovulating you can go straight to hell." I say this nicely.

"When did you last see it, the notebook? Try to reconstruct."

This is the problem. I don't know. A week ago, maybe two weeks ago. It was on my bookshelf. It's been on my bookshelf for several years now, part of the decor, resting on a copy of V.S. Pritchett's autobiography, casually abandoned as if it were worthless, under-appreciated — only now that it's lost, it suddenly vibrates with uniqueness and value. I should have kept it in a safe-deposit box — which is what Brownie does with his *Plastic Man* collection — or at least in a locked desk drawer.

"What about your office?" Brownie suggests. (I can tell he's bored with the topic, his tongue on his teeth like that.) "Or in your brief-case?"

"I never take it to the office."

"Maybe you wanted to show it to someone." The contours of his face are unreadable, and make me feel like a child, on my honour to behave.

"No, I don't think so." Wavering now.

"Your mother's place? On Sunday?"

"Of course not," I snap. This is getting us nowhere.

"It'll turn up," Brownie croons.

His face rearranges itself, shifting from pinkness to something more determined. His arm is around me, his fingers dancing on my bare arm, and for some reason I am unsettled by his phrase, *it'll turn up*. Perhaps because it's the same phrase my mother used. A placebo, a mindless tablet of optimism, *it'll turn up*. Did they think it was going to leap out of the walls?

Brownie rubs my back and tells me how, when he was twelve, he lost an envelope of stamps an uncle had sent him from Mexico. The loss was so grievous to him — not because he collected stamps or even liked stamps, but because he felt stupid and careless and unworthy — that he had actually wept, privately of course, with his head in his pillow. Later the stamps were found pressed inside his school dictionary where he must have placed them for safe-keeping. (Ah, Brownie; I imagine a slim boy with brown woolly hair cut short over sunburned ears, sitting alone in a small room, opening a book with a blue cloth and lifting from its pages a small glassine packet.)

"It's bound to turn up," he says again. "And besides" — his words form a calm electric buzzing at the nape of my neck — "besides, it's been photocopied."

Yes, of course, I admit it; the *contents* have been photocopied, but *it* is lost.

"You can't say it's really lost," Brownie says, giving me a fine ironic smile. "Not if there's a copy in the archives."

"A copy's not the same thing. As you know perfectly well." And I yawn to show him I'm sleepy and ready to climb into bed, ready to bury all this fuss in the creases of his body. A muscle inside me unclasps itself.

"You're tired," Brownie says. "I'd better not stay tonight." And he grabs for his coat. Quickly.

There's no talking him out of going, not without pleading. So I get into bed alone and toss for several hours. My trick of timing my breath to match a line of iambic pentameter fails and so does my other trick of reciting the ingredients for blanquette de veau, one large onion, one carrot quartered, two celery stalks. Two o'clock comes and goes, then three o'clock. I entertain myself with miniature horror stories. Could the notebook have got mixed up with that bundle of newspapers, those same bundled papers I used to start a fire in the fireplace last week, the night when frost was predicted and Brownie came through the door with a nimbus of cold around his hair and — or maybe I picked it up with the offprints on Sara Teasdale and took it to the office and maybe Lois Lundigan, thinking it was scrap paper — no, ridiculous. But not impossible. Four o'clock, four-thirty. I go over and over the possibilities until they strum a rusty plinked tune in my head, one of those old half-lisped songs from the sixties that are all refrain and three-quarters nonsense. Lost, lost, lost, gone.

11

It's possible to be brilliant without being profound — or, in Mary Swann's case, profound without being brilliant.

Think of brilliance as sunlight sparking off salty little waves, as particles of glare or shine that tease the eye. Then think of the underwater muscle of a very large ocean or the machinery of the earth's shifting plates.

Reading Mary Swann's poetry for the first time (Wisconsin, that screened porch, flies buzzing) I found myself suddenly grabbed by an elemental seizure of the first order. I was instantly alert, attenuated, running my fingers under the words, writing furiously in the margin (and recognizing at the same time the half-melancholy truth that this was what I would always, somewhere or other, be doing.) I read *Swann's Songs* at one sitting. Then I sat perfectly still for a few minutes, and then I read it again. A note on the back of the book said only that Mary Swann, 1915–1965, had lived in Nadeau, Ontario.

A week later I was back in Chicago packing my bags. I rented a car and drove up through the state of Michigan and after that across the little humped hills of western Ontario. In twenty-four hours I was standing in front of the town hall of the village of Nadeau, population 1,750, a village with a cheese factory and a knitting mill and a dozen or so quiet green streets shaded by maples and poplars and elms.

The first person I saw — this was very early on a Sunday morning in the month of August — was a balding old guy in a wrinkled cotton suit, Mr. Homer Hart (as I later found out), retired school principal, recovering (though I didn't know it then) from a nervous breakdown, his third. He was walking a large golden retriever, and he and the dog, Spanish Jim, had paused beneath a half-dead elm, the dog to raise his leg and Mr. Hart to peer up sorrowfully into the lattice of drooping branches. We froze, the three of us, as though we'd taken our assigned places on a small grassy stage. All around us I could hear the twittering of bird-song and feel the cool stirring of morning air. Then Spanish Jim opened his mouth, yipped excitedly, danced over to where I was standing and began sniffing at my jeans, pulling back a meaty lip and huffing hard so that I felt his breath through the cloth. "He won't hurt you," Mr. Hart called in a tissuey voice, his hands flapping in his pockets. "That's his way of saying good morning to you."

I explained — while Mr. Hart nodded and nodded — who I was and why I'd driven all the way from Chicago up to Nadeau, Ontario. "What I'd really like," I said, "is to talk to someone who actually knew Mary Swann."

"The person you want to talk to," Homer Hart said, composing himself, "is the one and only Rose Hindmarch."

"Rose Hindmarch?" I bared my teeth, a sort of smile, but not too eager, I hoped. Spanish Jim had left off licking my shoes and was chasing squirrels across the broad lawn. "Is Rose Hindmarch a relative?"

"Oh, dear, no, there aren't any relatives, afraid not. You see, Mary Swann's people came from over Belleville way. Oh, there's a daughter, but she's out in California, on the coast, married, never comes back here, not since her mother passed on."

"Rose Hindmarch, you said?" Where was my tape recorder when I needed it?

"Well," he said, "Rose was a friend, you might say, of Mary Swann. Rose's our librarian, you see, also our township clerk, and she knew Mary Swann pretty well. Well, now, let me qualify that last statement of mine. Let's say that Rose knew her as well as anyone did. Mrs. Swann wasn't what you'd call a mixer. She more or less kept to herself, a farm woman, only came into town every couple of weeks."

"Every couple of weeks?" I squeaked, wondering if I could remember all this to write down later.

"Did her shopping and then went over to the library to borrow herself a couple of books to read. She was a reader, Mrs. Swann, a real reader, as well as quite the celebrated poetess. Had a real way with words. Could spin off a poem on any subject you could mention. Snow storms, the lake when the ice was going. A really nice one she did about an apple tree, I believe. Wish I could remember just how it went. 'De dum, de dum the apple tree.' Something like that. You read that poem and all of a sudden you can see that tree in your own imagination, the blossoms coming out, a picture made out of words. It was extraordinary what that woman could do with hardly any schooling. Well, as I say, Rose Hindmarch is our librarian. We have a dandy library for a place this size, and if anyone can tell you about Mrs. Swann, it's Rose."

Rose Hindmarch turned out to be a little turtle of a woman with a hair on her chin like a hieroglyph, quintessentially virginal, mid-forties, twinkly eyed, suppliant, excitable. We spent all of Sunday afternoon together, sitting in the sweltering living-room of her apartment — her suite as she called it — which was the second floor of an old frame Nadeau house. I marvelled that Mary Swann's only friend should be a librarian with a little escutcheon face and a nervous laugh. I could see right away that I frightened her.

I often frighten people. I frighten myself, as a matter of fact, my undeflectable energy probably. I did what I could to put Rose at her ease, praising the ferns in her window, the lamp on top of her colour TV, the afghan on her sofa, the crocheted runner on her oak table, her method of brewing tea, her enthusiasm for spy stories, and for local history, and, especially — I approached the subject delicately — especially her interest in the poet Mary Swann.

In an hour she was won over, so quickly won over that I winced with shame. Rose seemed a woman inseparable from the smell of face powder and breath mints, and on that powdery, breathy face was the dumb shine of stunted experience. But she was, and there is no other word for it, a good woman. A true sense of humility, the sort I would like to claim for myself, made her open and truthful. I knew I could trust her. As she talked, I took notes, feeling like a thief but not missing a word.

It came out slowly at first. Yes, she had known Mary Swann. Their mutual love of books had brought them together; she actually uttered that face-powdery phrase, looking straight into my eyes: *our mutual love of books.* I pressed for details. How well had she known her? Well, she said, better than most folks. Most folks only saw Mary Swann from a distance, a farm woman buying groceries, wearing a man's old coat and an awful pair of canvas shoes. But Mary Swann liked to linger at the desk in the library when she could and talk about her favourite writer who was Bess Streeter Aldrich. Oh, and Edna Ferber, she was a true-blue Edna Ferber fan.

Later in the afternoon Rose offered me a drink of rye whisky and ginger-ale in a juice glass. She went into a hostessy flutter, bringing out a bowl of potato chips, and also a bowl of sour-cream dip. Her tongue loosened and she told me about Mary Swann's husband, who was a dirt-poor farmer, an ignorant man given to rages. He begrudged his wife's visit to the village library, that much was clear. He told anybody who'd listen that women had better things to do than gobble up time reading story books. He waited outside for her in his truck, giving her only a few minutes to get her books, honking the horn when he got impatient, and letting her check out just two books at a time. That was his limit. He had a beaky red face and button eyes. No one could figure out why she stayed with him. He didn't have so much as a single friend. People shied away from him. Their daughter, though, a smart girl, did well in her schooling, her mother's influence likely, and won herself a scholarship. She got away, but not Mary. Some people in the district said Angus Swann beat his wife up regularly. Once she appeared in town with a black eye and a sprained arm. It was also said he burned some of her poems in the cookstove and so she took to hiding them under the kitchen linoleum. A regular scoundrel, a monster. "And of course you know what happened in the end," Rose Hindmarch said.

"What?" I asked.

"You mean to say you really don't know?"

"No."

Rose's eyes glistened. Then she said, "Why that man put a bullet right through her head and chopped her up into little pieces."

12

I stayed in Nadeau for two days, getting myself a room at the Nadeau Hotel over the beer parlour. Rose Hindmarch, along with Homer Hart and his wife, Daisy, accompanied me out to the cemetery to see where Mary Swann was buried. There was a pretty piece of sloping land with a neat stone, a modest block of granite, and the words "Mary Swann, 1915-1965, Dear Mother of Frances." (Angus Swann was cremated and his ashes went unclaimed, so Daisy Hart righteously informed me.)

The four of us, chatting away like old friends on a holiday, next drove over to the Swann farm, which was deserted. A tattered For Sale sign stood in front of the house. It had been there for close to ten years, Rose Hindmarch told me, and it looked like the place would never sell. We waded through overgrown grass. The house and barn were of unpainted grey wood, their roofs sagging. The porches, back and front, were shaky and the windows were boarded up. Towering above the bleak outbuildings was the silo where Angus Swann had dumped the dismembered body of his wife — head, trunk, and severed legs — before shooting himself in the mouth as he sat at the kitchen table.

No one knows for sure what happened between them. There was no explanation, no note or sign, but one of Swann's last poems points to her growing sense of claustrophobia and helplessness. The final stanza goes:

Minutes hide their tiny tears
And Days weep into Aprons.
A stifled sobbing from the years
And Silence from the eons.

Rose Hindmarch — by now she was my devoted guide — offered
to get the key from the real-estate agent so I could see the inside
of the house, but for once I demurred. This surprised me, since
demurral is not my usual stance, far from it. But standing on that
front porch, watching the wind whip across the overgrown yard, I
felt the queasy guilt of the trespasser. The fact that art could be
created in such a void was, for some reason, deeply disturbing. And
what right did I have to dig up buried shame, furtive struggle?
Besides, I'd seen enough; though later, hearing about the poems
Willard Lang discovered under the linoleum, I had regrets.

Whatever had swamped Mary Swann in her last days — suffocation, exhaustion — now engulfed me, and I think the others felt
it too. Homer Hart leaned heavily on the fragile railing, panting,
his face white, and Rose's hand was travelling back and forth across
her chin as it had done when we first met. Even the ebullient Daisy
Hart, a broad-busted woman in her bristly mid-fifties, snugged into
a seersucker suit — she would have called it a two-piece — was reduced to a respectful, repetitious murmur — *that poor woman, her
head cut off even*. We got back into the rental car and drove to
Nadeau in silence. I yearned, all at once, to get back to Chicago,
and decided I would forget about meeting Mary Swann's publisher,
Frederic Cruzzi, in Kingston. I would leave as soon as I got my gear
together.

As a parting gift, to say thank you, I gave Rose a small bottle
of French perfume. (It was unopened, still in its box, a gift from
Olaf that I fortunately had brought along in my suitcase.) She held
out her hand, then hesitated. Her eyes watered with sentimental
tears. It was too much, she said. She couldn't imagine wearing such
extravagant perfume. She'd seen the adverts in *Woman's Day*. But
if I insisted . . . . I *did* insist. I was firm. I pressed it into her hand.
Well, then, she would treasure it, save it for special occasions, for
her bridge nights, or her trips to Kingston. She shook her head,
promising me that every single time she dabbed a little behind her
ears she would think of me and remember my visit.

Effusiveness embarrasses me, especially when it's sincere. The gift of perfume was little thanks for the help and insight Rose had been able to give me, but it was hard to convince her that this was true. Her mouth worked; the little hair on her chin vibrated in the breeze. We stood beside the rental car, which I had parked in front of her house, and I wondered if we would presently shake hands or embrace. A good woman. A courageous woman.

"Wait a minute," she said suddenly. "I'll be right back." She dashed into the house and returned a minute later with two objects, which she insisted I take with me. Both had belonged to Mary Swann and had been given to Rose, along with two overdue library books, by the real-estate agent for the Swann farm.

The first was a small spiral notebook, the kind sometimes described as a pocket scribbler. I opened it and saw its little ruled pages covered with dated headings and markings in blue ink. "A diary!" I breathed, unable to believe this piece of luck.

"Just jottings," Rose Hindmarch said. "Odds and ends. I couldn't make heads or tails of it myself, it was such a mishmash. But *here*'s something you'll find really interesting."

She held out a cheap paperback book, a rhyming dictionary. It was titled, if I remember, *Spratt's New Improved Rhyming Dictionary for Practising Poets*. Rose's face glowed as she handed it over, suffused with her own sense of generosity. "Here you are. It would only be wasted on me. What does someone like me know about real poetry?"

I think I thanked her. I *hope* I thanked her. We collided stiffly, I remember. A tentative self-protective hug. The top of her head struck hard on the side of my jaw. My shoulder bag banged on her hip. After that I got into the car and drove slowly away. I drove out of town under a cool lace of leaves with the dictionary and notebook beside me on the seat. Soon I was on the open highway heading west.

A lake flashed by with one or two outboards on its calm surface. Then there were fenced pastures, barns, and long sloping groves of birch. I thought of Sylvia Plath, how someone had told me she used a thesaurus when writing her poems. I was surprised I even remembered this. And sorry to be thinking of Sylvia Plath's thesaurus on such a fine day.

Mary Swann's rhyming dictionary and notebook rested on the seat. I could reach out and touch them as I drove along. My thoughts were riveted on the notebook and what its contents would soon reveal to me, but the dictionary kept drawing my eye, distracting me with its overly bright cover. It began after a few miles to seem ominous and to lend a certain unreality to the notebook beside it.

I stopped at the first roadside litter box and dropped it in. Then I headed straight for the border.

13

Standing up in a lurching subway car, clutching a plastic loop and looking healthy, young, amiable, and strong is Stephen Stanhope, my former lover. His shoulder bag is full of Indian clubs, rubber rings, lacrosse balls and other paraphernalia of the professional juggler. He's on his way to a juggling gig, he tells me, a Lions benefit in Evanston. "Why don't you come along and keep me company?" he says, and I say, "Why not?"

It's Saturday. I'm on my way home from a morning of marketing, my shopping bag bulging with sensuous squashes and gourds. The old restlessness has come back, my spiritual eczema as Brownie calls it. (Brownie is out of town, as usual on weekends, scouting the countryside for Plastic Man comics and for first editions of Hemingway or Fitzgerald — or second editions or third — which are becoming harder and harder to find.)

At the Lions benefit I sit on the sidelines and watch Stephen perform. A big man, six-foot-four, he wears loose cotton clothes and, on his feet, white sneakers. Soundlessly, with wonderful agility, he moves about on large white feet, elegant and clownish. He has the gift of enchantment, my Stephen, the ability to cast a spell over the children, some of whom are in wheelchairs, and to put the awkward, hovering parents at their ease. He fine tunes them to laughter. "If you watch very, very carefully," he tells the audience with lowered voice, "you might see me drop this club on my toe." An instant later he deliberately drops one and hops up and down in voiceless agony while the children howl and applaud. Then he executes a quick recovery and goes into his five-ball shower, followed by his reverse cascade, and finishing with the famous triple-torch fire feat. I've seen it before, but today he performs with special artistry. He's a master of his comic trade, this thirty-five-year-old son of a billionaire grain investor.

Clever men create themselves, but clever women, it seems to me, are created by their mothers. Women can never quite escape their mothers' cosmic pull, not their lip-biting expectations or their faulty love. We want to please our mothers, emulate them, disgrace them, oblige them, outrage them, and bury ourselves in the mysteries and consolations of their presence. When my mother and I are in the same room we work magic on each other: I grow impossibly cheerful and am guilty of reimagined naiveté and other indulgent stunts, and my mother's sad, helpless dithering becomes a song of succour. Within minutes, we're peddling away, the two of us, a genetic sewing machine that runs on limitless love. It's my belief that between mothers and daughters there is a kind of blood-hyphen that is, finally, indissoluble. (All this, of course, is explored in Chapter Three of my book *The Female Prism*, with examples from nineteenth- and twentieth-century literature liberally supplied.)

The experience of men is somehow different. I look at Stephen and at Brownie and all the other men I know and marvel at the distance they manage to put between themselves and their fathers. Stephen's father, whom I met only once, presides in a boardroom so high up in the Corn Exchange that he might be on a mountain top, while Stephen, his only son, this big, soft-footed boy, blithely plucks wooden clubs out of the air, rides the subway, and lives in a rented dump in Maywood, unwilling, it would seem, to enjoy the material plenty showered on him. And Brownie, his wonderful little scowl, his scowling eyes and scowly concentration — I'm sure these are his own inventions and not an inheritance from his poor but smiley father (as I imagine him) tramping around up there in his loamy fields. Brownie's life, like Stephen's, seems designed to avoid his father's destiny, while mine is drawn with the same broad pencil as my mother's.

Stephen asks me how my mother is. This is later, over toasted sandwiches and beer in a downtown bar. I explain about the lump in her side, how it sometimes keeps her awake at night, but at least it doesn't seem to be growing, and how next week she'll check into the hospital for a day of tests. There's a possibility of surgery, but in all probability the lump is benign.

"I've missed you," Stephen says, folding and unfolding his hands. "I've missed the amazing times we used to have."

"So have I," I say, a little surprised, and then, spontaneously, invite him to spend the night.

What I've missed is his face, the composure of it, its unique imperviousness, the fact that it's a face for which no spare parts seem possible and beneath which nothing is hidden. It's a face, too, that has profited from the shedding of youth. "An open face," my mother said the first time she met him. "The kind of face that gets better and better with time."

I remember just how she said this. Generally I remember everything she says. The connective twine between us is taut with details. I have all her little judgements filed away, word perfect. There's scarcely a thought in my head, in fact, that isn't amplified or underlined by some comment of my mother's. This reinforces one of my life theories: that women carry with them the full freight of their mothers' words. It's the one part of us that can never be erased or revised.

14

A graduate student called Betsy Gore-Heppel in my seminar on Women in Midwestern Fiction had a baby today, a seven-pound daughter. We've all chipped in to buy her a contrivance of straps and slings called a Ma-Terna-Pak so that Betsy, after a week or two, will be able to attend class with her child strapped to her chest. The decision about the gift, the signing of the card, and a celebratory drink afterward with the members of the seminar made me two hours late getting home. Supper, therefore, was a cup of tomato soup, which I sipped while reading my latest letter from Morton Jimroy.

As in his other letters, he is all caution and conciliation. He "understands perfectly," he says, about my reluctance to "share" the contents of Swann's notebook. He begs me once again to forgive him if his request appeared "impertinent," and hopes that I understand that his wish to have "just a peek" proceeded from his compulsion to *document, document, document!*

On and on he goes in this vein, his only vein I suspect, ending with a rather endearing piece of professional exposition: "The oxygen of the biographer is not, as some would think, speculation; it is the small careful proofs that he pins down and sits hard upon."

I ask myself: is this statement the open hand of apology or a finger of blame? I have denied him one of the "small careful proofs" he requires if his biography is to have substance. Should I, therefore, feel that I've interfered with the orderly flow of scholarship by asking him to wait a few additional months before seeing it? Yes. No. Well, maybe. Even if I were willing to set aside my own interests, it's hard to see what difference it would make. He's going to see Mary's notebook eventually, at least a photocopy of it, and what he's sure to feel when he examines its pages is a profound sense of disappointment.

Profound disappointment is what I felt when opening that notebook for the first time. What I wanted was elucidation and grace and a glimpse of the woman Mary Swann as she drifted in and out of her poems. What I got was "Creek down today," or "Green beans up," or "cash low," or "wind rising." This "journal" was no more than the ups-and-downs accounting of a farmer's wife, of *any* farmer's wife, and all of it in appalling handwriting. I puzzled for days over one scribbled passage, hoping for a spill of light, but decided finally that the pen scratches must read "Door latch broken."

Mary Swann's notebook — Lord knows what it was *for* — covered a period of three months, the summer of 1950, and what it documents is a trail of trifling accidents ("cut hand on pump") or articles in need of repair (a kettle, a shoe) or sometimes just small groupings of words (can opener, wax paper, sugar), which, I decided, after some thought, could only be shopping lists. Even her chance observations of the natural world are primitive, to say the least: "branches down," "radishes poor," "sun scorching."

This from the woman whose whole aesthetic was a piece of grief! The woman who had become for me a model of endurance and survival. I felt let down, even betrayed, but reluctant to admit it. In the weeks after I acquired the notebook from Rose Hindmarch I turned over its pages again and again, imagining that one day they would yield up a key that would turn the dull little entries into pellucid messages. Perhaps I hoped for the same dislocation of phrase that frequently occurs in the poems, a skewed reference that is really a shrewd misguiding of those who read it. Her apple tree poem, for instance, which is actually a limpid expression of female sensuality, and her water poems that trace, though some scholars disagree, the clear contours of birth and regeneration. She is the mistress of the inverted image. Take "Lilacs," her first published poem. It pretends to be an idle, passive description of a tree in blossom, but is really a piercing statement of a woman severed from her roots, one of the most affecting I've ever read.

Naturally I opened her notebook hoping for the same underwatery text, and the reason I've refused to share it casually with Morton Jimroy, or anyone else for that matter, is that I still hope, foolishly perhaps, to wring some meaningful juice out of those blunt weather bulletins and shopping lists.

I haven't yet decided how I'll present the journal at the symposium, whether to cite it as a simple country diary ("Swann had one foot firmly in the workaday world and the other . . .") or to offer it up as a cryptogram penned by a woman who was terrified by the realization that she was an artist. Nothing in her life had prepared her for the clarity of vision visited on her in mid life or for what *things* she was about to make with the aid of a Parker 51 and a rhyming dictionary. (I won't, of course, mention the dictionary, long since returned to dust and, I hope, forgotten.)

But no matter how I present the notebook, the responses will be one of disappointment, particularly for Morton Jimroy with his holy attitude toward prime materials. He will be disappointed — I picture his collapsed face, its pursed mouth and shrunken eyes — disappointed by the notebook itself, disappointed by Mary Swann, and also, I have no doubt, by me.

But haven't I been disappointed in turn by him and his biographical diggings? As yet he hasn't turned up a single thing about Mary Swann's mother, not even her maiden name, and he shows not the slightest interest in pursuing her. Doesn't he understand anything about mothers? "Childhood," he wrote in his second to last letter to me, "has been greatly overestimated by biographers in the past, as have family influences."

It's hard to know if this is a tough new biographical tack or if Jimroy is papering over a paucity of material. But one thing I'm sure of: Mary's poems are filled with concealed references to her mother and to the strength and violence of family bonds. One poem in particular turns on the inescapable perseverance of blood ties, particularly those between mothers and daughters. It's a poem that follows me around, chanting loudly inside my head and drumming on the centre of my heart.

> Blood pronounces my name
> Blisters the day with shame
> Spends what little I own,
> Robbing the hour, rubbing the bone.

15

What I need is an image to organize my life. A flower would be nice, an iris, a tender, floppy head of petals and a stem like a long green river. I could watch it sway, emblem of myself, in the least breeze, and admire its aloof purply stare. The frilled mouth, never drooping lower than a few permitted degrees — it would put to shame my present state of despondency.

Just why am I sad tonight? I address this question to the Moroccan cushion on the end of my sofa, a tender triangle of soft white leather. (Come on, lady, stop being precious; and what have you got to be sad about anyway?)

Because it rained all day today, because I'm jealous of Betsy Gore-Heppel, because I'm worried about my mother's health, because I still haven't found Mary Swann's notebook, because I had "words" this morning with dear old Professor Gliden about the intertextuality of Edith Wharton's novels, because my only mail today was an oil bill, because Stephen Stanhope sent me flowers, because of Nicaragua, because the Pope made a speech on television reminding me of my lost faith, because I'm sick of my beautiful clothes (those shoulder pads, those trips to the dry cleaners), because the rain continues and continues — because of all this I broke down tonight and phoned Brownie, who hasn't phoned me for two weeks.

He's been incredibly busy, he explains. (All my senses gather to a fine point of attention.) He has had to hire three new assistants at the Brown Study and a full-time accountant. He has just spent two days in Peoria going through a lady-and-gentleman library (his phrase) that was up for auction. After that he made a dash for St. Louis to look at some Wonder Woman comics, which were in lousy condition, though he *did* pick up an excellent signed first edition of Disraeli's *Sybil*, for which he has a buyer already committed. Next week he has an appointment in Montreal to look over some sizzling love letters written more than a hundred and fifty years ago.

Being eclectic keeps him hopping. He's busy, *too* busy, he says. He's exhausted. Depleted. A wreck.

Why then this frisson of exaltation running beneath his complaints? I can hear it in every word, even in the little spaces between words, his busy air of enterprise or cunning. "Why don't you come over?" I suggest. "I'll make a fire. We could talk."

The pleading in my voice dismays me. Oh, Lord, why do I love Brownie?

A good question. His crinkly hair, ending in snaky ringlets. The crinkly way he talks and thinks at the same time. His wrists. His wristwatch and the way he's always checking the time as if comparing it to that other clock inside his brain that runs to a different, probably threatening, rhythm. His cool impartial stare. His little shoulders, the Einsteinian hunch of them. His sweaters with their tender broken elbows. His helpless need for money and his belief that he'll never get enough of it salted away for his old age — which he doubts he'll reach. His fingertips on my shoulder, tapping out messages, subliminal. The strength and shortness of his legs, so short that when we walk along in the park together I can hear the rush-rushing of his feet on the gravel. His collection of costumes, Victorian capes, military jackets and the like. The shrewd way he handles his thready old books, his willingness to sock them away for ten years, twenty years, until their value multiplies and zooms. *Treasure, treasure,* his ridgy brow seems to say, meaning by treasure something very different than I would ever mean. The way his mouth goes into a circle, ready to admit but never promise the possibility of love. That almost kills me, his blindness to love.

"Next week for sure," he promises.

After Montreal he goes back to California to have a look at the Stromberg collection of Plastic Man comics, the only cache he knows that rivals his own. There's a rumour out that Stromberg's ready to deal. "I'm getting a cash package together just in case," Brownie tells me. "But after this is over, I'm definitely going to slow down."

Brownie told me once about an economist who cornered the world market on Mexican jumping beans. That impressed him. Now *he's* out for control of *Plastic Man*, every last copy, but after that he's going to relax, he says. He's planning to take it easy, maybe read some of the books in his store. He hasn't read a book in ten years, he tells me. Another reason I love him.

There must be something perverse about me. *You are perverse*, I tell myself; and fill up my head with Brownie, the way he winks when he makes a deal, licks his lips, rolls his eyes like a con man, fooling.

The thought is cheering, and so, buoyed up, I make myself a cup of ginger tea and wander off to bed. It looks like the rain's going to keep on like this all night. I lie on my back and imagine myself applying aggressive kisses to Brownie's warm mouth. The rain continues, sweet, sweet music on my roof.

16

Enough of this shilly-shallying, it's time for me to get my paper for the Swann Symposium knocked together and into the mail. Willard Lang in Toronto has been breathing down my neck; a letter last week, a phone call yesterday afternoon, pipping away in his so awfully polite mid-Atlantic squeal, reminding me of what I already know perfectly well, that he's extended the deadline twice (and only because I'm a member of the Steering Committee) and that November 15 is absolutely (eb-sew-lutley) the cut-off date if I want my paper included in the printed proceedings.

The title I've decided on is "Mary Swann and the Template of the Imagination," not the blazing feminist banner I'd planned on, but a vague post-modern salute, demonstrating that I can post-mod along with the best of them. Begin, begin! I take a deep breath, then punch my title into the word processor.

I bought this word processor from a friend, Larry Fine, the behaviouralist, who was trading up. He had a pet name for it — Gertrude. I paid over my fifteen hundred bucks, cash, always cash, cleaner that way, and promptly dechristened it, not being one to stick funny names on inanimate objects. Larry came over one evening and helped me install it in a corner of the kitchen, which is the room where I work best — a dark, fruity confession, but there it is.

So! The counters are wiped clean. It's Saturday, exceedingly frosty outside. The yellow tea-kettle, a gift from sister Lena, gleams on the stove. Only a sister gives you a kettle. Only an older sister. Get going, I instruct myself, you're such a hot-shot scholar, what're you waiting for?

It would be a big help if I had my copy of *Swann's Songs* on the table beside me, but Brownie hasn't returned it yet. He tells me he's "quite enjoying it." *Enjoying!* Probably he's taken it west with him. Lord, he'd better not leave it behind in a hotel room or on the plane — but he wouldn't do that, not a book. Books he holds very sacred. If only—

Never mind, I don't need the book. I can close my eyes and see each poem as it looks on the page. For the last few years, haven't I lived chiefly inside the interiors of these poems? — absorbed their bumpy rhythms and taken on their shapes? They're my toys, if you like, little wooden beads I can manipulate on a cord.

Unworthy that. Settle down. Enough. Write!

I've already made up my mind to skirt the topic of the Swann notebook. A gradual discounting is what I have in mind. Perhaps I'll just note — "allow me to note in passing" — that Swann's journal-keeping prefigured her poetry only in that it linked object with word, experience with language. A bit loose that, but I can come back to it. Put in a paragraph about "rough apprenticeship" or something gooky like that.

I drum on the table. Pine. It might be a good idea to use that queer little poem on radishes as an example, not her best poem, not one that's usually cited, definitely minor, twelve lines of impacted insight of the sort that scholars frequently overlook. I'll do a close textual analysis, showing how Mary, using the common task of thinning a row of radishes — the most grinding toil I can imagine — was able to distil those two magnificent, and thus far neglected, final lines, which became almost a credo for her life as a survivor. "Her credo," I toss into the word processor, "found its form in the . . ."

Noon already. I'm due at an anti-apartheid rally in four hours. Hurry.

I try again. (Oh, that miraculous little green clearing key!) "Thinning radishes was for Swann an emblem for . . ."

Wait a minute, hold on there. There's a gap that needs explaining, a synapse too quickly assumed. What kind of express train am I driving anyway? Radishes to ultimate truth? — that's the leap of a refined aesthete. How did Mary Swann, untaught country woman, know how to make that kind of murky metaphorical connection. Who taught her what was possible?

"Mary Swann was deeply influenced by . . ."

Back to the same old problem: Mary Swann hadn't read any modern poetry. She didn't *have* any influences.

Thinking of Swann makes me think, with the kind of double-storied memory that comes out of family annals, of my grandfather, my father's father, a machinist by trade, a man who worked with his hands, long dead by the time I was born. He was a quiet contemplative man from all reports, who ran his small business out of a shed behind his house in what is now Evergreen Park. Over the years, cutting and shaping sheets of metal, he noticed that there existed peculiar but constant relationships between the different sides of triangles. He kept a record of this odd information, and after a time he was able to discern measurable patterns. Keeping the discovery to himself, he spent several years working up an elaborate table of numerical relationships that was, in essence, an ordinary logarithm chart. He had reinvented trigonometry, or so my father used to say, and when, years later, he found out that it had already been done, he just laughed and threw his charts away. An amazing man. A genius.

In somewhat the same manner, I like to think, Mary Swann invented modern poetry. Her utterances, the shape of them, are spun from their own logic. Without knowing the poetry of Pound or Eliot, without even knowing their names, she set to work. Her lines have all the peculiar rough thrusts and the newly made syntactical abrasions that are the mark of the prototype. You can't read her poems without being aware that a form is in the process of being created.

"Poetry at the forge level," I hurl into the word processor, and then I'm off, shimmying with concentration, tap-tapping my way down the rosy road toward synthesis.

17

The first words my mother utters when she comes out of the anaesthetic are: "Your face is dirty, dear."

My hand flies to my cheek.

It's a bruise actually, the result of a scuffle at the rally, a brief, confused scuffle now that I stop and think about it, a case of my own steaming exuberance, then turning my head at the wrong instant and meeting an elbow intended for someone else. Not that my mother needs to know any of *this*. Anyway, she's drifting back to sleep now with her large, soft, dolorous hand tucked in mine. With my free hand I fish in my bag for the chocolates I intend to leave on her bedside table.

She's in a room with four other patients, but I passionately resist the notion that she has anything to do with this moaning team of invalids. I've already spoken with Dr. LeBlanc and with the surgeon. They were smiling, the two of them, leaning against a hospital wall, freshly barbered as doctors always seem to be, their thumbs hooked in the pockets of their greenies. The news they imparted was good, wholly positive, in fact: the lump removed from my mother's side this morning was not, as they had feared, the pulpy sponge of cancer but a compacted little bundle of bone and hair, which, they told me, was a fossilized fetus, my mother's twin sibling who somehow, in the months before her own birth, became absorbed into her body. A genuine medical curiosity, one of the devilish pranks the human body plays on itself from time to time.

She's carried her lump all these years, unknowing, a brother or sister, shrunk down to walnut size and keeping itself quiet. Now it has been removed, and my mother's unsuspecting skin sewn neatly back in place. A pathologist will perform some tests and in a week the results will be confirmed, but there's no real doubt about what it actually *is*.

It doesn't seem possible, I said at least three times. Dr. LeBlanc, however, assured me that though unusual, the phenomenon is not at all rare.

I still can't believe it: my own mother spread out here on her hospital bed, as calm and white as a cloud, my own mother the unwitting host to a little carved monkey of human matter, her lifelong mate. This fleshy mystery drives all other thoughts from my head.

Nelson Mandela is forgotten, the chanting demonstrators with their banners in the air, and an unknown elbow catching me under the eye — it no longer aches, by the way. Also forgotten is my completed paper on Mary Swann, now winging its way to Toronto, sadly late and less definitive than I would have wished. Template of the Imagination! — precious, precious. And Mary's lost notebook, still resolutely lost, no longer gnaws at me — yes, the gnawing has definitely eased — nor does Brownie's silence reach me, though I'm sure he must be back in Chicago by now.

All these recent events, these *things*, seem suddenly trivial and rawly hatched in the light of what has happened: my mother's strange deliverance.

Soon she'll be waking up again. In her sleep her lips move, mouthing a porous message. I watch her eyelids, the way they flutter on top of what must be a swirl of rolling dreams, drug-provoked dreams, and in the middle of that swirl must be imbedded, already, the knowledge of separation and loss. Or is it?

There's no telling how my mother will react.

I regard her large, trunky, sleeping body and think how little I know it, how impossible it is to gauge her response when told about her "lump."

She may shudder with disgust, squeeze her eyes shut and shake her head from side to side, *not me, not me*. She has always been a fastidious woman, not much at peace with the body's various fluids and forces. I can imagine her clearing her throat, ashamed and apologetic.

Or she may surprise me by laughing. I remind myself that she has sometimes demonstrated signs of unpredictable humour — witness her chesty retelling of family stories or the cartoons she occasionally clips from the newspaper and pins up in the kitchen. She may bestow on her little nugget a pet name, Bertie or Sweet Pea, and make a fully rounded story out of it, her very own medical adventure, suitable for the ears of her canasta cronies, more interesting, more *dramatic* than a gall bladder or thyroid condition and a lot more cheerful now that it's out and sitting in a jar of formaldehyde. Would she ask for such a jar? Keep it up on the shelf next to her Hummel figurines? There sits my little Bertie. Or Sweet Pea. Laughing.

Or she may grieve. Lord, *I* would grieve. I *am* grieving. Just thinking of this colourless little bean of human matter sharing my mother's blood and warmth all those years brings a patch of tears into my throat. My mother was the only child of elderly parents. She had a gawky girlhood, married, bore two children, was widowed, grew heavy, grew old; and all the time she was harbouring this human husk under the folds of her skin. It wasn't my father, it wasn't my sister or me, but this compacted little *thing* who followed her through her most secret rituals, bonded to her plunging moods and brief respites, a loyal *other*, given a free ride and now routed out.

Under the hospital sheets her body already looks lighter, making my body — hovering over her, adjusting her pillow, checking the i.v. needle in her arm — correspondingly heavy.

I'm tempted to grope under the band of my skirt, grab hold of my flesh and see what it is that's weighing me down — whether it's Mary Swann who has taken up residence there or the cool spectre of loneliness that stretches ahead for me. Because it does, *it does*.

My mother, still sleeping, breathes unsteadily, grabbing little, light girlish puffs of air. For the first time in my life I envy her, wanting a portion of her new lightness. Probably she'll sleep like this for another hour. Relief begins to settle around me. The bruise on my cheek resumes its faint throbbing. When she wakes up we'll talk for a bit, and after that I'll slip off to the telephone to call Stephen as I promised.

18

Letters; I've fallen behind in my letter writing, but nevertheless they arrive at the door in bales.

Willard Lang has written me a brisk, cosy little note saying my paper has arrived and been reviewed by the program committee and deemed very suitable *indeed*. A place on the agenda has been given to me, one hour for my lecture and twenty minutes for questions from the floor, should there be any. (He warns me not to go beyond the time limit since a buffet lunch is planned for 12:30, after which there will be a varied program of workshops.) I am to speak at the opening session immediately after the coffee break that follows Dr. Morton Jimroy's keynote address. There is an implication of honour in this.

Morton Jimroy has written a long, disjointed, and somewhat paranoid letter from Palo Alto. He distrusts Lang and dreads the unveiling of the four love poems, fearing they will spawn absurd theories. His own work is going well, despite the fact that Mary Swann's daughter, Frances, has become inexplicably hostile. He despairs of getting anything more from her. Furthermore, the continual California sunshine is oppressive, and there are roses blooming all around his rented house, he says, too many roses, which give the effect of vulgar profusion and untimeliness. He would like to lop off their heads with a pair of shears, but is afraid this might violate the terms of tenancy. Three times he tells me he is looking forward to meeting me: in the first paragraph, again in a middle paragraph, and once more in the closing paragraph. "We will have so much to say to each other," he suggests, declares, promises.

Frederic Cruzzi writes, agreeing, reluctantly, to attend the symposium. A stilted letter and faintly arrogant, but he praises my handwriting.

Rose Hindmarch from Nadeau, Ontario, has sent me a note on the back of a Christmas card, though it is only the first week in December, the Holy Family bathed in spears of blue light. "If my health permits," she writes, "I will be going to the symposium in January. Hope you'll be there so we can have a good gab." This letter stirs in me separate wavelets of emotion: pleasure that she's been invited; guilt (the free-floating variety) at the mention of her poor health; concern, in case she remembers Mary Swann's rhyming dictionary and mentions it to someone; and anticipation at the warm mention of a "gab," my needy self being fed by all manifestations of sisterhood.

A woman in Amsterdam (signature illegible) writes to say she has just finished reading the Dutch edition of *The Female Prism* and that it has changed her life. (Immediately after my book was published I received about two hundred such letters, mostly from women, though three were from men, crediting me with changing their lives, liberating them from their biological braces and so on. Nowadays, I sometimes see my book for sale in second-hand bookstores, and I'm always surprised at how little pain this gives me.)

A letter comes from Larry Fine who has gone out west to interview witnesses of the Mt. St. Helens eruption. "Temporary danger breeds permanent fears," he informs me, "but surprisingly few people can recall the exact date of the disaster."

My sister, Lena, writes from London — at the bottom is a string of pencilled kisses from my adored little Franklin, aged six — begging me to keep close watch over our post-operative mother, which she herself would do if she weren't so far away and hadn't just changed jobs again, abandoning the handcrafted bird-cage business for the more people-oriented field of therapy massage, chiefly whacking the daylights out of forty-year-old Englishmen, nostalgic for their boarding schools.

Olaf writes, reporting on his happiness/unhappiness quotient, describing a decided list toward gloom and outlining three positive steps planned to correct it; for a start he has regrown his beard. "And how are you getting on?" he asks in a postscript.

"How are you?" asks Stephen Stanhope on a little postcard from San Diego (windsurfers on a blue sea) where he's performing for a horticultural convention. No "wish you were here." No jokes. Just: "Hope to see you Thursday night."

"A little token," says a note from Brownie, a note tucked inside a lovely old book of essays by Anna Jameson. It arrives in a padded envelope. A second edition, 1880. Cover: a soft shade of brown with gold thingamajigs on the corners. Title: *Characteristics of Women*. "Sorry I couldn't make it last week," says Brownie in his artful printing. "Up to my neck with the book fair."

"A thousand thanks," says a note from Betsy Gore-Heppel. "Emma loves her little sling and is slowly adapting to life outside the womb. If my mental health holds up I should be back in class some time after Christmas."

A mimeo letter, folded and stapled: "The Free Nelson Mandela Action Committee will hold its next meeting at 6:30 in the back room at Arnies. WE need YOU."

"You rat," writes my friend-and-sometime-mentor, Peggy O'Reggis, who has gone to Mexico City to teach printmaking. "You promised to write and . . ."

"Just a scrawl to inquire whether you've broken your right wrist," writes Lorenzo Drouin, the medievalist, on sabbatical in Provence.

"Finally tracked down that quotation," says a note from dear old Professor Gliden, "which I think may shed some light on the point I was trying to make . . ."

Another postcard from San Diego (seals sporting in emerald water). "Rained out in Calif. Coming home Weds instead of Thurs."

"Dear Dr. Maloney," says a typewritten letter from Dora Movius at the university archives. "We're experiencing some difficulty tracking down the material you requested. Will you please phone me at the above number between the hours of . . .''

"I haven't heard from you in some time," writes Morton Jimroy, charmingly, the second letter in ten days. "I expect I've offended you by being overly familiar. I've always been such a terrible dolt."

Finally: "Please copy this letter three times and send to above address. In one week you will receive six (6) single earrings of good quality. To break this chain is to invite disaster."

19

Dora Movius who looks after the literary records on the third floor of the archives is an immensely cross woman with solid pads of fat under her eyes. Her heavy lower jaw juts forward as though guarding a mouthful of bitter minerals. Over the years I've run into her a number of times, particularly during the period when I was working on my thesis, and I've never been able to understand how I came to offend her so deeply. A sister in the struggle, I say to myself, blinking and denying.

People who work in libraries, like those in bakeshops, ought to be made peaceful and happy by their surroundings, but they almost never are. Today Mrs. Movius looks preoccupied and impervious in a black gabardine jacket, one hard fabric scouring another. Because she has bad news for me — I sense it already — she produces a small ghost of a smile, or at least the muscles around her mouth move in an outward direction.

"I've looked everywhere for the copy you requested," she says. (A perfumed, high-pitched voice, tense with vibrato.) *"We've* looked everywhere," she adds, as though to dilute blame.

A feeble dignity keeps me from replying at once. Then I tell her in my most reasonable tone, "But I'm sure it's here, Mrs. Movius. I brought it in myself for safe keeping. If you'll remember, it was not to be circulated but—"

"I'm afraid we've been unable to locate it. We've spent most of an afternoon, my assistant and I, looking—" The perfume falls out of the air.

"Maybe I could look—?"

"I'm afraid that's not possible. I'm sure you understand, Dr. Maloney, that we can't let people just walk in off the street and—"

"But it has to be somewhere," I insist.

"Undoubtedly." Arms locked across a hard front. Always ready with admonishment.

Shove and push, push and shove. I try again. "I don't want to appear melodramatic, Mrs. Movius, but I really do need that copy for a paper I'm presenting next month. I mean, people are counting on me. The Swann symposium, maybe you know, is meeting in Toronto and I'm scheduled—"

She waves her hands to shut me up.

"I can only suggest you use your original. We could photocopy it again for you if necessary, but we cannot—"

"But you see," I take a mouthful of air, humbled, a fourteen-year-old girl again, whimpering with guilt, my iris-in-a-glass-vase nowhere to be seen. "The problem is that the original's been lost."

"Lost?"

"Lost."

"You don't mean you—?"

"Yes."

She pauses at this, a deadly ten seconds, and then righteousness transforms the hard putty of her face. "Well" — shrugging — "that's always the risk we run."

"I know but—"

"As you know, Dr. Maloney, we strongly suggest that the originals be filed with us and the copies be retained by—"

"I know, I know. But surely it's with . . . isn't it filed . . . filed with the rest of the Swann material?"

"That's the problem, I'm afraid." The top half of Mrs. Movius' face gives a little reflective twitch and then softens. For a moment I think she is going to pat me on the shoulder. "We can't imagine how it happened, but *all* the Swann material seems to have disappeared. It's simply" — her voice drops angrily; she looks ready to strike me — "it's simply *lost.*"

20

There are times when the stately iris fails, when it's necessary to take a hot curling iron to life's random offerings. Either that or switch off your brain waves and fade away, as Mary Swann suggests doing in the first of her water poems.

> The rivers in this country
> Shrink and crack and kill
> And the waters of my body
> Grow invisible.

Tonight, on Christmas Eve, a night of wet snow and dangerous streets, Stephen Stanhope and I were married. The wedding was at five-thirty, in the living-room of my house. We had a roaring fire going, and it got so hot that Stephen and his father and Gifford ("Whistling Giff") Gerrard, the judge who performed the ceremony, had to remove their jackets the minute the ceremony was over.

Stephen's father's new wife, who is the same age as I, wore pink silk overalls and a pale grey blouse. My mother, looking tired and ill at ease, wore her best blue crepe dress and, notwithstanding the heat, a cream stole stretched over her shoulders. Lois Lundigan wore Paisley, and Virginia Goodchild, who came all the way from New Orleans on three days' notice, wore a kind of suede tuxedo cinched by a braided sash. I wore a white challis smock and wonderful white lacy stockings.

Stephen's father came in a suit of boardroom blue, "Whistling Giff" in courtroom black, and Stephen in a borrowed blazer of a colour I cannot now remember. Professor Gliden (in grey knitted vest and maroon tie) proposed the toast to the bride ("our very own irrepressible Sarah") and read aloud the pile of telegrams: from Lena wishing me happiness and from Olaf wishing me contentment and from the women in my Wednesday seminar wishing me success. We all ate and drank a good deal, and Stephen and I sat in the middle of the floor and opened gifts, the largest being a self-assemble perspex table from Lois Lundigan and the oddest being a cham-

pagne bottle from Larry Fine filled with Mt. St. Helens ash. Brownie
sent us a wooden bowl covered with strange tear-shaped gouges,
beautiful, and a printed note that said, "Happiness and prosperity."
My mother presented a set of Fieldcrest sheets, and Stephen's father,
executing a kind of tribal pounce, gave us a stock certificate worth
several times my annual salary.

At midnight, after much embracing, everyone went home in taxis,
and Stephen and I took off our clothes and dove into bed.

"Well," said Stephen. His large soft-footed voice.

"Well," said I.

Well, well, here we lie, side by side, two exhausted twentieth-
century primates, bare skin against bare skin. What in God's name
have we done?

For a fraction of a second, Doubt, that strolling player in my life,
stares down from the ceiling, a flicker of menace. I give it a com-
plicit wink, then wonder if this is the same shadow that foreclosed
on Mary Swann. But no, the steady unalarming breathing beside
me convinces me otherwise. Strange how the whole of this man's
body seems to breathe, as though equipped with gills. *Reprise,
reprise*; that lovely word mixes with the shadows. A number of
thoughts come toward me at full sail, an armada of the night, blown
by happiness.

A week ago Morton Jimroy wrote a letter in which he said: "We
live in a confessional age."

But he's wrong. This is a secretive age. Our secrets are our
weapons. Think of South Africa, those clandestine meetings. Think
of the covertness of families. Think of love. How else can we express
mutiny but by the burial of our unspoken thoughts. "I love you,"
says Stephen with his uncomplicated breath. "I love you too," say
I, biting into silence as though it were a morsel of blowfish and
keeping my fingers crossed.

"As long as it's what you really want," Brownie said politely when
I phoned to tell him I was marrying Stephen Stanhope. "I need
to have a few things settled in my life," I told him, refusing to
take on the tones of a penitent. "And maybe have a baby."

Recently, during these rainy dark fall days, I've grown a little
frightened of "the irrepressible Sarah." Her awful energy seems
to require too much of me, and I wonder: Where is her core? Does
she even have a core?

I want to live for a time without irony, without rhetoric, in a cool, solid metaphor. A conch shell, that would be nice. Or a deep pink ledge of granite. I've tried diligence, done what I could; I've applied myself, and now I want my sweetness back, my girlhood sugar. Not forever, but for a while. I'd like to fix my blinking eye on a busy city street and take in the flow of people walking along hypnotically and bravely, bravely and hypnotically . . .

At last, at last, I feel my limbs begin to relax. The world is both precious and precarious. All I need do is time my breath to match Stephen's. How easily he sleeps, entertaining, no doubt, long chains of dreams in his brain and the mumbled charms of Indian clubs and tennis balls. Clearly he's not given to nightmares. What a miracle that he utterly trusts this sloping roof. There's no real reason why he should. Safe as houses. That odd expression. Where in God's name did it come from? Middle English from the sound of it. Tomorrow I'll look it up. Tomorrow.

I turn on my side, intoxicated now by the gathering weight of my body as it pushes the old worrying world away, my breath adding its substance to the heaviness and safety of the house. Almost there, my lungs tell me; a gateway glimpsed; a dream boiling on a slow burner.

And then, through the thin clay walls of a dream, I hear the telephone beside the bed ringing. Once, twice. On the third ring I catch it and hold it to my ear.

"Hello," I say, stiffening, knowing I am about to be stricken with unbearable news. My mother. The icy streets. Brownie. "Hello," I say again.

But there's no sound at all from the telephone, only the flatness of my own voice striking the painted walls. "Who is this?" I ask. "Who is this please?"

The bedroom is freezing. I am sitting on the edge of the bed, and the cold has invaded my back and shoulders and is causing my hand to shake. "Hello," I say into the silence, and then hear, distinctly, a soft click at the other end.

"Hello, hello, hello," I sing into the wailing dial tone.

First to come is a sense of reprieve, which yields an instant later to panic. I am shivering all over, my eyes wide open.

Morton Jimroy

JIMROY WAS FEELING LONELY his first month in California and decided to go one evening to a student production of *The Imaginary Invalid*. Why he should do this was puzzling; Molière's plays had always seemed to him a waste of time. But his spirits had taken a sudden dip, and he reasoned that an evening out would do him good.

It was not unusual for him to take his pleasures in this way, as though they were doses of medicine. Bookishness had kept him narrow, or so his ex-wife had complained. "You look like a bloody monk," she accused him once, putting her long, purplish neck around the door of his study — she never did learn to knock. "You ought to get out now and then," she scolded. "Mix a little. Have more fun. It'd cure what ails you."

Dear old Aud. Well meaning, sensible, but a woman whose intuitive thrusts had invariably reminded Jimroy of metal shelving screwed to a wall. It was like her always to think she knew what ailed him. He smiled at the thought. Audrey with her frizz of red hair, her narrow shoulders and flat front. And her elbows, the way they went scaly in winter so that she had to rub them with Jergens before she went to bed, his dear, greasy Aud. He thought of her often, especially in the early evenings, especially in the fall of the year, and yet it was an indulgence thinking about her, one that brought him sharp little arrows of pain. But yes, he admitted it. He missed the cups of strong tea she used to bring him after dinner, and even the way she set them down — hard — on his desk.

Well, time dulled petty irritations. Time had even brought a perverse rosy appreciation for those acts of Audrey's that he'd found most annoying, so that now it was with autumnal nostalgia — certainly not love — that he recalled her voice, clamorous and hoarse from too much smoking, and the white tea mug grasped in her chapped hand.

There was no autumn in California, which Jimroy found disorienting. Here it was, the third week in September, and all around him trees and shrubs were keeping their shrill green. Numbers of dripping eucalyptus gave a blue roundness to the air, a roundness cut by the ubiquitous highways with their terrifying loops and ramps. Stanford bloomed. Everywhere along the campus walls and walkways flowers swayed; and what flowers! — like open mouths with little tongues dragging out. Oppressive, Jimroy thought, but was careful not to say so aloud.

He reminded himself that there would be no winter to cope with; he wouldn't miss that, not for a minute. Back home in Manitoba it made his head ache to hear his acquaintances exclaim year after year about the beauty of trees in their winter dress or the music of snow crunching underfoot. This year he had escaped all that, as well as the kitsch outpourings it seemed to inspire. A snowless year. His *annus mirabilis*. He would be able to sleep all year round with the windows wide open. For this coup he congratulated himself, thinking happily of his heavy, hairy coat and gloves and overshoes left back in Winnipeg in a bedroom closet, locked away from the young tenant who had rented his house. Let him freeze.

This year, his fifty-first, he would be spared the drift of snow around his windows and that confusing ritual with the antifreeze that he had never felt easy with. Californians were spoiled and fortunate, and this green place was clearly paradise, and yet, and yet . . . . When he looked around him at the people he had met in the last few weeks, he could not imagine how they regulated their lives or what it was that kept them buoyant.

The Molière play at the Stanford Student Center began at nine o'clock. This would not have been the case in Winnipeg, where things got under way at eight-thirty. And there were other differences. Here people drifted in, a surprising number of them alone, wearing soft clothes and looking sleepy-eyed and dreamy as though they had just risen from their beds. The girl who showed him to his seat wore old faded jeans and a navy cardigan with the buttons mismatched. This seemed to Jimroy a fey affectation, and so did the high sweet western voice. "There," she crooned to Jimroy, as though he were a person of no consequence. "There at the end."

He was handed a program printed on what looked like a section of newsprint, an immense limp sheet too big to be held on the lap.

The ink rubbed off on his fingers, and after the house lights dimmed he let it slide to the floor.

Molière had no heart. Even the French, he was told, admitted that Shakespeare outdid Molière in largeness of heart. There was no worthwhile philosophy, either, and no real intelligence. Surfaces and madcap mischief, coincidence and silliness, hiding in armoires or scrambling under beds; that was the sum of it. Still, once or twice toward the end of the first act he caught himself smiling, and he welcomed his own smile with a sense of reprieve, thinking in Audrey's insipid phrase that this might, after all, be good for what ailed him.

During the intermission Jimroy remained in his seat and studied, from the corner of his eye, a man who had come in late and was sitting to his left. He was a man in his late twenties, perhaps a little older, with curly brown hair brushed back from a pale forehead. There was an expression about the eyes that was close-hauled and secretive — probably he'd been drinking. The nose was beaky; no, the whole face was beaky. On his chin was a brown mole, which protruded slightly, though it wasn't large enough to be disfiguring. But the surprising thing about this man was that he was wearing a full Scottish kilt. Jimroy took in the soft reds and greens of the tartan and reflected that the cloth looked both old and authentic, and there was one of those little leather purses hanging from his belt. (There was a name for them. What was it, now?)

Jimroy pondered the significance of this Scottish costume. Probably there was none. Half the people in Palo Alto seemed to drift about dressed as characters out of a play. Yesterday, crossing the campus, he'd seen a bare-chested youth in satin track pants coming toward him on a unicycle, balancing an armload of books and flashing the tense nervous smile of an actor. The Creative Sandwich Shop where he'd eaten lunch today had been filled with long-skirted gipsy-like girls, and one of them, barely out of puberty, had worn what looked like a width of carpeting belted around her hips. Another girl behind the counter, scooping out avocado flesh and smashing it onto slices of bread, was dressed in blue bib overalls covered with tiny embroidered flowers and the stitched message over one breast, "Taste Me." (Jimroy had stared boldly at this message, wanting to show that he did not find it in the least shocking — which indeed he did not.)

"Pardon me." It was the man in the kilt.

"Are you speaking to me?" Jimroy heard his own voice, priggish and full of Canadian vowel sounds.

"You've dropped your program." Then, "At least I believe it's yours."

"Thank you, very kind." His snorty laugh, never intended, but always ready to betray him.

"Interesting production, wouldn't you say?" The man in the kilt said this in a bright, liturgical, surprised-sounding voice. A Scottish accent, Jimroy noted, though certainly muted, perhaps even counterfeit.

"Quite good," Jimroy said, feeling friendly because of the ambiguity of the accent. "Especially the notary."

"Ah, yes, the notary. Wonderful. Great sense of maturity. And the maid, what do you think of the maid, little Toinette? Now that's a role to conjure with."

"Very demanding, yes," Jimroy said, and rested his gaze on the Scotsman's knees, which were clutched tightly together. Nervous type. Perhaps the kilt eased his limbs and that was the reason he wore it.

He considered his own clothes, the light green cotton pants and the checked shirt, not at all what he might have worn for an evening out at the Manitoba Theatre Centre. They were emergency clothes, bought three weeks ago when the airline admitted, finally, that both of his suitcases seemed to be temporarily lost. (Temporarily—what a joke.) They had gone astray somewhere between Manitoba and California. No one was able to account for it. He phoned the airline office every day or two, but nothing had turned up yet, and meanwhile he alternated between two sets of clothes he'd purchased in a men's store in the Stanford Shopping Mall. The clothes were cheap, but the colours pleased him, these minty green pants and a second pair in a sort of salmon. He had also bought himself a minimal supply of underwear, some white socks — when had he last worn white socks? — and a pair of pyjamas made in Taiwan.

With this limited wardrobe he had managed well enough and, in fact, rather liked the clean feeling of owning so spare a closet of clothes. But soon he would need a suit and a dress shirt or two. More alarming was the loss of some papers he needed for his work and, of course, the photograph of Mary Swann. He would give the airline another week and then begin to press them harder. Luggage didn't disappear into thin air. It had to be somewhere. He realized now that he should have made more of a fuss in the first place.

At the end of the play, after the applause faded, the man in the kilt turned abruptly to Jimroy and said, "I wonder if I could persuade you to join me for a drink."

Jimroy hesitated a second, caught off guard, confused by the Scottish accent, which seemed not quite as Scottish as before, and the man quickly amended, "Or a cup of coffee perhaps. They make a very good espresso at a place not far from here."

He had feared something like this. The moment his neighbour had uttered the word "little Toinette," he had been alerted. Certain kinds of people were inevitably attracted to him; he possessed a lean body, neat shoulders, hips that were unusually small; it was probably not a good idea under the circumstances to go in for green pants. "I'm awfully sorry —"

"I just thought. Since you seemed to be alone."

"Very kind of you." Jimroy rose hurriedly, at the same time mumbling a brief apology, which was courteous, deferential and, in its way, he supposed, convincing: the lateness of the hour; an early morning appointment; and a delicate suggestion that he was expected elsewhere, that someone awaited his arrival.

No one awaited his arrival. He was living alone in a house he had rented from a famous physicist, a Nobel Prize winner, who had left, months earlier, for a year in Stuttgart. The house was small, just two bedrooms, a single-storey California-style house with white siding and redwood trim. The rent was entirely reasonable considering how close it was to the university, so close he was able to manage without a car. The famous physicist's wife, Marjorie Flanner, had been anxious to join her husband in Germany and was happy to find a tenant like Jimroy who was mature and responsible.

She showed him the large tiled bathroom and the stacks of folded sheets in the linen cupboard. In the bedroom she pressed down on the mattress with the heel of her hand to demonstrate its firmness and told him whom he might phone if there were problems with the air conditioning. The only thing she really cared about, she said, was the garden. Things needed pruning. Occasionally, depending on the weather, it was necessary to water certain of the plants or spray for spiders. The gate at the back of the garden had to be kept latched so the children in the neighbourhood would stay out of the roses. "I hope you like roses." She smiled at Jimroy. Her middle-aged face was soft and puffed, rather like a rose itself.

He knew nothing about roses. He knew none of the names for any of the flowers in the garden or even the name of the bent little tree that stood protected by its own low wall of pink brick. The yard in Winnipeg, his and Audrey's, had contained nothing but a patch of grass, a pair of lilac bushes and what Audrey liked to call her veg patch, her rows of onions and radishes and runner beans. "I hope you like roses." Mrs. Flanner turned her pink face in his direction.

Reluctant to crush her open look of hopefulness, he exclaimed in his awful voice, "I adore roses," and heard himself continue, "Roses, as a matter of fact, happen to be my favourite type of bloom."

Already he was imagining himself carrying his morning coffee into the Flanners' garden, along with his books and papers. There were several garden chairs grouped on the flagged patio. And the little brick wall would serve nicely as a kind of desk. He felt certain that the sun — a whole year of sun — would do him good. As for the Flanners' roses, he would put up a notice somewhere, perhaps run an advert in the local paper. There must be thousands of gardeners in this part of the world.

Marjorie Flanner did *not* treat him as though he were a person of no consequence. She made him a gin and tonic, stirred it carefully, and decorated it with a frilled lemon slice, and they sat for an hour on the wrought-iron garden chairs discussing details about the house. The neighbours were "tremendous," she said, all of them Stanford people; he would be besieged with dinner invitations. Hmmmmm, said Jimroy, who intended to ignore the neighbours. About the rent, she said, would he mind very much giving her postdated cheques. Not at all, Jimroy said, and immediately pulled out his chequebook, asking in a polite, faintly stagy voice, if she would like a bank reference.

At this she almost, but not quite, giggled. "Heavens, no. I mean, in a way I *do* know you. That is," she adjusted her pretty legs, "that is, my discussion group's just done your book on Starman. Someone in the group suggested, way back last year I think it was, that we try one of Morton Jimroy's books."

He fixed his eyes on the brick wall and tried not to look pleased. "So you're hardly a stranger, Professor Jimroy. But I'm afraid I haven't read your other book, the one on Pound."

"Don't apologize please—" Jimroy began, conscious of a small pink wound opening in the vicinity of his heart, a phenomenon that occurred always when such blithe confessions were brought forth. Irrational. Paranoid.

"But then—" Marjorie Flanner gave a small laugh — "I haven't really read Ezra Pound either. I mean, not really."

"Pound can be difficult," he said kindly. Even more kindly he added, "And he can be an awful old bore too."

Then they both laughed. He imagined their laughter and the blended tinkling of their ice cubes floating through the lathe fence and reaching the ears of the friendly neighbours, the ones who soon would be pressing dinner invitations on him. He dared another look at Marjorie Flanner's warm brown legs and wondered if he should suggest dinner some place. No.

She was back on the subject of roses. Five years ago she and Josh had brought in a load of special soil. Roses liked a sandy loam with just the right balance of minerals. Whenever Josh came home from one of his trips he always brought back a new rose cutting. It was illegal, of course, bringing rose cuttings into the country, and so he had become adept at smuggling. There was this little loose piece of lining in his suitcase, and it was under this flap that he hid his contraband.

Josh the Nobel Prize winner, a smuggler of rose cuttings. Jimroy found the fact discreditable but humanizing. (Later, after he moved in, he would wander about the little house thinking: a Nobel Prize winner sat in this armchair, lay on that pillow, occupied this toilet seat, adjusted this shower head.)

Mrs. Flanner, her face flushed — clearly she liked her drinks — poured him a second gin and tonic and asked what it was that had brought him to California for a year. "Are you working on a new biography?"

"I'm afraid so," he said. Eyes downcast, expression modest. Ever the man possessed, the body snatcher.

"And is it to be another poet?" She asked this in her merry voice.

"I'm afraid so," he said again.

"I don't suppose I really should ask who—"

"I doubt very much if you've heard of her," he began.

"Ah!" she said, and clapped her hands together. Brown hands with rather short fingers and an old-fashioned wedding ring in reddish gold. "A her! A woman! How wonderful. I mean, my group will be thrilled that—"

"As I say, though, she is not well known. Hardly in the same class as Starman or Pound. Still she was quite a remarkable poet in her way—" He wished to appear forthright, honest, but out came the old sly evasions.

"I wonder if I might know her," Marjorie Flanner said. "I used to read a lot of poetry when I was younger. Josh and I—"

"Mary Swann."

"Pardon?"

"Her name. Mary Swann. The poet I'm working on at the moment."

"Aahhh!" A look of mild incomprehension. She took a rather large gulp of gin and then asked politely, "And did she have a fascinating life?"

"I'm afraid not," Jimroy said, feeling a quickening of his body. "I think you would have to say she had one of the dullest lives ever lived."

She looked at him with new interest. "And yet she was a remarkable poet."

"That *is* the paradox," he said, giving a laugh that came out a bark. "That was, I suppose, the thing I could not resist."

"I can imagine," Marjorie Flanner said. She smiled. Her teeth flashed, and Jimroy could see the grindings of an old eagerness. "Well, that's quite a challenge, Professor Jimroy."

Quite a challenge. Jimroy wondered in an idle way if Marjorie Flanner had ever uttered those words *it's quite a challenge* to Joshua Flanner as he sat contemplating the mysteries of mass and energy that glued the universe together. Probably she had. Probably Joshua Flanner, humanist and smuggler of rose cuttings, had not found the phrase objectionable. Why should he? Who but a throttled misanthrope would object to such a trifling remark?

Later, at the motel where he was staying temporarily, falling asleep in his buttoned, made-in-Taiwan pyjamas, Jimroy remembered the brief bright expansion of Mrs. Flanner's face as she handed him the house keys. It had seemed artificially lit, a social expression only, as though she were concealing some minor disappointment she felt toward him. Perhaps she *had* expected him to invite her to dinner, or even to stay the night. It was a failing of Jimroy's, not knowing what other people expected.

Like many an introvert, Jimroy distrusts the queasy interior world of the psyche, but has enormous faith in the mechanics of the exterior world of governments and machinery and architecture and science — all these he sees as being presided over by anonymous but certified authorities who are reliable and enduring and who, most importantly, are possessed of good intentions. He is able to step back from the threat of acid rain, for instance — every softy in Canada is babbling about acid rain — certain that ecologists will arrive any day now at a comprehensive solution. He *trusts* them to find an answer; they will find it chiefly because the burden of their care demands it. AIDS will be conquered too, Jimroy has no doubt about it, what with the piles of research money and all those serious ready faces turned together in consultation.

And on a more self-interested level, he reasons that someone or other will always come forward, ready to defend *his* civil liberties, and someone else will keep him relatively safe on the highways and even flying through the air. A race of incomprehensible (to him) men and women have assumed responsibility for *his* safety, have been willing to make regulations, set standards, and bring into being an entire system of checks and counter checks. When he flicks the switch on the Flanners' microwave oven to warm up his taco dinner he takes it for granted that the tiny crinkled rays will permeate the food and not him, and that the tacos themselves, though tasteless, will be free of botulism. Thus, when he thinks about his lost luggage, he is no more than marginally worried.

His two large vinyl suitcases, one black, one tan, are not, after all, metaphysical constructs, but physical objects occupying definable space. The number of places where these suitcases might reasonably be is finite. It is only a matter of time before they are discovered and identified and shipped to him in Palo Alto, accompanied by official apologies and an entirely plausible explanation, which he will, of course, believe and accept with grace; this is not a perfect world — how well he knows that — but a world, at least, turned in the general direction of improvement.

Besides, he sees now that his Manitoba clothes would be out of place here. Those suits of his, those heavy laced shoes; it would be an act of brutality to bring such dark colours and such thick materials into the delicate latticed light of California. He wears open-weave shirts now, pure cotton preferably, and finds he can get along perfectly well without a tie, even when invited out to dinner. The sandals he bought for $4.95 are about to fall apart after one month — it seems they are stapled rather than sewn — but he is prepared to buy another pair, and another — they are surprisingly comfortable, too, especially when worn over a pair of heavy cotton socks.

It's true he's been inconvenienced by the loss of some of his papers, but it was an easy matter to telephone Mrs. Lynch in Winnipeg and have her send photocopies. His first-draft documents are safely locked away in a desk drawer in his study at home, which is a relief. He does, though, suffer intermittent worry over the photograph of Mary Swann. It had not been a good idea to bring it. It cannot be replaced and is one of only two known photographs of her in existence. (The other, much the inferior, is still in the Nadeau Museum, a blurred snapshot of Mrs. Swann standing in front of her house with her eyes sealed shut by sunlight.) The loss of the photograph would be serious, tragic in a sense, if indeed it is lost, but Jimroy persists, even after days and weeks have gone by, in thinking that his luggage will reappear at any moment.

This occasional nagging worry about the photograph is, in any case, tempered by the relief he feels that at least he has the letters from Sarah Maloney safely in his possession. What amazing luck! He can't help wondering what bolt of good fortune made him decide at the last minute, packing his things in Winnipeg, to put Sarah's letters in his briefcase rather than with his other papers in his luggage. When he thinks of it, he shakes his head and feels blessed.

He needs the letters more than ever now that he has been uprooted; they stabilize him, keeping away that drifting sadness that comes upon him late in the evening, eleven, eleven-thirty, when the density of the earth seems to empty out. It's then that he likes to reread her letters, letters that pulse and promise, that make his throat swell with the thought of sex. He props himself on the headboard of the Flanners' outsize bed, cleansed from his shower, toenails pared, a cup of hot milk at his elbow. (Half his stomach was removed the winter Audrey left, and he admits to anyone kind enough to inquire that the hot milk and the early nights are needed now; besides he likes to think of his homely habits as a precaution against hubris.)

"Dear Morton Jimroy," runs her first letter, sent to him more than a year ago in Winnipeg. "Will you allow me to introduce myself? My name is Sarah Maloney, and a mutual friend, Willard Lang, has told me that you too are interested in the work of Mary Swann. I am writing to ask you . . ."

"Dear Mr. Jimroy," the second letter reads — Jimroy keeps the letters in chronological order, each one in its original envelope with its U.S. stamp and the Chicago postmark. "I am amazed and delighted to have a letter back from you so quickly, amazed in fact that you replied at all after my cheeky intrusion—"

"Dear Morton," reads letter three. "Your cheerful letter arrived on a day when I particularly required a cheerful letter—"

He is glad she waits a decent interval before answering his letters. The silence torments him, but endows her with substance.

Ah, Sarah, Sarah. He sings her name aloud, so round a sound, so annulated — to the walls, the ceiling, the open window. The smell of flowers floats in from the garden, and he wonders if it could possibly be jasmine at this time of year. (The neighbours have mentioned jasmine; he himself wouldn't recognize a jasmine bloom if it were right before his eyes, another admission. The neighbours have also cautioned him about leaving the windows wide open. Hasn't he ever heard of burglars?)

From nowhere comes an overpowering wish to share the fragrant air with Sarah Maloney of Chicago. He inhales deeply — the stillness of uncommunicated rapture! — releases his breath in a long sighing moan, like a man gasping out the richness of his cravings, and then picks up Sarah's letters again. They bring him — what? — solace. And connection with the world, a world redolent with intimate pleasures, sight, sound, touch, especially touch. His tongue tests the sharpness of his teeth. He imagines Sarah Maloney's soft lips, and how they must enclose small, white, perfect teeth, opening and speaking, her teasing voice. *Take off that ridiculous shirt, she says, and helps him with the buttons. Hurry, she commands, now those silly green pants, let me do the zipper for you. There. That's better.*

Ah, how soft. How adorable. Like a little bird, all fluttery. Let me put my mouth there for a minute. Please. See, I told you I'd be gentle.

It is not quite sane, Jimroy knows, these images, this caressing of a strange woman's words, but the warmth they carry has become a necessary illusion, what he appears to need if he is going to continue his life.

In October Jimroy was asked to address a group of graduate students and staff.

As a Distinguished Visitor, his official title for the year, he knew he would be required from time to time to "share" his experience as a writer of literary biography. The word *share* is an irritant, nevertheless, for what would these hundred or so naked faces in the audience share with *him*? Their gaping incredulity? Their eagerness for "advice"? What?

Back in Winnipeg he had demanded a year's leave of absence, hoping his life might hold one more surprise. Leave had been granted without a murmur, one of the rewards of fame, and Stanford, also without a murmur, had given him the Distinguished Visitor title, plus office space — if that little cinderblock cube with cracked floor tile could be called an office — and provided him with the services of a typist, as though he would for a minute let anyone, anyone but Mrs. Lynch, handle his personal correspondence. He had, moreover, been "welcomed to the Stanford community of scholars," as Dean Evans put it in his introduction to Jimroy's afternoon talk.

Welcomed? A nebulous word. An ingratiating word. An oily, blackened coin. Community of scholars? Equally cut-rate, and ludicrous, too, since they all looked like tennis players arrayed before him. A ripple of faces, eye slits and dark combed hair, a collage of open-necked T-shirts, muscular forearms, healthy hands gripping biceps, and the conditioned eagerness of beagles, the fools, the idiots.

Stop, Jimroy hissed to himself, in God's name, desist.

He longed for Sarah in Chicago, serene and responsive and saying the right thing, the only thing; he longed for autumn, for the indulgent sadness that autumn brings. He longed for Manitoba and his bumbling starch-fed students who conceived of literature as a comical family product to be gnawed upon between real meals,

Shakespeare's Richard, a nutty Oh Henry bar for a vacant Saturday afternoon. And why not?

Didn't these monied Stanford sharpies realize that literature was only a way for the helpless to cope. Get back to your tennis courts, he wanted to shout. Out into the sunshine. Live! Universities are nothing but humming myth factories. Dear God. How we love to systemize and classify what is rich and random in life. How our fingers itch to separate the tangled threads of theme and anti-theme, moral vision and moral blindness, God and godlessness, joy and despair, as though all creativity sat like a head of cabbage on a wooden chopping block, ready to be hacked apart, first the leaves, then the hot, white heart. Scholarship was bunk — if they only, only knew. It was just a matter of time before the theoreticians got to Mary Swann and tore her limb from limb in a grotesque parody of her bodily death. But he could not think about that now; now was not the time.

His talk, entitled "The Curve of Life: Poetry and Principle," went well. The applause was prolonged and vigorous, even from the back of the lecture hall, where a number of people had been forced to stand throughout the hour. When Dean Evans called for questions from the floor, Jimroy was flattered to see so many hands in the air. Such strong brown arms, flailing the air, beseeching. Rather touching in a way.

"Can you tell us if you think a biographer has a moral obligation to his or her subject?" This from the slenderest of young women, lovely, lovely, those frail shoulders. Crushable. And such hair. A voice clear as bouillon. Pour forth, my beauty.

"What kind of moral obligation are you thinking of?" Jimroy asked her in his most tender, questioning manner.

She hesitated, raised her lovely shoulders an eighth of an inch. "I just mean, well, if you're looking at someone's life, say, and you feel that there's something, like, well, private, would you—"

"Respect it." Jimroy supplied. Gentlemanly. A thin smile playing on his lips, but nothing committal. He liked to think he had eyes that expressed irony.

"Exactly. Yes. Well, sort of, yeah."

"I think that that would depend on whether the subject was still living. One certainly must respect the living, that goes without saying. And perhaps this will explain why my work, so far anyway, has focused on deceased poets."

Laughter. Right on cue. Discouraging.

"But," cried a young man, excitedly leaping to his feet, "What if the body of work is still alive and breathing? Don't you feel that the work *is* the poet? Take Sylvia Plath—"

"Rexroth says—" came a carroty-textured voice from the front row.

"I believe," said Jimroy, squelching the untimely intrusion, "that you must be alluding to the central mystery of art. Which is—" he paused and sent his long visionary look out over the heads of the audience, "which is, that from common clay, works of genius evolve. That is to say, the work often possesses a greater degree of dignity than the hand that made it."

"But isn't—?"

Jimroy cut him off. Crapshooter! Dunce! "Of course a biographer of a writer must pay as much attention to the work as to the life. But the life is more than gossip and disclosure. It is what the work feeds on. One's own experience, before it is tainted by art."

"Tainted?" A challenge like gunfire.

He was being doubted; that same shouting voice. "Yes, in a sense." (Give the lad his orotund best.) "The highest work, the most original work, comes, I believe, out of an innocent, ignorant groping in the dark."

The young challenger was on his feet, but now he was seeking reconciliation. "Would you say, sir, that Pound had a sense of innocence?"

Sir? That was better. But Jimroy paused, always defensive about Pound, always sensitive to the sin of apostasy. "In the beginning, yes. Later on, quite definitely no." The old equivocation, the old yes-and-no trick. Dear Christ, it shamed him to think he could still get away with it.

"But Dr. Jimroy—"

"It's plain mister, I'm afraid—." He gave the audience his expansive look, hands held out to his sides, palms up, fingers crabbed, as though caught on invisible wires.

"Mr. Jimroy, then. In your book on Starman, you said something or other about his ability to sustain the elegiac by—"

"Up to a certain point."

The afternoon was a success, yes, definitely. Jimroy spoke for some minutes about the mystique of elegy, leaving behind a cloud of allusions for the astute to sniff out, and a final silver *aperçu* that never failed, an after-dinner mint, sinuously phrased, to hold in their mouths while their hands applauded. Dean Evans, summing up ("our speaker is far too modest . . . ") was kind enough to mention Jimroy's three honorary degrees, one of them from Princeton.

Coffee was served, also chocolate doughnuts — an odd choice, Jimroy thought, but enthusiastically consumed. Californians! The young woman — concupiscence — with the blade-carved shoulders came up to him and took his hand and said, "You must feel so close to Pound and Starman. Writing on them like that. You must feel, really, you know, in sync with them. As real people, I mean."

Jimroy detests the popular fallacy that biographers fall in love with their subjects. Such cosy presumption; its very attractiveness makes it anathema to him. So easy, so coy; this romance between writer and subject, so cheerful, so *dear*, such a convenience, such an invitation to sentimentality. And it is, in a sense, brother to that other misconception people hold about the writing of books: that after a certain point a book acquires a life of its own and begins, as they love to say, *to write itself*.

Why in the name of God, Jimroy asks himself, does the world seek so anxiously to lighten the writer's burden by pretending that writing is the product of a grand passion, that it is the effluent of love and ease? That it is *fun*?

Writing biography, as Jimroy perfectly well knows, is the hardest work in the world and it can, just as easily as not, be an act of contempt. Think of the Sartre writing on Flaubert. Ah, God. And— closer to home—who could *love* Ezra Pound? Certainly not he, not Morton Jimroy, moralist *manqué*.

The longer he spent closeted with the Pound papers—and his book on Pound took the better part of five years *(oh waste)*—the more he desired to hold the man up to ridicule. Those long months sitting at his oak table in his study in south Winnipeg, crowded by books, crowded almost to the point of suffocation, he had felt himself being slowly crushed to death by Poundian horrors. And as the horrors accumulated he became convinced that lovers of Pound's poetry should not be spared the truth about their poet. Far from buttering over Pound's nasty little racial theories, Jimroy found himself going out of his way to expose them. This was easy enough; all that was required was that he pile massive incriminating quotations onto the page, worrying not a whit that they might be out of context. What was the point of context anyway? Wasn't Pound, he said to himself, wasn't the flatulent flabby Ezra Pound always and fatally out of context himself? Yes, oh yes! And poor Dorothy, did anyone ever spare a thought for Dorothy?

From time to time, exhausted and appalled by some fresh revelation, Jimroy stopped and demanded of himself why he had ever decided to write about Pound in the first place. Apotheosis? Never! There must have been some initial tinkling attraction—but what? He was unable to remember. But he was certain that he had never had any desire to be Pound's apologist. Meticulously, then, patiently, and with a minimum of annotation, he set out Pound's spacious social prescriptions so that they sat on the crisp typescript in all their deadpan execrable naivety for all the world to see. When a line of Pound's poetry failed to yield to analysis, he left it for the stubborn little nut of pomposity it was. Let Pound be his own hangman, Jimroy decided early on, and the correspondence alone was enough to hang him—the pettiness, the fatuous self-stroking, the hideous glimpses into a mind swollen with ghastly ambitions and believing in his tissues that he was a genius. Yes, Pound wrote to one friend, he would remain in Italy until the United States of America established a Department of Beaux Arts and "called him home" to be its director. Dear God. Elephantiasis of the ego, the horror of it.

How is a biographer to respond to delusions of this scale, to this ninny who insisted on performing cartwheels on the tremulous and silly edge of vainglory? "Make it new," the old goat exhorted young poets, tricking them into acts of foolishness. Why should a biographer be expected to explain, justify, interpret or even judge? These are acts one commits out of love, or so Jimroy has always believed.

Nevertheless the willingness, the *glee* with which he offered Pound up to ridicule frightened him slightly and forced him to modify his disgust into a mild and sour sense of distaste. (Miss Lynch, his typist, usually reticent, encouraged these modifications.)

Flinching only slightly, Jimroy observed the disgust he felt, and indeed he recognized a moral ungainliness in himself that vibrated with a near-Poundian rhythm. His original attraction to the old fart, he supposed, must lie in this perverse brotherly recognition. Like persons who in secret sniff the foul odours of their bodies, he had been mesmerized by Pound's sheer awfulness, by his *own* sheer awfulness.

He had had to rethink the book's structure. Certain vivid anecdotes had to be withdrawn or consigned to small temperate type
or worked into the inky compression of footnotes where they would
scream less shrilly for attention. The rewriting of the book—the
neutralizing of the book was how he thought of it—required an
additional six months, but the result was a biography that had been
regarded, and was still regarded, as being balanced, dispassionate,
scholarly, humane. The reviewer in the *New York Times,* describing it as *Ellmanesque,* cited its "marriage of decency and
distance"—delicious phrase. Jimroy likes to chant it to himself as
a kind of mantra on sleepless nights. Decency and distance, decency
and distance.

After a three-month vacation (during which he took Audrey back
to Birmingham for a visit; and what a disaster *that* was), he began
his book on John Starman who, in the beginning, had seemed less
detestable. The poetry, at least, with its intricacies and gymnastic
daring, appealed to him as Pound's never had; but there was no
avoiding the man's greedy seeking after fame or the slurpy lushness
of his *pensées.* Even his suicide note had a hectoring wonderful-
me, beautiful-me clamour. There was no way, either, to overlook
Starman's childish misogyny (poor Barbara) since the clod insisted
on wearing it as openly as a pair of overalls. That line in his love
series about keeping his genitalia in a vasculum for all the world
to gaze upon and admire! Dear Christ. And finally, at Starman's
centre, there was nothing but shallow and injured feelings, a gaping self-absorption that rivalled Pound's. Though Jimroy diligent-
ly chronicled the famed acts of generosity and the long lists of kindnesses to friends and fellow poets, the hollowness rang loud. And
it rang with a double echo for Jimroy, announcing not only deadness
at the centre of life, but a disenchantment with surfaces. The
discovery of emptiness affected him like the beginning of a long
illness. Once again he seemed to be looking in a mirror. (It was
during this time that Audrey finally lost all patience with him.)

Three long years. Despite the fact that the Starman book was
highly thought of, almost up to the Pound some said, it seemed
to Jimroy that the writing of it had drained away too much of his
energy. Three years with the exasperating, unhappy, unswervingly
self-regarding John Starman; a thousand days of hanging each
morning over his oak table, long hours of shifting notes, idly,
despondently, feeling sick, feeling the gnawing of an incipient ulcer,
and losing weight he could not afford to lose, and reflecting that

this was a man he would not have wanted to spend so much as an hour with.

He told himself that perhaps it was just poets he was weary of, poets from mean northern states, Minnesota, Idaho. Working on the Starman proofs (while the situation with Audrey deteriorated even further), he asked himself whether it was poetry itself he had come to despise. Certainly he was suspicious of it, its scantiness and shorthand. It was so easy for a poem to be fraudulent, for what was the difference, really, between an ellipsis and a vacuum? What indeed? Even when the words of a poem fell together in rough, rumbling, delectable rhythms, there might be nothing beneath them that spoke of thought and feeling. For this reason he had always distrusted the flashy line and kept a chilly eye on pyrotechnics, on the hollow stem of the dead narcissus. Speak to *me*, he wanted to say to poets. To poetry.

It had always seemed something of a miracle to him that poetry *did* occasionally speak. Even when it didn't he felt himself grow reverent before the quaint, queer magnitude of the poet's intent. When he thought of the revolution of planets, the emergence of species, the balance of mathematics, he could not see that any of these was more amazing than the impertinent human wish to reach into the sea of common language and extract from it the rich dark beautiful words that could be arranged in such a way that the unsayable might be said. Poetry was the prism that refracted all of life. It was Jimroy's belief that the best and worst of human experiences were frozen inside these wondrous little toys called poems. He had been in love with them all his life, and when he looked back on his childhood, something he seldom did, he saw that his early years, those passed before the discovery of poetry, had drifted by empty of meaning.

Even the failures strike him as touchingly valiant. *That*, if the truth were known, is what seduces him, the poet's naive courage. Keats, visiting the rough cottage where Robert Burns had lived, had wept to think a man had lived in such a place and tried to be a poet. (When Jimroy tells this Keats story to students, he comes close to weeping himself.) Which is why, despite everything, he is always moved when his thoughts settle on the riddlesome nature of his two large, imperfect men, Pound and Starman, thick-fingered, crippled by provincialism, morally clumsy—but made graceful, finally, by their extraordinary reach.

And so it was natural (inevitable, he told himself) that when he came to write a third biography, he should choose as his subject another poet: not a muling modernist with Left Bank pretensions this time, but a woman named Mary Swann, a woman who had lived all her lean, cold, and unrewarding years in rural Ontario, a place more northerly and restrictive than the most northern state. The decision to write about Mary Swann had been made sitting in his Winnipeg study. (Audrey had departed.) He had felt a momentary sense of elation, the by-now-familiar nascent ritual. A new beginning. Rebirth. The egg, the genes, the reaching out.

Marvellous Swann, paradoxical Swann. He would take revenge for her. Make the world stand up and applaud. It would happen.

Jimroy's nose feels tweaked by tears when he thinks of Mary Swann's reddened hands grasping the stub of a pencil and putting together the first extraordinary stanza of "Lilacs." (But he romances; it is believed that even her early poems were written with a fountain pen—and how can he assume the fact of those reddened hands?)

The discovery of her poems a few years ago had rescued him from emotional bankruptcy, and at first he *had* loved her. Here was Mother Soul. Here was intelligence masked by colloquial roughness. Her modesty was genuinely endearing and came as a relief after two monomaniacs. He treasures, for instance, her little note written to the Nadeau *News* in 1955. "Dear Mr. Editor," she began in that tiny, flat, unmistakable hand of hers. "I've just opened that letter you sent about printing my poem and can't believe my eyes. What a thrill to have something in print. As for the dollar bill, I'm going to frame it and hang it up for inspiration."

Naive, pathetic, obsequious, but certainly sincere. Jimroy has no reason to doubt the letter's sincerity. Mary Swann was forty when "Lilacs" was published. Probably she thought life had passed her by, though her despair was sharp rather than heavy and, oddly, she seemed always to be keeping back little smiles. She may have been menopausal. Even as recently as thirty years ago, women reached menopause earlier, or so Jimroy has read, especially country women. Something to do with diet. He supposes he will have to deal with the biological considerations in his book, though the thought makes him tired and reawakens his ulcer. And he will have to deal also with the peculiar ordinariness of Mary Swann's letters and even the subjects of those letters. Pleading letters to Eaton's returning mail-order underwear. Letters to her daughter, Frances, in California,

letters full of bitter complaint about the everlasting Ontario winter—
these from the woman who wrote "September Night" and "Apple
Tree after the Snow." What can be done with such unevenness?
Nothing. (Though Jimroy had decided to withhold the underwear
letter from his book, and he had "misplaced" another, which
referred to a "nigger family" the astonished Mary Swann saw in
Elgin one summer.)

The fact is—and why deny it—Jimroy has come to distrust Mary
Swann slightly. In recent weeks he has felt his distrust turn to dislike.
Here was an impenetratable solipsism. One was always straining to
catch her tone. Furthermore, she was unreliable about dates, con-
tradictory about events, occasionally untruthful. A Poundish falsity
was creeping into her life, drowning her, obliterating her. Starmanes-
que delusion was gaining on her, dear Christ. She was about to
become famous at last, a woman who a few years ago, balanced on
a thimbleful of praise. And when she was killed in the winter of
1965, there was hardly a person in the world who recognized her
for the rarity she was.

Jimroy's days have fallen into a pleasing rhythm.

Disjointed by nature but orderly by choice, he spends his mornings
as he had orginally hoped, in the Flanners' garden. Around him
are clustered flowers, their colours so brightly pink, so lightly blue
and yellow, so moist and silken that they seem to be telling him
something. He holds a pencil in one hand; a cigarette burns in the
other. How joyous it is to be working again, to set his thoughts adrift
on the scholarly sea. How puny they are, these thoughts, but how
precious, tossing like flecks of foam, his little loves, his little
discovered truths.

The sun falling on his head and arms convinces him that he is
entering a period of good health, although instead of the chestnut
tan he hoped for he has acquired an oily shine to his face and dry
colonies of freckles on his forearm. He has never had freckles before.
Well, he is fifty-one, he reminds himself, and changes in the
pigmentation of the skin are to be expected. *C'est la vie.* Et cetera.

He wonders at times, and worries, how his fifties and sixties will
go, admitting he has no talent for the avuncular and that he feels
uneasy in the role of wizened philosopher or generous mentor. A
fatigued and coarsened cynic? He hopes not. Love is the word he

whispers to his listening self, *love*. He is aware, he alone probably in all the world, of the membrane of sweetness that encases his heart. Well, sweetness perhaps is putting it too strongly. But there is—he is sure of it—a scrap of psychic tissue that he guards and knows to be hopelessly malleable. Audrey once or twice jabbed her careless fingers into its softness, dear old Aud. If he'd tried harder to hang on to her, she might be here now, puttering in the trim little California kitchen, coming out the back door with her shears in hand, eager to prune the flowers and hedges and perhaps start a row of radishes by the lathe fence. Unthinkable, yet he thinks it.

Jimroy can scarcely believe how quickly the garden has gone out of control, and he has given up his search for a gardener. There wasn't so much as a single reply to the ad he placed in the local rag. The neighbours tell him, with puzzled kindness and a hint of amusement, that the people who used to do garden work are now pulling down fat wages in the computer plants. This is Silicon Valley. Who would want to potter away in someone else's weedy yard? These same neighbours insist, with a chauvinism Jimroy finds irritating but charming, that West Coast gardens more or less look after themselves.

Maybe. But the hedge has become grossly misshapen, sending green spiky shoots over the top of the fence. In the cracks between the patio stones, weeds have sprouted. Jimroy nudges at them with the toe of his new plastic scandals and finds them toughly attached. Marjorie Flanner's roses bloom brilliantly; he watches the buds open. The flowers last a few days, then darken. With a flick of his fingers he sends the petals flying to the ground. He likes their perfume, but otherwise ignores them. He hopes the neighbours aren't writing letters to the Flanners in Germany telling them their garden is in ruins.

Normally he works at his improvised desk in the garden from nine each morning until one o'clock, and then he walks a distance of four blocks to Lester's Steak House. The curving domestic green of the street gives way brutally to traffic and a busy shopping centre where Lester's is located. There, every day, he eats a hamburger and drinks a glass of cold beer. A sign on the restaurant door says "Members and Non-members Only." Another sign inside says "Under Three Million Burgers Sold," and Jimroy thinks how these signs—open, disrespectful, collegiate—typify California humour. Sitting at a booth with his hand closing on the cold glass, he feels transported back to Manitoba. He rejoices in his homesickness, always happy to find something in himself to like. (He had forgotten whether he suffered homesickness in Rapallo.) Here at Lester's there are no avocados or sesame seeds. The walls are damp, greasy, knotty pine, dark and smelling like someone's basement rumpus room. When a door is opened to the outside, the sunlight cuts across the floor bright as a knife.

Each Wednesday after lunch he walks to the house where Mary Swann's daughter lives. It is a mile away, and he stumbles along blindly, not because of the beer but because of the shock of bright sunlight after the dark hour inside. He is forced to walk along the side of an extremely busy thoroughfare since, for some reason, there is a shortage of sidewalks in California, an unwillingness to serve those who must go about on foot. Jimroy feels rebuffed by the passing cars that come perilously close to him, sending up choking clouds of dust and carbon monoxide. He thinks as he walks along how pridefully Californians parade their barbarisms; every day he sees a small chapel, lit up even in the daytime, with a sign on its roof that says "The God Shop." And almost every day he is overtaken by a horde of perspiring runners, young men stripped to the waist and wearing sweat bands around their heads. (It was several weeks before he realized it was the same group every day.) They pass him on both sides, never breaking stride, calling back and forth to each other between breaths (" . . . theory of applied mechanics" . . . "monitoring the fucking test results . . ."). Gradually he is beginning to recognize individual faces as they surge grunting past him, and he nods to them now in a friendly way, breathing in the smell of human sweat that briefly pierces the automobile fumes.

Mary Swann's daughter lives on a street called Largo Lane in a house that is one of the most beautiful Jimroy has ever seen. Well, he asks himself roughly, what had he expected?

He'd expected something hideous. A bleak sitting-room with sagging furniture. Cheap siding damaged by sun. A picnic table in the front yard. Weeds. He'd expected a stubborn fecklessness and a narrowness to correspond with the narrowness of that farmhouse outside Nadeau, Ontario, where Frances Swann Moore (1935–) grew up. He had not allowed for upward mobility and the miracle of the one-generation leap. He had not expected this, this lovely house, these green moist grounds. Where was the river of loud traffic now; where the exhaust fumes and the sweaty joggers? Even the gravel of the Moores' driveway looked freshly washed. Large palms framed the wide front door, a dark luminous slab of wood without ornamentation of any kind; it had been a challenge, on Jimroy's first visit, to find the doorbell; ah, but there it was, cunningly concealed in the bronze moulding.

When he asked Mrs. Moore ("Please call me Frances") about the style of the house, she told him it was a blend of Japanese and West Coast. "The architect was ____" and she said a name that meant nothing to Jimroy but that seemed to carry the heft of international reputation. Low spans of laminated wood rested on rough stone and supported the large coolness of tinted glass. And inside, such calm; the polished oak floors islanded by Navaho rugs or by the small perfect orientals that Frances Moore and her husband collected. Is it, Jimroy asks himself, true connoisseurship, a knowing eye that gluts on carved shapes and intricate shadow? Or is it only Californian acquisitiveness gone mannerly? The Moores also collect antique cars—there are three in the garage—Peruvian baskets, which are displayed on the dining-room wall, and Egyptian pottery, which is arranged on shelves at one end of the wide foyer. The pottery is the first thing Jimroy sees when Frances opens the door to him on Wednesday afternoons.

He cannot understand her availability, why she is always at home, always serenely ready when he arrives, spotless in her pressed blouses and well-fitting golf skirts. An attractive, smooth-faced woman, still slender. Her coil of dark hair contains quite a lot of grey, and Jimroy remembers that Mary Swann is reported to have gone grey before she reached her forties—was it Rose Hindmarch who told him that? Yes, probably; who else would have known? Frances, Mary Swann's daughter, is a woman in her early fifties. Her fingernails are pink and polished and cut short. Her eyes hold the blue of Nordic summers, although Jimroy is impervious to such eyes, and to such metaphors. When she smiles, wrinkles fly into her face. His questions take a long time to reach her. She reflects, touches her earlobes with those pink fingers of hers, then speaks slowly.

She is always alone. Her only son is away at Princeton; her husband, an economist at Stanford, travels a great deal giving lectures and consulting for the government. ("You must meet him," Frances Moore has said, but this meeting has not yet occurred, and Jimroy senses that it never will.)

She leads him to a low, rough-textured sofa and settles beside him, crossing her legs at the knee, a swift elegant series of motions. They sit before a coffee table on which rest a stack of magazines

(*The Smithsonian* on top, *The Atlantic* peeking out below), a small stone carving (Tibet, Frances tells him), a lovely, locally made ceramic ash tray (Jimroy has not dared drop an ash in it, nor even light a cigarette) and a pot of freshly brewed green tea.

"And now," she says in that melodious voice that holds only a faint echo of rural Ontario, "now, where did I leave off last week? Oh, yes, I remember. You asked about Ma's relationship with the neighbours. I've been trying to recall. We didn't have a telephone, of course, and it wasn't until 1949 that we had a car. Well, a truck, really. But you know that already. So there wasn't a great deal of neighbouring. We were twelve miles out of Elgin and two out of Nadeau and ten from Westport—which is just a kink in the road, as you know. Mostly my mother didn't bother with neighbours. I believe she went to a wedding shower once. She grew up in Belleville—you've got all that—and in those days that was like coming from the other side of the moon. You've been to Belleville, Mr. Jimroy? Well, then, you know. Are you ready for some tea?"

Dazed he holds out his cup and wonders why he is afraid of so charming a woman. Frances Moore's voice, rhythmic, smoothly modulated, possesses a tonal slant that makes him want to close his eyes, but he doesn't dare for fear of being dismissed. Only the strange disruptive word *ma* ties this exquisitely relaxed woman to Mary Swann; not mother, not mama, but *ma,* a word that breaks from her lips like a barnyard squawk. He gulps his tea and says, "Neighbours?" to prompt her.

"There were the Hannas, of course. I think Ma rather liked Mrs. Hanna, though she wasn't very bright. I don't think she could read or write. I remember once, coming in from school, that she, Mrs. Hanna, was sitting in our kitchen, and Ma was reading her something out of one of her library books. I think I told you, Mr. Jimroy, that there was a library in Nadeau."

"Oh, yes, in fact I've visited—"

"This was the old library, of course. Just two hundred books or so, no more than that. On a shelf in the post office. Ma used to get those books when she went to town, just two each time. You were allowed more, but she only took two."

"I wonder why?" Jimroy feels the need to question her minutely, to pin her down, if only to assure himself that he is really sitting in this room. He is not at ease as an interlocutor; he remembers with impatience his difficulties with Starman's widow. Then, too, he has had little to do with women like Frances Moore.

"Heaven only knows. She's dead now, Mrs. Hanna. I don't know what book it was Ma was reading to her. *Gone With the Wind*, perhaps. Or, Edna Ferber. She liked Edna Ferber."

Jimroy makes a noise that signifies regret and writes this down in his notebook. Of course he is disappointed. Has he foolishly hoped for Jane Austen? Yes, though he knows better. "And you don't remember that she ever read poetry?" He has asked this question before.

"Not that I can remember. Unless you count Mother Goose as poetry. She certainly knew all those nursery rhymes. Her favourite was 'A Man in the moon/ Came down too soon/ And asked his way to Norwich.' Remember? 'He went by the south/ And burnt his mouth/ From eating'—what was it?—'Cold pease porridge.'"

"I remember," Jimroy says, and makes another note.

"She read to me, too, now and then. In the evenings."

"Ah." His pencil is at attention, his voice affects insouciance. "Can you possibly remember the titles of any of the books she read to you?"

"*Five Little Peppers*. I loved that. And the Bobbsey Twins books. Not what you'd call great literature. I never heard of *Winnie the Pooh* and the *Wind in the Willows* until I had a child of my own. But there we'd sit in the evenings, on the couch in the kitchen, the two of us. We never used the living-room, or the front room as we called it, in the winter. It was just too cold. In the kitchen there was the woodstove, which we kept going all the time. I suppose it sounds rather idyllic, the cosy little family gathered in the kitchen. The wind would be howling outside. We had a couple of those gas lamps. Ma used to get quite carried away with some of the Bobbsey Twins' adventures. She'd put this ferocious expression in her voice. Very dramatic. There was little Flossie, forever getting lost in the woods. I think Ma enjoyed it all as much as I did."

"And your father?"

"I think we went through the whole series. Awful stuff, I don't know why the library carried them—"

"Was your father there, too? In the kitchen, I mean?"

"If you don't mind, Mr. Jimroy—"

"I'm terribly sorry. I just—"

"I think . . . I'm sure I made it clear when you first wrote to me about these interviews that I was not willing to discuss—"

"Please forgive me. The scene was so vivid and I . . . I'm afraid I forgot—" A shamed stutter.

"Under any circumstances."

"I understand. I do understand." He held his lips together.

"More tea?"

"I would, yes, please, I'm becoming quite addicted to green tea. I never—" He hears his voice foolish and passionate, his ninny laugh.

"The neighbours. Now, let me see. Mrs. Hanna I've already done. There was one other family. The Enrights. They had a bigger farm, not far from us. A modern barn."

Jimroy, worshipper of images from a disjointed world, is writing as rapidly as he can: "The Enrights. Large farm, modern barn."

He found the evenings difficult at first; what was he to do with these long soft evenings?

In the Flanners' microwave oven he warmed himself meals. He switched on the news as he ate; Californians seemed mired in their own crises, their mudslides and earthquakes and city politics and major art robberies. After dark he went for long walks and felt his lungs expand in the moist evening air, pure oxygen topped with the scent of petroleum. Pollution's cordial edge. The moon, rising, seemed rimmed with Vaseline. What a puzzle California was, even Palo Alto. There was no easy way to understand it. He felt reassured, though, by the lights going on in neighbouring houses. The domesticity of others sometimes made him envious but, as he zipped up his new light windbreaker, he told himself that he had come to feel at home inside his loneliness. In truth he half believed this, and the thought kept Audrey at bay.

After a few weeks he was invited next door to a buffet supper. There the Lees introduced him to the Krauses, who lived on the other side of him. "Meet Morton Jimroy, he's in the Flanners' house." He met at least a dozen other people too. "So you're in the Flanners' house, we've been wondering. So you're the biographer. Well, how're you adapting to the coast?"

They were hospitable people, and soon he was being made welcome in their houses too. He was grateful for these low-key social evenings, even though he sensed he would never have been asked had he not possessed at least a degree of celebrity with which to advertise himself. These people were accustomed to success. Dr. Lee next door (Ian) was forever being driven to the airport by his wife, Elizabeth (a strenuous, combative woman possessing a large elastic mouth, but very kind), so that he could fly half way around the world to lecture on arcane branches of mathematics. And Dr. Krause was a world-class philologist (the expression *world-class* was sprinkled like cayenne on the Stanford community). Krause's heavy body seemed to Jimroy barely able to move beneath its weight of knowledge. His wife, Monique, a psychologist, was an expert on cheesecake and national parks hiking trails. These kind people accepted Jimroy, inviting him in for platefuls of roast beef and baked ham, teasing out of him opinions and anecdotes and asking for his comments on the methodology of biography. Ian Lee pressed him about how a biographer knew when he had at last reached the essence of personality—"Does a light go on or what?" he asked Jimroy, snapping his fingers. August Krause pursued him about the gap between the private and public person. "Ah, but what *is* a public person?" Monique Krause cried, clapping her little hands together. "Only a nude body wearing slightly better clothes."

What good people they were: middle-aged, civilized, tolerant, travelled and tanned and united, all of them, in their contempt for Ronald Reagan. They offered Jimroy, without a thought of return, their delicious food, their good-to-excellent wine, their recorded music, and their conversation, and they sent him home well before midnight.

Jimroy, thankful, could only think: thank God for their honest cuts of beef and the little pings of laughter that leapt from their mouths when he produced his "first impressions" of California. He was less lonely than he had been in Winnipeg, although he knew similar couples there, the Swensens, the Zieglers, the Mullocks. He marvelled at the steadiness of love that seemed to flow between these husbands and wives. Most of them had been married for well over twenty-five years, and still they maintained toward each other an attitude of courtesy and tenderness. He tried to imagine them coupling in their beds—Ian's plump penis stuck up there between Elizabeth's legs—and couldn't; but that scarcely seemed to matter. Love was what mattered, that enduring, mysterious refuge. Returning home alone to the flatness of the Flanners' bed, he carried some of their circumambient warmth with him.

He reflects on one such night that it has been some weeks since he's surrendered to that hideous weakness of his, which is to make anonymous phone calls to Audrey in Florida. Perhaps he's getting over the need to hear her croaking voice erupting from sleep. "Hullo?" she yawks into the phone, like someone testing the depth of a cave. He shuts his eyes and tries to imagine the trailer she's living in, what her bed is like, if she requires a blanket in that ridiculous climate, how she looks sitting on the edge of the bed with the receiver in her hand.

"Hullo, I said. Who is this?"

He never speaks back; just holds the receiver, listening.

"Who is this anyway?" she demands roughly. That Midlands snarl.

More silence. He is careful not to breathe. He would never stoop to being a breather. And he doesn't really want to frighten her. Dear old Aud.

"Who is this, for the love of God?"

A long pause, and Jimroy waits for the voice that will surely come and fill it. Instead she often bangs the phone down hard.

Once she shouted, "You can't fool me. I know who it is, you bugger."

His hands had trembled, but he managed to hang on to the receiver. His lips brushed against the mouthpiece, fear and love entwined. He thought of her large mouth, not an attractive woman, not at all.

It's been several weeks since he's phoned Audrey in the middle of the night. A good sign. He should celebrate, like an alcoholic after a dry month.

If only he could expunge—ah, but he can't. He promises himself, a solemn pledge, that he will make no more phone calls to Sarasota. His work on Mary Swann is coming along; every week he mails a sheaf of papers off to Mrs. Lynch for typing. Fragrant air drifts in through the open window. He's sleeping well. He has just returned from a charming evening with cheerful, intelligent friends who regard him, he knows, as a minion from the North, a role he fancies. And, after all, he doesn't love Audrey any more. That was over years ago.

But he is, he admits to himself, deeply in love. He is sodden with love, foolish with love. And the woman he loves is Sarah Maloney of Chicago whom he has never met.

October 24

Dear Morton,

I knew you'd relent! So! We'll meet at last—I'm delighted. You should be getting your tentative program in a few days, hot off the press. What would our Mary have thought of all this? I'm afraid that when I try to imagine her sitting in the audience listening to someone discussing her use of the caesura, it all seems suddenly laughable. You may not agree. Do you? Or not?

Toronto in January—it sounds like a piece of misery. I do agree with you, yes, that it would have been more appropriate to hold the thing in Nadeau, and the Steering Committee did look into it. (Isn't Steering Committee, a curious expression? Fascist almost; invented no doubt to give us false notions of power.) The problem with Nadeau was hotel space—none. Unless you count the six rooms over the beer parlour. And, yes, Elgin was a possibility, though the hotel is one of those drafty old country places, as you must know. And the highway between there and Toronto is sometimes closed in January because of storms. It was agreed that Toronto would have to do if we wanted to attract people. And, astonishingly, it looks as though there will be sixty of us, and maybe more. Who would have believed it? Herb Block is coming from Harvard. When I heard that, little silver bells rang in my head. Herb Block! I suppose you know we invited Frances Moore. "Not quite my thing," she replied. A cool one.

And now, Morton, I want you to know that I was deeply touched by what you said in your last letter, how important it was to you to receive personal mail. Yes, I know about what you call the "loneliness of the half famous"—not, by the way, a category I would place you in. I think a lot about loneliness, surely the most widespread of modern diseases—don't I know! As a matter of fact, it was the spectre of loneliness that first attracted me to Mary Swann's work, that she and I shared the same bad cold. Of all her poems, the one that speaks to the very center of my heart is "Alone in the House."
Especially those lines—

Pity my blood hidden and locked
Pity my mouth shut tight.
Pity my passing unclocked
Hours, pity my unwatched night.

Not her best stanza, but when you think of the anguish behind it! How that poor woman needed someone to "watch" her. How we all do! I don't, by the way, think she's being self-pitying here as Professor Croft suggests in her *PMLA* article. (By the way, Croft is coming to the symposium, a sure sign that our Mary has arrived.)

I'm so glad you weren't miffed by my reluctance to let go of the Swann notebook at this time. If I thought there was material in it that you could use for your book, of course I'd send you a copy. But mostly it's just notes, ideas for poems, lots of scribbles—all of which I'll be talking about in my presentation. I feel rotten about this, damn it. But then you know about the selfishness of scholars. What a lousy bunch we are.

All good wishes,

Sarah

Most of the letters that arrive for Jimroy are business letters from his publishers in New York or from his colleagues in Manitoba. These typed communications, though welcome, hurt his eyes. Too casual, this plinking of print, too easily accomplished. The battering of mechanical keys seems to convince most people that they are witty, when, in fact, they are only verbose. The result, Jimroy finds, is exasperating prolixity and an excess of little dots between sentences, or else that gassy kind of nervousness that came blithering off Ezra Pound's typed notes to his friends—Jimroy always imagines that these letters of Pound's, even the gayest of them, were written with his teeth tightly clenched. Sarah Maloney's envelopes bear jaunty angled stamps and are, Jimroy dares to hope, lovingly licked. The letters themselves are handwritten. Her crisp—but not too crisp— off-white paper suggests harmony and resilience. The ink is deep blue and flows from a medium-tipped pen, what to Jimroy looks like a nylon nib. He loves the calm way Sarah Maloney writes *honor* and *center* —these words, with their plain American spellings, seem to grow rounded and luminous. Her wide-open a's and o's enchant him. Her capital w's are innocent well-fed young birds, ready to try their wings. She is twenty-eight years old; he knows because the date of her birth was included in the biographical data that accompanied her first published article, but in any case he would have guessed from her handwriting that she was still in her twenties, the lucky age, the emancipated age. One has only to look at Mary Swann's cramped hand or at his own squashed loops. Her tone is murmurous, womanly.

He distrusts the photo on her book jacket, long hair falling over a long face. A talky mouth and libidinous eyes. A neat little chin, though, redeems her. She might, he thinks, be the kind of woman who hangs prisms or pieces of coloured glass wistfully in her windows. He imagines that she shuns crimson nail polish. A certain bodily stockiness? He fervently hopes not. (At least Audrey had not been stocky.) He knows that Virginia Woolf is Sarah's favourite novelist— as a rule he distrusts a Woolfian bias in women—and that V.S. Pritchett is her favourite essayist. The books of these two authors, he imagines, are placed side by side on a little painted shelf close to the desk where she works, the place where she sits (in a pool of sun?) writing her lovely handwritten letters, licking with her soft tongue, honey at its core, the gummed envelopes and stamps—ah, Sarah. *The soft tongue, pink, travels across his body. For heaven's sake, take off your pyjamas, Sarah whispers, foolish buttons, hurry. Oh, how sweet, let me lick, lick, lick. There now, isn't that what you needed? What you wanted? Yes, of course it is.*

He is sure she has mellowed, changed utterly in fact, since the publication of her big, beefy, angry book, *The Female Prism*. Her letters are all soft edges and crisp corners. Her refusal, for instance, to part with Mary Swann's notebook was tenderly phrased, so that the sting of denial was scarcely felt. Well, only a flick. And only for an instant.

Her most recent letter is the tenth one she has written him. Jimroy places it at the bottom of the pile under the others and replaces the rubber band with a glad snap. Tonight, since the Lees' party ended even earlier than usual, he will get into bed, pull up the light cotton blanket, and treat himself to the whole oeuvre.

He admits that her style leaves something to be desired; only occasionally does it tilt toward the kind of persiflage he admires. He wishes she wouldn't use that phrase *deeply touched;* he imagines reddened nostrils, dampness, appalling *sincerity*. The word *lousy* offends him slightly. She seems unable to produce the long, many-branched sentences he most admires, but he hasn't the heart to cavil at something she can't help. And her phrases *do* have a certain sonority, a stubbornness, her own kind of reckless heat. More than that, the words seem to be shaped for him and for him only. He imagines that the letters she writes to others—Herb Block, that lightweight fake—are thinner and deficient in vitality.

When he writes to Sarah Maloney he is careful not to smoke. He doesn't want her to open his envelopes and inhale staleness. Another thing: he makes a point of inserting one, and only one, personal message that he knows will elicit a personal response. He tries for something self-deprecating, the admission of some minor failing or misadventure, for he knows he is most likeable when he is being second rate. He rations himself, anxious that this relationship not turn soppy. He wants hardness, sharpness, *net,* with just the occasional soft spot, rapidly opened and just as rapidly closed. In a recent letter he told her about the guilt (a mild exaggeration, but no matter) he suffers over the Flanners' roses, how he sits among them but ignores their beauty, how they bloom without his appreciation.

"They don't need appreciation," Sarah wrote back, absolving him—and, furthermore, she wrote, "nature worshippers are vastly overrated as human beings, particularly in their own estimation."

It was what he needed to hear. Sweet impunity. Everything Sarah (Sarah! Sarah!) writes is what he needs to hear.

Of course he knows this can be explained as a trick of love, that every word spoken by a lover becomes radiantly relevant and overlaid with gold.

Sporran.

Jimroy is awakened in the middle of the night by this word, which appears suddenly spelled out in his dream.

The rest of the dream fades quickly—he has never been able to retain his dreams—leaving only this single word: *sporran.* The letters dance with a garish blue light behind his closed eyelids. There is a background of dull grey and a sensation of shrill music being played off stage.

The image is surprisingly persistent, and in order to make it disappear Jimroy is forced to reach over and turn on the bedside lamp. The alarm clock on the table says 3:00 A.M.

Sporran. Of course. It is the word he was trying to remember, the name of the little purse that Highlanders wear in front of their kilts. He saw one not long ago on that odd young duck of a Scotsman sitting next to him at the University Theater.

This is something that has happened to him fairly frequently. A word or phrase or piece of trivia will completely slip out of his mind, only to reappear later when the need of it has passed. Objects mislaid, an appointment overlooked. It happens to everyone, of course—he knows that—and gets worse with age. From time to time, especially in the middle of a lecture, it has caused Jimroy a flutter of embarrassment. The phenomenon had to do with the breakdown of the oxygen supply to the brain cells. Somewhere he has read an article about it. Was it *Scientific American*? No, must have been *Harpers*. Or else he's seen a television program about it. He hopes he won't become the kind of doddering old fool who forgets to zip up his pants or has to have his phone number pinned inside his shirt.

Probably it's a good sign that the forgotten word or phrase always does come back to him eventually, usually when he's relaxed or even, as tonight, in the middle of sleep. What a curious thing the brain is really, with its intricate circuits and cross channels, all embedded in inches of damp, unpretentious, democratic tissue. Sometimes Jimroy thinks of his brain as a rather thick child, wilful and mischievous and dully unaccountable, that he must carry atop an awkward body. But tonight he is grateful for the sudden flashpoint of memory.

Wide awake now, he tries to recall something that has happened during the day to produce this sudden revelation, this illuminated word *sporran*. There is nothing. And it's been weeks since his encounter with the Scotsman, weeks since he's asked himself what the term was for the little pouch the man wore around his waist. Of course, it's not a particularly common word. One could go years and years without hearing it. But still he should not have forgotten.

It isn't as though this word was something he was trying to suppress, not like the time he was filling out the divorce papers and quite suddenly couldn't remember Audrey's middle name. In a case like that he was willing to admit there might be an element of unconscious blocking.

Audrey Joan Beamish Jimroy. The name *Joan* came to him the day after he mailed in the papers to the lawyer, when he was sitting in a tub of hot water. He immediately got out, dried himself off and phoned the lawyer, saying that he "might possibly have neglected to include my estranged wife's middle name."

Then he got back into the tub, telling himself, making light of it, that he was thankful *his* parents had chosen not to give him a middle name or he might very likely have forgotten that, too. After his bath he sat down in a chair by a window and made himself recite some of the Cantos; on one line only, but a line that had once been a favourite, he faltered. He would have to watch himself. In his *métier* a good memory was essential. Vitamin E was helpful, so some people believed. It was something to look into. If a man was going to go around forgetting his wife's middle name . . .

Sporran, sporran. He turns out the light and tries to go back to sleep, but the word bleeps in his head. He wonders what its origin is. Irish, probably. It has that sound. Nothing to do with spores certainly, though it is hung on the body in a conspicuously spore-related place.

Audrey Joan Beamish. He clearly remembers the first time he saw her name, a signature at the bottom of an application letter. All spring he had been looking for a research assistant, and Audrey, who didn't know research from beans, had applied. Typical of Aud to think she could master anything she put her mind to. At least she could type a little, that was something. And her Birmingham accent had an invigorating effect on him. Her boniness, her rawness—she had the kind of reddened nose that was always pressed in a wad of damp tissue—invited his tenderness. He wanted to protect her from herself. Poor old Audrey.

Often, even here in California, homeland of long-legged American beauties, he sees extraordinary unattractive women—sallow or bent or overweight or in some way deformed—riding on buses or dragging through department stores. Their shopping bags and the children they tug along confirm without doubt that these women are married. Who would marry such women? Jimroy has asked himself. Then he remembers: *he* married Audrey. He was even drawn to her *because* of her long horse's face, her knobbed wrist bones gleaming like pickled onions above her hands.

Even her ignorance gave him pleasure in the early days, telling him he was not alone in his failings. He had amused himself by mumbling inanities to her: Isn't this the most celestial sky, isn't this the most urban city, isn't so-and-so forever putting his foot in his Achilles' heel, wasn't somebody-or-other always looking back in retrospect. Then he would watch her face in canny delight as these remarks bounced off her like rubber bullets. She would frowningly turn her eyes upward in thought or else give her sideways nod; one shoulder would go up. Yes, yes, she would say, riding roughshod over his *jeu d'esprit*, his prickliness, blind to it, oblivious as only Audrey could be oblivious.

What he loved her for, if love in its defective mode can still be called *love*, was her stubborn though unspoken belief that there existed an order to the universe and that she was part of the human army who propped it up. *Soldiering on* was the phrase Audrey lived by, soldiering on blindly, bravely, doing those thousands of things she deemed worth doing. With a wild flailing of arms, with an inexhaustible noisy flow of energy, she had wallpapered the hall of the ugly old house Jimroy owned in Winnipeg, scraped paint from the woodwork, planted her "veg patch" in the scrubby backyard. He admitted that she was simple-minded—but there was such *kindness* in the way she misread him. To her he was not a crippled cynic with a talent for misanthropy; to Aud he was no more than a poor sap who needed cheering up. A coarse, awkward woman, but something in her nature appealed, even her sense of righteousness. He once in conversation used the word *poleaxed*, and she took him to task for being derogatory about the Polish people.

When he married Audrey Beamish he had been prepared for pity from his acquaintances. He braced himself for their questioning faces. Why in his fortieth year had he saddled himself with a wife, particularly a wife like Audrey?

Instead of pity there was rejoicing. She was just what he needed, people said, this noisy good sport of a woman with a heart the size of a watermelon. (Someone or other had used those exact words.)

Moments of lamentations. Everyone has them, Jimroy supposes. His are conducted late at night. *My wound is that I have no wound.* This is just one of those things Jimroy chants to himself, not sure how fitting it is—introspection distorts even the sharpest mind—and extremely doubtful about its originality. (The phrase, the rhythm of it, sounds suspiciously like something someone else said, someone starkly confessional and melodramatic—Rupert Brooke, someone of that ilk.) Nevertheless Jimroy proceeds: *My wound is that. . .*

His wound, or woundlessness as it were, is a small organism curled inside him, patient, docile, like a sleeping spaniel, a dwarf spaniel. It refuses to identify itself, and the only reason Jimroy knows of its existence is that he sometimes, though rarely, encounters it elsewhere, curled inside another human body where it is, to his surprise, instantly recognizable. That student he once had at the university, Ely Salterton, fresh off a wheat farm; from Ely Salterton he had kept his distance. And "more recently" that queer fellow in the kilts—well, *he* was not a clear case. But Audrey; in Audrey he had seen it at once, only instead of being repelled by it, he had reached out, a man who at forty was in danger of drowning.

"Never mind, love," Audrey said after his first (and last) sexual attempt. "It doesn't matter in the least, love."

Amazingly, it hadn't.

A miracle. He had been free to withdraw his hand from the damp coarseness of Audrey's pubic curls, from the folded old-man confusion of her wet labia—at least he supposed those spongy tissues were labia.

The relief was awesome. Even more awesome was his conviction that Audrey felt the same exalted sense of relief. The failing between them was recognized at once and surrendered to. Afterwards they lay quietly in the dark, their arms around each other, the happiest hour Jimroy has ever known. Plenitude. A rich verdure, richer than he had ever imagined from his reading of love poetry. And where did it come from? From Audrey. Dumb Audrey with her grating voice. Audrey who thought Shakespeare was "snooty," Audrey who had never even heard of the poet John Starman, Audrey who pronounced Camus so that it sounded like Cam-muss; at that moment, at that level, hidden away in a dark Fort Garry bedroom, they met. Their silence settled on the hairs of his released hand and on Audrey's sadly smiling mouth. Dear Christ, what happiness.

After the divorce a surprising number of their friends sided with Audrey. (There were those who cruelly joked that she was the first of their acquaintance to divorce a man for sarcasm.) Of course she felt rejected, people said, this with small lip pursings and an upward glance. They could understand exactly how it must be from her point of view. Even now Jimroy knows that these old friends receive postcards from Sarasota from time to time. Good old Audrey reporting in.

And what does he get? Nothing.

Eastern Airlines was unable to trace Jimroy's lost luggage. They were sorry. They gave him a number of new forms to fill out and told him not to abandon hope entirely. There were hundreds of wild stories about baggage turning up in out-of-the-way places. Of course he would receive a cheque for the replacement value of the contents and for the two pieces of luggage themselves. Was Jimroy absolutely sure that the luggage had been weighed in at the Winnipeg airport? (He had to say no to this, remembering that Miss Lynch had looked after the luggage.) Had he, when arriving in the San Francisco airport, gone directly to the luggage pickup or had he stopped somewhere, at the men's room perhaps, or at a coffee machine? (Jimroy could not be sure of this, not after all this time.) Luggage, he was told, was rarely stolen, but on occasion . . . well . . . it was certainly not unknown. Mrs. Myrtle, the adjuster, was sorry about the lost papers, which she realized were extremely valuable as well as being irreplaceable, but with luck, these might still surface. There was a woman just last year who lost her vanity case on a flight between Santa Barbara and L.A., and six months later, after an unexplainable detour to Hong Kong, the case was returned to her. Anything could happen. It could turn up at any moment.

And on November 10—there was a fall of rain, which prevented Jimroy from working out of doors—it *did* turn up, though no one was able to say exactly how it had happened. Mrs. Myrtle from the airline phoned Jimroy and informed him in a rocking jubilant contralto that his baggage appeared to have been found. Would he come out to the airport to identify it?

An hour later he was there, inspecting his suitcases. Inside were his clothes, his folded suits and shirts, his shoes still wrapped loosely in the newspaper he had put around them two months earlier. He looked inside his toilet case and saw that his toothbrush had gone green with mould, but that everything else was in order. His neckties were still rolled neatly around his black nylon socks. There was his battery shaver—a gift from Audrey; one of her good ideas—and the striped swimming trunks he had put in at the last minute. A set of towels and face cloths, a knitted vest for chilly days. He reached a hand under the vest, searching for his papers and for the photograph of Mary Swann. His fingers struck glass, then the hard metal frame. "Everything's here," he told Mrs. Myrtle, a heavy black woman with large swinging earrings. "The photograph too."

"Photograph?"

"Of a woman." How silky he sounded saying this: *Of a woman*. "Who unfortunately is no longer alive." Her blue-black forehead became a sheet of crinkles. "Yeah?"

"A wonderful woman." His happiness had made him silly.

"Can I see?"

He held up the picture for her inspection. "The love of my life," he said recklessly.

He observed that her eyes rolled back slightly and that she blew softly through her teeth. "Far out," she said, a phrase that injured Jimroy with its aroma of doubt.

"This is an extremely rare photograph." He heard himself turn weak with pleading. "The only copy in existence."

"Hey." She sounded soft, smoky. He could swear she was laughing at him. "Didn't I tell you we'd find your stuff, Mr. Jimroy?"

When he reached home he unpacked his suitcase and hung his clothes carefully in the closet. He set the photograph on the bureau and then sat down on the bed, his hands icy despite the heat. A moan bubbled its way through his closed lips. She had changed. Her face was hard, unreasonable, closed, and invoked in him a fever of shame. I am a relatively famous man, he said to himself, seeking comfort. My name is well known, and I have no reason to be ashamed.

The sense of shame was surprisingly poignant, and the fact that it was genuine gave Jimroy a perverted stab of pleasure and bestowed on him an odd little capelet of authenticity. But what he could not set aside was the fear that drilled through his shame, for it occurred to him that the photograph had altered and that Mary Swann had, unaccountably, become his enemy.

The thought, irrational and paranoid—he admitted the paranoia, at least—frightened him. He became jumpy, he spilled coffee in his saucer and down the front of his pants, he avoided thinking about it as much as possible. He tried instead to think of South Africa, Nicaragua, the Middle East. His little twisted wordy world; what did it amount to?

Nevertheless his fear persisted. After a week he decided to put the photograph away in a safe place, and then he buried himself in his work as he always did when his life was going badly.

During the past two years Jimroy had conducted extensive interviews with the following people:

Willard Lang, professor and critic (Toronto). Jimroy detests Lang, who has a benighted concept of *art naïf* and who has so far refused to publish the four poems, love poems he claims he found under Mary Swann's kitchen linoleum. A lumpish man. A man whose thought waves come in unindented paragraphs. And vain. Would like to be thought mercurial. But never will.

Frederic Cruzzi, retired editor of the *Kingston Banner* (small-town paper) and the Peregrine Press. Pompous old boy, fond of the sound of his own voice. Fund of wisdom, etc.

George Hanna, nephew of Elizabeth Hanna, neighbour of Mary Swann (Nadeau). Cretin.

William and Alma Lardner, neighbours of Mary Swann (Nadeau). Unreliable. Possibly insane.

Rose Helen Hindmarch, librarian (Nadeau). Lachrymose woman, tears in her eyes saying goodbye. Helpful, of course, more helpful than anyone else, but three days of that whinnying voice. An unpretty woman. Bent on imparting to him her feeble meditations and moony recollections. Small mouth gobbling air. Greedy. No, too harsh. Needy. Awful in a woman, being needy.

The Rev. W.A. Polson, retired (Nadeau). Nothing came of that.

Homer Hart, school principal, retired (Nadeau). Confused. Unreliable.

Grace Saltman, retired teacher (Belleville, now of Victoria, British Columbia). Bulbous nose.

Richard Eckhardt, town clerk (Belleville). Memory intractable.

Susan Hansen Kurtz, niece of Mary Swann (Belleville). Seemed to be retarded. Or senile.

Rupert "Torchy" Torchinski, baker, retired (Belleville). Hopeless.

Frances Swann Moore, daughter of the poet (Palo Heights, California).

In addition to these interviews, all patiently typed out like plays by the faithful Mrs. Lynch, there have been long, reasonably profitable days in the public archives in Toronto gathering background material. He has also spent a few intensely lonely and wasted days in the National Archives in Ottawa gathering nothing at all but a severe headache and an infection in his upper intestine. In the end he abandoned background research—it seemed to have little to do with Mary Swann. The problem was not to reconcile Swann with her background, but to separate her from it, as the poetry had done.

He wills himself not to think about Swann's notebook, which is in the keeping of his beloved Sarah. Not that he has much faith in it. He has seen diaries before and knows how little light they shed, but still there may be some subterranean detail that will throw light on . . . but why think of that now? He can feel the stitch of his old ulcer picking away.

He had read and reread her only book of poems, *Swann's Songs,* published by the Peregrine Press in 1966. (Idiotic title.) He knows these poems so well that he could, if he were called upon, recite most of them by heart. Some of Mary Swann's lines rise spon-

taneously in his thoughts while he shaves his chin in the morning
or tramps along the gravel-edged roadway to Frances Moore's splendid house.

> A green light drops from a blue sky
> And waits like winter in its jar of glass
> Tells a weather-rotted lie
> Or stories of damage and loss.

Jimroy murmured these lines one afternoon to Frances Moore who
looked at him blankly and moved her teacup, swiftly, to her lips.

The fact is, the poems and the life of Mary Swann do not meld,
and Jimroy, one morning, working in the garden, spreads his handwritten notes in the December sunshine and begins to despair. The
sky today is bordered at the top with streaks of weak-looking blue.
He is not such a fool, he tells himself, as to believe that poets and
artists and musicians possess an integrity of spirit greater than other
people. No, of course he has never gone in for that kind of nonsense.
What an absurdity is that critical term *unity of vision,* for instance—
as though anyone in this universe ever possessed such a thing, or
would want to.

And yet—he shifts his papers, which are weighted down this cool
and breezy morning by small pebbles dug out of the flower border—
how is he to connect Mary Swann's biographical greyness with the
achieved splendour of *Swann's Songs?* He has gone over and over
the chronological events of her life. He has even made a detailed
chart, hoping his inked boxes and arrows and dotted lines may yield
the one important insight, the moment in which she broke her way
through to life. He does not, of course, really believe in the institu-
tion of childhood, and this, he knows, is a somewhat daring reversal of prevailing biographical theory. Freudians! But what precisely
is the value of childhood? he asks himself. It is a puzzle not worth
solving, a primitive time predating literacy, a dulled period presided over by dull parents. Nevertheless, he flips through his index
cards once more.

Birth of Mary Moffat Swann: at home, near Belleville, on a hundred-
    acre farm. Parentage unremarkable. (As he knew it would be;

genius owes no debts to parents; one has only to look at his own sad set, their memory not so much suppressed as simply not thought of, and his lack of eccentric aunts and funny uncles. A Sahara.)

Childhood: narrow, poor, uneventful; at least nothing recorded to the contrary.

Schooling: minimal, a meagre, one-room-schoolhouse education; one surviving report card indicating Mary Moffat had not excelled even in that limited environment.

Work: one year selling bread in the Belleville Golden Sheaf Bakery, defunct since 1943.

Marriage: to a farmer, Angus Swann, a Saturday-afternoon service in the Belleville United Church, no existing photographs, but an eyewitness (the dim niece) recalls that the bride wore a blue gabardine dress, buttoned down the back. (How had she met this farmer? No one knows, but the notebook may reveal—when Sarah deigns to release it.)

Later life: Moved to an unproductive farm near Nadeau, Ontario; gave birth to one child, Frances. Never ventured farther than Kingston, and there only occasionally.

Died: violently, at the age of fifty. A cynic might call her death the only dramatic episode in a life that was a long surrender to the severity of seasons.

Buried: outside Nadeau. In the Protestant cemetery.

Even with the background material and critical commentary, this will be a thin book. A defeat. Jimroy is now thinking in terms of a long article.

In desperation he rummages about one chilly day for the photograph of Mary Swann, hoping it will impart the little jolt of insight he requires. He looks first on the closet shelf, then in his bureau drawers, then, a little frantically, in the linen cupboard, under the Flanners' stacked sheets and blankets. He remembers that he put it in a safe place, a particular place, a place where he was unlikely to come across her slyly withholding eyes. But where? It must be somewhere. This is a small house, smooth-surfaced and without secrets. Where? He spends all of one afternoon looking, wearing himself out, wasting his valuable time.

He accuses himself of senility. He accuses himself of hubris, of burying Swann's grainy likeness, keeping her out of sight and shutting her up, a miniature act of murder.

And now that he needs her again, she's bent on punishment. She is a sly one, a wily one. Women, women. Endlessly elusive and intent on victory.

He admits it: for the moment at least, Mary Swann has defeated him.

It is the fact of *seasons,* Jimroy finally decides, their immensity and extremes, that blocks out Swann's personal history. Each year of her life seems a paroxysm of renewed anonymity, for although he is a careful interviewer, his proddings and probings have not yielded much that is *specific* about her. Recollections of those who knew her—except for Rose Hindmarch, thank God for the moist, repulsive Rose—are maddeningly general and adhere always to the annual cycle, those *seasons.* "In the spring Mary Swann always . . ." or "Usually round about late fall Ma busied herself with . . ." or "In the summers there was the garden to dig and weed and then the canning . . ." The power of these recurring seasons overwhelms the fragile scurryings of that obscure farm wife, Mary Swann, and what is left is a record of dullness and drudgery. And a heartbreaking absence of celebration, a life lived, as the saying goes, in the avoidance of biography.

Of course he can surmise certain things, influences for instance. He is almost sure she came in contact with the work of Emily Dickinson, regardless of what Frances Moore says. He intends to mention, to comment extensively in fact, on the Dickinsonian influence, and sees no point, really, in taking up the Edna Ferber influence; it is too ludicrous.

At times he aches for the notebook, which on good days he imagines to be filled with airy reaches of thought. He's tired of pretending that his partial vision carries a superior and intuited truth. And it pains him, too, to think of the lost love poems in the hands of the lightweight, egregious Willard Lang, who strikes him as a man sweaty with ambition. The bushel of peaches, or was it half a bushel (he has forgotten and anyway he despises involutions), but it was peaches Lang gave the real-estate agent, a bribe, in exchange for vital documentation that by rights belongs to the biographer. To him.

But what Jimroy yearns for even more than the notebook and the love poems is to be told the one central cathartic event in Mary Swann's life. It must exist. It is what a good biography demands, what a human life demands. But now, December, he had begun to lose faith in his old belief that the past is retrievable. He would give a good deal even for a simple direct quotation from Mary Swann, but even Rose Hindmarch, the only real friend she ever had, is halting about direct quotations, and Mary's own daughter, Frances, is unable to recall with accuracy anything her mother ever said. "Oh, she used to get after me about mud on my boots and doing my homework, but Ma wasn't a great one to talk, you know."

Jimroy curses Mary Swann's silences and admits to himself, finally, that he's disppointed in her. Some of this disappointment he shifts to her daughter, Frances; he has, after all, come to California hoping that their conversations might spring open an unconscious revelation, something that will expose the key to Swann's genius. It hasn't happened, he might as well admit it. Frances's revelations, though she furrows her brow convincingly and bites her lower lip in concentration, are too detached for revelation. Her memory is opaque and lacks detail, and Jimroy can't make up his mind about this; is it a personality defect, this bent for invisibility, or a daughterly reflection of the larger opaqueness that was Mary Swann's life? She refuses to talk of her mother's death, and Jimroy knows that it will be impossible to enter that life without understanding its final moment. Reticulated detail is what he needs, and that is being systematically denied. A single glimpse, and the poems would open out and become clear.

On the other hand, he feels a perverse admiration for Frances, especially for the distance she has placed between the harsh, limited scene of her girlhood and her glowing sun-streaked California livingroom. She has an aptitude for distance. She remains distant from Jimroy, too, after all these months still cool, still polite, never for a moment presuming friendship, closed in that patrician way Audrey could never master. The hand she holds out to be shaken, though its dryness is oddly intimate, is as exquisitely bent as for a royal handshake.

And then, unexpectedly, one afternoon a week before Christmas, settled on the sofa in the dancing light, she violated this distance for the first time by saying, "You know, Mr. Jimroy, I'm a little surprised you've chosen a woman for a subject."

"Why is that?" he asked her. "We are living in the age of women."

"Well, it's only—" she stopped, gave an awkward flick of her hand.

"Only?" He fixed his glance on hers, waiting for a response, preparing himself for injury.

"Well, only that you seem to be a man who isn't, well—"

"Yes?" He held his breath.

"Well, a man who's not . . . overly fond of women."

Jimroy's eyes flew to the small curled fingers of a terracotta figure on the coffee table. Neither he nor Frances Moore spoke for a moment, and the silence grew so heavy it seemed to him to be turning into water. He felt a distinct sensation of drowning. His nose and throat and lungs were filling with water. He was afraid to open his mouth for fear of it spilling out.

"I think—" he began.

"I'm sorry. I've spoken out of turn," Frances Moore said quickly. "It's a bad habit of mine, spouting nonsense—"

"If I've given you the impression—" He felt himself groping for balance. "If I've said anything that gave you the idea that—"

"No, of course not. It's nothing you said. Or did. It's nothing at all. I was just being—well, frivolous. Please, forgive me."

"There's nothing at all to forgive. It's just that—" and to his horror he gave out a sort of snuffling laugh.

"Can I warm up this tea, Mr. Jimroy? It's gone stone cold."

"I—"

"Surely you'd like a little more. I know *I* would. It'll just take me half a minute to boil some more water."

"Well, yes." He coughed hideously. Something seemed to have entered his throat and lodged there, an avocado pit, oily and dense. Indignation seized him, but indignation at whom?—at this graceful, smooth-haired California matron rising and lifting a pretty teapot from the table? Or with himself, his awful quagmire heart, his flapping hands.

In a few minutes she was back with the teapot, and she had something else in her other hand, a little narrow jeweller's box covered with blue velvet. "I thought you might want to see this," she said.

She opened the box. "It's Ma's Parker 51."

Jimroy made a suitable sound and asked if he might examine it.

"It was sent to me after she died. I don't know why, but the house agent thought I might want it. At any rate, when Ma was given this pen, it was quite something. What I mean is, in our part of the country it was unusual to own a pen like this. It was a gift, a birthday gift, just after the war, I think. Fountain pens were expected to last a lifetime in those days as you must know, and Ma always kept it in this box when she wasn't using it."

"Was it from—?" He stopped himself in time. The biographer's shameless silky greed.

"She'd write her poems out in pencil and then copy them over in ink. Then she'd burn the pencil copies in the woodstove."

"Such a loss!" Jimroy had already heard this story of the burnt poems, but couldn't stop himself from murmuring, "They would have been of great interest to scholars today—"

"Well yes, but—"

"First drafts are highly prized, almost—"

"Yes, well—"

He went on, relentlessly. "How wonderful it would be if one or two had survived."

"They didn't, though." She said this firmly and snapped the case shut. "I think that tea should be steeped now. You will have a little?"

"Please."

"I'll just get you a clean cup—"

"Please don't bother."

"It's no bother," she said, and excused herself.

What he did next simply happened. He found his hand on the rounded velvet top of the box. Then he lifted the lid, marvelling at the strength of the spring. After all these years, to open so stiffly! It twinkled against the satin lining, a dark blue pen with a fine marbled finish. Then it was in his hand, then in the inside pocket of his new denim sports jacket. He closed the box and positioned it on the table between the bowl of wet flowers and the stack of magazines.

Thief. Robber. He knew he was taking a shocking risk. Frances Moore would suspect him at once. Even if several weeks went by before she reopened the box, she would remember that he had been the last person to see it.

But she would never believe him capable of common thievery, not Morton Jimroy, biographer, Distinguished Visitor. She had given him hours of hospitality, hours of her shared recollections. She had trusted him, and why not? A man of his reputation. He would never bring himself to abuse such a trust!

She would search for the pen under the woven sofa cushions, run her hand across the patterned rug. She would ask herself if there had been a newspaper on the table and if she might have placed the pen on top of the paper and, later, tidying the room, thrown it out? In the end she might decide that that was what had happened, the only explanation.

She would blame herself for her carelessness, berate herself—a thought that made Jimroy shiver a little with perverse pleasure. She would remember that she had been flustered; and now Jimroy was grateful for their awkward scene. Still, she might decide to question him directly. He would have to be prepared for that. Did he remember that afternoon she had shown him the Parker 51? Yes? Did he remember her replacing the pen in the case afterward? It seems to be lost, she would say mournfully, and he would exclaim, "What a pity!" Had she looked under the sofa, under the rug? Perhaps when she was tidying the table . . .

He relaxed against the soft cushions and awaited his cup of tea. A sharp sigh, almost a whistle, escaped his lips, and his hand reached inside his jacket and touched the fountain pen. The pen of Mary Swann. The pen that had written:

Ice is the final thief
First cousin to larger grief.

He would probably not be seeing Frances Moore again. There was nothing more she could tell him, she said, and she would be occupied in the days ahead with Christmas preparations, the return of her son from Princeton, the return of her husband from a lengthy lecture tour. And he himself would soon be off to Toronto for the Swann symposium.

At the door they shook hands gravely. A tinted mirror on the foyer wall sent back a reflection of cordiality.

"Merry Christmas, Mr. Jimroy," Frances said, her composure restored, her strong, finely veined hand extended.

"Merry Christmas," he returned, once again his extravagantly amiable self, and hurried down the flower-lined driveway, almost running. He imagined the wind rubbing the hair on his head and exposing spots of pinkness, a soft baby's scalp. The smell of eucalyptus was in the air. Green, green, everywhere he looked it was green. He gave a queer little leap into the air as he rushed along his way.

How extremely kind of Ian Lee and his wife, Elizabeth, to include him in their Christmas Eve festivities next door. A last-minute invitation to be sure, but his unpressed pants gave off, he hoped, a creditable air of self-forgetfulness, of social ease. We adore having you, Elizabeth Lee said, and planted a holiday kiss on his cheek. Would he mind helping mix the punch? Would he take the cheese tray around for her? Isn't the tree a dream! Visitors from other parts of the country are always surprised that Californians have Christmas trees, aren't they? Of course they cost the earth. Had he met the Gordens, the Kapletters? Yes, that was real holly, not the imitation stuff. Was he sure he wouldn't like a little more to eat himself, one more plateful? Surely another glass of wine, Ian's special wine, the one he only drags out for Christmas; it goes down like velvet. She was stunned by the news from Africa. This was a violent world. It seemed only yesterday that she and Ian had lighted a Christmas candle for Poland, though they'd both thought it a Reaganesque gesture, empty and theatrical; but, well, why not? Christmas was the time to be aware of others less fortunate, the time to be at peace. No one should be alone on Christmas Eve, didn't he agree? Ah, yes, he did agree; emphatically. (The irony bit, but not deeply.) Yes, yes—his uxorious voice, coming on like corn syrup.

And then he was home again. It was midnight, and he was heating himself some warm milk, hoping he would be able to sleep. There was such a weight of silence in the little house, such chilly stillness. He had slipped his old knitted vest on over his pyjamas (blessings on Mrs. Lynch) and happened to catch a glimpse of himself in the bedroom mirror. How shockingly like an old man he looked tonight. He was white-faced and thin, the wormy, rheumy, pink-eyed old gent of his nightmares, mouth dragging down, cheap pyjamas crushed around the collar and not very clean. He was only fifty-one, he reminded himself. Almost fifty-two actually. He looked again in the mirror. It must be a trick of the hour or perhaps the season. "Old," he said noisily. "Old, old." In the frame of the mirror he had stuck the Christmas cards he had received, six in number. One was from the moony, cheese-faced Rose Hindmarch in Nadeau, Ontario. A snow scene, hills, a barn, and a little boy pulling a sled.

Old, old. He had drunk too much of Ian and Elizabeth's wine. Well, why not, it was Christmas after all—as Elizabeth had remarked at least three times in that rather tedious hostessy voice of hers. (There it was, surfacing again, his caustic self, that sour maliciousness rearing up even on this night. Yes, but it was a *regulated* malice; he *did* practice abstentions, did hold back, aware, even if nobody else was, of that pool of unformed goodness at the bottom of his being. And poetry, thank the gods of poetry, without poetry what kind of monster would he have been?)

Down, down his throat went the warm milk. Ah, better, much better. What was it Dr. Johnson had said about the power of warmed liquids?—something or other. He felt a surge of strength akin to munificence. Merry Christmas, cheery Christmas, glad tidings, the time when no one should be alone. His hand was already on the telephone, already dialling the magic digits that connected with Audrey's mobile home *(quel euphémisme!)* in Sarasota. How amazing that he should know her number by heart. In the back of his brain he offered up congratulations. Not bad, Jimroy, a man of your years. You may lose valuable possessions and forget names, but the real juice is still running.

Audrey's telephone rang and rang. He checked the clock and calculated the time difference. She was probably too lost in sleep to hear the ringing of the phone, though he remembered that she had always been a light sleeper. Even the clicking of the electric blanket used to disturb her sleep. Audrey, Audrey, Audrey, dear Audrey. If he had been a little more patient, if his nature had been inclined toward . . . what? . . . instead of always belittling, accusing, haranguing, those thunderous verbs of incompatibility. If he had waited, been kinder, Audrey might be here now.

He dialled her number again, and once more the phone rang and rang. He felt the old anger returning, damn her, but then the thought of her fuzzy corona of hair, her large kind hands. He would never be able to sleep now. He would be awake all night, shivering and staring into the mirror and listening to the sound of his own breath.

And then, from nowhere, came the thought of Sarah Maloney, asleep in Chicago. He could get her number from the long-distance operator. Why not? It suddenly seemed the most important thing in the world to know what Sarah Maloney's voice sounded like. He loved her, he loved her. He had every right to the sound of her voice. He was a lover, a fifty-one-year-old man, slightly drunk, with a slightly drunken heart that was reduced, through no fault of his own, to a shuddering valentine. Darling Sarah, beloved.

No, it was a despicable thing to do, especially at this hour. It was worse than that: it was perverse. He went to the mirror again, peered at himself and said without mercy, "This is unspeakable." He noted with interest that the colour had come back into his face. A sense of disgust refreshes the spirit, a fact that always inspires chills of uneasiness in Jimroy. That trembling of his hand, was that lasciviousness or was he only nervous? Nerves, he decided, congratulating himself yet again. How troublesome but indispensable the body is.

On his first attempt the lines to Chicago were busy. Of course, it was Christmas; of course the lines would be busy on this night of all nights. Families and friends calling each other from every part of the country; lovers, husbands, wives, children, even the most wayward of them reaching out for affection. He could picture them all in their millions, standing in shadowy hallways, dialling into the darkness with faces that were composed and hopeful. What a wonder it was, the bond that joined human beings. An act of faith, really, faith over reason. Over bodily substance.

The second time he dialled, the call went straight through. On the third ring he heard the phone being lifted. A woman's voice—it could have come from the next room—was saying, "Hello? Hello? Who is this please? Hello."

Enough. Quietly, happily, he replaced the receiver.

Unspeakable. Unpardonable.

And yet, in the fresh morning sunlight it seems to Jimroy entirely harmless. What damage has he actually done, and whom has he hurt? He has never understood the science of casuistry, its fierce labours and silly conclusions.

There he is, sitting in the Flanners' backyard feeling ruddy and healthy. He has risen early, a smallish act of atonement, then eaten a bowl of instant oatmeal and drunk a mug of hot coffee, and now, with one of his Winnipeg cardigans buttoned up to his chin and a pair of warm socks inside his sandals, he is working on his book in the quiet of the garden. Christmas morning. *I saw three ships . . .* He breathes deeply, offers up an earnest prayer to the blue sky. Astonishing, that blueness. The flowers and weeds around him have coarsened with new growth, and the trees have a fresh lettucey look—how absurd, how delightful that growth should continue even in the month of December.

He is going over some notes covering Mary Swann's middle period (1940–1955) and making a few additions and notations with a freshly sharpened pencil. *It is highly probable that Swann read Jane Austen during this period because . . .*

The sun climbs gradually and warms the backs of his shoulders. By noon he is able to unbutton his cardigan and fold it over the back of his chair.

He hears a sharp rapping and looks up. It's Elizabeth Lee next door, waving at him from an upstairs window. A moment later Ian appears, a muzzy bulk behind her, and they both wave. It seems to Jimroy that they are mouthing something at him. Merry Christmas? Yes.

He knows what they're thinking. There sits Jimroy. Alone. Working, and on Christmas Day. Actually working. Sad. Pathetic. That life should come to this. Later they will embrace—already Ian's hand is on Elizabeth's breast, or so it appears from this distance. They have each other, their erotic transports, but poor Jimroy loves no one and must do without the solace of Christmas Day sex and domesticity—poor sad Jimroy.

Ah, but how mistaken they are. How he would like to tell them of his happiness. But the condition embarrasses him; he would never be able to describe it. Even if he could they would never believe him, thinking instead: Jimroy's being brave, one of your hard-bitten Canadian stoics.

This is happiness, he wants to tell them, these scrawled notes, these delicate tangled footnotes, which, with a little more work, a few more weeks, will evolve into numbered poems of logic and order and illumination. The disjointed paragraphs he is writing are pushing toward that epic wholeness that is a human life, gold socketed into gold. True, it will never be perfect. There are gaps, as in every life, accidents of silence and misinterpretation and the frantic scrollwork of artifice, but also a seductive randomness that confers truth. And mystery, too, of course. Impenetrable, ineffable mystery.

Jimroy believes, or is beginning to believe, that the intervening mysteries compensate for the long haul between birth and death, bringing into balance early deprivation and enhancing the dullness of stretched-out days and nights. Always authenticity is registered by the inexplicable. He thinks gratefully of the kilted stranger with his—what was it?—his *sporran,* who sat by his side and reached, albeit feebly, for his friendship. He thinks, warmly now, of the return of his luggage by the airline. Of the lost photograph he will surely stumble upon tomorrow or the next day. Of these fragrant West Coast roses, budding, blooming, replacing themselves without complaint. Of the healing perplexity and substance of Sarah Maloney's voice. Of the small solid fact of the fountain pen that Mary Swann, poet extraordinary, once held in her human hand, and that now rests uniquely beneath his cotton socks in a bureau drawer in the state of California, amazing, amazing; he is skewered with joy.

The Lees, his neighbours, these fine people, his generous friends, are waving to him across the tops of the rose bushes and the tall weeds, and he longs to shout out to them that he is in the embrace of happiness. The proof of it is flowing out of the graphite of his pencil, out of his moving hand.

They won't believe it; not they with their stubborn contentment. Impossible. Nevertheless he lifts an arm in salutation, shouting, in his cheery broken tenor, "Merry Christmas," and smiling broadly at the same time to show them that his life may be foolish, it may be misguided and strange and bent in its yearnings, but it's all he has and all he's likely to get.

Rose Hindmarch

Rose's Hats

Rose Helen Hindmarch wears a number of hats. "I wear too many hats for my own good," she has been heard to say.

For instance, if you want to check on surveying details of a piece of farmland in Nadeau township, or if you want to know when your next tax instalment is due, all you have to do is go to the township office on the first floor of the old school any weekday morning between ten and twelve o'clock, and Rose Hindmarch, the town clerk, will be glad to interrupt her typing or bookkeeping, or whatever, to help you. One of her hats.

In the afternoon she moves across the hall to the library. (She takes a packed lunch to work, a sandwich of tuna fish or egg salad, which she eats at the library desk, and afterwards she makes herself a pot of tea, boiling the water on the little hotplate in the storeroom at the back. It is almost, one might say, ordained for women of Rose's age and occupation to huddle over hotplates in ill-ventilated storerooms.) Some winter days it's so quiet in the library she has to keep drinking tea all afternoon in order to stay awake. The sunlight coming through the windows, the dry air, the sulphuric sting of the printed bookcards mailed from a supply centre in Ottawa—all these things tend to induce sleepiness, but luckily business gets brisker after two o'clock when the younger married women, looking fat in their parkas and stretch jeans, drop in with their babies in tow. Quite a number of them—Cathy Frondice, for instance, jigglingly obese but with a clear pink face—are addicted to light romance. Cathy always stops at the desk to ask Rose Hindmarch what she recommends, and it's a rare day when Rose hasn't got a suggestion at the ready.

Later in the afternoon, between four and five o'clock, numerous school children stop by, and Rose helps them look up things in the *Encyclopaedia Britannica* and tries to locate pamphlets for them in her famous pamphlet file. This can be a hectic time of day. She has to keep after the children, the boys in particular, so they don't tramp into the library with their wet boots on, trailing in mud and soaked yellow leaves; and she has to keep a sharp lookout so they don't walk off with books without checking them out first, and all of these things have to be done in the firm, friendly placid manner that people have come to expect of her.

Then there is her role as curator of the Nadeau Local History Museum. The museum has no set hours; if visitors come, Rose simply leaves her desk in the town office or her post in the library and escorts them upstairs to the second floor, first asking them to sign the guest book in the foyer. She is also responsible for classifying donations to the museum—such things as old kerosene lamps and unusual plates and glass sealers—and arranging for insurance and for the small operating grant from the federal government. When the flurry of interest in Mary Swann began five years ago, it was Rose Hindmarch who conceived the idea of the Mary Swann Memorial Room, and it was Rose who spent her spare time scouting around for the articles on display there. Another hat.

And as if this weren't enough, every Wednesday evening at eight sharp she must appear in the Sunday-school room at the Nadeau United Church in the guise of church elder. She and Mrs. Homer Hart (Daisy) are the only women on the board, and Rose takes her position seriously. On the subject of replacing the communion trays or changing altar clothes, she is hearkened to as few others are, though she has to watch her step so as never to betray for a minute the fact that she is no longer a believer in the sacrament of communion, or even, for that matter, in the existence of a heavenly host. It has been some years since Rose's conversion to atheism was accomplished. She had been sitting at home one night, still a relatively young woman, listening to a philosophical debate on the radio, when she suddenly heard one of the debaters say, "Who can really believe there's a God up there sitting at a giant switchboard listening to everyone's prayers?" Rose had laughed aloud at this, and her loss of faith occurred at that moment, causing her not an ounce of pain and scarcely, for that matter, a trace of nostalgia. Only the nuisance of remembering to keep it to herself.

Her changing of hats gets even more confusing on the fourth Monday of every month when she returns to the town clerk's office, having had a light supper of soup and toast, to take her place as a village councillor. She is one of seven and has held the post for fifteen years. Her position is a complicated one, for she must report to herself in a sense; first the library report, then the report of town clerk, then the museum report. For the last twelve years she has also served the council as recording secretary, and this places her in the ludicrous position of writing up minutes in which she herself is one of the starring actors. She writes: "The minutes were read by Rose Hindmarch, and then Rose Hindmarch presented the interim library report," just as though Rose Hindmarch were a separate person with a different face and possessed of different tints of feeling. The Rose she writes about is braver than she knows herself to be. "Stout of heart" is how she thinks of her, an active woman in the middle of her life. (This much is true; Rose at fifty *is* in the middle of her life; her grandmother lived to be a hundred and her mother eighty-five. Those are her other hats, you might say, daughter, granddaughter, though she no longer is obliged to wear them.)

For a brief time after she finished high school Rose worked as the local telephone operator, sitting at the same kind of switchboard over which the nonexistent Ontario God is believed by good-hearted people to preside. To her surprise she found that working for the telephone company was arduous and, contrary to popular belief, she was not privy to tantalizing circuits of gossip. Mostly she heard nothing but farmers ordering machine parts and housewives exchanging recipes for jellied salads. Still in her twenties, she started to grow old, sitting on the uncushioned stool in her telephone office, pulling out plugs, then stabbing them in again. She began to notice, during this period, that she was lonesome all the time.

The town clerk's job fell vacant and she applied. It provides her with respectability. Even the men in Nadeau repect her calm rows of figures and her grasp of recent by-laws. Her post as librarian has given her something else: an unearned reputation for being a scholar, for it is assumed by people in Nadeau that Rose must read the books that fill her library shelves, so easily is she able to locate these books for other people, so adroitly does she thumb the index, so assuredly does she say, her forehead working into a frown, "Here it is, just what you're looking for."

But if you were to ask Rose which of her hats means the most to her, she would say her role as museum curator. It has, in fact, rescued her from the inexplicable nights of despair she once suffered. This is especially true in recent years, ever since she's taken an interest in the life of Mary Swann. Curiously enough, this new historical interest has not so much opened the past to Rose as it has opened the future. Her life has changed. She has connections in the outside world now, the academic world. Quite a number of scholars and historians have come to Nadeau to call on her.

What a dirty shame she never married: this is what Nadeau people occasionally say, but Rose has never inspired hard pity. Some delicacy of hers, some fineness of bodily tissue or sensibility, the way she moves her hands down an open page or pronounces certain words— with an intake of breath like a person caught by surprise—make it appear that she has *chosen* to remain unmarried.

A woman of many hats, then, which she feels herself fortunate to own and which she wears proudly, almost vaingloriously, though there are moments when she experiences an appalling sensation of loss, the naggy suspicion that beneath the hats is nothing but chilly space or the small scratching sounds of someone who wants only to please others.

When she walks home from work, down Broadway as far as Second, down Second to the corner of Euclid, she moves with an air of purpose and amiability, stepping through the dry leaves like a woman accustomed to making choices. Today something twinkles at her feet: a penny, a lucky penny. She stoops to retrieve it, then continues on her way. Her cinnamon suede coat and smart new boots (bought last year in Toronto) ask you to guess at an inner extravagance, but not one that inspires either envy or pity. Other Nadeau women, looking out their front windows and seeing her pass, think affectionately, "There goes Rose. It must be five-thirty, time to put the potatoes on."

Some Words of Orientation

People are often surprised to find that the geographical centre of the North American continent lies not in Kansas or Minnesota or Indiana, as they've always thought, but farther north—across the 49th parallel, in fact, well within the boundaries of Canada.

If you were to place your finger on the map of Canada where this geological centre is located, and then move it an inch or two to the right (and one-quarter of an inch downwards) you would discover yourself touching the dot that represents the small Ontario town known as Nadeau (pronounced naa-dough, the two syllables equally accented).

Nadeau, with a population of 1,750, has only two main streets, that is to say, streets that comprise the business section of town. Broadway Avenue takes you past the cheese co-op and into town, and then there is Kellog Street (on which is located the feed mill and knitting factory), named for the Kellog family, who were the original settlers in the area, not the Nadeau family as it is often thought. (This is a place whose social strata creak with confusion, but a confusion balanced by tolerance, by habit, by a certain innocence it might be said.)

At the crossing of Broadway and Kellog you will find, on the north-east corner, the Esso garage, closed a year ago but soon to be reopened as a Burger King franchise, and on the second corner, the lovely, slender, grey and white stone tower of the United Church. There are weeds standing knee high in the front yard at the moment, a disgrace, but these will be taken care of presently. On the third (south-west) corner is the Red and White, which sells groceries and a complete line of hardware, plus men's work clothes, caps, and so forth. And on the fourth corner, facing onto Broadway but set back on a wide stretch of lawn, is the old two-storey red-brick building that for many years served the community as a high school. This was before the new consolidated school was built out on Highway 17.

The old school in Nadeau—and there *are* still those in town who refer to it as the old school—dates from 1885 and is constructed in a style sometimes known as lean-to Gothic or box-and-beam village Victorian. Distinguishing characteristics include a dressed limestone foundation, which reaches to the first-floor windows and joins, at the front of the building, a handsome set of exterior steps leading up to the main entrance.

The double front doors deserve particular attention, being of heavy oak framing and fitted with long panes of bevelled glass on which are etched charming oval designs of dogwood interwoven with trillium. The hinges on the left-hand door have seized up—this was years ago—but the right-hand door opens easily enough, as you will discover when you turn the door handle.

Notice that the first floor of the old school is divided into two areas, one (on the left) for the Office of the Town Clerk and one (to your right) for the Public Library. The library—open Monday through Friday, 1:00 to 5:00—is surprisingly comprehensive for a small village, but it is not the library that has brought you here and certainly not the town clerk's office.

Turn to your right and ascend the broad set of old wooden stairs that lead to the second floor. You'll find that these stairs yield a little under foot, pretty much what you would expect of an old school stairway when you stop to think of all the young feet that have pounded these boards smooth. The steps, for all their elegance, look faintly dusty, but in truth they're not; it's only the *smell* of dust that somehow lingers in the old, hollow-sounding stairwell. Be sure to stop at the landing and read the plaque that records the fact that in the year 1967 the Nadeau High School (as such) ceased to exist. The same plaque tells you of the simultaneous coming-into-being of the new Nadeau Local History Museum.

This museum, taking up all of the second floor of the old school, is small by anyone's standards, though it manages to attract more than five hundred visitors annually. The two rooms on the right are lined with glass-fronted display cases inviting you to examine some of the astonishing old arrowheads, fossils, and coins unearthed in the region. You can also look at such curiosities as a spinning wheel, a set of cards for combing wool, and a collection of crockery, some of it locally made (at the end of the last century). Be sure to see the interesting old washing machine, *circa* 1913, and to take in the various articles of clothing that include a christening gown from the "nineties" and a woman's grey wool walking costume, piped in red (1902). You will want to spend at last half an hour looking at these interesting exhibits and also at the framed maps and land certificates in the hall, not to mention an outstanding group of old photographs, one of them labelled "Sunday School Picnic, 1914," illustrating the simple recreational pastimes of bygone days.

On the left of the hallway are the two remaining rooms (the former classrooms for grades 11 and 12). One of these rooms has a small placard over the doorway (the door itself has been taken off the hinges and carted away) that reads: The Mary Swann Memorial Room.

Who on earth, people ask, is Mary Swann?

The answer to their question can be found on a neatly typed sheet of white paper tacked to the doorframe. The late Mary Swann, 1915–1965, was a local poet who spent most of her life, at least her married life, on a quarter section of land two miles from Nadeau.

Well-known in the area for her verse, some of it originally published in the now defunct *Nadeau News*, she has lately been recognized as a distinguished, though minor, contributor to the body of Canadian literature, and there are those who have gone so far as to call her the Emily Dickinson of Upper Canada. The Mary Swann Memorial Room, established only two or so years ago, contains a number of mementoes of Mrs. Swann's life—a kitchen table and chairs, a golden oak sideboard, an iron bed, handmade quilts, and many household articles (notice particularly the well-worn wooden turnip masher). In addition, there are some examples of her handiwork (chiefly crochet) and a photograph (blurred unfortunately) of the poet herself standing on her front porch, her arms folded on her chest, facing into the sun. If you have time you may want to linger and read a few examples of Mrs. Swann's verse, which are framed and mounted on the wall. Especially recommended is the prophetic poem entitled "The Silo," which was originally printed in the *Athens Record*, June 4, 1958, just seven years before the poet's untimely demise.

Next to the Mary Swann Memorial Room is the room that has proved to be the most popular with the public. Visitors can stand in the roped-off doorway and admire what is, in fact, a re-creation of a turn-of-the-century Ontario bedroom. Of interest is the floral wallpaper, an exact duplicate of an authentic Canadian wallpaper of the period. There is a length of stove pipe running across the room near the ceiling, carrying heat from the woodstove that can be imagined to exist in an adjoining room. The pine washstand in the corner is typical of the period (note the towel rack at the side) and so is the wooden blanket box at the foot of the bed. The bed itself is unusual, an Ontario spool bed, handmade it would appear, in a wood that is almost certainly butternut. There is, of course, the inevitable chamber pot peeping out from beneath. The mattress on the bed would have been stuffed with goose feathers—or so a notice on the wall tells you—or perhaps straw.

The extremely attractive quilt on the bed was made by the Nadeau United Church Women in 1967 as a Centennial project. It is composed of squares, as you can see, and each square is beautifully embroidered and signed by one of the women of the congregation. From the doorway you can admire the individual embroidered designs (mostly flowers and birds) and you will be able to make out some of the signatures, which are done in a simple chain stitch.

Mrs. Henry Cleary, Mrs. Al Lindquist, Mrs. Percy Flemming, Mrs. Clarence Andrews, Mrs. Thomas Clyde, Mrs. R. Jack Rittenhouse, Mrs. Floyd Sears, Mrs. Frank Sears, Mrs. Homer Hart, Mrs. Joseph H. Fletcher, and so on. Seeing those names, you may smile to yourself, depending of course on your age and situation. You might think: didn't these women have first names of their own? Hadn't women's liberation touched this small Ontario town by the year 1967? You may even form a kind of mental image of what these women must look like: lumpy, leaden, securely wedded, sharp of needle and tongue, but lacking faces of their own and bereft of their Christian names. Sad, you may decide. Tragic even.

But wait. There's one square near the centre of the quilt, just an inch or so to the right—yes, there! — that contains a single embroidered butterfly in blue thread. And beneath it is the stitched signature: Rose Hindmarch.

Here Comes Rose Now

Here comes Rose now, a shortish woman with round shoulders and the small swelling roundness of a potbelly, which she is planning to work on this fall.

Never mind the leather coat and boots and gloves, there's something vellum and summery in Rose's appearance, and she almost sings out the words, "Good evening." As you stand talking on the corner you see, behind her softly permed head, a fine autumn sunset dismantled in minutes by pillars of deep blue cloud. "Such gorgeous weather," she cries, stretching an arm upward and compelling you to agree.

She asks about your bronchitis and whether you've been into Kingston lately to see the new shopping centre; she comments on how lovely your house looks now that the porch and framework have been painted that nice soft shade of grey, how riotously the geese have been flying over town this past week, how the lake is higher than in recent years, how the Red and White is once again offering discounts on quarters of beef—not that she needs a quarter of beef, not her for heaven's sake, she's just about turned into a vegetarian!

Generalities and pleasantness, the small self-effacements and half-apologies and scattered diversions that fit so perfectly the looped contours of Rose's middle life. She does not tell you anything about herself, not about how she will be spending her evening tonight—a Friday evening—or about the recent cessation of her menstrual periods or the lucky penny in her pocket or the square beige envelope she is carrying home in her purse, an envelope containing, if you only knew, an invitation to a symposium (yes, a symposium) on the works of the poet Mary Swann to be held in Toronto during the first week of the new year.

And why doesn't Rose confide any of this to you? You've known her for years, all your life in fact.

Perhaps she detects a lack of interest on your part, sensing that you are already wearying of this casual, peripheral chitchat, that you're shifting from foot to foot, anxious to be on your way, into your own house where a familial disarray awaits and affirms you, where you can sink on to a kitchen chair with your sack of groceries and say. "Oh, for heaven's sake, Rose Hindmarch *does* go on and on, and she never says *anything*."

Or does Rose, so open, so helpful, so stretched by smiles, protect her secrets like a canny nun? For in a sense you might say that her Friday nights *are* a kind of secret, though an innocent one, and that her menopause, except for the headaches, has brought her a flush of covert pleasure, a deserved but shameful serenity, almost dispensation; at last she's released to live freely in the kind of asexual twilight that most flatters her. As for the printed invitation in the silky inner lining of Rose's purse, it glows like a reddened coal, precious, known only—as yet—to her.

Just fifteen minutes ago, on her way home from the library, she stopped to collect her mail from the post office. There were three items for her today—not unusual, not at all. There was her telephone bill; there was a postcard, close to indecipherable, from her friend Daisy Hart who is visiting her sister on the gulf coast of Florida; and there, puzzlingly, was the large square beige envelope (quality paper) addressed simply: Rose Hindmarch, Nadeau, Ontario. No box number, not that that mattered. No Miss or Ms., just Rose Hindmarch, the sturdy wily Rose, the energetic leading lady of the Nadeau township monthly minutes.

She opened it on the spot—never mind what Johnny Sears thought—but taking care not to destroy the creamy wholeness of the envelope. A symposium? On Mary Swann. January. Toronto. She was invited to attend a four-day symposium. (That must be a meeting or a convention, something along those lines, she will look it up in Funk and Wagnall's when she gets home.) Also included was a small, rather cunning-looking reply envelope, the kind that comes with wedding invitations, already stamped, too, a thoughtful gesture given the current postage rates.

Rose calculated quickly. September to January, four months away. A long time. Hallowe'en, Thanksgiving, Christmas; a very long time. Her excitement dwindled to dullness and she felt a pressure like tears rushing behind her eyes. But no, on second thought, four months would give her time to lose ten pounds—all she'd been waiting for was a good excuse. Five pounds off each hip and a little off the stomach. And time to make a shopping trip into Kingston to find something appropriate to wear, a suit maybe, something in that burgundy colour everyone is so crazy about these days, though Rose can't see why. Turquoise, her old standby, is hardly to be found.

The Harbourview Hotel. Toronto. January. That nice Sarah Maloney might come from Chicago. It wouldn't be any trip at all for her, not the way she travels about. And Professor Lang. Certainly he'll be there, no doubt of that. And maybe, but it would be silly to count her chicks, and so on, but maybe Mr. Jimroy would be there. Morton; he had, on that very first morning they met, asked her to call him Morton. "All my good friends call me Morton," he'd said.

His good friends. That is what Rose Hindmarch is: one of Morton Jimroy's good friends.

Where Rose Lives

Here we are, coming to where Rose Hindmarch lives. This is her suite, her apartment, 16½ Euclid Ave. Not, probably, the kind of place that comes to mind when people think of the word *apartment*; that is to say, there aren't any concrete towers or elevators or underground parking facilities here. This is a three-room suite (living-room, bedroom, kitchen) on the second floor of an eighty-year-old frame house on the corner of Euclid Avenue, a house owned by a young couple, Howie and Jean Elton (originally from Cornwall), who both happen to teach out at the new township school on Highway 17. (Howard teaches science; Jean, Phys. Ed.) Eventually the Eltons are planning to put in a separate outside entrance for Rose, but for the time being she goes in through their dark narrow front hall. "Hi ya, Rose," Jean calls from the kitchen, where she's usually throwing together something for supper; that's the expression she uses, *throwing something together.* "How are ya, Rose?" Howie will yell. He might be helping Jean make hamburgers in the kitchen or else sitting in the living-room having a beer and watching something on television. "Hi," Rose says in her merry voice, and hurries up the stairway.

She's glad there's a proper door at the top of the stairs, even though there's no lock. She likes Howie well enough and loves Jean, but privacy is important. She senses that they feel this way too.

And now what? She hangs up her coat on its special wooden hanger, glancing at the elbows for signs of wear. Owning a suede coat is a responsibility. Then quickly, in one long unbroken gesture, she puts on the tea-kettle and turns on the little kitchen radio, just in time to catch the six o'clock news. About once a week, usually on a Friday—and today *is* Friday—Rose will treat herself to a small rye and ginger-ale, which she sips while stirring up an omelette; two eggs, one green onion minced, a quick splash of milk. And just one slice of toast tonight. If she's going to lose ten pounds by January she'll have to start getting serious. But a little butter won't hurt. Only twenty-five calories in a teaspoon of butter, less than people think. There's a tiny mirror on the kitchen wall that Rose sometimes stands in front of, demanding: is this face going to turn into dough like Mother's did? Granny's too.

The news these days always seems to be about Libya or South Africa. When Rose thinks of South Africa she pictures a free-form shape with watery sides way down at the bottom of the map. The Dutch people went there first, she recalls vaguely, or else the English. In South Africa untidy policemen in shirt sleeves are always stopping people, black people, from going to funerals or forming labour unions. Well, Rose thinks, that doesn't seem like too much to ask for, though she's grateful she doesn't have to deal with unions herself. Howie and Jean belong to the teachers' union, but Howie says it's mostly bullshit, just two or three troublemakers trying to stir things up for everyone else. In South Africa there's a man called Nelson Mandela, a family man, stuck in jail. Rose has seen pictures of him on television, and pictures of his wife, too, a handsome woman with a grave face and a kerchief on her head.

From habit she eats slowly, daintily. Then she opens the refrigerator door and helps herself to a scoop of chocolate ice cream for dessert. Tomorrow morning she'll go down to the Red and White and buy a carton of yogurt. Jean and Howie both recommend yogurt, and Jean has even offered to lend Rose her electric yogurt maker. But Rose loves chocolate ice cream. Her mother used to make ice cream out on the lawn on summer evenings—that was when they were still in the house over on Second where the Harts live now. Rose remembers being twelve years old, turning the crank, waiting for the ice cream to form. A little rock salt, a little elbow grease, and the miracle took place. Almost the only miracle she can recall witnessing.

Rose is a happy woman; her routines make her happy. When in the early morning she pulls the sheets and blankets smooth and fluffs the pillow on her bed, she feels hopeful about the day ahead. A parade of minor pleasures—like the lucky coin today—reassure her, let her know she's part of the world. And on Friday nights she gets into her pyjamas early and crawls into bed to read. It's only seven-thirty and still fairly light outside. She cleans her face with cold cream and brushes her teeth and creeps under the covers. Her bare feet stretch out contentedly. She might read until midnight or later. Tomorrow is Saturday; she can sleep as late as she likes.

This is the bed her mother and father slept in, though Rose can't recall anything about her father who was a soldier—his mother was a Nadeau, a descendant of Martin Nadeau—who died at Dieppe. It's a comfortable double bed with a walnut-veneer headboard and has a good firm mattress that Rose bought after her mother's last illness and death; and smooth fitted sheets, cotton and Fortrel, a cheerful checked pattern. When Rose reads in bed she props herself up in the middle so that the pillows on each side embrace and warm her.

Only once has she shared this bed with another. That was two years ago, on a Friday night like this. She was reading as usual. It must have been eleven or later when she heard someone tapping or scratching lightly on her door. Then there was a hoarse whisper. "Rose? It's me, Jean. Can you let me in?"

Big bony Jean with her muscular shoulders and arms protruding absurdly from the lacy sleeves of a pale blue nylon nightgown. Her large feet were bare and her hair was pulled back as always by a heavy wooden barrette. That night her wide mouth gleamed in the dim hall light, a rectangle of anguish. "Oh, Rose. Oh, Rose," she was whimpering.

Sitting in Rose's kitchen she wept helplessly, and while she wept she beat her fist softly and rhythmically on the kitchen table.

Rose made her drink some rye, a good inch, straight, out of a juice glass.

"I hate him, I hate him." Jean made a wailing sound and put her head on the table. Rose, sitting beside her, stroked Jean's heavy hair, awkwardly at first, tentatively, and then she got up and made some tea.

"Oh, he's such a fucking bastard, oh Rose, he's a bastard, a first-class bastard, if you knew what he was really like. You don't know how lucky you are. Oh, my God, oh, my God."

Rose herself drank some tea, but poured another inch of rye for Jean. She wanted to say, "Can you tell me what happened?" or "Do you want to talk about it?" This was what people said in such situations. But a lump of stone had lodged itself in the centre of her chest and kept her from speaking. The pain was terrible. What a ninny she was.

Jean's nose burned bright red, and large Paisley-shaped blotches formed on the sides of her face. Rose supposed—hoped—they were caused by the weeping and the rye whisky, and not by the force of Howie Elton's fist. With both hands she passed Jean a box of Kleenex. "Here," she said.

After a minute Jean blew her nose. The light from the fluorescent fixture sharpened her somewhat vulpine cheeks and lips. She drew herself up and said "What am I going to do?" Then she said, "He doesn't know I'm up here. He thinks I ran out the back door."

"You can stay here," Rose said, "as long as you want." She felt heroic at that moment.

"Oh, Rose, can I? Really? Are you sure you don't mind?" Jean began sobbing again. The sobs sounded like water bubbling up from a deep lake, and Rose put her arms around her. It seemed to her that Jean was like a daughter or a sister.

Neither of them mentioned Rose's living-room couch. They slept together—it seemed perfectly natural—in the big double bed; or at least Jean slept, her copious kinky hair, wild and perfumy, loosened from the barette and spread out wide on the pillow. Rose lay awake most of the night, staring at the dark softenings in the corners of the ceiling and feeling herself in a daze of happiness. Her nose twitched with tears. She had no desire to touch the heavy, humming, sleeping body beside her. A narrow, exquisitely proportioned channel of space separated them and seemed to Rose to be a breathing organism. When Jean turned, Rose turned. When Jean murmured something from the depths of a dream, Rose heard herself murmuring too, a wordless, shapeless burr of pleasure. The wonder of it. The bewildering surprise. So this was what it was like to feel another human being so close. Inches away, so close she could feel the minute vibrations that were the sounds of Jean's inhaling and exhaling. Dear God. At almost fifty years old she at last divined that a body was more than a hinged apparatus for getting around, for ingesting and processing food, for sustaining queasy cyclical assaults. The same body that needed to be washed and trimmed and tended, and sometimes put to sleep with the help of a wet finger, also yearned to be close to another. How could she have failed to know something as simple as this? There was nothing to be wary of, there was nothing dangerous at all about this, lying here in bed with Jean Elton beside her.

In the morning Jean was gone. A note on the kitchen table said: "Thanks."

Nothing was ever said. Howie and Jean disappeared to Cornwall for the weekend and came home late on Sunday night; Rose heard them in the kitchen downstairs making coffee, Jean's familiar heavy voice, always on the verge of swelling into horsy laughter.

What had happened? What was it that Howie had done? Rose didn't know, or, more accurately, she *did* know, or at least suspected. Women, other women, opened their bodies trustingly. Howie must have done something unspeakable, something that appalled Jean, something vicious and sexual, something less than human; he must have climbed on top of her and taken some dark animal presumption. What that violation might be, Rose didn't know, didn't need to know. She regarded Howie after that with a certain awe. Jean, she loved.

It didn't happen again, but even now, after two years, Rose spends her Friday nights reading and waiting. She turns the pages of her book slowly, one ear tipped for the sound of Jean Elton scratching on her door. She feels it important to be there if Jean needs her.

Oh, she loves her Friday nights. During the week she's too tired to read, and it's all she can do to keep her attention on the television. But Friday nights: a pot of tea by her bedside, the satin binding of the blanket at her chin, the clean cotton-and-Fortrel-blend sheets moving across her legs, her book propped up in front of her. Amid this comfort she speaks harshly to herself. "Well, Rose kiddo, you're getting to be a real old maid, tucking in here like a hermit Friday after Friday. You should get out, go to a movie in Elgin now and then, the bingo even. What about the Little Theatre in Kingston, you used to go along with the Harts to all the shows. You're getting downright anti-social. Set in your ways and that's a bad sign."

It has crossed Rose's mind that someone should do a survey of what the librarians of small villages read in their spare time. Librarians are, after all, the ones who order new books and the ones who are always recommending such and such to someone else. "You'll love this," they cry, trying to remember who likes thrillers and who goes in for war stories and who opts for heavier things—though only Homer Hart in Nadeau reads books that might be called heavy.

It can't be said that Rose Hindmarch is a narrow reader. At the library, whenever she has a minute, she's dipping into this and that, a little local history, a Hollywood biography, the new mysteries, the new romances, the latest bestsellers, two inches thick—though these are getting so expensive Rose orders only one or two a month—and even the occasional volume of modern poetry.

Poetry, though, poses a problem for Rose. Except for Mary Swann's book, she has trouble understanding what it's about, and even with Mrs. Swann she's not always sure. "The rooms in my head are bare/Thunder brushes my hair." Now what's she trying to say in that poem? Of course rooms are a symbol of something, but thunder? "The mirror on the other side/Opens the place where I hide." Who can make heads or tails of that? Mr. Jimroy maybe. Morton.

Poetry, biography, romance, travel—Rose will read anything. But what she craves, and what she saves up for her Friday-night reading binges, are stories of espionage.

She tells herself she should sit down some day and make a list of all the spy stories she's read. There must be five hundred at least. Intrigue, escape, foghorns in the harbour, duty and patriotism. She knocks one back every week or so depending on the number of pages.

Ian Fleming—but she scorns him now, his bag of tricks—Ken Follet, John le Carré, Robert Ludlum, these are her favourites. The delicious titles, the midnight blueness of them, and the heroes with their hair curling over their ears, their intricate disguises and quick thinking, the cipher clerks labouring away by night in the back of an electrical supply store, the plump Munich prostitute with the radio receiver strapped to her thigh.

What Rose Hindmarch appreciates in most tales of espionage is the fine clean absence of extenuating circumstances—not that she would put it in those words—and the way the universe falls so sparely into two equal parts, good on one side, evil on the other. There's nothing random about the world of espionage. Evil is never the accidental eruption it is in real life, far from it. Evil, well, evil is part of an efficiently executed plot set into motion by those unnamed ones who possess a portion of dark power. And death? Death is never for a minute left in the hands of capricious gods (the morose, easily offended Ontario God included). Death is a clean errand dispatched by a hired gun. A slender man enters a brilliantly lit room, his wide velvet collar spilling charm, but his right hand moving meaningfully toward an inner pocket.

And Rose is drawn, too, toward that black confusion that pulsates behind the Iron Curtain—the tricky, well-guarded borders, the deep Danube, the cyanide pellets concealed in Polish fountain pens and lipstick cases, the rendezvous in shabby Warsaw bars or under flickering Slavic streetlamps. The swift-running trains that cross Germany and Hungary, always at night, transport her too, her chugging heart, her dry hands, carrying along a carload of ideological passion, none of which matters in the least to Rose, and the obsession to get to the heart of evil, to follow orders, to risk all. Mr. X (greenish skin beneath a greenish suit), a man of no fixed profession but protected nevertheless by hooded guards and German shepherds with open mouths. Why? Rose reads on. Because he is part of a gigantic plot to take over the Western world, that's why. The linkages glow like jewellery below a mirrored surface. Solutions arrive in the final chapters, cleansing as iodine, though Rose has read so many spy stories by now that she sees, halfway through, how it will go for her special envoy. This doesn't prevent her from reading on.

Another chapter, another poisoned gin rickey ("She had only taken a swallow when she realized . . . "), another undelivered message—and an hour has been subtracted from Rose's life. Her eyes intensify and shine. There's no turning back now. "My name is Smith," she reads. "I have been sent to warn you."

Rose's bedside clock says 2:00 A.M. The hour and the grey chill of the room augment the airlessness that enters her throat. Just one more chapter, she promises herself, but she can't stop. Through a crack in her curtains she can see the moon, shaved down to a chip. The tea in her cup has been cold for hours, but she sips a little anyway to relieve her terrible thirst. "You aren't the real Smith, my friend. I happen to know that you are really—" Rose postpones a trip to the bathroom, though her bladder is burning. "Here is an envelope. You will find plane tickets and a small map—"

Then the last page. It's 4:00 A.M. Jacob Smith is really Count Ramouski, as Rose suspected all along, and his double agentry has placed him on the side of good, as Rose hoped it would. He receives a commendation at a small private ceremony, and his nights are only slightly troubled by the number of assassinations the case necessitated. But part of his cover has been blown. A new code name will be assigned. This he accepts with a shrug. *C'est la vie.* Rose turns out the light, expecting to fall asleep immediately.

But for some reason she doesn't, not tonight. Something is nagging at her, making her restless. Then she remembers: the invitation to the symposium. The thought of it flicks on in her head like the burst of a cigarette lighter. (For Rose, who was a smoker before signing up last year for the Elgin Non-smokers Buzz Group, this is an appropriate image.) Click, click, the obedient flame leaps up.

It burns a small bright orange hole in the future. *Symposium. Symposium.* Her blind, sealed bedroom is set floatingly adrift by the single word, and her long night ends with a rush of joy.

A Saturday Night in Nadeau

In Nadeau, Ontario, as in other towns and villages on the continent of North America, and indeed around the world, there is a social structure that determines more or less how people will spend their disposable time. A social historian would be able to plot this leisure factor on a graph. Certain activities seem suited for certain people, while others seem inappropriate, even unthinkable. Rose Hindmarch, for instance, would feel almost as ill at ease having a drink at the Nadeau Legion as you would on arriving in town for the first time and stopping in there for a few relaxing beers. (Even so, you would not be turned away. You would be able to find yourself a chair in the damp beery coolness, and Susan Marland Jones, aged nineteen and sleeping with young Dick Strayer from Elgin, would bring you a drink and favour you with one of her vague, loopy smiles.) But unlike Rose Hindmarch, you will be unable in a single visit to take in the *sense* of the Nadeau Legion. The faces floating before you and the brief scraps of conversation you overhear will be dissociated from any meaningful context, just as though you were observing a single scene plucked at random from an extremely long and complex play. For every ounce of recognition provoked, there would be an answering tax of bafflement; a glimpse of "Life in Nadeau on a Saturday Night" conceals more than it reveals. Although you listen intently (and perhaps take notes), the scene before you never rounds itself out into the fullness of meaning. Too much is taken for granted by the speakers—Hy Crombie, Sel Ross, the Switzer twins, and their large smiling wives—and the allusions tossed up are patchy and fleeting and are embedded in long, shared histories. True they are careless of strangers down at the legion, and besotted by beer, but there is no thought of unkindness and no wish to suppress information. The same thing would happen if you stopped off at the Buffalo Bingo in the basement of the Nadeau Hotel or dropped in at one of the gracious old houses on Second Street where people (two or three or four, the number varies) have gathered to spend a Saturday evening.

Fat, tender-faced Homer Hart, for instance, sits in his living-room shuffling cards and listening to Rose Hindmarch rattle on about the symposium in Toronto. Then he says, "I once attended a symposium. At Lake Placid. I found it very interesting, if I remember rightly."

"What I can't imagine is why they bothered inviting me," Rose says, and looks around the bridge table at the others. She and her mother lived in this house before the Harts bought it, but that seems centuries ago.

"Your cut, Rose," Belle Waterman prompts, sighing and tutting. She's been invited tonight to replace Daisy, who is still in Florida. This happens every year about this time.

"Don't know why the heck they shouldn't invite you," Homer says. "Why, you're the expert, Rose. If anyone knows about Mary Swann, you're the one. The only one who really got to know her."

"Well," Rose allows, "maybe. But when I think about who's going to be there! It gives me the shakes. They're all scholars, and so on."

"Scholars, eh?"

"All of them. Eminent in their field. Morton Jimroy, he writes books, biographies, life stories of famous people. And Professor Lang. He was here in Nadeau once. No, twice. And probably Sarah Maloney will be there."

"Ah, Sarah!" This from Homer who met Sarah Maloney when she came to Nadeau five years ago.

"She's really Dr. Maloney," Rose explains to the others "I found that out after she was here. The Ph.D. kind of doctor. But you'd never know it."

"What do you bid?" Floyd Sears says. He's a regular at Saturday-night bridge, a man with a red, papery face. His wife, Bea, goes to bingo.

"Two clubs."

"So. We're back in clubs, are we?"

"This isn't my night. Not a good hand all night."

"Well, I think it's absolutely fantastic, Rose. And you deserve it, to get invited, I mean. Look at all the work you did, getting a room set up at the museum."

"Sounds real la-de-da."

"There was Plato's symposium," says Homer. "I remember—"

"Okay, I'm going to four clubs."

"Pass."

"As long as they don't expect me to contribute to the discussion," Rose says. "I wouldn't dare open my mouth if they did."

"I don't blame you a bit."

"Now, Rose, that doesn't sound like you. I've never known you to be shy or hold back."

"Well—"

"Well, if you ask me," says Belle, "you're more of an expert than any of them. Sure, so maybe they write these books and what have you, but you're the one who actually knew Mrs. Swann. Did any single one of *them* ever meet her? Face to face, I mean? No."

"Well," Rose answers slowly, looking around the table. "No, I guess not."

"See! You're the one with the real know-how, the firsthand knowledge. You've got it right over all those professors and book writers. You knew Mary Swann. In person."

"That's true, Rose," Homer says. His tone is fond. His face too.

"Still—"

"Trump."

"Damn. 'Scuse my French."

"It isn't as though I knew her all that well."

"No one knew her all that well when it come to that. I never said more'n two words to her. Well, maybe 'nice day,' something like that, if she happened to come into the post office. Not that she'd say anything back much."

"Wasn't much of a talker, Mrs. Swann, that's for sure."

"She used to make those dolls for the Fall Fair. Remember?"

"Only once, I think."

"Queer in her ways," Floyd Sears says. "That's what Bea used to say."

"I wouldn't say queer exactly."

"Odd?" Rose looks around her. She has known Homer since she was six, Belle Waterman since she was five, Floyd Sears for—she can't remember; she has always known Floyd Sears.

"Well, what the heck, poets are supposed to be odd, aren't they?"

"She didn't seem all that odd to me. Just one of your nervous types. And ashamed of how she looked, those clothes of hers."

"Remember the poem she did on the big snowstorm? When was that, anyways?"

"Good grief, yes, I remember that."

"Fifty-nine, November. Twenty-two inches we got. Boy oh boy, what a dump of snow. I'll never forget that."

"Where's the time go."

"Older I get, the faster—"

"It was a nice poem. Real nice. You know the one I mean, Rose? It was in the paper. All about white—"

"Buried under bridal white," Rose says. "That's how it starts out anyhow."

"Bridal white?"

"Like a bride's dress. She compared it to—"

"Oh."

"Anyone for coffee?" Homer offers, rising heavily. "Or is tea okay?"

"Here let me give you a hand."

"She was kind of shy, I think. Mary Swann, she was one of your shy women. Sort of countrified, if you take my meaning. Didn't take to shooting the breeze."

"Well, she sure is famous now. Wouldn't you say so, Rose?"

"Well—"

"She sure as heck must be famous if all these people're getting together in Toronto for a—what was it again?"

"A symposium."

"Plato's symposium, I can remember—"

"Poor Mrs. Swann. She always looked scared to me, a regular rabbit-type woman. Never had two nickels to rub together. Used to buy her postage stamps one at a time. Of course folks did in those days."

"Those were darn tough times."

"One at a time. Imagine!"

"Sorry, folks," says Homer. "Store cookies is all we've got. Chocolate chip."

"Tasty, though."

"Thanks, Homer, I will."

"Well, she went and put this town on the map, Mary Swann. You never know."

"Nadeau, Ontario, home of Mary Swann."

"World-famous poetess."

"Remember that black coat she used to wear?"

"I remember the running shoes. The poor woman. She'd come into the Red and White in those darned old running shoes."

"Poor old soul."

"She wasn't really that old. I wouldn't call fifty exactly old."

"Not nowadays."

"Not then either."

"Who knows, she might of written a lot more books of poems if she'd lived another ten, twenty years. Boy, that woman could sure write the poems. There was one that really got me. About a calf drowning. Any of you remember that one?"

"That was in the Elgin paper if I'm not mistaken."

"Real sad. But kind of touching, too."

"She had a gift. Writing poems is a genuine gift."

"You never know, do you, when you look at a person, I mean. What kind of talent they're keeping under their bushel basket."

"What was she like, Rose? She must of warmed up to you some. When she came in to borrow books."

"Not all that much. This was when the library was in the church basement. After it got moved out of the post office—"

"Well, what *was* she like? Like in a nutshell, how'd you describe her?"

"Oh, we used to chat about this and that. About the weather. I knew her daughter, Frances, a little at school. I used to ask her how Frances was getting along out in California, that kind of thing."

"A good-looking girl, Frances."

"Still is, probably. Not one of your glamour girls, but a smart-looking girl when she was young."

"And she got the Queen's scholarship. Not bad when you think—"

"Her husband's a big shot, I hear. Goes around telling folks how to invest their money. Wrote a book—"

"Really?"

"She must of had a tough time, Mrs. Swann, bringing up a kid with never two nickels to rub together."

"Frances was always clean. And polite. You could say that for her."

"Poor Mrs. Swann. What kind of life was that for a woman of her talents? Stuck out on that good-for-nothing farm with that good-for-nothing husband—"

"She married him. She must of thought he was okay. In the beginning at any rate."

"Well, she found out different, didn't she?"

"She sure did. The hard way."

"Of course we'll never know the whole story."

"That's true, that's so true. It takes two. That's what Bea said at the time."

"Two to tangle."

"Poor Mary Swann."

"Funny the way things turn out. You just never know what's going to happen in this life. From one day to the next."

Drifting Thoughts of Rose Hindmarch

We no longer care about the lives of the saints, yet we long for a holiness of our own.

This, or something like this, is what Rose Hindmarch is thinking as she bows her head during silent meditation on Sunday morning. And such a lengthy silent meditation! The new minister, Bob Holly, who drives up from Kingston on Sunday morning to conduct holy worship in Nadeau (his young wife sits outside in their Pontiac doing a crossword puzzle, a picnic lunch beside her on the seat) imposes, for reasons of his own, uncomfortably long periods of silent prayer, sometimes as long as five minutes. This morning he directs the congregation to pray for the struggle in South Africa, which is all very well, but Rose is unable to compose her thoughts. Black townships, barbed wire; something swims into the pious hush of the church, an oily substance, green in colour, then slides away. "Our father," Rose begins, and is filled with unrest.

She shouldn't have come, not this morning, not in this condition, nagged by the betrayal of her own leaking body. She likes to sail into this church with the lightness and dryness of a pressed oak leaf. But early this morning she awoke to find a pool of blood between her legs. After eleven months—this! The odour and the stickiness brought tears to her eyes and, rinsing out her sheets in the bathtub, she gave way to a single sharp cry of anguish. This! "You okay, Rose?" Jean Elton yelled up the stairs.

"I'm fine," Rose called down gaily. "Just dandy."

She would stay home from church, she decided. Then changed her mind.

Despite her atheism, or perhaps because of it she almost never misses church. On those few Sunday mornings when she *has* stayed home, she's sat stiffly on her brocade chesterfield in the front room as though glued there and felt loneliness blow through her body. The longest hour of the week is the one wrenched from the machinery of habit.

Holy, holy, holy, Lord God Almighty,
Early in the morning, we raise our song to thee.

It was better, far better, despite everthing, to be seated here in the austere waxy light, head inclined, praying. "Our Father—"

As always Rose leaves her eyes half open and directs her prayers toward the railing that encloses the pulpit, a railing composed of four pine panels topped with a pretty moulding of carved leaves. The prettiness of the carving, which by rights ought to be neutral, seriously challenges the few moral choices made by Rose Hindmarch in her life. From where she sits, row six this morning, she can see light shining between the leaves, and it is to these lighted spaces that she addresses her prayers, or rather her questions. *Why?* is what she usually asks, the *whys* coming like a bombardment of electrons —why, for instance, is she thinking about Mary Swann this morning instead of Bishop Tutu and Nelson Mandela?

It is a surprising fact that Mary Swann never, at least as far as anyone knows, attended church. Surprising because in every one of her poems there is one line at least that can be interpreted as sacred. It was Morton Jimroy who pointed this out to Rose when he visited Nadeau a year ago. No, it was closer to eighteen months ago. How time flies, Rose thinks. He was extraordinarily kind, lingering in the museum, plainly enchanted by the exhibits, particularly by the two photographs of Mrs. Swann, and asking questions, nodding his head, taking notes, He invited Rose out to dinner at the old hotel in Elgin. "You don't have to do that," she protested. "But I want to," he said. "I really do."

He brought his copy of *Swann's Songs* to the restaurant, a rather battered copy and not very clean, and after they had ordered the double pork chop platter with mashed potatoes, turnip, and a mound of apple sauce, he showed Rose those lines of Mary Swann's that he felt demonstrated her deep religious impulse. "There," he said, pointing with a patient finger, "and there. And there."

"I see what you mean," Rose said after a minute, disoriented.

"Look at this line," Morton Jimroy said. "This reference to water—a stunning line, isn't it?—which clearly expresses a yearning for baptism, for acceptance of some kind. Or even forgiveness."

"You don't think—" Rose began. "I mean, perhaps you know that there's no well out there on the Swann property."

"Of course, of course, but then"—he switched to his instuctor's voice—"serious poetry functions on several levels. And in Swann's work the spiritual impulse shines like a light on every detail of weather or habit or natural object. The quest for the spiritual. The lust for the spiritual."

Spirituality from Ma.y Swann? That rough-featured woman who never once came to church? (Though she had, Rose told Morton Jimroy, always donated some of her handmade crochet work to the Fall Fair.)

"But why not?" he pressed her. He was facing her across the little table, one hand curling a corner of the paper placemat, the other reaching in his breast pocket for a pencil. "Why do you think she stayed away from church so religiously?—if you'll pardon my little joke."

"Clothes probably," Rose said this boldly. She was conscious of a noisy brimming of happiness. She had only once before in her life been taken to dinner by a man, and that had been Homer Hart, years ago, before he married Daisy.

"Clothes?" His pencil moved busily.

"Well, she probably didn't have the right clothes. For church, you know."

"Do you think so? Really?"

She could see he was disappointed. "Yes," she said. "I think that must have been the reason."

"You don't suppose," Jimroy said, "that Swann felt her spirituality was, well, less explicit than it was for regular churchgoers in the area. That it was outside the bounds, as it were, of church doctrine?" He regarded Rose closely. "If you see what I mean."

"I see what you mean, Mr. Jimroy. Morton. But I really think, well, it was probably a question of not having the right kind of clothes."

"She told you this?"

"Oh, heavens, no. It's just a feeling I have."

"Oh?"

"I know it sounds silly, but a few years ago it was different. You just didn't set foot in church without a hat, not in Nadeau, not in the United Church. And gloves. Mrs. Swann didn't have a hat or gloves. Well, just work gloves, and she wouldn't have had a decent Sunday dress or stockings or anything like that."

He put his fingertips together. "I suppose I see her," he paused, "as someone whose faith was exceedingly primitive and mystical. Is that how you saw her, Miss Hindmarch?"

"Rose," she reminded him.

"Rose, of course. Is that how—?"

"I, well, I think so, yes." She gave a nod, implying tolerance and generosity.

"As in this passage?" He opened the book again and read aloud. (Rose was glad there was no one else in the dining-room.)

Blood pronounces my name
Blisters the day with shame
Spends what little I own,
Robbing the hour, rubbing the bone.

Rose waited, respectfully, her hand touching her brooch.

"Well," Jimroy said, speaking rather loudly. "This seems to be—now you may disagree—but to me it's a pretty direct reference to the sacrament of holy communion. Or perhaps, and this is my point, perhaps to a more elemental sort of blood covenant, the eating of the Godhead, that sort of thing."

Rose said nothing, not wanting to disappoint him a second time. She was unable to utter the word menstruation. She would have died first. It was a word she had always been uneasy with. She nodded, first hesitantly, then vigorously. And chewed away on her meat. She had trimmed away the fat, feeling it would be indelicate to eat it—but it was a sacrifice, she loved it so!

For dessert there was a choice of rice pudding or rhubarb pie. It seemed to Rose that Morton Jimroy shuddered slightly when presented with this choice, but after a moment's indecision, he accepted the pudding, and when it arrived, a formless cloud stuck with currants, he sat pushing it from side to side on the plate with the back of his spoon, still pursuing the substance of Mary Swann's blood poem. "A poet," he told Rose, "is able to speak of those states of consciousness of which he or she has no personal knowledge."

"But how—?" She waved her arm, a little too gaily.

Jimroy's eyes shot upward to the pressed-tin ceiling as though its patterned squares contained the key to his theory. "This is something I've thought about a great deal," he said. "What sets poets apart from the rest of us—and I'm talking about those rare poets who stand head and shoulders above the simpering 'little mag' people, the offset people—true poets carry a greater share of the racial memory that do we lesser beings.''

Rose smiled, not displeased to be cast into the category of lesser being, where Mr. Jimroy, Morton, clearly placed himself.

He went on. ''Their actual *experience*, what happens to them in their lives, is really beside the point. It's their genetic disposition, a mutation, of course, which urges them forward and allows them to be filters of a larger knowledge.''

''I'm afraid you're a little over my head,'' Rose said.

This was not strictly true. She was following what he said, yet sensed that humility was called for.

Jimroy continued, his hands jabbing. ''This is the central mystery of the poets, Miss Hindmarch. We examine the roots of our poets, their sources, the experiences they draw upon, and it never adds up. Never. There's something that you'' —he looked directly into Rose's eyes at last—''that you and I can't account for. Call it an extra dimension if you like. A third eye.''

For some reason Rose felt unworthy of this insight. A gust of real humility struck her, and she wished Jimroy would remove his gaze. ''I see,'' she said foggily.

''Take Swann's profound sense of Angst,'' Jimroy said.

''*Angst*?'' Rose looked down, then cut into her pie. She was conscious of Mrs. Ryan in her large apron standing in the doorway to the kitchen. Normally the hotel dining-room closed at 8:00 on week nights.

''Perhaps despair is a better word,'' Jimroy said kindly. ''I don't suppose our Swann read the existentialists, at least there is no concrete evidence that she did, but she was most assuredly affected by the trickle-down despair of our century.''

''I think we all are,'' Rose said. ''All of us. I know I have my low moments—''

Jimroy pushed aside his uneaten pudding. He leaned forward. ''But you see, Swann had that rare gift of *translating* her despair. She wasn't writing poems about housewife blues. She was speaking about the universal sense of loss and alienation, not about washing machines breaking down or about—''

''Oh,'' Rose said, ''the Swanns didn't have a washing machine.''

''I beg your pardon.''

"A washing machine. They didn't have one." She felt obliged to explain. "Of course there *were* people in the country who did have washing machines, even then, but the water supply out at the Swann place—"

Jimroy looked tired. "I was using a washing machine as an example," he said. "It was just a metaphor for, well, for all that's nonspiritual in life if you like." Nevertheless he pulled out his pencil and made a brief note. "What I meant was that great poets write from large universalized perceptions, and Mary Swann's blood poem seems to me to be her central spiritual statement." He paused, making sure Rose was following his argument. "The blood, you see, is a symbol. It stands for the continuum of belief, a metaphysical covenant with an inexplicable universe."

"Yes," said Rose, and closed her mouth.

Courage, courage, she said to herself, a word she has learned to unfurl in her head whenever her awful timidity rises up. Her voice immediately grew louder—she hoped not shrill—and her shoulders gathered force. "But you see," she began, "Mrs. Swann was a woman and—"

"Yes?"

"It isn't important."

"Everything's important."

"I can't remember what I was going to say." She looked down at her rhubarb pie and pledged herself not to jeopardize what was left of the evening.

"Our Father," she says on Sunday morning to the carved leaves on the pulpit railing. "Take it away, take it away. When I come out of church today, make it be gone."

Mr. Jimroy wrote a lovely letter thanking her for all her help. She wrote back "But I'm the one who should be thanking you. It was such a pleasure—"

Such a pleasure. Such an honour. Morton Jimroy—he was a famous author. She hadn't realized how famous he was until later. He was in *Who's Who*. She'd looked him up. He was a world authority. He knew everything there was to know about poetry, including what it all meant. Except for that poem of Mary Swann's—he couldn't seem to get the drift of that. Of course he was a man, an unmarried man at that, or at least separated—he'd mentioned something about a former wife—and perhaps men have a tendency to overlook what is perfectly obvious to women. Or perhaps he found it embarrassing or messy; she wouldn't blame him a bit if he did. It had seemed so clear to Rose, but then she was no authority, and poetry could be so . . . so vague. Still, she was sure, a hundred per cent sure, of what Mary Swann had been talking about. Rose supposed she had made do with old rags as country women still did occasionally. Never two nickels to rub together, poor woman. And no clothes suitable for Sunday service, something else Mr. Jimroy hadn't quite cottoned onto, though in the end maybe he had. At least he'd made a number of notes as she talked and talked.

It was wonderful really, how he listened to her, to every little thing she had to say about Mary Swann, no matter how small or trivial. Sitting there, talking and talking, she realized she didn't really like him. But she wanted him to like *her*. He was too anxious, too greedy somehow, but underneath the anxiousness and greed there was something else, a green shoot that matched her own unfolded greenness. *Courage*, she said to herself, and began another anecdote. "One day Mrs. Swann and I—"

He wanted to hear it all. Tell me what she looked like, this famous author and scholar had begged Rose Hindmarch, local librarian. How did Mary Swann wear her hair? How did she walk? What was her voice like? Did you ever talk about poetry? What did you usually talk about? And what else?

He was patient, waiting until she found the words and put her recollections in order. His eyes had burned. "Remarkable," he said, and made a note. "Priceless." Then, "Go on."

He filled one notebook and started another. "Now tell me, Miss Hindmarch, Rose, did you ever discuss . . ."

He seemed altogether happy sitting there in the dining-room of the Elgin Hotel, leaning forward so eagerly, his rice pudding forgotten. And she? She felt a happy, porous sense of usefulness, as though joined for once to something that mattered. *Slim-shouldered Rose Hindmarch, local expert on Mary Swann, a woman with an extraordinary memory and gift for detail, able to remember whole conversations word for word, able to put precise dates on . . . episodes that were years in the past . . . and . . .*

He shook her hand in farewell. She wanted him to linger, but his handshake was hurried, as though he could hardly wait to get back to his typewriter before the things she had said faded. A little let down, a little tearful in fact, she had wanted to hang on to his hand and blurt out something more. Anything. "I forgot to tell you about the time Mary and I . . ."

Later, in church, after Morton Jimroy returned to Winnipeg, she begged forgiveness from the pine pulpit rail. She had never meant to be untruthful. She had not intended to exaggerate her friendship with Mary Swann. Friendship! The truth was that she had scarcely done more than pass the time of day with Mrs. Swann. Good morning, Mrs. Swann. Nice weather we're having, Mrs. Swann. Won't be long till the snow flies.

The two of them had *not* gone for long walks together. They had *not* discussed—not even once—the books Mary Swann borrowed from the library. Mary Swann had *not* give Rose Hindmarch copies of her poems to read and comment upon. They had *not* —not ever—discussed their deeply shared feeling about literature or about families or about nature. None of this had taken place. It is a myth that people in rural communities are all acquainted with one another and know all about each other's business. Mary Swann had been a virtual stranger to Rose Hindmarch, just as she was to everyone else in Nadeau, Ontario. A woman who kept to herself, that was Mary Swann.

Forgive me, forgive me. Forgive me the sin of untruthfulness.

Our unlikeliest prayers are answered. Within weeks Rose felt herself to be absolved. Her guilt receded with surprising speed in the days following Jimroy's visit, and before long she felt the balm of complete forgiveness. This came not in the usual way through a cycle of confession and mortification, penalty and pardon, but through the roughly weighted balance of mutual transgression. Human beings are not stainless; this is a fact. Rose is far from possessing moral perfection. So too is Morton Jimroy. Their imperfections, colliding in a blue sky somewhere between Ontario and Manitoba, merged and cancelled each other out.

For Morton Jimroy took—stole, that is, no use to shilly-shally—the photograph of Mary Swann from the Nadeau Museum. There could be no doubt of this. He probably, Rose believes, slipped it under his jacket while she was looking the other way. Yes, she is sure this is what happened. There were two photographs: one rather blurred, showing Mary standing in the sunshine; the other, much clearer, showing the unsmiling matte face, eyes wide open, a mouth that was intensely secretive; it is this second photograph that vanished. There were no other visitors to the museum that day, not one.

Her first thought was to write Jimroy a letter and accuse him directly. "Dear Mr. Jimroy, I am afraid I must ask you to return . . ."

But the impulse died almost at once. Weeks passed. Months went by. Now, if she thinks of the photograph at all it's with the sense that it is in the hands of its rightful owner. (Just as it is right that Mary Swann's notebook is with Dr. Maloney, Sarah.) Knowing this, she experiences a quiet tide of relief. An act of restitution has taken place, an undefined wrong set right, and as for Jimroy, her fondness for him has increased steadily. His friendship, his *confidence*, is the anointing she has longed for, and the evening in the Elgin Hotel glows like one of those stained-glass birds people hang in their windows, the two of them together, chaste, joyful, the book of Mary Swann's poems between them on the table. There was a moment when his hand, reaching for the bill, brushed hers. It shames her that she should savour this moment, since she knows it is the sort of accident others cast away as valueless. Nevertheless it is hers, and nothing will persuade her to give it up.

Rose Hindmarch Is Visited by the November Blues

The water tower at the edge of town wears a crown of snow, though it's only mid-November. It has been snowing steadily for two days now. The lake is full of snow. The back roads are full of snow, and so are the small straight streets of Nadeau and the whitely blowing late-afternoon sky that hovers over the village. A water-colourist attempting to capture the scene would need only a minimal palate: blue, white, and a slash of violet. The violet, especially in the late afternoon, carries the power of melancholy.

Coming through the snow is a human form that can barely be distinguished. Yes, it is female; yes, it is someone no longer young, a figure bundled against the snow and walking with an awkward and seemingly painful gait. It's only Rose Hindmarch with a sack of groceries in her arms. Wouldn't you think some kind person would offer her a lift?

Now, around the corner, comes a blue Volkswagen van with its jumpy, nervous little windshield wipers going like fury. Homer Hart is behind the wheel, a kindly, fat-chested man squashed into an old-fashioned overcoat. He brings the little car to a sliding halt, rolls down the window and says in that quavering tenor of his, "Rose? Is that you? Climb in and I'll run you home."

Before Homer's breakdown he was principal of the Nadeau High School. Then the shock treatments wiped away his Latin and French and left behind only his sputtering, faltering high-pitched English. "This is no weather to be out in, Rose," he natters. "This is no kind of day to be walking around out of doors."

"Thanks a million, Homer," Rose says, getting in beside him. "I needed a few things from the store so I thought I'd—" Then she stops herself and says, "Any news from Daisy?"

He takes the corner slowly. "Not a word for two weeks. You know Daisy when she gets down in the Florida sunshine."

"Didn't she say when she'd be back? In her last letter, I mean?"

"End of next week, she said, but you know Daisy." He gives Rose a shrewd, unhopeful smile. "Gets a little longer every year."

"It won't be long now," Rose says. Then she adds, sighing, "Just look at all the snow she's missed! Have you ever seen snow like this?"

Homer offers to carry up the bag of groceries, but Rose says no, she can manage. "Thanks anyway, Homer." Then "Let me know if there's anything I can do for you."

A lot of people say this to Homer. It's a natural gesture, offering aid to an older man who's keeping house on his own for an interval and who's lonely and disoriented. Of course Homer is chronically disoriented and, therefore, the recipient of many small kindnesses, which he has learned to accept meekly. This is especially the case when Daisy is off on her annual trip south.

Rose is waiting for Daisy to come home from Florida and feed some life into her. Daisy with her leathery tan will bring her a new fund of stories: the people she's met at her sister's trailer park, the bridge hands she's played, the new restaurants she and her sister have discovered in the Sarasota area. She'll have bought herself two or three new outfits, and for Rose a rainbow-coloured scarf or a shell necklace from St. Armand's Key. Rose is hoping to persuade Daisy to go into Kingston with her for a pre-Christmas shopping spree. Not that Daisy will need much persuading; she loves to go shopping with her friends, taking them by the arm and coaxing them into

Eaton's, offering advice and sharing precious threads of information. This'll wear well, she'll say, but this won't. This flatters you, this brings out your complexion, covers your neck, hides your upper arms, conceals the bust. Daisy has an eye. Some say a wicked eye.

Six months ago, just after Easter, Rose received a note in the mail. There was a local postmark on the envelope. A shower invitation, Rose thought happily; she hadn't been to a shower for ages. Inside was an attractive little hasty note with a blue flower in one corner. The note was printed. "Dear Rose: I am a friend and can't think of any way to tell you this, but there is a little hair growing on your chin. It's been there for a while now, and I thought you might want to know."

Of course the note wasn't signed. Of course Rose knew it could only have been sent by Daisy Hart.

She felt sick. She would never be able to look Daisy in the face again. In the bathroom mirror she peered at herself, tipping her head back as far as she could. There it was, a little grey hair about an inch long, a small wiry hair, curly like a pig's tail. She removed it with a manicure scissors and immediately felt better, and also more kindly toward Daisy, and now, every night she looks to see if it has grown back in. She has replaced the bathroom lightbulb with one twice as bright and has also purchased a small magnifying mirror into which she can scarcely bring herself to look, so suddenly present are the colony of pores at the side of her nose and the webby flesh under her eyes. When Daisy comes home from Florida, Rose intends to consult her about buying a new makeup base. She wants to look her best for the Swann symposium, which is now only two months away. She would like to lose her tired, wan look and appear lively and knowledgeable, not exactly a fashion plate, that would be ridiculous, but someone who possesses the brisk freshness of the countryside. *"You're looking just the same, Rose,"* cry Sarah Maloney, Morton Jimroy, Professor Lang, too.

At least she's managed to lose some weight. Twelve pounds so far, and without the pain of going on a special diet or eating yogurt. Mysteriously, she seems to have lost her appetite for chocolate ice cream, and has just about given up her evening omelettes, too. Toast and tea are all she bothers with these days. Her blue skirt hangs on her, and she feels tired at the thought of taking in the side seams. When she looks in the mirror she sees only a blur, but accepts the fact that aging means estrangement from one's own face. She's tired most of the time lately, what with the long hours at work and the evening meetings and so on. Of course people slow down at this time of year—Homer was saying something like that not long ago, something about iron deficiency. On top of everything else there's the worry about her periods starting up again.

It's exasperating the way they start and stop, stop and start. Only today, on a Saturday afternoon, she had to go down to the Red and White to buy a new box of pads. Naturally, Stan Fortas was at the cash register with his big hands gripping the box and dropping it into the grocery sack, talking a mile a minute about how he was planning to do some ice fishing this winter, just as though it was Rice Krispies she was buying and not sanitary pads which she required to staunch this new, thick, dark-red outpouring.

She should see a doctor. Women her age are always being told to have annual check-ups. Daisy Hart goes twice a year to a women's clinic in Kingston. She will ask Daisy when she gets home where the clinic is and perhaps make an appointment. She certainly doesn't intend to go back to Dr. Thoms in Elgin, not if she's bleeding to death.

"Just slip off your panties," he said in his crackling young man's voice, "and try to relax." As though anyone could relax with that rubber glove pushing away up inside her. She whimpered a little with the pain, a bleating sound that surprised her, but the rubber glove plunged even farther, twisting and testing the helpless interior pulp of her body. Afterwards he sat her down in the little office and asked, without preliminaries, "Would you say your sex life is satisfactory?" She was tempted to whimper again. Something like a nettle rash came over her larynx. His pen wagged in the air, impatient. She managed to nod. "No pain during intercourse?" he pursued her. She shook her head and he made another check mark. "Libido falling off at all?" He was relentless—to this last question it seemed she could neither nod nor shake her head, so she grimaced stupidly and gave the smallest of shrugs and was rewarded by another check mark on her chart. A moment later he was taking her blood pressure and inquiring about her diet, and she was giving him curt, icy replies, which he seemed not to notice.

For a day afterward, her stomach churned with humiliation. She resolved never to go back. That he was new in the area only made it worse, for he was bound to find out who she was sooner or later, the virgin village clerk, the old-maid librarian. She wondered if he could guess how she put herself to sleep some nights, her finger working.

He pronounced her a healthy specimen, but that was five years ago. What should she do now about this pouring blood?

She's going to have to buck up, she tells herself with a shake of her head. Start taking an interest in things the way she used to. Buck up, Rose girl. Mind over matter. The new John le Carré on the bedside table is only half read, but this one doesn't hold her interest the way the others did. Everything in the story is happening so far away that she has a hard time imagining it. It all seems a little silly, in fact, all jumbled up, though probably it will come together in the end. But the end lies somewhere beyond her strength at the moment. It's such a big book, so many pages. Were his other books this long? She finds it curiously heavy to hold. That's the trouble with a hardcover book, of course. A paperback wouldn't draw the strength from her arms like this, making her shoulders ache and her fingers go numb.

She decides she will abandon le Carré for tonight and browse through her copy of *Swann's Songs*. She's familiar with most of the poems, of course, even if she doesn't understand them, but it's been a while since she's read the book straight through. She has been intending to give it some serious attention before the symposium actually rolls around. She doesn't want to look ignorant. People there will be looking at her—her!—as an expert.

But the little book isn't in its usual place under her magazine rack. Probably it has slipped through onto the floor behind. Well, she'll look for it in the morning. Right now she's too tired to bend over.

Her eyes especially are heavy and tired; sometimes Rose thinks they're like two hard stones perched there on a face that's half dead.

Rose and Homer Take a Sunday Drive

"Feel up to taking a drive over to Westport?" Homer says to Rose two weeks later. It is the middle of a cold, windless Sunday afternoon when he phones. At this moment Jean and Howie Elton are quarrelling loudly downstairs. Some heavy object has been dropped on the floor, an act of carelessness on Jean's part, it seems, and Rose can hear Howie shouting and slamming cupboard doors, and the shrill counterpoint of Jean defending herself. (It has been going on for more than an hour; at first Rose listened with a disabling sense of excitement and eagerness. Then there was another loud crash and the sound of weeping; Jean's of course.) Rose puts her lips close to the telephone and whispers to Homer that yes, she would love a drive over to Westport, that he is a godsend—which seems to please him inordinately.

The road to Westport is clear of ice, and the running glare on the snow-filled fields is so bright that Rose feels herself grow buoyant. "Oh, I love it," she says. "It's a wonderful day for a run. I love it."

People in Nadeau, at least those older people who still subscribe to the idea of a Sunday "run," quite often travel the twelve miles to Westport. Westport is a smaller village than Nadeau, a prettier village. Its white houses with their shining windowpanes and painted doors are arranged not in neat rows as in Nadeau, but charmingly, haphazardly, along the lake shore. In Westport you can stand by the side of the lake next to the old ferry shed and get a fine view of the ice fishing out on the bay. Afterward, if you like, you can stop in at Lou's Antique Barn where blue glass insulators and pink glass relish dishes are arranged on rustic shelves, and then you can warm yourself up with a cup of coffee and a muffin at the Westport Luncheonette.

Homer Hart, buttering his second muffin, is in a merry mood. He has a feeling in his bones, he tells Rose, that Daisy will be home by the end of the week. He is ninety-nine per cent sure that there will be a letter from her Monday morning telling him when she'll be arriving.

Anticipation makes him adventurous, and he proposes to Rose that they go back to Nadeau by way of the back road. He feels sure that the snowplough has been through by now. It's still early, just three-thirty, and the road is prettier that way.

"Well," Rose says, "I don't know." But after a minute she agrees. She's feeling uneasy now about Jean, and wondering if she's done the right thing leaving the house. On the other hand, the back road is prettier, just as Homer says, even if it does take a little longer.

For the first mile or two it follows the lake and then cuts north, wandering back and forth gaily between low rounded hills. Rose often thinks to herself what a pleasure it is, the flash of scenery through a car window, how it infects her with an ancient rush of innocence and holds in abeyance more difficult daily chores and dealings. A tent is thrown over her thoughts. Scenery gliding past the eye doesn't need worrying about. It passes, that's all, quick as a wink, and asks nothing in return.

One by one the old farms come into view along the back road, and Rose, because of her position as town clerk, is able to put a name to each of them, as well as being able to comment on the acreage and the taxes paid or owing. There's the old Hanna place. And that's where the Enrights used to live. Mainly these are poor farms, though the deep layer of snow gives them a false look of prosperity. The soil beneath is thin and stony, good for nothing but grazing animals or planting a few acres of hay or corn. It's a wonder, Rose observes, that people stay on these farms and continue to eke out a living somehow.

The farm where Mary Swann lived with her husband and daughter is one of the smallest and poorest of the area, though it's encouraging to see that the new owner, a young man from the States who bought the place as a weekend retreat, has at least had the fences repaired and a new roof put on the house. The sight of the dull silvery silo poking up next to the barn always affects Rose. What she feels is some unnamed inner organ flopping in her chest and squeezing her breath right out.

"Poor Mrs. Swann," Homer says, as though reading Rose's thoughts. He slows the car just a bit.

"It's a wonder," Rose says, thinking of the new owner, "how he could bring himself to buy a place where something awful happened."

"Probably never thinks about it," Homer says. "That was a long time ago."

"Not that long."

"People forget. And he's not from the area. Didn't know the family."

"But still." Rose lifts her gloved hands helplessly in the air, then drops them on her lap with a sigh.

"As a matter of fact," Homer goes on, his tender mouth moving, "I don't suppose that young fellow cares about the farm. Probably just a tax shelter. Looks like he's letting the fields go wild."

"A hobby farm," Rose says, "That's what Mr. Browning said when he came into the office. Just for weekend. Not that he ever seems to come."

The countryside around Nadeau is full of weekend farmers these days. Rose, going over her tax sheets, is familiar enough with the phenomenon, but she still finds it strange. She can remember that as a child it was a rare treat to be taken to Kingston. Now people think nothing of driving all the way from Montreal or Toronto or up from the States just for a weekend.

"Well," Rose says to Homer, "he sure couldn't make any kind of living off this place. And the silo. What would he put in it?"

Both Rose Hindmarch and Homer Hart remember the year when Angus Swann amazed his neighbours by erecting a silo on his farm. There was talk. The news travelled fast and met with wide disapproval. There was a feeling that an injustice had been done. Mary Swann had no washing machine and no refrigerator. She cooked the family meals on a blackened wood-burning stove right up until the day she was killed—though it was said she owned a Parker 51 fountain pen with which she wrote her poems. But, the pen aside, she lacked those conveniences that had become common even on the less-prosperous farms, those conveniences that were said to "make a woman's lot easier."

How were these daily domestic deprivations, a washing machine, a refrigerator, to be balanced beside Angus Swann's new silver-clad silo? Because it was obvious even to the disinterested eye that the Swann farm didn't merit such a dignifying emblem. Silos belonged on prosperous dairy farms, keeping company with roomy, wide-raftered barns and graceful rows of elms. But not on the old Swann farm, or rather, the old Swann *place,* for it was an exaggeration to call this tumbledown habitation a farm. The crippled rail fences, the teetering shed, the broken machinery rusting in the weedy, chicken-maddened yard, the sopping clothes perpetually dripping from a sagging line, the shame of cardboard over a broken bedroom window—and all this presided over by a new concrete-and-steel silo paid for, it was said, in cash.

It mustn't be thought that the Swann place resembles in any way those paintings of run-down farms so popular in suburban living-rooms during the late fifties and early sixties, a fad that quickly bankrupted itself, for where can decay go but down toward deeper decay? In the silvery dilapidated farms of popular art there's little suggestion of the real sourness of old back sheds or the reek of privies or the sucking mud between house and barn. Even if you could pry open the door and enter into the kitchen of one of these houses, chances are you would get no glimpse of that kind of cheap patterned linoleum that soon flaked underfoot and somehow never got replaced. One of Mary Swann's poems, one of those published by Frederic Cruzzi after her death, and one that is a puzzle to scholars goes:

Feet on the winter floor
Beat Flowers to blackness
Making a corridor
Named helplessness

Rose Hindmarch has visited the Swann farmhouse twice. The first time was with Sarah Maloney and Homer and Daisy Hart, but they didn't go inside that time, just walked around the yard and stood for a few minutes on the porch. The second time was two years ago when she was setting up the Mary Swann Memorial Room in the old high school in Nadeau. Russell Donegal, the good-natured, semi-alcoholic real-estate agent who operates out of both Nadeau and Westport, drove her out there in his Oldsmobile (a cold Sunday afternoon, much like today) and let her wander at will through the house.

That, of course, was during the time when the house was up for sale, before the new owner came up from the States and bought the place. ("Who the hell wants to buy a house where a murder's been done?" So said Russell Donegal.) Rose moved silently from room to room, walking hesitantly on tiptoe: the verandah (where Mrs. Swann had once stood smiling into a camera), the kitchen with its suspended smell of cold and its torn linoleum, beneath which Professor Lang had found a number of poems that had been hidden away. The sitting-room had plastic sheeting on its windows. There was a crude, railingless stairway leading to two upstairs bedrooms. Russell followed close behind Rose, and she was both flustered and relieved to have him there.

"Well," he said at last in his meaty salesman's voice. "What d'ya think, Rose?"

She waved a limp arm, then asked boldly, "What happened to everything?" To herself she said: What did you expect? The word that floated to her lips, like a child's balloon bobbing crookedly to the ceiling, was not the word *squalor* and not *trash*. Those are middle-class words, heavy with judgement. (And by now you will have realized that Rose Hindmarch lacks the spirit, the haemoglobin, for judgement. She is afflicted with social anaemia—though she does possess something else, which might be termed *acuity.) Poor* is the word that came to her, *poor*. A spare, descriptive, forgiving term, thin as a knife blade and somewhat out of fashion. *Poor.*

In Mary Swann's house there were a few straight chairs, a painted kitchen table, another table in the sitting-room with an old Westinghouse radio on it, a single cheap armchair missing one arm, iron pipe beds in the bedrooms, and old cheap bureaus of the kind that are *not* stripped down and sold as antiques at the Antique Barn in Westport.

"Where is everything?" she asked Russell Donegal, and he replied with a level grunt, wagging his broad, empurpled-with-whisky face, "This is it. Such as it is." Then he said, "We've got a saying in the business that a house sells faster when it's furnished. Well, this place is an exception. I'd like to clear the damn place right out."

"I suppose some of the things, the family mementoes and so on, went to Mrs. Swann's daughter in California." Rose ventured this hypothesis with only half a heart. Except for the two photographs and the drawerful of crocheted doilies, there appeared to be no family mementoes. Unless Professor Lang, when Russell had showed him through the house, carted off more than a sheaf of crumpled poems.

"Nope," Russell said. He lit a cigarette with a match struck directly on the kitchen wall. "He just took what he found under the linoleum. This is the way she was. Except"—he gave his goofy laugh—"except for the blood. We had that cleaned up before the place went on the market. Needless to say."

"Of course," Rose said. Then she added with a tincture of shame, "I suppose there was an awful lot of blood."

"The old boy was just about emptied out when they found him. Every last drop. Head wounds are the worst for blood, you know, and he'd put the bullet right through his. So you can imagine the mess. Of course there was no telling how long *she'd* been dead."

A week, the coroner had reported.

And so Rose was forced to use her imagination when it came to furnishing the Mary Swann Memorial Room. She was fortunate that the Nadeau town council had appropriated $300 for acquisitions (she embraced that wonder-word *acquisitions)* and that a second grant from Ottawa brought the amount up to $500. Russell Donegal encouraged her to help herself to anything in the house, saying she was welcome to the lot for all he cared. He'd thank her, he said, to tote off what she could. Rose took the kitchen table, two of the better kitchen chairs (pressbacks, Daisy Hart informed her) and a few cooking utensils, pathetic things with worn handles and a look of hard use. She left behind the bent rusty carving knife and the nickel-plated forks and spoons.

As for the other articles in the Memorial Room, she bought them from the Antique Barn and from Selma's Antiques in Kingston: a pretty wooden turnip masher, a wood and glass scrubbing board, a cherrywood churn, a fanciful, feminine iron bedstead, and a walnut bookcase and the set of tattered dull-covered books (Dickens, Sir Walter Scott) that came with it. At an auction in the town of Lynd-hurst she bought three old quilts and a set of blue-and-white china and a framed picture of a cocker spaniel. A measure of pride flow-ed around her not-quite-secret purchases, and she watched with joy, with creative amazement, as the room took shape, acquiring a look of authenticity and even a sense of the lean, useful life that had inhabited it. Yes, Rose could imagine the figure of Mary Swann bent over the painted table scratching out her poems by the light of the kerosene lamp. (The table had been repainted, and the kerosene lamp she found at a rummage sale in Westport.)

Redness of cold, circle of light
Heating the heart when the hour is late

If you suggest to Rose that her room has been wrenched into being through duplicity, through countless small acts of deception, she will be sure to look injured and offer up a pained denial. These articles, after all, belong to the *time* and the *region* of which Mary Swann was a part, and therefore nothing is misrepresented, not the quilts, not the china, not even the picture of the cocker spaniel. She may admit, though, that she has considered, then rejected, the idea of placing a small card in the doorway advising visitors that the contents are *similar* to those found in Mary Swann's rural home. But quite rightly she has decided that such a notice would be a distraction and that it might inject a hint of apology, of insuffi-ciency. (The charm of falsehood is not that it distorts reality, but that it creates reality afresh.) With all her heart Rose would like to have on display the papers found by Professor Lang under the linoleum—and the Parker 51 fountain pen that Mary Swann was reputed to have owned; but this article (according to Russell Donegal who heard it from Cecil Deacon, the trust officer in Kingston who handled the estate) was sent as a keepsake to Frances Swann Moore in California.

The missing pen is a void that sucks away at Rose. A number of times she has been on the verge of writing to Frances in California to ask if she would care to donate or at least lend her mother's pen to the museum. Meanwhile Rose is keeping a lookout at local flea markets for one of a similar vintage.

It is a mystery why Angus Swann hacked his wife Mary to death in December of 1965. Homer Hart and Rose Hindmarch, driving by the old Swann farm, discuss the various theories. Angus Swann was a violent man. No one ever denied that. It was known he butchered his poultry crudely with an axe and bragged about it. Also that he once went into a rage at the Red and White over the price of a ballpeen hammer. Another time Mary Swann was seen in town with a bruise over one eye and an arm in a sling. Some people say he was jealous of her poetry, the little bit of local celebrity that came her way, and that he begrudged her the postage when she sent her poems to local newspapers. But there is no proof of any of this, and other people say that, on the contrary, he was proud of her in his way, that it was he who gave her the fountain pen for a birthday present.

The last person to see her alive—other than her husband and possibly the bus driver—was Kingston publisher Frederic Cruzzi. According to the testimony Mr. Cruzzi gave the coroner after Mrs. Swann's body was discovered, he was sitting quietly at home one wintry afternoon when she suddenly appeared at his doorway. She thrust a bulky bag at him and, kind man that he was, he invited her inside and read through the loose sheets of paper that constituted a manuscript, later to form the bulk of *Swann's Songs*.

It was said he realized at once that the poems were remarkable. "I'd like to publish these," he told her, but she seemed ill at ease, puzzled, anxious about getting her bus home. The bus driver, not the regular driver, but a holiday replacement, half remembers dropping her at the side road near the Swann farm, and then, presumably, she walked into her house and was bludgeoned to death by her husband.

Rose came close to telling Homer as they drive along the back road that she sometimes dreams about this scene of horror—mazy dreams of splashing blood and thin-walled vessels hacked open and strewn on kitchen linoleum.

Homer said into the silence, "It must have been something pretty bad to set him off like that. Well, we'll never know."

"No," Rose says, and gazes at the glare-filled hills.

She doesn't tell Homer—she has never told anyone—that it was she who suggested to Mrs. Swann, in their one and only extended conversation, that she should show her poems to Frederic Cruzzi. Rose had read about Frederic Cruzzi and his wife and their publishing company, Peregrine Press, in *Library News*. Peregrine Press was interested in regional poets whose work was not sufficiently recognized. When Mary Swann came into the library one December day in 1965 to return a book, looking feverish and wearing her running shoes and her terrible coat and with her hair matted and uncombed, Rose was stricken by the wish to do her a kindness. She pulled the article about Frederic Cruzzi out of her clipping file and showed it to Mrs. Swann. "You should mail him some of your poems," she urged her. "Or better yet, go and see him."

Mrs. Swann looked dubious, but Rose detected a nervous stirring of interest and cut out the article then and there with her library shears—not without a stitch of regret—and placed it inside the book. It was the last book Mary Swann ever borrowed from the Nadeau library, *The Ice Palace,* by Edna Ferber.

It might be thought that Rose Helen Hindmarch suffers anguish over this episode and the part she may, inadvertently, have played in Mary Swann's murder. But oddly enough she doesn't. She thinks about it from time to time, and wonders about it, but feels no sense of responsibilty.

What protects her from guilt is the simple balm of modesty, of self-effacement. She cannot possibly be the one who set in motion the chain of events that led to Mary Swann's death since she has never been capable of setting anything in motion. Never mind her work in the town office, in the library, and in the museum—she has always known, not sensed, but *known,* that she is deficient in power. So many have insisted on her deficiency, beginning with her dimly remembered soldier father who failed to come back home to Nadeau to take his place as her parent, and her grandmother who told her, moving leathery gums stretched with spittle, that she had the worst posture ever seen in a young girl, and her mother who said looks weren't everything, and a teacher back in the early grades who said she was a silly goose; and then Daisy Hart who noticed the hair on her chin, and Dr. Thoms who slyly inquired about her libido, and the United Church God who deserted his switchboard, and Morton Jimroy who, except for one little letter, has not answered any of her perky little notes or cards, and Jean Elton who has never come back to share her bed, and even Homer Hart who has not had the goodness to inquire about the Swann symposium for some time now, and the seditious blood that is pouring out of her day after day after day, making her weaker and weaker so that she can hardly think—all this has interfered with her life and made her deficient in her own eyes, and it is this that mercifully guards her against self-recrimination, from believing she is someone who might possibly have played a part in the death of the poet Mary Swann. Rose is a person powerless to stir love and so she must also be powerless in her ability to hurt or destroy.

Rose Receives a Letter and Also Writes One

Rose very often gets postcards from vacationing friends and neighbours: cards that come all the way from White Rock, B.C., or New York City and, of course, from Daisy Hart in Florida. She also receives a fair number of small, dainty pastel envelopes containing shower invitations or thank-you notes or the like. And then there's her official mail: from the National Library Association, from the Department of Cultural Affairs, from the OATC (Ontario Association of Township Clerks) or from the CCUC (Committee of Concern for the United Church).

Seldom, though, does she receive a real letter. The one that comes for her today, from Professor Willard Lang in Toronto, brings a mixed flush of pride and apprehension. "Gotta letter for ya, Rose," Johnny Sears at the post office calls when Rose pops in after work. "Boy oh. boy, you sure get lots of mail."

Her hand shakes; Willard Lang, his name on the envelope. Writing to tell her the symposium has been cancelled. Or that her presence is not required after all. Or that that some mistake has been made; she should never have received an invitation in the first place. Some administrative bungle. She will understand. He hopes.

Rose opens the letter, cheerfully chatting all the while to Johnny, how is his mother doing, what about the hockey game last Friday night, those roughnecks from Elgin, the weather.

"Dear Miss Hindmarch," Professor Lang has written. "We are delighted you are to be with us at the symposium. Will you allow me to ask two very special favours of you."

The first favour is that she bring along her photograph of Mary Swann so that it can be included in a special display the committee is setting up. "As you know, it is the only photograph we have of our poet."

The second request is more complicated. Professor Lang writes:

The rather elderly Frederic Cruzzi from Kingston, after considerable persuasion, has agreed to attend the symposium and perhaps say a few words about his role as Mrs. Swann's publisher. I am not sure what his travel arrangements are, but at his age there may be difficulties, and it occurred to me that since you live only a stone's throw from each other, and no doubt have met, perhaps you wouldn't mind offering the old fellow a lift to Toronto. He is well past eighty, I believe, and not in the best of shape since his wife died (she was a charming woman, very intelligent). Here, at any rate, is his phone number in case you feel like giving him a buzz regarding travel plans.

Rose would sooner put a sack over her head and jump down through a hole in the ice on Whitefish Lake than give Frederic Cruzzi a "buzz" on the phone. Mr. Cruzzi is the retired editor of the *Kingston Banner*; she once heard him deliver an address at the National Library Association annual meeting. He is tall, angular, has a foreign accent, quotes Shakespeare, and wouldn't be able to make head or tail of a phone call from Rose Hindmarch of Nadeau, Ontario.

Instead she writes him a letter, a long letter, which takes her all of one evening to get right. She introduces herself: Rose Hindmarch, librarian and former friend of Mary Swann. She will be travelling up to Toronto by train for the symposium, she explains, and she thinks perhaps the two of them might keep each other company. (She apologizes twice for not being able to offer him a ride for the very good reason that she has never learned to drive a car.) She mails the letter in a mood of gaiety, uneasiness, and disbelief, gaiety because she is overtaken by a sense of abandonment, unease because she fully expects a rebuff from Mr. Cruzzi, and disbelief because she is unable now to hold in steady focus an image of herself actually sitting on a train bound for Toronto.

It is not to be. She may go on and on pretending, packing her bag, buying her train ticket and so on, but the blood secretly leaking from her body leaves her a future that is numbered in days now, not weeks. Every morning she wakes up and repeats the cycle: desolation, a brief buoyancy, and again desolation. It is laughable. By the first week of January there will be nothing left of Rose Hindmarch but the clothes in her closet, her row of paperbacks on the TV set, half a carton of cottage cheese in her refrigerator, and her bed with its checked sheets and chenille spread. She could leave a note saying goodbye. But to whom? And for what reason?

Rose Hindmarch Gives a Party

Rose Hindmarch's Christmas Day eggnog party is something of a tradition. Even when she and her mother lived in the Second Street house, they always "asked people in" for a glass of eggnog and a slice of Christmas cake between 5:00 and 7:00 P.M. on Christmas Day. (Christmas dinner is taken at about 2:00 or 3:00 in Nadeau, and so Rose's guests arrive already stuffed with turkey and drowsy from overeating.)

Rose makes better eggnog than her mother did. She's more generous with the rum, for one thing, and she also offers the alternative of rye and ginger-ale to those who prefer it, and most do. Her Christmas cake is store bought, but she has canned baby shrimp in a glass bowl on the table and a plate of Ritz crackers, and she serves her famous Velveeta Christmas Log, full of glittering green pepper bits and slices of stuffed olives.

Despite the fact that she's feeling *punk* —her word—she has decided to go ahead with the party, and her living-room looks surprisingly merry this dull snowy Christmas day. She has strung her

Christmas cards, one of them from Sarah Maloney in Chicago, on a cord over the window, and set up her little artificial tree by the window between the radiator and the television set. Her tree ornaments always bring her pleasure: that little smudged cotton Santa with his beady eyes, the tiny straw donkey Daisy once brought her back from Florida, and the red glass reindeer she herself bought on Markham Street in a store called "Things." She has even put up the string of lights this year, something she hasn't done since her mother died.

The first person to come is Homer Hart, huffing up the stairs, looking bulkier than ever and bearing a box of Laura Secord chocolate almonds, Rose's favourite. He arrives at the party alone; Daisy has, at last, written from Sarasota to say that she and a divorceé called Audrey Beamish, a woman she met in her sister's trailer court, are about to embark on an auto trip to the southern states and that she won't be back to Nadeau before February at the earliest.

Next to arrive are Jean and Howie from downstairs, Jean wearing the dusty-pink velour track suit Howie gave her for Christmas, and Howie the navy blue track suit Jean gave him. Their gift to Rose is an electric yogurt maker and a booklet of instructions and recipes. Other years they've gone to Cornwall for Christmas, but this year, since Jean is three months pregnant, they've decided not to risk the icy roads. Howie seems enormously pleased about the baby. He breaks off in the middle of discussion on the regime in Libya and pats Jean's stomach, saying, "Ha! Won't be long before we have our own little dictator." At this Jean smiles dreamily. She's hoping for a boy, she tells Rose privately, for Howie's sake.

Also at the party are Floyd and Bea Sears. Floyd is in good spirits, winding up his second term as reeve of Nadeau Township. Bea, his wife, a woman often described for want of a more specific title as "an A-one housewife," has brought Rose a gift of a homemade cushion crocheted with ribbon. Belle Waterman, who was widowed years back, has come along with Floyd and Bea and has brought Rose a dried-flower-and-driftwood arrangement to put on her TV. Percy "Perce" Flemming and his wife, Peg, are with their three-hundred-pound son, Bobby, who has twice attempted suicide and cannot be left alone, even for an hour. Joe and Marnie Fletcher are a little late because Marnie was slow getting the turkey in the oven this morning, and for this she takes a good-natured ribbing from her husband and from Floyd Sears. "We just this minute got up from the table,'' Marnie says, refusing a piece of Velveeta Log. Vic Brower, a lifelong bachelor, huddles with Homer on the couch. Someone once hinted to Rose that Vic frequents a house of prostitution in Kingston, but Rose, when she looks at Vic, his shy eyes and small mouth, doesn't see how this can be. Hank Cleary, his wife, Agnes, and his sister, Elfreda, who is visiting from Sarnia, all get quite merry on eggnog, the three of them, and Hank tells a long Libyan joke, mangling the punchline and getting shouted down by his wife, who then dissolves into a fit of laughter.

Merriment, merriment, Seasonal joy, Time slips away. Rose thinks how glad she is she decided to give her party after all. People come to depend on certain traditions in a small town, and this may well be a farewell to her old friends, a farewell to life.

Happiness seizes her, exhausted though she is by the loss of blood and by the preparations for the party. In recent weeks she has had a feeling that some poisonous sorrow has seeped into her life, and now, this afternoon, from nowhere comes a sudden shine of joy.

What is Homer saying to her? Into her ear he is whispering how he has suffered terrible loneliness in the last month and that he is extremely doubtful whether Daisy will be home before spring. Vic Brower has fallen asleep, resting his head rather sweetly on the new crocheted cushion. Joe and Marnie look at him, winking at each other and grinning like mad, and Marnie laughs her watery laugh and says very softly into Joe's ear, ''Let's go to bed early tonight and have ourselves a high old time.'' Bobby Flemming is telling Floyd Sears about a new diet the doctor has put him on. Starting January first, only three hundred calories a day, mostly lemon juice, club soda and strawberries. Bea Shears is telling Howie that fatherhood should be taken seriously. Her own father, she confides for the first time in her life, never once asked her a single question about herself, not once. Jean is chewing a shrimp and watching Howie and trying to imagine the little shrimp-shaped organism inside her, how she will teach it the meaning of charity and gentleness, how if it is a girl she will not be disappointed.

Elfreda is telling her sister-in-law that the real reason she's taking early retirement from the post office in Sarnia is because her supervisor hinted that her breath was less than fresh, and she has been unable, for some reason, to absorb this terrible accusation. ''Perce'' Flemming tells his wife, Peg, about a recurrent nightmare he has, a lion chasing him and nipping at his heels, and Peg pats him on his stringy arm and says, "Next time wake me up and I'll give it a bop on the head." Rose hands Homer a glass of ginger-ale and tell him about the blood that's been pouring out of her for two months straight and of how she refuses to go to the doctor in Elgin because his brisk scrutiny reminds her of how lonely she is, and that she is one of the unclaimed, and Homer responds by taking her hand on his lap and promising that on Monday morning he will drive her into Kingston where they'll head straight to the clinic where Daisy goes and find out what's causing the trouble.

Rose gazes about the room, at her friends, at the table of food, the little tree, and in the corner the television set, its sound off but the screen flickering with the dark, coarse, stiffening face of Muammar Gadaffi, and then, out of the blue, she remembers a line from one of Mary Swann's poems. It just swims into her head like a little fish.

A pound of joy weighs more
When grief had gone before

Frederic Cruzzi

A Circuitous Introduction

The world claps its hands for the intellectual nomad: the Icelandic scholar in Cuba, patiently translating his sagas into Spanish, or the Quaker lesbian traveller in Peru with her backpack and her flute and her notebook full of compassionate poems, or the young barmaid in Dubrovnik with a degree in physics who serves rum cocktails with a monologue that dilutes and reconstitutes the seven languages she speaks, or the French existentialist in his Irish cottage, contemplating local flora and folktales and extracting from them a message that will soon convert hundreds, or at least a handful, to a simplified, nourishing vision of the oneness of things. We love these wanderers for their brilliance, their adaptive colouring, their many tongues and tricks of courage; but chiefly we love them for the innocence and joy with which they burrow into the very world so many of us have given up on.

Retired newspaper editor Frederic Cruzzi of Grenoble, Casablanca, Manchester, and Kingston, Ontario, aged eighty, is such a one—equally at home grafting an apple tree or poaching a salmon or reading a page of Urdu poetry or writing one of his newspaper columns on the diabolism of modern technology. Recently he has come out against the telephone. Vile instrument of slander and babble. Rude interrupter of lamp-lit evenings. Purring flatterer, canny imposter, silky lover, sly mendicant, cunning messenger of unwelcome news, of debts, of dinner parties. "We are dialling our way direct to an early death," says the outspoken octogenarian Cruzzi, who has a weakness for alliteration. Buzzed, bashed, kept on hold. Welded to copper wire, bonded to slippery plastic. Recorded, pre-empted, insulted, seduced, and finally, ultimate injury, presented with a bill as long as your femur.

Sitting in an upstairs bedroom of a hundred-year-old house (limestone, creepers) in Kingston, Ontario, F. Cruzzi, who has risen at half-past seven, is typing his weekly column on a 1950 Under-wood, a large, muscular office model, solid and unmusical. He leans over the keys, heated to a fine frenzy. By now, although he fiercely believes people must compromise with the history they are born into, he is persuaded by the crescendo of his own rhetoric that telephones must go. What a sight he is, surrounded by his hundreds and hundreds of books, with that sail of white hair, that turkey neck, those bobbling shoulders, the stub of a pencil gripped between his strong old teeth. He has a hard humorous face and oaken hands. Down beneath his wine-dark dressing gown his spindly old-man legs poke out, and his long narrow yellowed feet slap away at the dusty floor. A ladder of sunlight climbs his sleeve, reaches the triangularity of busy eye sockets. Wham goes the carriage, plink-plunk go the keys. It's a wonder steam isn't pouring out of his ancient orifices, a wonder his heart doesn't give way. Sorry, wrong number—. O execrable telephone pole, despicable wire and vulgar coin box. The wound the world inflicts on itself is ringed by automatic answering machines. The barbarous disembodied yoking of human voices, the chattering, battering, shattering of pure air. Desecration. Shame. Gossip in the treetops, alarm in the night.

One paragraph to go and he'll have his five hundred words for this week.

His dressing-gown gapes, revealing shrunken testicles and penis. His foot keeps time. A delicate web gathers at the left side of his mouth. He has come to the last sentence, the final word.

He chooses it with care. As always.

Frederic Cruzzi: A Few of His Friends

Frederic Cruzzi of Kingston, Ontario, former newspaper editor, journalist, traveller, atheist, lover of women and poetry, tender son of gentle parents, scholar, immigrant, gardener, socialist, husband, and father—he is also a man who can be said to have been lucky in friendship. His friendships, he sometimes thinks, are all he has to forestall the pursuing chaos of old age. They give him interludes of calm as well as moments of exhilaration and reverence. Now and then he recalls the slightly overwrought words of a nineteenth-century Indian poet describing friends:

Jewels of uncertain colour
Flowers of evasive scent
Stars of shifting distance
And hands that hesitate never

The opaque ironies of the poet appeal to Cruzzi, since they emphasize the steadiness of friendship and reject the current jejune notion of soul-baring and abandonment of self. There's something devouringly selfish, he believes, about the wish to know someone "through and through."

Of course, by now many of his friends have been taken from him by death: his brother Hilaire, dead at twenty in a climbing accident; Herve Villeneuve, friend of his student days in Grenoble, a suicide at forty-six; Professor Nicholas Guincourt, a colleague of his father, who gave him the gift of the English language: Sami Salah, his Moroccan cousin who travelled with him for a year in the Far East and was later killed in a hotel fire in Cleveland, Ohio; Tante Maleka, his giggling, indulgent Casablanca aunt, a prodigious smoker of cigarettes who worried about bronchitis but died instead of measles; Max Robinson, literary editor of the *Manchester Guardian* in the thirties, a man of bountiful imagination and easy tears; and Max's wife, May, contemplative, spiritual, alluring; Estelle Berger, Jungian therapist, whose plangent voice still visits Cruzzi in dreams; Glen Forrestal of Ottawa, tonsured sybaritic physician, essayist and poet, sanguine sipper of whisky sodas; Monkey La Rue of Kingston, naturalist, fisherman, skier, composer; Barney Ouilette, also of Kingston, amateur painter and brilliant mathematician (despite the tide of vodka between his ears), and many many more, but of all of these dead friends Cruzzi misses most his wife, Hildë, who in fifty years sometimes exasperated him but never once gave him a moment of boredom.

It's true that Cruzzi is at an age when he can count more friends among the dead than the living, but he is still a man who lives in the midst of friendship. More and more, to be sure, he seeks solitude, is out of sorts, is impatient with confidences, feels put upon, feels weary and oddly restless; but he cannot imagine a life in which friendship is not the largest part.

He is slightly in awe of those who manage their lives without friends and wonders where these unfortunates find their strength. In all of Mary Swann's poems, for instance, the word *friend* is found only once, and even then it is used reflexively and all but buried in a metaphor, pointing, he believes, to a terrifying ellipsis.

> Like a cup on the shelf
> That's no longer here
> Like the friend of myself
> Who's drowned in the mirror
> The hour is murdered, the moment is lost,
> And everything counted except for the cost.

Those things that kept Mrs. Swann friendless—fear, crippling shyness, isolation, drudgery—are as foreign to Frederic Cruzzi as such bodily afflictions as impetigo or beriberi. His life has always been organized, and is *still* organized, so that he is in the midst of people who possess "hands that hesitate never."

Bridget Riordan is one of those friends, even though he has seen her infrequently during the last forty years. Seductive, rangy, managerial, she is master of all the arts of love and all the modes of loving. Only recently retired from the theatre, she lives in a London flat furnished with airy furniture and heavy paintings, and writes endless letters to friends, including Cruzzi—letters full of wit, skepticism, memory, gossip, tact, and cheerful lewdness.

Cruzzi also counts among his friends a man named Bud McWilliam, former linotype operator on the *Kingston Banner*, a man who loves guns, hunting dogs, machinery, hearty food, and speculative conversation. (Some physical provision or deficiency— Cruzzi doesn't know which—has separated Bud McWilliam from the need for women, but he is able, nevertheless, to cackle at the paradoxes his life has held up.) Nowadays he's more or less confined to bed, and he welcomes Cruzzi's weekly visits. A number of operations have left him with a gnarly larynx and a throat full of scar tissue, but he steadfastly refuses to indulge in the quavering warble of the aged. His struggle to overcome his bodily infirmities strikes Cruzzi as heroic, and he has often been tempted to remark on it. Last week their discussion centred on the emergence of certain sprightly neologisms in the popular press, the week before on the refraction of light.

He loves, has always loved, Pauline Ouilette. Her passion for perfume, pedicures, and expensive underwear gives an impression of frivolity that is false. Sometimes when the two of them sit talking, usually in Pauline's pink and grey sunporch, Cruzzi shuts his eyes for an instant and breathes in, along with her fragrance, the skirted merriment of her voice, the way her vowels tumble out, an engaging spill of music forming little hillocks that signal the beginning of laughter. If Pauline should see him close his eyes, she would never be offended or suspect boredom. She is fully conscious of her powers, appreciates the importance of good food, knows that books, particularly fiction, form a valuable core of experience, and believes she can trust Cruzzi absolutely to understand and follow the intricacies of her observations.

He wonders sometimes how he would manage without Dennis and Caroline Cooper-Beckman, who live with their three children in the brick house across the street from him. Dennis, aged forty, brings him clippings from obscure journals, fresh raspberries, and iconoclastic views on universities and governments. Caroline, thirty-five, brings the terrible sincerity of her social concerns and a slightly skewed sexual ambivalence that suggests faint, flirtatious arcs of possibility and stirs in Cruzzi memories of buried passion. He would do anything for Dennis and Caroline, and they for him.

Mimi Russell, otherwise known as Sister Mary Francis, has won Cruzzi's heart. Not yet fifty, not yet out of a long childhood, she is breezy and articulate and in love with English literature. She can recite most of Keats by heart (except for "Endymion," which she considers a piece of kitsch). In literature she sniffs a kind of godly oxygen that binds one human being to the next and shortens the distance we must travel to discover that our most private perceptions are universally felt. In this, Cruzzi believes, she is right. (They lunch together weekly and speak often on the phone, or did until Cruzzi's phone was disconnected.) Mimi Russell's biography of Laura Jane Oldfeld, the nineteenth-century Ontario pioneer, is impeccable; also lively and suffused with a rare amiability. When Mary Swann's biographer, Morton Jimroy, visited Kingston a year or so ago, Cruzzi arranged a dinner so the two of them might meet and talk shop; never had such sweetness met such sourness. (Cruzzi supposes the sad, sour, spluttery Jimroy will be in attendance at the Swann symposium and mentally braces himself.)

Simone Cruzzi is Frederic Cruzzi's daughter-in-law, not that he attaches that clumsy title to so slim, so blonde, so vivacious a woman. She lives in Montreal, has a neat, organized face and dresses snappily. Often she comes down to Kingston for the weekend, and between visits she writes Cruzzi fond little notes on company stationery. For a number of years she has worked as a travel agent and tour guide, and she is forever setting off for Salzburg or Bejing or Oslo with her "little chicks" in tow. From these distant points on the globe she mails Cruzzi postcards crowded with stamps (which he pretends he collects). The messages scrawled on the back are always in animated counterpoint to the scenes—sunsets, fountains—displayed on the front. She almost never alludes to her husband, Armand (only son of Hildë and Frederic Cruzzi) who died of a brain tumour at the age of thirty-six.

There is also Frank Hurley who owns Hurley and Sons, Funeral Directors, of Kingston. In his nether-world Frank embalms bodies and sells coffins sheathed in bronze and lined with satin. Otherwise he scours the countryside on foot (five miles is nothing) for wild flowers and grasses. His need to observe and classify operates like a busy little buzz-saw in his brain, and it is partly for this ever-humming busyness that Cruzzi loves him. He has no humour, but is prodigiously kind and something of a metaphysician. Human society, he says to Cruzzi in his soft burr, is distinguished by four manifestations: the existence of tools, the presence of art, a respect for the dead, and a compulsion to give names to natural phenomena. At eighty-four he is Cruzzi's brother in old age.

And one more: Tom Halpenny, who now edits the *Banner*. He is an American by birth and education, is forty-four years old, speaks in a loud voice, sometimes of matters he knows nothing about. He has a quacky laugh, yawns in public, wears a black T-shirt and a gold chain around his neck, and is famous for his explosive farts, manifested most recently while he was addressing the Ontario Bay

Jaycees at their annual fall banquet. Two wives have left him. Of his four children, only one is still in touch. His hair, what remains of it, hangs raggedly on the ears. Laziness, or perhaps the withdrawal of love, has caused his shoulders to slope. His roots are in the old New Left which means they are nowhere. New England puritanism runs through him like a seam of coal. He worships Cruzzi, adored Hildë, thinks Kingston is heaven and the *Banner* the banner of heaven.

At least once a month Tom Halpenny tries to bully Cruzzi into writing his life story. "Before it's too late," he goads wickedly.

Today, a Tuesday in early November, the two of them are eating lunch in Kingston's Old Firehall Restaurant. Cruzzi is part way through a plain omelette, sipping his Perrier, wishing it were wine, and refusing to be bullied. Tom Halpenny, who has just savaged a nine-dollar lobster salad, is gulping cold milk. From the bottom drawer of cleverness he produces what he considers the ultimate argument, which is that an unrecorded life is a selfish life.

Cruzzi shakes his head at this piece of foolishness but says nothing. (Bad enough to be wobbly and squint-sided at his age, but to be encumbered with garrulousness too!) The truth is that except for those of Orwell and Pritchert, autobiography is a form that offends him. The cosy cherishing of self is only part of the problem. There is the inevitable lack of perspective, not to mention hideous evasions, settlings of scores, awesome preciosity, and the appalling melted fat of rumination, barrels of it, boatloads. Most of the people in the world, he tells Halpenny, could write their autobiographies in one line.

"Ha!" Tom shouts, spraying milk. "Impossible."

"One sentence then," Cruzzi concedes.

"Jesus, God," Tom breathes. "The cynicism, the cheap cynicism. You of all people. I don't believe it. And you a humanist."

"Ex-humanist."

"Since when ex?"

"Since . . ." Cruzzi looks evasively to the ceiling.

"You honestly can sit there and tell me that a whole human life can be boiled down to one shitty little fucking sentence?"

"How about one *long* sentence then?" Cruzzi suggests slyly.

Frederic Cruzzi: His (Unwritten) One-Sentence Autobiography

Frederic Georges Cruzzi was born eighty years ago in the French city of Grenoble, the second son of happily mismatched parents (Mohammed Cruzzi, formerly of Casablanca, a professor of middle eastern languages, and Monique Roche Cruzzi, a shy, pretty, musically able woman), and in that exquisite mountain-ringed city, now bitterly contaminated by the chlorine industry, the young Cruzzi was educated, formally and informally, by exposure to languages and to the arts—though not to science—and to people who were for the most part kind, following which he spent a number of years travelling and testing the shock of strangeness in such places as Morocco (a second home to him), Turkey, India, Japan, and the United States (the world being in those days, before the invention of work visas and inflation, more accessible, more welcoming) and acquiring along the way a taste for women and for literature and supporting himself by becoming a journalist, a profession that was continually carrying him to unlikely places, one of them being, ironically, the French town of Gap, not far from his home city of Grenoble, where he happened to meet at a small supper party a young student by the name of Hildë Joubert, a rather large-boned girl with straight yellow hair parted in the middle, who had grown up in the hamlet of La Motte-en-Champsaur (where her father kept goats) and who was possessed of a shining face in which Cruzzi glimpsed the promise of his future happiness, though it took him a week before he found the courage to declare his love—in the museum at Gap, as it happened, standing before a hideous oil painting, even then peeling away from its frame, depicting Prometheus being fawned upon by a dozen lardy maidens—after which the two of them lived for some years in England, Hildë finishing her dissertation on the poet Rilke, and Cruzzi working on the staff of a newspaper in the city of Manchester, where they bought a semi-detached suburban house (Didsbury) with a garden and fruit trees, produced a baby son, Armand, and decided one midsummer night when the English sky glowed lavender in the west and seemed to beckon, that they would emigrate to Canada (where they naively believed they might keep a foothold on the French language), an excellent choice, as it turned out, since a newspaper in the small (population: 50,000) lakeside city of Kingston (King's town; the name promised history) was at that time looking for a new managing editor, a position offering that extremely rare combination of independence and security, and which Cruzzi—despite his socialism—was to enjoy for more than three decades, though the death of Armand came near to breaking his heart, and would have if he hadn't had his work at the paper to occupy him, as well as a small literary venture, the Peregrine Press, which he and Hildë launched in order that they might print the work of a number of new Canadian poets who had come to their attention, Mary Swann of Nadeau Township being perhaps the most singular, a poet that Hildë found endearingly "rough" in technique, but as fine a poet in her way as the great Rilke—a rather extravagant comparison, but one with which Cruzzi partly concurred, though both he and Hildë kept their estimation to themselves for reasons they avoided mentioning even to each other, and that Cruzzi, now eighty years old, must carry alone.

Frederic Cruzzi:
Some Recent Invitations and Replies

September 5

Dear Editor Cruzzi:

Once again it's the fall of the year and we of the Ontario Bay Jaycees are getting together for our annual blast-off banquet. September 30 is the big day, and as usual we're going all out for a great evening. It is my special privilege to invite you to be this year's banquet speaker, and we hope you'll do us the honours. What we usually appreciate by way of talk is something short and snappy and full of humour. Fifteen minutes is the absolute maximum. We've found that after turkey and trimmings nobody's in the mood for deep thoughts. Rumour has it your after dinner speeches are a barrel of laughs and appreciated by one and all. Your own meal will of course be gratis. Hoping you will reply soon due to the fact that we have to get our program to the printers pronto.

Yours truly,

J. Wade Hollinghead (Hollinghead Hardware), Bath, Ontario

September 8

Dear Mr. Hollinghead:

Thank you for your kind invitation, but I am afraid you and I
have both been ill-served by rumour. I am no longer *Editor* Cruzzi,
having retired from the *Banner* more than ten years ago. Laughs
by the barrel have never been my commodity. I am a strict vegetarian,
eschewing fowl as well as other animal proteins. I am long-winded
and bad-tempered and, since suffering a slight stroke, unpleasant
in appearance. In short, I am afraid I will not "do" for the Ontario
Bay Jaycees.

Yours,

F. Cruzzi

September 7

My dear Freddy,

Come and give me some cheer. I promise you roast lamb and
a good bottle of wine. Possibly artichokes. Certainly my usual
mustard sauce. Any evening will do, but make it soon. Forgive me,
Freddy, but you've been alone too much since Hildë died. (I miss
her too, and, selfishly, I miss your company.)

Yours,

Pauline

September 8

My dear Pauline,

I've just this minute written a shameful and pompous letter to
a Mr. Hollinghead of Hollinghead Hardware in Bath, declining an
unwanted unvitation and claiming to be a vegetarian and cur-
mudgeon. I hope I can be better company in your presence. Would
next Friday do?

Your uncivilized old friend,

F.C.

September 15

Dear F,

I'll come right to the point. I think it's time you stirred yourself and came to Montreal for a visit. Thanksgiving to be precise. Come! I can't bear to think of you in that big house by yourself with time hanging on your hands. And I can't imagine why on earth you had the phone disconnected. What if there is an emergency? What if you need a doctor or something? And how would I get hold of you? Think about it. And think about coming for Thanksgiving. You could take the train. You used to love the train.

Take care,

Simone

October 3

Dearest Simone,

Many thanks for your card. Thanksgiving is impossible, I'm afraid, much as the thought of family tempts me. I'm loath to leave home for long these days. I seem to require certain things around me, my books especially. And I still look in at the *Banner* now and then, and there's the Friday column, of course. The column is fast becoming a burden, since (to tell the truth) it is increasingly difficult to be genial and carping at one and the same time, or even to think of topics worth rumbling and rambling about. In the last month I've covered false gentility, technological insult, the crimes of local politicians and sins against the language—and now must thrust about for something freshly abhorrent. I enclose my piece on telephone tyranny, which partly explains my present state of disconnectedness. (The real problem, if you insist on knowing, is the press of invitations from long-lived widows, Hildë's dear old friends, chiefly, who beseech me daily to come for suppers, lunches, bridge games, concerts, picnics, whatever. They believe me to be in need of comfort, and, as you know, comfort has always been the focus of my deepest skepticism.) And then there are the antiquarians, *les bouqinistes* (one in particular) who pester me via the telephone about selling my books and other oddments—as if I ever would.

Your loving,

F.

October 8

Dear Frederic Cruzzi:

I have been trying to reach you for some time by telephone, but without success. As Chairman of the Steering Committee for the Swann Symposium to be held in January at the Harbourview Hotel in Toronto (tentative details enclosed) I would like to invite you to be our Keynote Speaker. We on the Committee are all fully cognizant of your role as Mary Swann's first (and only) publisher and one who early glimpsed her extraordinary (to my mind) textual genius. It seems, therefore, eminently appropriate to the members of the Committee (unanimous, in fact) that you be given a leading role in this first—though not, we hope, last—scholarly gathering to be held in her honour.

I understand that you have not been in the best of health recently, but we do, nevertheless, hope you will do us the honour of accepting. Will you be kind enough to contact me as soon as possible?

Yours very truly,

Willard W. Lang, Chm, Dept. of Eng.
University of Toronto

P.S. You probably don't remember that we met some four years ago when I was bold enough to knock on your door while passing through Kingston. We had a most interesting (to me) discussion on modern poetics, as I recall, and on the work of Mrs. Swann. Please give my regards to your wife who, I remember, was kind enough to give me a cup of tea and a magnificent slice of walnut cake.

October 15

Dear Professor Lang,

I am sorry to say I am unable, for reasons of health and temperament, to take part in your "symposium." It has always seemed to me that the glory of Mary Swann's work lies in its innocence, the fact that it does not invite scholarly meddling or whimsical interpretation. As a close reader of her "text," you will remember the lines that conclude her second water poem:

Let me hide.
Let this kneeling-down pain.
Of mine
Wait safe inside.

Of course it would be ludicrous to interpret these lines as a plea that we not read her work. Poets, after all, write in order to show others their singleness of heart and mind. But I do believe Mrs. Swann would resist with all her "kneeling-down pain" any attempt to analyse and systematize what came out of her as naturally as did her own breath. I often think of the sage who commented, "Critics are to art as ornithologists are to birds." I remain grateful for the words and rhythms Mrs. Swann left us, and I have no wish to tamper with their meaning. Furthermore, it would cause me grief to hear others doing so.

Yours,

F. Cruzzi

P.S. My late wife would have been pleased, I know, that you have remembered her, *and* her walnut cake. As for me, I do indeed remember your visit and have often wondered what became of the poems you discovered under Mrs. Swann's kitchen linoleum.

October 20

Dear Freddy,

The flowers are lovely and you are a dear to have sent them. I'm sure the sight of them will speed my convalescence and bring me good cheer. But I can't help wondering if *you* aren't the one who needs cheering. When you were here the other evening you seemed somehow quieter than usual, a little sunk in your thoughts. Are you still dwelling on South Africa? I hope not, for what can any of us do? Let's you and me have a cheery drink together next Friday, any time after five. I'm afraid, though, I'll have to ask you to bring along the gin since I won't be allowed out on these wretched crutches for another ten days.

Yours,

Pauline

October 23

My dear Pauline,

Just a note to say I'll be there on Friday with a bottle of Beefeater. We can console each other. I will question you about your poor fracture and your insomnia, and you may pry if you like into my current vexations, most of which I've brought upon myself. I miss my telephone for one thing, but hubris prevents me from contacting Ma Bell. And I've recently turned down, viciously, mockingly, arrogantly, and with a wide scatter of sneering quotation marks, an invitation to a symposium on Mary Swann that I now think I might rather have enjoyed. (What wickedness makes me so eager to snub the academic world?) Some of the spiritual poison has overflowed into my column—don't tell me you haven't noticed—and certainly my last piece on free-roaming dogs has caused hard feelings. It was Hildë, you know, who kept my malice under control, her daily innoculations of goodness, something in her more delicately balanced. Ah well . . .

Until Friday,

F

November 1

Dear F.C.,

Bravo and keep it up for crissake. The mail's been raining down steadily since the famous dog piece (pro, con, midfence, you name it). And the thing on abolishing the senate got good vigorous waves too. Judy and Fran and I were sitting around the other day going through the mail sack and got to wondering if you'd maybe do us two columns a week instead of the one. Say, Tuesday and Saturday kind of thing. I know it would be a break with tradition, but it's terrific for circulation and gives the poor folks out there something to chew over besides the bloody Middle East. Let me know what you think. I don't suppose there's any chance of your getting your phone reconnected, is there? You might as well be on the moon instead of across town.

A suggestion for a future column!! How about pouring a little timely vitriol on pink plastic flamingos? Judy sends her love. Fran too. Also me.

TSH

November 6

My dear Tom,

Your note has just arrived; that's six days for a quarter of an ounce of paper to travel half a mile. The moon indeed!

I'm afraid I must gratefully decline your twice-weekly column suggestion, since it's difficult enough gathering ire for one. My ability to become incensed declines along with my various other physical parts, and I find that working up a lather even once a week is landing me in difficulties. The fact is, I *like* dogs. I believe, to a certain extent, in the senate. I admire courtesy, false *or* genuine. The majority of politicians *are* well-intentioned, strange as it seems. The English language *must* be kept pliable and open and out of the hands of pedants like myself. And the telephone is one of the world's greatest conveniences. (I intend to get hooked up again in the New Year, as soon as the fuss has died down.) As you can see, my venting of spleen, now that it has become an artificial exercise, is depriving me of those beliefs and pleasures that have sustained my life. Nevertheless I will continue the Friday column for another year at least, a creaky perseverance being the prime disease of old age. But I'm thinking seriously of coming out *in favour* of something next week, just to see if I'm still capable of writing a piece that doesn't "take umbrage."

If I may make a suggestion, Tom, one syndicated column of advice for the lovelorn is quite enough in my opinion. And you may want to think about cancelling that "Advice to Golden Agers" fellow. We're all going down the chute anyway, and that idiot's little rays of sunshine are insulting.

F.C.

P.S. Afraid I cannot throw my heart into a condemnation of flamingos, nor the casual effrontery of garden elves, nor even Black Sambo at the gatepost. I feel quite sure these trinkets are purchased and displayed in an innocent attempt to ornament a bleak world, and how can one attack an impulse so simple and human as that?

November 7

Dear Mr. Cruzzi,

I apologize for bothering you once again with what at first glance may appear to be a commercial inquiry. You may remember that we spoke on the phone two or three times early in the fall and at that time you made it quite clear that you were not interested in selling any portion of your personal library, nor were you anxious to avail yourself of the sort of inventory and evaluation services in which our firm specializes.

This letter is written, frankly, in the hope that you may have reconsidered and may now want to liquidate your holdings and enjoy the benefit of alternate investment or disposable income for travel, charity and so on. It has been our experience that many people wait too long to dispose of their valuables, so that at the time of settling an estate, those articles most treasured and revered during a lifetime become neglected and overlooked by heirs. Instead of finding their way into the hands of those who would most appreciate them, cherished collections (books in particular) are broken up and scattered, or sometimes even destroyed by careless handling.

The special focus of our firm is the matching of books with discriminating collectors. While we are happy to consider entire inventories, we also deal in partial collections and even with individual volumes. At the moment for instance, we have a buyer keenly searching for first-edition Hemingway. Another active collector whom we represent has a special interest in the poet Mary Swann, whose work you yourself published in the not-so-distant past.

I can assure you that our firm appreciates and pays the top market price for such volumes. Indeed, in certain cases, such as Mrs. Swann's rather curious little book, we are prepared to offer well above the going price, depending on condition, of course.

We invite you, at least, to consider our services and to contact us at the New York mailing address or to telephone the toll-free number indicated in our letterhead.

Yours very truly,

Book Browsers Inc.

November 11

Dear Book Browser:

I address you as such since you offer no other name. Please do not worry yourself further about what will befall my "estate" after my death. I have an extremely alert daughter-in-law who appreciates fully the value of the library that my late wife and I spent fifty years accumulating. What she will do with the collection when it becomes hers is up to her, but while I am still alive, and I expect to remain alive for some time, I intend to see that the library remains intact. My books, dear Book Browser, are a comfort, a presence, a diary of my life. What more can I say?

If it will ease your mind and prevent further communication, I will assure you that nothing of the Hemingway school occupies my shelves. As for the four remaining copies of *Swann's Songs* (all that are left of the original 250 copies my wife and I published under the Peregrine Imprint), I have made provisions in my will that they are to go to the Queen's University Library here in Kingston.

And so I am afraid, Book Browser, that I cannot be of help to you, nor you to me.

Respectfully yours,

Frederic Cruzzi

November 16

Dear Mr. Cruzzi,

My name is Sarah Maloney, and I'm a fellow Swannian. Recently I've had a phone call from Willard Lang, chairman of the Steering Committee for the Swann Symposium, saying you had declined the committee's invitation to be our keynote speaker. I can tell you that we are all downcast at this news.

I'm writing to see if I can possibly persuade you, instead, to take part in an informal question-and-answer session concerning the original publication of *Swann's Songs* by your own Peregrine Press. This hypothetical event might take place on the second or third day of the meetings, after the academic stiffness has been leached from our bones. Those of us in the Swann industry can endlessly speculate, but you're the one who midwifed the original text and the only one to lay eyes (and hands) on the manuscript—which I understand was grievously lost some years ago. What a tragedy.

Speaking selfishly, I'd like very much to meet you and hear your impressions of Mary Swann. To me she remains maddeningly enigmatic, not only her work but herself. How did all those words get inside her innocent head? Perhaps you know. I think you may. I hope you'll tell me. Please reconsider and come to the symposium. We can talk and talk.

With sincere good wishes,

Sarah Maloney (Ms.)

November 26

My dear Ms. Maloney,

Your charming letter arrived today. (Forgive me for suspecting that you make rather a specialty of charming letters. Certainly you flatter me with your suggestion that I understand the secret of Mary Swann's power; in fact, I am as baffled as the next person by her preternatural ability to place two ordinary words side by side and extract a kilowatt, and sometimes more, much more, from them.) At any rate, I am both seduced and persuaded by your invitation, and feel this crisp fall morning decidedly anticipatory—though I will probably regret my decision in a week's time.

As for my possible contribution, perhaps it would be useful to those at the symposium if I were to talk for a few minutes in a generalized "midwifely" way about how I came to know Mrs. Swann, though I expect the story of her bringing me her poems on that long-ago snowy day is fairly well known. I might also describe briefly, if it would be of interest, the odd clutter of paper, or "manuscript" as you call it, on which the poems were written. I'm not at all sure myself that I would call such a heap of scraps a *manuscript*, and I cannot agree with you that the loss of it is "tragic." (As a matter of fact, my late dear wife used it for wrapping up some fish bones after a particularly fine meal of local whitefish, but I believe that story too is well documented.)

Furthermore, as an old newspaper man, rather than a professional scholar, I may have rather less reverence than you for the holiness of working papers. If you are familiar with Urdu poetry, or indeed with the oral tradition of most of the world's literature, you will know that this cherishing of original manuscripts is a relatively new phenomenon, and one that I find puzzling. A manuscript is, after all, only a crude representation of that step between creative thought and artefact, and might just as usefully be employed as kindling for a fire or in the wrapping of fishbones.

Frankly, the endless checking of one text against another, this tyranny of accuracy that rules the academic world, is all rather tiresome. I have found that it is sometimes better to look at the universe with a squint, to subject oneself to a deliberate distortion, and hope that out of the jumbled vision, or jumbled notes if you like, will fall the accident that is the truth. So please, Ms. Maloney, don't "grieve" for the loss of a few shreds of paper. As you surely know, there are other things to spend your grief upon.

Yours,

F. Cruzzi

P.S. May I compliment you on your handwriting—the almost engraved quality of your upper-case C's in particular, and the deep whimsical, old-fashioned way you indent your paragraphs—very pretty indeed.

December 7

My dear Freddy,

Let me say first that you have nothing, nothing, nothing to reproach yourself for. I am not, as you suggest in your note, offended, and I am sure Hildë and my own dear Barnie, too, would think it the most natural thing in the world. You are not ready yet for mellow avuncularity, and why should you be? I was only a little startled, that's all—it's been so long. Oh, my dear, I am finding this difficult to put down on paper. What I know is that words are rather pathetic at times and that what we need most is to reach past them and touch each other. That's all that happened, such a little thing, but what happiness it brought me, though you seem to have thought otherwise.

Please come on the 17th. I am going to do partridges with that sauterne sauce you're forever talking about, and with luck there'll be strawberries in the market.

Yours,

Pauline

December 10

My sweet Pauline,

I will be there, bearing a walnut cake, just this minute out of the oven and ready for its brandy bath.

Until then,

F.

December 11

Dear Mr. Cruzzi,

You probably won't remember meeting me at the Library Association meeting a few years back, when you were the guest speaker. We had a little visit afterwards. Maybe it will jog your memory if I tell you that I am the librarian (part-time) out in Nadeau and that I was a great friend of Mary Swann's before she passed away. Wouldn't she be surprised how famous she's got to be? I hope there's some way she knows.

Not so long ago I received an invitation to her symposium in Toronto, and last week I had a nice little note from Professor Lang saying you would be coming too and would be giving one of the speeches, in fact.

To get to the point, Professor Lang suggested that if I was driving down to Toronto maybe I could give you a ride, but the problem is, crazy as it seems, I've never learned to drive a car, and so I'll be taking the bus into Kingston on Monday morning (Jan.3) and then getting the 10:00 A.M. train. Whenever I go into Toronto, which isn't half as often as I wish I could go, I take the train. Once I took a bus all the way and didn't like it half as much and got bus sick part way there to make matters worse.

This may seem awfully forward of me, but I thought maybe we could take the train together and keep each other company on the way. We could meet at the train station in Kingston about 9:30 or so, in plenty of time to buy our tickets, unless we get them earlier, which I always do. So as you'll know who I am, I'm five feet, four inches, and people say I'm on the thin side these days due to being a bit under the weather of late, though I'm bound to pick up before too long. I've got glasses with blue-grey frames and I'll be wearing a brown suede coat if there's no snow, but if it's snowing, as it probably will be, I'll be in my old down-filled blue coat with a grey fur collar (just artificial).

By now you've probably made other arrangements for getting there, so please don't think my feelings will be hurt if I get there (the train station) and you're not there. It was just that Professor Lang asked if I could drive you down, but as I explained, I don't drive a car. Which is ridiculous living out in the country like I do.

But anyway, I love the train, every minute of it, especially the part along the lake.

Sincerely,

Rose Hindmarch

P.S. Merry Christmas

December 18

Dear Ms. Hindmarch,

I expect Lang wrote and told you I was elderly and infirm and muddled and needed looking after, all of which is true or partly true, and so it is with gratitude that I accept your kind invitation to be your travelling companion.

I too love the train, especially at this time of the year. We can gaze out the window and you can tell me all about your good friend Mary Swann, whom I am sorry to say I met only briefly. It has been some years since I've passed through Nadeau, but I have been told that the local museum has a special Mary Swann display.

I send you best wishes for good health and for a happy Christmas.

Yours,

F. Cruzzi

P.S. Since we've met before, you'll recognize me easily, though I am somewhat more tottery than I was when we talked at the Library Association.

Frederic Cruzzi: His Dreams

Everyone is familar with the Persian poet Rashid and what he has written about the power of dreams, how if all the dreams dreamt by men on a single random night were gathered into a bundle and hurled into the early morning sky, the blaze of it would:

> . . . put to shame
> The paltry shrivelled,
> Fires of the sun.

When Frederic Cruzzi's wife, Hildë, was alive, the two of them occasionally made gifts to each other of their dreams as they moved about in their large old-fashioned kitchen preparing breakfast. Hildë, rhythmically buttering toast, described wild animals, brightly coloured food, sudden nakedness, and misplaced objects, objects that remained stubbornly unidentified.

Cruzzi himself, ever the editor, was sometimes guilty of polishing his disjointed dreams for Hildë's benefit, giving them a sense of shape and applying small, elegant, decorative touches. (There are many modes of estrangement, the poet Rashid has observed, and elegance is one.) Cruzzi's dreams, as conveyed to Hildë, were filled with flowers, with long healing conversations, with the whimsical or heroic defiance of gravity. A lack of linearity lent charm, and still does. He is forever in his dreams bumping his forehead against some surprise of texture or weather or, even at age eighty, watching his hands, which are the symbols, the messengers, of his whole self, travelling across a landscape of undiscovered female bodies, breasts, clefts, thighs, ankles—and all these mountains and vales pinned down by the patient cobalt eyes of his wife, Hildë.

Ever since her death a year ago—a single cataclysmic explosion of the cranial artery—Cruzzi has kept his dreams to himself. He would sooner plunge his hand into boiling water than bore his good friends with his dreams. (Whereas these same friends approach the subject of *their* dreams rather frequently, and whenever they do Cruzzi knows he's in for a dull time of it.).

Nevertheless, his dreams continue, and are, if anything, more varied, more vivid, more Dadaist in their narration, and more persistent in their reaching after odd tossed chunks of history. Their pursuit of him into old age amazes him, and he is perplexed always by their utter uselessness, sometimes comparing their substance to the magically soft, recurring skin of lint he peels from the steel mesh in the door of the electric clothes dryer. (There's a certain pleasure in this peeling, he thinks; but to what use can the clean, gathered handful of fluff be put?)

The idea that dreams are the involuntary poetry of the mind appeals to him, but he rejects it. He is also by nature skeptical of that theory that dreams accumulate and become part of the making and unmaking of the universe, and equally distrusts the notion that dreams exorcise guilt or fear or mend the imagination. He doesn't know what he believes, and remains as baffled as the poet Mary Swann (cosmic cousin to the great Rashid) who felt herself tormented by:

What seems
A broken memory that tears
At whitened nerves
Like useless dreams
The night preserves
In sealed undreamed-
Of jars.

Early in September, or perhaps late in August, after a short afternoon's walk in the woods that begin behind his house, Cruzzi fell asleep in an armchair by an open window, and in his first breath caught a glimpse of his mother's white hand attempting to open a bottle of mineral water and, after making a struggle of it, handing it to her husband. In the foreground, a red cloth is spread on the grass, a picnic is in progress, and the sleeping Cruzzi catches with his second breath the round Muslim face of his father—soft, slightly overripe, as smooth and hairless as a pear, and made even rounder by a wonderful spreading candour. How they smile, the two of them! The radiance of their smiles forms the melody that keeps this dream aloft, even as a fly buzzes in Cruzzi's ear, threatening to whisk the picnic cloth out of sight and overturn the bottle of mineral water. The smiles of the two picnickers are directed upward into the leaves of a small dusty tree, at each other, at the rippling water poured from the bottle, and at Cruzzi himself who is somehow there and not there.

Walking through this dream, and through all Cruzzi's dreams, are the stout, sun-browned legs of his wife, Hildë. Mahogany is how he thinks of those legs, solid, polished lengths of hardwood between walking shorts and laced boots, legs brought to full strength on her annual hiking tours in the Appalachians or along the Bruce Trail. The roundness of Hildë's brown thighs on the picnic cloth overwhelms the multiplicity of other forms and gestures and brings a whimper to Cruzzi's groin, breaking through the fragile arrangement of sandwiches and fruit and pulling him slowly and painfully to consciousness.

In October, on that particular Saturday night when clocks are officially turned back one hour, Cruzzi sleeps soundly, thanks to a nightcap of warm whisky. It is almost as though the fibres still strong beneath his aged, flaking skin are fused to those other fibres that make up the smooth cotton sheets of his bed.

But toward morning, perhaps because of the dislocation of the single unaccommodated hour, his sleep is invaded by violence. The violence comes in the form of a voice that achieves a loudness rare in dreams. It goes on and on, booming against the tight weave of the sheets, and Cruzzi, sleeping, his hands curled into fists, struggles to hear what the voice is saying, but can hear only a roar of anger and injury. It is his own voice, of course, and this makes his inability to distinguish words all the more frustrating. An old-fashioned clock strikes the hour and announces that the floor—for a patterned floor has suddenly established itself in the void—is tilting dangerously. Hildë is running, her strong brown legs frightened, trying to keep her balance; but the voice, loud enough now to tighten a muscle in Cruzzi's shoulder and bid him turn on his side, threatens to pull down the floor along with the slippery tiled walls and the beautiful ceiling tracked with blue-black hieroglyphics, which, because of their astringent colour and configuration, remain maddenly unreadable.

Cruzzi, still sleeping, shifts the whole of his body and brings a bony thumb into the cavity of his mouth.

Landscapes, earthquakes and sharp cliffs give way suddenly to an Alpine meadow and warm sunlight. (It is a cold night in Kingston, the temperature reaches minus ten, low for this time of year, and Cruzzi gropes in his sleep for the wool-filled quilt he keeps at the foot of the bed.)

Hildë is laughing, pulling away from him, and showing a smile that has turned provisional. Then she is arranging fruit in a bowl, placing the plums carefully so that the soft blue cleft that marks each one catches a streak of lustre from the sun. But no—it's not the sun, but the moon. She dances lightly into his arms, giving him the kind of embrace that promises nothing, then whirls away on legs that are thinner, whiter, that shine from calf to thigh with a strange lacteal whiteness. (Cruzzi wakens briefly, scratches his genitals, acknowledges soreness in his joints, and is carried with his next exhalation through the doorway of a cottage where he discovers a stairway, corridors, a great hall brilliantly lit, a table set for twelve, and stately music.)

The face on the television screen has been talking for several minutes now. The subject is Libya, a hijacked plane, a terrorist's telephone call, impossible demands. Gadaffi appears briefly, peers with fanatical eyes into the camera, then wavers and flickers. After a minute his wide retreating image seems to float. Cruzzi can feel his own face begin to fade and dissolve into a miasma of dots— then his brown-speckled hand on his coffee cup and then the length of his arm. He is being eaten up by light. He is a young man standing in the corridor of a train and in his hand is a postcard. Hieroglyphics again, but this time he struggles harder to make them out. The words are in French, written very large, and they promise foolishness, gaiety, passion, love . . . especially love.

Snow is everywhere, filling up the woods behind Cruzzi's house and the crevasses between the drifts of his breath. From nowhere comes a saving hand, warm, pale in colour, talcum enriched, a gold ring gleaming, a few muffled words that point toward a dream inside this dream, a house-like cave built into a hillside.

But the door is sealed by pressure, his bladder again, then a seizure of coughing, and numbness in the feet, and his loud voice filling the kitchen. Hildë is weeping, her brown arms over her eyes, and he is striking out at her with his voice, with his hand, even his fist, so that she falls under the snow, which is deeper than ever now and so heavy that he must scramble like a madman in his effort to rescue her.

Frederic Cruzzi: His Short Untranscribed History of the Peregrine Press: 1956–1976

The *Kingston Banner*, even before Frederic Cruzzi arrived from England to be its editor, had perforce been something of an anomaly as a regional newspaper, its constituency being an uneasy yoking of town and gown, farmers, civil servants, and petit-bourgeoisie. Its advertisers were the owners of such small, conservative family businesses as the Princess Tearoom and Diamond Bros. Colonial Furniture Emporium, but its most vociferous readers were revolutionaries and progressives of the academic stripe. The *Banner*'s editorial policy, as a result, tended to be skittish, gliding between pragmatic waltz and feinting soft-shoe, and for that reason was always, and still is, perused with a knowing wink of the eye. This is accepted by everybody. It is also accepted that the real battles are fought on the Letters-to-the-Editor page, which occasionally spills over to a second page and once — in 1970, with the War Measures Act — to a third. Here, despite quaint temporary alliances and retreats into unanimity, the struggle assumes those classic polarities between those who would stand still and those who would move forward.

The boisterous, ongoing warfare of the Letters page has mostly been regarded by Cruzzi as analogous to a healthy game of societal tennis, both amusing and lifegiving. Sometimes, too, it yields an inch of enlightenment. But warfare abruptly stops at the Entertainment page. Even among those readers who would never dream of subscribing to the Kingston Regional Theatre or the fledgling Eastern Ontario Symphony, and who would rather dive naked into a patch of summer thistle than be caught reading one of the books reviewed in the *Banner*, there is a silent consensus that *art* is somehow privileged and deserving of protection. A dirty book discovered in a school library may raise a brief fuss, but the general concept of art is sacred in the Kingston region, and lip service, if nothing else, is paid to it.

When Cruzzi took over the *Banner* he was bemused, and so was Hildë, by a long-running feature on the Entertainment page known as "The Poet's Corner." A number of local poets, mostly elderly, always genteel, vied for this small weekly space, dropping off batches of sonnets at the *Banner* office on Second Street, as well as quatrains, sestinas, limericks, haiku, bumpity-bump, and shrimpy dactyls, all attached to such unblushing titles as "Seagull Serenade," "Springtime Reverie," "Ode to Fort Henry," "Birches at Eventide," "The Stalwart Flag," "Old Sadie," "The First Bluebird," "Sailors Ahoy," "Cupid in Action," "The Trillium," "The Old Thrashing Crew," "The Eve of Virtue," and so on. Payment, regardless of length or verse form, was five dollars, but this rather small sum in no way discouraged the number of submissions. Cruzzi, in his first month in Kingston, looked carefully at both quantity and quality and immediately announced plans to terminate "The Poet's Corner."

What a fool he was in those days, he with his heavy tweed suits and strangely unbarbered hair, his queer way of talking, his manners and pronouncements. The public outcry over the cancellation of "The Poet's Corner" was unprecedented and appeared to come from all quarters of the community. He was labelled a philistine and a brute journalist of the modern school. The word foreigner was invoked: Frenchy, Limey, Wog — there was understandable confusion here. Readers might be willing to tolerate the new typeface imposed on them, and no one seemed to miss the old "Pie of the Week" feature when it disappeared from the Women's page, but they refused to surrender Li'l Abner and "The Poet's Corner." Culture was culture. Even the advertisers became restless, and Cruzzi, in the interest of comity and suffering a heretic's embarrassment, capitulated, though he let it be known that there would be a two-year interregnum on seagull poems.

In time, because the Kingston literary community was small, he and Hildë befriended and grew fond of the local poets. Cruzzi even took a certain glee in the awfulness of their product. Herb Farlingham's poem "Springtime Reverie," for instance ("Mrs. Robin in feathered galoshes/Splashes in puddles chirping 'O my goshes!' "), gave him moments of precious hilarity that were especially welcome after a day spent composing careful, pointed, balanced, and doomed-to-be-ignored editorials on the arms race or the threat of McCarthyism.

In 1955, toward the end of a long golden summer, Cruzzi opened an envelope addressed to "The Poet's Corner," and out fell a single poem, typed for once, titled "Anatomy of a Passing Thought" written by one Kurt Wiesmann of William Avenue, just two streets from Byron Road where Cruzzi and Hildë lived. The sixteen-line poem possessed grace and strength. Light seemed to shine through it. Cruzzi read it quickly, with amazement. One line, toward the end, briefly alarmed him by veering toward sentimentality, but the next line answered back, mocking, witty, and containing that spacey necessary bridge that in the best poetry joins binocular clarity to universal vision. Extraordinary.

It was 5:30 in the afternoon. He took a deep breath and rubbed a hand through his thick, still-unbarbered hair. Hildë was expecting him at home for a picnic supper with friends. Already she would have set the table under the trees, a red table cloth, wine glasses turned upside down, paper napkins folded and weighed down by cutlery. Nevertheless he sat down at his desk and wrote Mr. Wiesmann a letter telling him why his poem was unsuitable for the *Banner*. It was unrhymed. It had no regular metre. It did not celebrate nature, or allude to God, or even to Kingston and its environs. It did not tug at the heart-strings or touch the tear ducts and was in no way calculated to bring forth a gruff chuckle of recognition; in short it was too good for "The Poet's Corner." He ended the letter, "Yours resignedly, F. Cruzzi," surprising himself; he had not realized his own resignation until that moment. (Rationality won't rescue this scene the way, say, a footnote can save a muddled paragraph, but it might be argued that Cruzzi, by this time, had acquired an understanding and even a respect for his readers' sensibilities.)

Kurt Wiesmann, a chemist with a local cooking-oil manufacturer, was delighted with his letter of rejection, and continued to send the *Banner* unprintable poems. In a year's time Cruzzi and Hildë had read close to fifty of them, and they both urged Wiesmann, by now a friend and frequent visitor in their house, to approach a book publisher. They were astonished, moved, and entertained by what he wrote, and felt he should have an audience larger than the two of them.

But it turned out that publishers in Canada found Wiesmann's poems "too European"; American publishers thought them "too Canadian," and a British publisher sensed "an American influence that might be troubling" to his readers. Hildë, exasperated, suggested one night — the three of them were in the kitchen drinking filtered coffee and eating cheesecake — that they publish the poems themselves.

In a month's time they were in production. It was Kurt Wiesmann who suggested the name Peregrine Press. He was a restless man, tied down by a family and job, but a traveller by instinct. His book was titled *Inroads* (Hildë's idea) and was favourably reviewed as "a courageous voice speaking with the full force of the alienated." A Toronto newspaper wrote, "The newly launched Peregrine Press must be congratulated on its discovery of a fresh new Canadian voice."

Their second poet was the elegant Glen Forrestal of Ottawa, later to win a Governor General's Award, who wrote to the Peregrine Press introducing himself as a member of the Kurt Wiesmann fan club and a veteran of several serious peregrinations of his own. Their third poet was the fey, frangible Rhoda MacKenzie, and after that came Cassie Sinclair, Hugh Walkley Donaldson, Mary Swann, Mavis Stockard, w.w. wooley, Burnt Umber, Serge Tawowski, and a number of others who went on to make names for themselves.

Printing was done during off-hours at the *Banner* and paid for out of Cruzzi's pocket. Hildë, who had set up an office in an upstairs bedroom, read the manuscripts that soon came flowing in. She had a sharp eye and, with some notable exceptions, excellent judgement. "Whatever we decide to publish must have a new sound." She said this in a voice that contained more and more of the sonorous Canadian inflection. To a local businessman, whom she attempted to convert into a patron, she said, "We have the responsibility as a small press to work at the frontier."

Along the frontier a few mistakes were inevitably made. Even Hildë admitted she had been taken in by Rhoda MacKenzie's work, that behind its fretwork there was little substance. And both she and Cruzzi regretted the title they chose for Mary Swann's book — *Swann's Songs*. An inexplicable lapse of sensibility. A miscalculation, an embarrassment.

For twenty years the press operated out of the Cruzzi house on Byron Road. Methodically, working in the early mornings after her daily lakeside walk, Hildë read submissions, edited manuscripts, handled correspondence, and attended, if necessary, to financial matters — though bookkeeping took little time since the Peregrine Press never earned a profit and print-runs were small, generally between two hundred and three hundred copies. Always, in the final stages before the publication of a new book, a group of friends, the official board as they called themselves, gathered in the Cruzzi diningroom for a long evening of plum brandy and hard work: collating pages, stapling, gluing covers, the best of these covers designed by Barney Ouilette, and remarkably handsome, with a nod toward modernism and a suggestion of what Hildë liked to call "fire along the frontier."

Her only agony was the problem of what to do with unsuccessful manuscripts. Tenderhearted, she laboured over her letters of rejection, striving for a blend of honesty and kindness, but forbidding herself to give false encouragement, explaining carefully what the press was looking for. These explanations gave her pleasure, as though she were reciting a beloved prayer. "New sounds," she explained, "and innovative technique, but work that turns on a solid core of language."

Despite her tact, there was sometimes acrimony, once an obscene phone call, several times scolding letters impugning her taste. Herb Farlingham, who would have financed the publication of his *Seasoned Sonnets* if Hildë had let him, wept openly. "I'm so terribly sorry," Hildë said, supplying him with tea and a paper towel for his tears. "It's nothing personal, you may be sure." The Peregrine Press, she explained, thankful for a ready excuse, had very early taken a stand on self-publication and was anxious to avoid even the appearance of being a vanity press.

This stricture was put to the test years later when Hildë herself began to write poetry. She had reached the age of fifty, her waist had thickened, and her hair, which was short and straight with a bang over her forehead, was almost completely white. She had a dozen interests, though her ardour, flatteringly, centred on Cruzzi. There was her schedule of reading, her music, her fling at oil painting, her tennis and her hiking, her work with the blind. She was robust, cheerful, impatient, amiable, always occupied, always determined and passionate in her undertakings, pleased as a child with her successes, and smiling with her round face in her failures. That round face of hers, friends said, was unique in its openness, and yet it was a year before she showed her husband what she had been writing. "Here," she said to him late one evening, thrusting a folder forward. "I want you to be absolutely honest with me."

"Poetry?" His eyebrows went up.

She shrugged. "An attempt." It had been years since they'd spoken French at home.

Her poems, he saw with sadness, had no edges, no hardness. The words themselves were pleasing enough, melodious and rather dreamlike, but there was also a quality in some of the lines that he identified as kittenish — and that surprised him. He was reminded of the year Hildë had leaped into oil painting and how her curious, wild abstractions whirled without regard for line or composition; these canvases, relics of a lapsed enthusiasm, were stacked now in the basement, keeping company with the summer screens and garden tools. He wondered if some natural amiability in his wife's nature blocked the imaginative vision. (He *knew* poets, their ever-expanding egos, their righteousness.)

"Well, what do you think then?" Hildë asked him. She was sitting tensely on a footstool inches from his chair. "I want you to be very, very severe."

"They're quite moving," he said. "Some of them."

She was not fooled. "Do you think the Peregrine might . . ." She let the suggestion drift off. One of her hands smoothed her skirt over a round knee.

He looked at her with amazed pity. A mingling of tenderness and caution dictated his reply. "You remember," he said slowly, "that we decided in the beginning that we would avoid —"

"They're not much good," Hildë said, more baffled than heartbroken. She gave one of her steep, explosive laughs. "I was just trying to express — well, I don't know what exactly. Maybe that's the problem." She got up with an awkward little jerk to make coffee, a gesture so self-protective that it lingered in Cruzzi's mind far longer than her words. "You're right," she said firmly. "We did make that decision, and we must stick to it."

By 1977 Hildë was engaged in the anti-nuclear movement, and the Peregrine Press began to languish. Then she died.

Twenty years, Cruzzi has since learned, is the usual life of a small literary press. The vital juices get used up, energy or a willingness to take risks. The manuscripts — they still arrive from time to time — begin to look creased and not very clean. The corners curl. Some of them bear coffee rings.

It's been quite some time since Cruzzi has seen anything that suggested "fire along the frontier." Every once in a while his conscience gets the better of him, and then he gathers up the accumulated manuscripts, attaches to each one a little printed fiche declaring that the Peregrine Press is no more, and mails them back to their owners. "Good luck elsewhere," he always adds, just as Hildë used to do when she was alive.

Frederic Cruzzi: An Unwritten Account of the Fifteenth of December, 1965

In his life Frederic Cruzzi has had two loves: the written word and his wife, Hildë. The two loves are compatible but differently ordered, occupying separate berths in his brain and defying explanation or description, something that bothers him not at all.

His own father once told him — and this conversation he now lovingly reviews as he walks in the woods behind his house — the trees bare of leaves, the low junipers underfoot snapping with cold — that love would not exist if the word *love* were taken from the language. At the time he had nodded agreement, happy to be included in his father's solemn abstractions, but destined to outgrow them.

Once in a while, walking like this in shadowed woodland at three o'clock on a winter afternoon, or hearing perhaps a particular phrase of music, or approaching a wave of sexual ecstasy, Cruzzi has felt a force so resistant to the power of syntax, description or definition, so savage and primitive in its form, that he has been tempted to shed his long years of language and howl monosyllables of delight and outrage.

Outrage because these are moments of humility, of dressing down, of rebuke to those, like Cruzzi, who perceive reality through print, the moments when those who are proudly articulate confess their speechlessness. It is as though some enormous noisy motor of which they had not ever been conscious, were suddenly switched off. These moments, and their ability to spring leaks at the edges of language, tend to be exceedingly brief, and Cruzzi has noticed, too, that they are shattered by the least effort to analyse them or extend their duration. Only this morning he stood naked in front of a mirror and regarded the body that both pleased and disgusted him. "Knackers," he pronounced aloud, cupping his balls in a mothy hand, and heard the word slip from its encasement of meaning, and fly, ludicrously, into the air.

Go back to love, he instructs himself, bending stiffly to examine the scars on a young birch. Rodents.

He and Hildë, from the beginning — that convivial evening in the city of Gap, seated around a supper table that was lit by an overhead gas lamp — had felt themselves separated from the others by a narrow arc of privilege. Each, it seemed, at once measured the other's need, though each had been grave, correct, addressing the other with a respectful *vous*, and shaking hands briskly when the party ended. But Cruzzi had not neglected to write down her address in a small notebook he carried, sealing in print that promise he could not have described. He asked if he might see her the following day; a long walk was what he suggested, a walk followed by tea in a café. He determined to take up as much of her day as possible. The cruder stratagems of the *célibataire* wearied him, but he would delight all his life in the miniature theatre of courtship, its gifts and entrances and phrases frozen out of meaning — all this Hildë seemed to grasp. Her response as she stood in the dim foyer had the quality of instinct. By all means a long walk, she told him directly, by all means tea in a café.

Already a brisk adjustment had been made, an understanding reached.

The hold most married people have on each other tends to dwindle fairly quickly, but occasionally accident and temperament, so strangely mingled, keep it buoyant. It might be suggested, in the case of the Cruzzis' marriage, that a curious, possibly shameful need to ameliorate the effects of their foreignness, first in England and later in Canada, was a further bond. Or that the death of their son had the effect of isolating them in their incoherence. Or that the health of the Peregrine Press, in its good years especially, imbued them with a spirit that even close friends judged to be a rebirth of love. Not one of these speculations, however, held much truth.

Their simplicity, their little routines, would always escape others, especially those who thought of passion in terms of appetite and rich, sad sighs of impatience. That even in midlife, and after, Hildë's face was often foolish with affection, that Cruzzi's hand rested frequently on the back of her chair at Kingston concerts or theatricals — these actions falsely signalled to others the devotion of habit that arrives after love's final retreat.

All these supposed mutations and gradations of love Cruzzi would have denied if the question were put to him (it never was), arguing that the regard he and Hildë had for each other was a simple, uncomplicated element like the air he took into his body or the print that swam into his head. Its force, fluctuation, and flavour were not even to be thought of, much less given expression. *They take each other for granted* — that curse hurled at those who embrace their good fortune wordlessly — has always seemed to Cruzzi an unfair challenging of fate. Furthermore, he would have considered it an act of arrogance to believe that he and Hildë had been served with something finer, stronger, and more enduring than the love he has observed between other married people. (A remnant of innocence convinces him that even those who practise public cruelties on each other, are tender in their private moments.)

He did not love Hildë because of her black-currant sherbet or her generous hospitality or her early morning cheerfulness or the way her rounded features took the light, or the graceful, energetic way she leaned over a bed and pounded the air back into a pillow, as though she were doing it a kindness and doing it with the whole of her heart. His range of response did not coalesce around such lists. He was not one to produce an informed rationale about a bond so simple and natural. Such dissection, such *counting of ways*, was frivolous and ignoble. He was, some might think, almost careless of his good fortune.

But just as everyday articles — preserving jars, teaspoons, loaves of bread — take on the look of sacred objects when seen in exceptional light, so he sometimes looked at his wife and saw her freshly and with the full force of vision. One of these "seizures of the heart," as Cruzzi might describe it (but never did), occurred early in the afternoon of December 15, 1965.

He awakened on that particular morning with a sore throat. Both he and Hildë had long since surrendered their first language, but maladies of the body continued to speak to them with their French names. *Mal à la gorge. Le rheum.* He had gone to bed in good health and wakened like this!

He decided he would spend the morning, at least, in bed. He was still several years from retirement, but not averse to letting the *Banner* run itself occasionally.

Hildë brought him a steaming infusion of thyme. She swore by it, especially for the throat. He drank it, then dozed. He heard her in various parts of the house as she moved about, talking on the telephone, playing the piano, concocting something in the kitchen — he knew before he saw it that it would be a thick soup made with cauliflower, milk, and butter. In times of illness she always made this soup. He ate a bowl of it for lunch, by now dressed and sitting at the kitchen table, and began to feel a little better. He fished in his pocket for a pencil and wrote down the first paragraph of an editorial that was to be a defence of a new piece of public sculpture. It was an exceptionally cold day. The wind blew hard against the old window frames of the house and, hearing it, he resolved to spend the afternoon, too, at home, sipping his hot tea and working on his column, which was going surprisingly well.

He looked up, slowly, and saw Hildë standing beside him. She was dressed in her warmest clothing — sheepskin boots, woollen ski pants, a bulky parka, her heavy fur-lined mittens, a knitted scarf, and a hat from which wisps of white hair poignantly escaped. "I'm going ice-fishing," she told him, smiling broadly.

She loved to fish at any time of the year, but ice-fishing in particular gave her pleasure, its clumsy paraphernalia and intrinsic paradox — the flashing bitter cold and the calm wait in a warmed hut. Sometimes she went with friends and sometimes alone. Usually she was lucky, bringing home fresh whitefish, which she expertly boned and grilled for dinner; fish never seemed so fresh to her as when pulled miraculously through an opening in the thick ice.

How he had loved her at that moment! More it seemed than at any time in their life together, her strength and imagination and, beneath the impossibly coarse outdoor clothing, her body, all polished wood and knowable clefts. She had removed one mitten, which she held between her teeth, and was bending over, checking the contents of her tackle box, mumbling a little to herself — utterly, endearingly, preoccupied — and the next minute she was gone, the heavy storm door shut behind her, leaving him alone in the house.

It was mostly for this abandonment that he loved her, the unlooked-for gift of an empty afternoon.

The living-room smelled of cold fireplace ashes and (very faintly) of cooked cauliflower. Outside it was dark for so early in the afternoon, a storm coming up, the first big one of the season, but the large, many-paned windows let in enough light to read by. From a bookcase Cruzzi took down his dilapidated copy of Rashid's *Persian Songs* and allowed his eyes to travel over a familiar page.

On your shoulder a bird alights
Singing, singing a song without words,
A song without meaning or wisdom or words,
A song without asking or giving or words,
Without kindness or judgement or flattering words.
On your shoulder a bird alights
Singing against your loud silence.

He thought to himself, as he had thought many times before, how little he demanded of eastern poetry. The poets of the East lacked western rigour, that ability to build up a universe with the nib of a pen. He conceded that much. The ironies were too slack, the music too rhythmically obvious. But, reading it, he felt himself connected to ancient rhythms that some less ordered part of his brain welcomed. Most of what he knew of love he found amplified in eastern poetry, not its application but its brief transports. Reverberations, he knew, were an aspect of love, which was why, when he picked up a volume of the great Rashid, he asked only for the affirmation of a single moment and no more. The moment stretched; he turned over a page, yawned, glanced out the window at the blown trees and heavy sky, and wondered if Hildë would return home early; he hoped so. After that he may have slept a little in his chair, because when he looked at the clock again it was after three.

The room felt more than usually drafty, and he stirred himself to organize a heap of kindling and dry wood in the fireplace. He had just got a blaze flickering when he heard the front doorbell. One faint ring, then the stutter of the door knocker, something of entreaty about it that sent him hurrying into the chilly vestibule.

Standing on the stone porch was Mary Swann, though of course he didn't ask her name or even what she wanted. It was far too cold for such preliminaries; later he discovered that the temperature had fallen twenty degrees since noon. He took her arm, murmuring a stream of comforting words, and drew her into the hall, then into the living-room, steering her firmly in the direction of the fireplace.

In those first moments, bewilderment gave her the look of an imbecile. She wore a shapeless black coat, hideous thick fawn stockings and rubber overshoes with buckles. She had no gloves. Around her face was tied a man's plaid muffler. Her face was small, purplish, the mouth working, the eyes squeezed shut as though the room were unbearably bright.

What was the mouth saying, those shrunken lips like rows of stitching? Something grotesquely apologetic. She was so sorry. Sorry to be bothering him. To just drop in like this. To arrive without, without —

He made her sit in a chair, which he drew up to the fire, and he insisted she remove her rubber boots. She drew back, reluctant, and so he leaned over to assist her, feeling like an actor in a fine old play, undoing the buckles, easing them off, ignoring her weak little mew of shame. "Frozen," he said, addressing the feet, now revealed in their thick grey work socks. An obsequious whimper came from her mouth, and he, still relishing his actor's role, continued to rub her feet between his hands, conscious of her acute embarrassment and also of his strange happiness. Under the socks her toes curled tensely; he massaged them, muttering inanities as one does to children — there, there, it's all right. He was beginning to drift in his thoughts, to think of the story he would make of this for Hildë's sake — *a stranger came to the door and* . . .

"Are you feeling any better?" he asked her.

She nodded mutely.

He offered her sherry, which she refused, shaking her head and looking at the floor.

Tea?

Her flow of apology began once again, mumbled and unintelligible. So sorry. Such a bother. She refused to meet his eyes. Her head bobbed and shook. She was taking up his valuable time, she said. She should have written a letter instead of arriving out of the blue like this. It wasn't proper. It wasn't right.

Tea, he asked again, and she nodded. Her face flushed with shame. She started to say something, but couldn't go on. She was so sorry. She never intended —

He fled to the kitchen, put a kettle on, took cups from the cupboard, giving her time to compose herself, making a fearful noise with the tea canister, forcing himself to hum a jaunty little tune, feeling still the shapes of her frozen feet in his hands. Sugar — he was sure she would want sugar. He found some fruit cake in a tin and put a large slice on a plate, then put milk in a little jug. For himself he poured a hefty brandy, which he sipped as the kettle came slowly to a boil.

He judged her at first to be a woman in her sixties, even her seventies, something about the hunched sweatered shoulders and the whiteness of scalp under scanty hair. As she lifted the teacup to her mouth, he saw that the wrist of her green cardigan had been mended with grey wool. She drank the tea greedily, adding milk and sugar and stirring with terrifying thoroughness, darting little looks in his direction. He decided at this point that she might be in her fifties, perhaps even her *early* fifties.

Did she behave in a manner that could be described as deranged? he was asked later. Was her speech incoherent? Did she mention any specific fears or threats? Exhibit paranoid signs? Did she at any time mention her husband?

Some of these questions came from the police, some from a reporter on Cruzzi's own paper, Freddy Waggoner, who later drifted off into television work. Other questions arose at the inquest, which was held in mid-January, 1966, and still others came from a Professor Willard Lang of the University of Toronto — this was more than fifteen years later — and still later from the egregious Morton Jimroy, who had recently appointed himself Mary Swann's official biographer.

To most of these questions Cruzzi said no. Signs of instability? No. Not even what you might call eccentricity? No. She was, of course, very, very cold, having walked more than a mile from the bus station in appalling weather. She was perhaps excessively anxious about the time of her return bus and several times asked to be told the time. And naturally, being a timid woman, she was nervous about how she and her bag of poems would be received.

But you say she gradually relaxed?

Yes, once she had warmed up and had drunk two or three cups of tea, she grew composed.

It was then, Cruzzi said, that he realized she was younger than he had originally thought. (In fact she was forty-nine. She would have been fifty years old the following February.)

Can you describe her physical appearance, her face, her way of wearing her hair? These questions from the indefatigable Jimroy.

The hair could be easily enough described, or rather, not described, since it was without shape or colour. Skinned back, the scalp barely covered. He could not, in fact, remember much about Mrs. Swann's hair. Medium brown, he told Jimroy. Slightly wavy over the ears.

Would you say she was tall or short? Fat or thin?

Difficult to remember. She was seated for most of the time, remember. Not tall, certainly not tall. Not fat either, no. She had a look of being wasted. Thin, but thin without the lankiness that accompanies ease and good health.

Wasted, you say? Jimroy at his most persistent, full of nerviness.

If the poor woman had had a driver's licence, there would have been a record of her height and weight. But, alas, she did not. And there were no doctor's records, none that could be found, at any rate. Apparently she wasn't in the habit of visiting a doctor, though once she had seen a dentist — in Elgin — where she had several teeth pulled. No x-rays, however.

Surely it's not possible for a person in this century to go through a life without being measured or weighed or x-rayed?

It seems it *is* possible. Her only child was delivered at home —
Incredible! You mean — ?

A doctor, yes, but no records were kept. And one could hardly ascertain her height and weight after her death.

No, quite. But the colour of her eyes — ?

That, too, would have been on a driver's licence if only she had had —

But perhaps you noticed?

Afraid not. I usually *do* notice such things, eyes, especially women's eyes, but —

But?

The room was rather dark that day. A storm coming up. And I didn't want to put the light on for fear of —

For fear of what?

Well, startling her. Her face —

She was very ill at ease then?

Only at first. She was not used to . . . to being served tea. One could see that. She was not used to being *served*.

Her face. You started to say her face —

(Rabbity. Rodentlike. Not that I intend to give you that for your tape recorder.) An ordinary face, I would say. No makeup, of course. Nothing like that.

Any distinguishing mannerisms?

Not really.

Nothing?

Well, two or three times she put her fingertips to her earlobes.

Why?

I've no idea. Nerves perhaps.

A nervous mannerism, then?

Perhaps. (And sensual for some reason, this touching of the ears. One kept hoping she'd do it again.) But as I said, after she had some tea she became more at ease.

Did you say two cups or three? Sorry to be so banal, but a biographer —

Three cups. Orange pekoe. Milk. And sugar.

And until then she had not mentioned why she had come?

That is correct.

Then how did she approach the subject of —?

I believe I eventually asked her if she had come to see me about anything special.

In fact, Cruzzi, who had drawn up a chair beside her, only gradually became aware of the paper bag she clutched on her lap. A white bag, or so he said into Jimroy's tape recorder. An ordinary bag, much folded and creased. At first he had been conscious only of some shapeless object cradled on her knees, which she did not set aside even while she drank her tea. Whatever it was, Cruzzi sensed it had to do with her reason for having come.

"I've come here about my poems," she told him when at last he asked. Her eyes went straight to the paper bag on her lap and stayed there.

"Ah," he said, and almost laughed with relief. She was *not* a madwoman. "So! You're a poet."

She seemed about to deny this, then confided shyly. "I've had some poems printed. In the newspaper. The Elgin paper took one just last month."

"I see," he said gently.

"About the first snow. That was what I called it. 'The First Snowfall.' "

"How pleased you must have been," he said.

"And they sent a cheque. —" She stopped herself. Up went her two hands, fluttering to her ears and then back into her lap.

He waited a few seconds, and then, to encourage her, said, "Perhaps you'll send something to the *Banner*. We have a poet's corner once a week —"

She opened her mouth, her expression loose, scattered, full of entreaty. "I've brought these," she said, holding up her shopping bag. "Someone said, someone told me you were looking for . . . and so I thought, well, I'll get on the bus and bring everything I've got. Well, almost everything. Here." And she handed over her bag.

He looked inside. It was half-filled with small pieces of paper in varying size. There seemed no order. It was a bag full of poems and nothing more.

"Would you like to leave these with me?" he suggested. "I could read them and give you a call. If there's something we can use."

"We don't," she said, "have a telephone."

"In that case, I could drop you a line."

"I was hoping —"

"Yes?"

"— hoping you could look at them now. I have to get my bus at half-past five, you see, so I don't have much time, but if you could —"

To himself he said: this is absurd. His throat was feeling raw, and the fever he had had in the morning had returned. An image of warmed brandy passed before his eyes. He longed for Hildë's return. He dreaded what he knew would be in Mrs. Swann's paper bag and what he would have to say to her.

"If you would please read a few." She said this in a voice that he found intimate and dignified.

He shook the bag lightly. "Is there any special order?"

"Order?"

"What I mean is, where would you like me to begin?"

Her hands rose again, barely grazing her earlobes. "It doesn't make a difference," she said. "They're all poems, all of them."

He reached in the bag and drew out a piece of lined paper. It had been torn from a spiral notebook and bore a ragged edge. At the top was written, "Thinning Radishes." The writing was in ink, at least, but was scarcely legible. His heart squeezed with pity, but he read the poem carefully, then set it aside and again reached into the bag. "Lilacs" was the name of the second poem. After that he read "Pears." Then "The Silo."

She watched him as he read, her eyes on his face. He thought once to offer her a newspaper or magazine to occupy her, but she shook her head at the suggestion.

After reading the first few poems he became accustomed to her unevenly shaped letters and her strange mixture of printing and writing. The spelling surprised him by its accuracy, but the words were crowded on the little pieces of paper as though an effort had been made to be thrifty. As he read he placed the poems in a little pile on the hearthrug. It took an hour and a half to read them all. Then he gathered them up — thinking how like fallen leaves they were — and lowered them once again into their bag.

"Did you know at once that you had stumbled on the work of an important poet?" Professor Lang had not carried a tape recorder or even a notebook, but he had had the hungry face of a man on whom nothing was lost.

"I knew the work was highly original. It was powerful. There was, you might say, a beguiling cleanliness to the lines that is only rarely seen."

"Did you tell her this?"

"Yes."

"What did she do?"

"She smiled."

"But what did she say?"

"Nothing. Just smiled. A soft, quite lovely smile."

Two of her upper teeth had been missing — Cruzzi found the sight piercingly sad — and slackness at the side of her face suggested the further absence of molars. "You have every reason to be proud of your work," he remembers telling her.

"My work?"

"Your writing. Your poems."

She continued to smile. He smiled back, and they sat together in silence for a minute or two.

"I suppose this was a moment of epiphany for her," Morton Jimroy had commented. "Hearing her genius confirmed in such a way."

"I've no idea," Cruzzi said, "what she was thinking."

"Is that when you mentioned publishing the work?"

"Yes."

"How exactly did you phrase this, if you don't mind my asking?"

"I told her I would like my wife to see her work. And that I would like to publish her poems in a book if she were agreeable."

"And she replied?"

"She agreed to leave the poems with me for publication."

"But what were her exact words?"

"Mr. Jimroy, this conversation took place in 1965. I cannot possibly, I'm afraid, reconstruct our conversation in its entirety."

"But she must have expressed some . . . jubilation?"

"If I remember rightly, she was a little confused."

"Perhaps she was overcome. By the suddenness of it. The idea of her poems forming a book, I mean."

"Perhaps."

"Can you remember — I know it's difficult after all this time, but can you remember what she said next?"

"She asked me what time it was."

"And?"

"I said it was a few minutes after five o'clock, and then I insisted on driving her to the bus station."

"And did she resist this suggestion?"

"I was very firm."

"Did she at any point mention having been threatened by her husband?" This was a question that came up several times during the inquest.

"She didn't mention her husband at all," Cruzzi told the court, "but she did express great urgency about catching the five-thirty bus."

"Would you say she was frightened?"

"I would say she showed anxiety. I assured her that I would get her to the bus station in time."

"Is it your opinion, Mr. Cruzzi, that her anxiety stemmed from the weather conditions or from some other unstated fear?"

"I'm afraid I wouldn't be able to say."

"While you were in the car driving to the station did she refer in any way to her domestic situation?"

"She was quite silent. And so was I. The snow was blowing directly into the headlights and visibility was very poor."

"What were the last words she said to you?" Morton Jimroy asked, pressing the release button on his tape recorder. "Before she got on the bus?"

"She said goodbye."

"And what did you say? If you'll forgive my asking."

"I said I would be in touch within a few days."

"And that, of course, was the last time you saw her alive."

"Yes."

"Were you deeply shocked to hear the news of her death?"

"Deeply."

"It is the kind of act," Jimroy said into his machine, "which is beyond the comprehension of ordinary people."

To which Cruzzi made no reply.

Cruzzi returned from driving Mrs. Swann to the bus station and found that Hildë was back home. Still ruddy-faced from the cold and wonderfully pleased with herself, she stood in the middle of the big kitchen holding high in one hand a string of whitefish. "Oh, I was a lucky one today," she cried out as he came through the door. "They came jumping up to meet me, I loved them all. Look! This one is smiling at you, just look at that smile, he's already dreaming about hot butter."

Cruzzi, whose happiness had been building all day, felt his skin ready to burst, and if his wife hadn't at that moment picked up her filleting knife—which she kept killingly sharp—he would have taken her into his arms and danced her through the house.

"Something's happened," he said. Then, more quietly, "Something truly remarkable happened while you were gone."

He remembers that he shivered with pleasure thinking how he would tell her about Mary Swann. "I have been visited," he began, "by a beautiful toothless witch. A glorious, gifted crone. She materialized out of the storm—"

She heard the excitement in his voice and turned her face toward him, always quick to catch his mood. "I want to hear it all," she said, and held up her knife. "But from the beginning. Just let me do these beautiful, beautiful fish, and then I can sit down and listen with both my ears."

At the table he told her what Mary Swann had looked like, what she had said. He ate with great happiness. Hildë possessed rare skill with a filleting knife and even greater skill with the cooking of lake fish. It came off the grill redolent of butter, a thin skin of salty gold on the outside, and tender, breaking whiteness within.

Along with the fish they drank glasses of very cold dry white wine, and he told his story as Hildë had requested, from the beginning. "It was about three o'clock. I had drifted off in the wing chair, but I heard the doorbell ringing and . . ."

She listened the way a child listens, with touching expectation, without a single interruption, her eyes rapt. "If only I'd been here," she said when he finished. "If only I'd had a chance to talk to her, too, to ask questions."

"But you will." He took her hand. He had promised, he said, to contact Mrs. Swann in the next week. Meanwhile he would show her the poems.

"She left them all?"

"All of them."

He reminded her, teasing a little, how she had once tried to persuade the owner of a local gravel pit to become a patron of the Peregrine Press by telling him they only published work that was mysterious and accessible at the same time. "You've never seen anything quite like these poems," he told her now.

"Wait till I make coffee," Hildë said. She loved surprises and loved even more to delay them, letting her anticipation rise and sharpen. It was an old game of theirs, a sexual game too, this greedy stretching out of pleasure.

Cruzzi, euphoric, feeling years younger than his true age, carried the coffee tray into the living-room. The smooth wood tray, the white cups, the small ovalness of the spoons—all these objects appeared that evening to be ringed with light. What he balanced so carefully in his arms, but with such ease, seemed suddenly to be the gathered entity of his life. Outside a storm blew, a blizzard of hard-driven pellets, but here was Hildë, his own Hildë, kneeling at the hearth, poking the fire back to life, reaching now for the little Swiss bellows they kept on a hook next to the fireplace. Her skill with fish, her skill with fires, the generous sorcery of her flashing elbows—what a void his life would have been without her. He could not even imagine it. She ought to be thanked, plied with gifts, as though anything would quite suffice.

He would make a presentation of the new poems. Benefice of the afternoon storm. Mary Swann's bag of poems. Providence from an accidental universe—from Nadeau Township, less than thirty miles away.

This thought, blindingly welcome, immediately blurred with another, the fact that he was staring at Hildë's round back and thinking, a little wildly, that she must be kneeling on the paper bag. Then she stood up, and he saw it wasn't there.

The room seemed to darken, and at first he thought he might faint, something he had never done in his life. His eyes closed, and what crashed in front of him was a boulder of depthless black. It had the weight of nausea. Hildë told him later that he cried out, "No!"

He *knew*, he was *sure* at that moment that Hildë had put the bag into the flames. It was this certainty closing over his head that sent him swirling into darkness.

For Hildë that terrible, involuntary "No!" meant only an arm thrown up in disbelief.

For Cruzzi, though he never came close to admitting it, not even to himself, it was a wail of denial. Because the darkness, or whatever it was that engulfed him, had dissolved for the briefest of moments, and what he glimpsed was the whole of his happiness revealed in a grotesque negative image. He was a man weakened by age and standing in a remote corner of the world, a man with a sore throat, a little drunk, and before him, facing him, was a thickish person without beauty. Who was she, this clumsy, clown-faced woman, so careless, so full of guilt and ignorance? He addressed her coldly as though she were a stranger. "There was a bag there," he said. "A paper bag."

Her mouth opened; puzzlement drifted across the opaque face. Then recognition. His beautiful Hildë, smiling and stepping toward him. "Oh, that," she said. "I put it in the kitchen."

Air and lightness returned. Lightness mixed with love. He lurched his way to the kitchen, unsteady on his feet, hideously giddy with something sour rising in his throat. His body seemed to drag behind him, an elderly man's deceived body that had been shaken and made breathless.

He found the bag on the kitchen table, gaping wide. Inside were the fishbones from their dinner, the ooze of fish innards, the wet flashing scales of fish skin, fish heads raggedly cut, fish tails, all the detritus of appetite, startlingly fresh an hour ago and already turned to a mass of rot.

Under the fish remains, under the wet heaviness of fish slime, were the soaked remains of Mary Swann's poems.

"Christ, Christ, Christ." He was moaning, lifting the stinking mess from the bag, hurling it in handfuls onto the floor. Bones dropped and shattered. Fish eyes glittered from the floor tiles. He was choking back tears. "Oh, Christ."

Hildë, who had followed him into the kitchen, watched this scene of madness. She saw a section of fish vertebrae, delicately formed, fly through the air and strike the wall. Then she saw her husband pulling pieces of soaked paper from the bottom of the bag, pulling them apart and gazing at them with sorrow.

She went to him and put her comforting arms around him.

It was a mistake, though not one she could have foreseen. He threw her off violently with the whole force of his body, and an arm reached out, his arm, striking her at the side of her neck. They both knew it was a blow delivered without restraint. It sent her falling to the floor, slipping on the fish guts, out of control, banging her jaw on the edge of the table as she went down.

The sight of her body on the floor brought Cruzzi back to himself. In an instant he was down beside her, cradling her head on his chest. A bubble of blood seeped from her chin, and he cupped it in his hands. "Forgive me," he said over and over, stroking her hair. The smell of fish rot deepened his sorrow immeasurably. In his arms Hildë was trembling and gasping for breath.

His first thought was a selfish one: he would not be able to live without her forgiveness.

He confessed to her his blindness and madness. He had not, he said, now firmly in the grasp of reason, struck out at *her*. He had struck at some fearful conclusion. Too much had happened in one day, too wide a swing of feeling to be accommodated.

As he spoke he realized this was true. Illness and fever and a secondary fever of happiness, and then the astonishing fact of Mary Swann's visit, the violent improbability of her arrival, the amazing offering of her paper bag. Then shock, followed too quickly by relief, then the sight of the ruined poems. He was not a young man. Something had come unbalanced. Something had snapped.

He knew that phrase—*something snapped*. He heard it every day; he deplored it. It was cheaply, commonly used, even in his own newspaper, in the reporting of crimes of passion. Something snapped. Someone was pushed over the edge. Temporary insanity.

He had never completely understood what constituted a crime of passion.

The bleeding at the edge of Hildë's jaw stopped. It was only a small cut, but he washed it carefully with a clean cloth and insisted on applying an antiseptic. She lifted her hand and, with her fingertips, attempted to steady his. He could not stop begging her forgiveness.

Hildë was never a woman who cried easily—her tears are collector's items, Cruzzi once said—but that night her sobbing seemed unstoppable. She was blind with tears. He was sure this meant she would never forgive him.

But of course she forgave him. She forgave him at once. It was only shock, she said, that brought the tears. An hour later they sat drinking brandy in the living-room, their shoulders touching. She had stopped crying, but she was still shaking.

Mary Swann wrote her poems with a Parker 51 pen, a gift, it was said, from her husband "in happier days." And she used a kind of ink very popular in those days, called "washable blue." When a drop of water touched a word written in washable blue, the result was a pale swimmy smudge, subtly shaded, like a miniature pond floating on a white field. Two or three such smudges and a written page became opaque and indecipherable, like a Japanese water-colour.

With great care, with tenderness, Cruzzi and his wife Hildë removed Mary Swann's drenched poems from the bottom of the paper bag. They by now had exchanged their brandy for coffee, planning to stay up all night if necessary.

First they used paper towelling torn into strips to blot up as much excess water as they could. Some of the little pieces of paper were so wet it was necessary to hold them at the edges to keep them from breaking apart. Some of them Hildë separated with the help of tweezers and a spatula. Then she and Cruzzi arranged the poems flat on the dining table, which they first covered with bath towels. When the table was full, they set up a card table beside it for the overflow. To speed the drying, Cruzzi brought in from the garage a portable electric heater.

At least half the poems had escaped serious damage, and these they worked on first, Cruzzi reading them aloud while Hildë transcribed them in her round, ready handwriting. At one point she raised her head and said, "I don't suppose there's any chance she has copies at home." It was a statement rather than a question. Neither believed that a woman like Mary Swann would have made copies. Her innocence and inexperience ruled against it.

A surprising number of poems became legible as they dried. From the puddles of blue ink, words could be glimpsed, then guessed at. If one or two letters swam into incomprehension, the rest followed. Hildë was quick to pick up Mary Swann's quirky syntax, and when she made guesses, they seemed to Cruzzi's ear laden with logic.

By midnight they had transcribed more than fifty of the poems. Cautious at first, they grew bolder, and as they worked they felt themselves supported by the knowledge that they would be able to check the manuscript with Mrs. Swann who would surely remember what most of the obliterated words had been. Already they were referring to Hildë's transcribed notes, and not the drying, curling poems on the table, as "the manuscript."

The seriously damaged poems worried them more. Lakes of blue ink flowed between lines, blotting out entire phrases, and they wondered about Mary Swann's ability to recall whole passages. Would she be able to reconstruct them line by line? They puzzled and conferred over every blot, then guessed, then invented. The late hour, the river of black coffee, and the intense dry heat in the room bestowed a kind of reckless permission. At one point, Hildë, supplying missing lines and even the greater part of a missing stanza, said she could feel what the inside of Mary Swann's head must look like. She seemed to be inhabiting, she said, another woman's body.

The manuscript grew slowly. It helped that Mary Swann was a rhyming poet—the guessing was less chancy. It helped, too, to understand that she used in most of her poems the kind of rocking, responsive rhythm borrowed from low-church hymns. Her vocabulary was domestic, hence knowable, and though she used it daringly, it was limited.

The last poem, and the most severely damaged, began: "Blood pronounces my name." Or was it "Blood renounces my name"? The second line could be read in either of two ways: "Brightens the day with shame," or "Blisters the day with shame." They decided on *blisters*. The third line, "Spends what little I own" might just as easily be transcribed, "Bends what little I own," but they wrote *Spends* because—though they didn't say so—they liked it better.

By now—it was morning— a curious conspiracy had overtaken them. Guilt, or perhaps a wish to make amends, convinced them that they owed Mrs. Swann an interpretation that would reinforce her strengths as a poet. They wanted to offer her help and protection, what she seemed never to have had. Both of them, Cruzzi from his instinct for tinkering and Hildë from a vestigial talent never abused, made their alterations with, it seemed to them, a single hand.

It was eight-thirty. The weak winter sun was beginning to show at the window.

Mary Swann, though they would not know for several days, was already dead. Her husband shot her in the head at close range, probably in the early evening shortly after she returned home. He pounded her face with a hammer, dismembered her body, crudely, with an axe, and hid the bloodied parts in a silo. It was one of the most brutal murders ever reported in the area, the kind of murder that makes people buy newspapers, read hungrily, and ask each other what kind of monster would do such a thing. It was the kind of murder that prompts other people to shrug their shoulders, raise their eyebrows, to say that we are all prey to savagery and are tempted often in our lives to wreak violence on others. Why this should happen is a mystery. "Something snaps" is what people usually say by way of explanation.

Frederic Cruzzi: The House in which He Has Lived for the Greater Part of His Life

You sometimes see, driving through small North American cities, those large symmetrical stone houses built years ago. The roofs are almost always in good repair, with chimneys that sit authoritatively; window boxes are painted black or white and in summer are filled with brightly coloured flowers; everything speaks of family and peace and security; and, oh, you think, they knew how to build houses back in those wonderful days! Such a house is Frederic Cruzzi's on Byron Road in Kingston, Ontario. Through those tranced decades, the forties, the fifties, the sixties, the seventies, each rich in weather and economic outlook and modes of music and dress—through all those years Cruzzi and his wife occupied the rooms of this house and persisted in their lives.

It is best if we enter through the wide front door, for this is the way Cruzzi's many friends come and go, and this is also the way the burglar entered on Christmas Eve when Cruzzi, happily unaware, was dining across the street with his good friends Dennis and Caroline Cooper-Beckman and their three children. What an agreeable evening! And what a quaint assembly they formed, they a modern agnostic family, and he, old and widowed, sitting in noisy scented air at a table brilliant with poinsettias and spilled milk, amid platters of sliced turkey and vegetables and the solid cone of a Christmas pudding, then fruit, then chocolates, then the snapping frizzle of Christmas crackers, a final brandy, a morsel of peppermint sucked to nothingness in his old teeth, then home, a little tottery but filled with the resolve to put himself at risk one more time. He entered the house, climbed the stairs, went directly to bed (still happily unaware) and dreamed of Pauline Ouilette, her fragrant flesh, her floury neck and arms.

Outside, the snow had been falling steadily all evening and with such fine driving flakes that the handsome porch was completely covered, even the intricate crevices of the stone balusters that enclose the porch. (*Portico* is the term sometimes used for this architectural feature, with its polite proportions and civilized air of welcome.) The main door of the house is solid and graceful, and the knocker is the kind that fits the hand and kindles hope. Above the brass housing of the door lock, there are several scratches and a deep gouge; these were made by the Christmas Eve burglar.

A clumsy entry, or so a Kingston police constable judged later. Clearly the work of a bungling amateur, yet he succeeded. He would have been assisted in his work by the carriage lamp next to the door, the type of lamp referred to by some area residents as a welcome light and by others, of different disposition, as a safety light. It had been the habit of Cruzzi and Hildë to turn this lamp on during the long evenings in order to greet friends and strangers and to prevent accidents on the slippery stone steps.

Inside the front door is a vestibule, that practical Victorian invention, the means by which the weather of the house is separated from the true weather outside. Beyond the vestibule is the large, high-ceilinged hall, full of the gleam of dark wood and containing a bench where one can sit while pulling on overshoes, a hall-tree of whimsical design, and a very beautiful maple dresser, the drawers of which had been left open by the burglar—though Cruzzi, on his way to bed that night, failed to take note of this fact.

The design of the Byron Road house, like many in the area, is generous, but dictated by strict symmetry, and thus the living-room, leading to the left off the hall, precisely corresponds in size and shape to the dining-room, which leads from the right. In the daytime these two rooms are filled with light, that most precious element in a cold climate. The wide curtainless windows stretch from the ceiling to the floor. Their sills are made of stone, delicately bevelled, and the same stone has been used for the hearth and mantel of the very fine classical living-room fireplace. It was here, in front of the fireplace, that Cruzzi observed the gap-toothed Mary Swann, how she moved her hands to her earlobes, and thought to himself that he had never seen a more seductive gesture. In this room, too, Frederic Cruzzi and his wife, Hildë, spent uncounted hours, hours that, if dissected, would contain billions of separate images, so many in fact that if one or two were perverse or aberrant, it would not really be surprising. The room is filled with modest treasures, a curious set of andirons on charming, ugly feet, four excellent water-colours, a superb oil by the primitive painter Marcus Hovingstadt, two very old brass candlesticks, an eighteenth-century clock with wooden works, and a valuable collection of early jazz records—all these things were mercifully left undisturbed by the Christmas Eve burglar.

The walls of the dining-room are white. The floor is polished hard-wood. Overhead a lamp of tinted glass, made by a local craftswoman, sends a soft circle of light down onto the broad oval table. So many, many meals have been eaten here. So many conversations, so much clamour of language. Upraised hands have bridged the spaces between words and sent shadows up the walls. There have been loud debates and cherishing looks, the ceremonial cutting of cheeses and cakes, celebrations and rituals, satisfaction and satiety. Here at this table more than fifty books published by the Peregrine Press were assembled, and here in that distant December of 1965 Cruzzi and his wife, Hildë, worked through the night in an attempt to rescue Mary Swann's ruined poems, and here, with rare, unsquandered creativity, Hildë made her small emendations. The dining-room con-tains silver from France, porcelain from Germany and a set of rare old chairs from Quebec, but none of these things attracted the atten-tion of the Christmas Eve intruder.

At the back of the house symmetry abruptly breaks down. There is an oddly shaped sunroom full of plants, comfortable chairs, and a piano. The kitchen is a hodgepodge, the various parts worn and mismatched, though the overall effect is one of harmony. Across uneven kitchen tiles and scattered fish bones, Cruzzi had looked at Hildë and watched the best part of himself fissure. Here the atoms of his wife's face had grown smaller and smaller, retreating from him in a width of confusion. The kitchen contains the usual elec-trical appliances, a blender, a toaster, and so on, but nothing appar-ently that tempted the uninvited visitor on Christmas Eve.

He—the unbidden guest—did, however, mount the broad stair-case, without a doubt running his fingers up the silky bannister and pausing in the dim upstairs hall. It was in this hall, between bathroom and bedroom, that Hildë suffered the stroke that killed her, a thunderbolt many times the force of the tiny haemorrhage that knocked Cruzzi off balance for a few minutes last summer, and that he at first thought was nothing but a touch of sunstroke.

Four doors open from the upstairs hall. One, of course, leads to a bathroom, but there is little in a bathroom, even a hundred-year-old bathroom, to excite the interest of a prowler.

A second door leads to the bedroom that Frederic and Hildë Cruzzi shared for so many years. What would catch a thieving eye in such a bedroom? Not the excellent new stainless-steel reading lamp, just two years old, not the wool-filled comforter from Austria, not the marble-topped bureau or the plants by the window or the pine-framed mirror, which can be tipped back and forth, or the comfortable wicker chair in the corner. The scenes that have taken place in this room are unguessable. Memory, that folded book, alters and distorts our most intimate settings so that passion, forgiveness, and the currency of small daily bargains are largely stolen from us—which may be just as well.

The very large room running across the front of the house is where Frederic and Hildë Cruzzi kept their books. (Because this room, forty years ago, was painted a brilliant yellow, it has always been known as the "Gold Room.") There are some chairs here and a desk that holds an old typewriter, but this room is mainly a resting place for books. They line the four walls and reach from floor to ceiling. Other rooms in the house contain odd shelves of books, but Cruzzi's most cherished books are kept here. They number in the thousands, and are arranged on the shelves according to language, then subject or author. Any reasonably intelligent adult entering this room could, in a matter of minutes, find what he or she was looking for. If, for example, a person were looking for one of the various editions published by the Peregrine Press between the years 1957 and 1977, it could be spotted easily by the logo—a set of blue wings—on the narrow grey spine. The four copies of Mary Swann's book, *Swann's Songs*, published in 1966, were in the middle of the Peregrine shelf, since their publication occurred about halfway through the life of the press. All four of these books were stolen by the Christmas Eve burglar, and the books on either side pushed together, presumably to make the gap less noticeable.

In the ordinary course of events it might have been weeks or months before Cruzzi noticed the missing books, but, in fact, he was alerted to the theft on Christmas Day. He wakened late after the revels of the night before, made himself coffee, which he drank sitting on a kitchen chair and listening to the mutters and rumbles of the house. After a while he went upstairs and was about to take up a volume of his beloved Rashid when he remembered that he had as yet done nothing to prepare for the little talk he had promised to present at the Swann symposium, now just ten days away.

He had, however, given it some thought. It was his intention to keep his remarks simple and tuned to a tolerant orthodoxy, to discuss the manner in which he had met Mary Swann, and the decision, not an easy one, of the Peregrine Press to go ahead with publication after her death. He planned also to comment, savouring the irony of it, on how little stir the book had originally caused. The notoriety of the Swann murder had been brief and confined to the immediate region. The poems in *Swann's Songs* were passed over by most reviewers as simple, workmanlike curiosities, and the 250 copies that the press printed sold poorly, even in Nadeau Township. In the end he and Hildë gave most of them away, keeping just four copies for themselves. It was these four copies that were missing.

Gazing at the shelf, Cruzzi felt pierced with the fact of his old age, his helplessness, and the knowledge that a long-delayed act of reprisal had taken place. It was unbearable; some menacing reversal had occurred, leaving him with nothing but his old fraudulent skin hanging loose on his bones. He felt his vision blur as he made his way to the little back bedroom that Hildë had once used as the Peregrine office. He opened the door. There was nothing in the room but a table, two chairs, and a rather large file cabinet. The drawers of the cabinet were open and the contents were scattered over the whole of the room.

It took him the rest of the day to put things back in order. As he sorted through twenty years of manuscripts and correspondence, he listened to Handel's *Messiah* on the radio and felt a feeble tide of balance reassert itself.

Occasionally he hummed along with the music, and the sound of his voice, creaky and out of tune, kept bewilderment at bay. The music soared and plunged and seemed to coat the little room with luminous, concurrent waves of colour. By late afternoon he was finished. Everything was in place, with only the file on Mary Swann missing. He supposed he should be grateful, but instead found his face confused by tears.

The Swann Symposium

DIRECTOR'S NOTE: *The Swann Symposium* is a film lasting approximately 120 minutes. The main characters, Sarah Maloney, Morton Jimroy, Rose Hindmarch, and Frederic Cruzzi, are fictional creations, as is the tragic Mary Swann, *poète naïve*, of rural Ontario. The film may be described (for distribution purposes) as a thriller. A subtext focuses on the more subtle thefts and acts of cannibalism that tempt and mystify the main characters. The director hopes to remain unobtrusive throughout, allowing dialogue and visual effects (and not private passions) to carry the weight of the narrative.

Fade in: Full screen photograph, black and white, grainy, blurred, of MARY SWANN, a farm wife, standing on the ramshackle porch of her rural house. She is wearing a house dress and bib apron; her lean face clearly indicates premature aging; her eyes are shut against the sun. TITLES roll across the photograph. SOUND: a sprightly (faintly Scottish) organ tune that gradually grows heavier as the CAMERA concentrates on Mary's face.

Dissolve to: Exterior shot, main street of Nadeau, Ontario. Early morning, winter, still dark.

The darkness gradually yields up a hint of light. Snow is falling. The main street of Nadeau becomes faintly visible. One or two cars pass, then a pick-up truck; their headlights glow yellow through the swirled snow. A Greyhound bus comes into view, then pulls to a stop at the side of the road. The CAMERA picks up a sign, NADEAU.

A woman steps from the shadows and boards the bus. She is small, middle-aged, somewhat awkward, and hesitant in the manner of someone who has recently been ill. This is ROSE HINDMARCH. She wears a too-large padded blue coat with an artificial fur collar and a wool muffler pulled loosely over her plastic headscarf.

CLOSE SHOT of driver's face. He is about thirty, with a fresh, alert face. Seeing Rose, his eyes widen.

DRIVER: Hiya, Rose. Hey you're up early, aren't ya? You off to Kingston?

He stands up, takes her suitcase and wedges it behind his seat. Rose opens her purse and takes out a five-dollar bill. The bus is nearly empty, with three or four shadowy figures dozing at the back.

ROSE (cheerful, newsy): I'm getting the ten o'clock train. For Toronto, as a matter of fact.
DRIVER (making change): You'll be in plenty of time. You'll be sitting around the station waiting. Couple hours anyways.

Rose, seating herself in one of the front seats, carefully removes her muffler and her plastic scarf and pats at her hairdo. The bus starts up slowly.

ROSE: Well, I didn't want to . . . you know, take a chance. And you never know this time of year—
DRIVER: Right you are, Rose. Don't blame you one little bit.
ROSE (still fussing with her hair): Wouldn't you just know we'd get snow today? I watched the forecast last night.
DRIVER: Yeah?
ROSE: Snow, he said. Of all days, just when—
DRIVER (shifting gears to climb a hill): S'posed to get six inches.
ROSE: —and I said to myself, just my luck, the roads closed and just when I have to get my train to Toronto for—

CAMERA pans open highway and fields. Snow is blowing across the road, but houses and barns can be glimpsed in outline. MUSIC, an alto clarinet, makes a jaunty counterpoint to the rather laconic conversation.

DRIVER: Jeez, yeah, the train's your best bet this time of the year. I mean, they tell ya six inches, but it looks to me like—
ROSE (chattily): I'd of worn my good coat, but with this snow, well, you can't wear a suede coat in weather like this. Oh, it's warm enough, that's not the trouble, but suede can't take it, getting wet.

Rose's natural garrulousness is augmented by the excitement of the journey to Toronto, and she sits on the seat tensely, jerking off her gloves and examining her nails.

DRIVER: So! You're having yourself a trip to Toronto, eh, Rose?

ROSE (still fussing): Just four days, that's all I can spare, what with having to shut the library down, and—

DRIVER: Fuck! (He swerves hard, brakes, barely missing a car.) Where the . . . did he come from? (Relaxing): 'Scuse me, Rose, but that bugger came out of that side road without even—

ROSE (staring dreamily out of the window, not hearing): You know, I do believe it's letting up. The snow. Maybe I should have— (She fingers her coat, questioningly, regretfully.)

The bus stops and a woman with a baby gets on. She greets Rose and the driver and makes her way to the back of the bus.

DRIVER (starting up again, adjusting the mirror): So I suppose you're going to hit the January sales, eh Rose? Go on a spending spree. (His tone is teasing; Rose is by nature a woman who is subject to good-natured kidding.)

ROSE (dreamily): Pardon? Sorry, Roy, you were saying?

DRIVER (louder, as though addressing a deaf person): Shopping spree, I said. You going on a spree?

ROSE (delighted at this show of interest): It's for a symposium. (She loves this word.) In Toronto.

DRIVER (self-mocking): A who?

ROSE: A symposium. (Apologetic now): It's sort of a meeting.

DRIVER (concentrating on road): Yeah?

ROSE: You know, people talking and discussing and so on. It's about—

DRIVER: Makes a change, I guess.

ROSE: It's about Mary Swann. She came from Nadeau, you know. A poetess. You probably never heard of her, but she's—

DRIVER (scratching an ear): She the one whose old man shot her up and stuffed her in the silo? Way back when?

ROSE (almost proudly): That's the one.

DRIVER: Whaddaya know!

ROSE: She's got real famous now. Not because of . . . that, but on account of her poems, her book of poems that was published.

Oh, people'll be coming from all over, the States, everywhere. She's got quite a reputation now. She's real well thought of, people writing books about her and—

DRIVER: Why'd he do it, her husband I mean. Do her in?

ROSE (ignoring the question): It's going to be at the Harbourview. The Harbourview Hotel, that's where the meetings are and that's—

DRIVER: The Harbourview, eh? (He negotiates a curve.) Was there another guy or what? I think I heard my dad saying once . . . anyways, I can't remember the details, but—

ROSE: How *is* your dad, Roy? Better? (Rose knows everyone).

CAMERA pans countryside, buried in snow. There are a few billboards indicating that the bus is approaching Kingston. SOUND of clarinet, cooler now.

DRIVER: Not bad. He's a lot better, in fact. You can't keep the old man down.

ROSE: Your mom? She taking it pretty well?

DRIVER: Oh yeah, you know Mom.

ROSE (regarding snow): Look at that, will you. Definitely letting up. I wish now— (She looks down at her coat mournfully.)

DRIVER: So whaddaya think of all this hijacking jazz, Rose? Real mess over there, people getting roughed up—

ROSE: Terrible. (A long pause.) Terrible. (She stares dreamily out the window as the bus enters town.) Terrible. (Dissolve.)

Fade to: Interior, the train station. Daytime.

Clearly this is the train station of a small city. There is a rather old-fashioned air about it: brown wooden benches, drab posters, and windows through which can be seen the double train tracks, this morning interfilled with snow. Rose, her muffler now neatly tucked into the neck of her coat, her plastic head scarf removed, is standing nervously and looking through the window to the platform. She looks at the station clock, which says 9:50, then at her wristwatch. She gazes about her. A few people come and go carrying luggage. She opens her purse, takes out a compact and looks at herself, pats her hair; she is obviously waiting for someone. She checks her watch once more, and then a voice takes her by surprise.

CRUZZI: Miss Hindmarch? (FREDERIC CRUZZI is a tall, thin, elderly man, wearing a long dark overcoat and a fur hat, and carrying a cane, which he clearly needs.)

ROSE (startled): You're . . . are you—?

CRUZZI (bowing very slightly): Frederic Cruzzi. How do you do?

ROSE (nervously): How do *you* do? (Her handbag slips to the floor; they both bend to retrieve it.) Thank you, but . . . oh dear, I've got such a handful. And that's all you have? (She gestures at Cruzzi's small carry-on.)

CRUZZI (smiling): A light traveller.

ROSE (rattled): I was . . . was starting to think, maybe you'd changed your mind, and, well, when I saw it was 9:50 on the station clock, I thought maybe you'd decided not to . . . meet me, the way we arranged like. (Her words are drowned by the sound of the train entering the station.)

CRUZZI: Shall we? (He offers his arm, but Rose, juggling her handbag, suitcase, and shopping tote, doesn't have a free arm. She attempts to rearrange things. Cruzzi picks up her suitcase.)

ROSE (alarmed): No! You mustn't. It's very, very heavy. No matter how I try I always end up with too much. And shoes weigh such a lot, and then there's my hair dryer and, well, what I need, I was saying to a friend of mine, what I need is one of those backpacks (laughs) like the kids wear nowadays.

CRUZZI (listening patiently, amused and polite): Ready?

They exit, arm in arm. MUSIC swells, a Scottish air, and the CAMERA follows them through the station window as they walk slowly, almost a matrimonial march, to the waiting train. Dissolve.

Fade to: Interior, SARAH MALONEY's bedroom, Chicago. It is early morning.

A very small bedroom is revealed in half-darkness, a room nearly overwhelmed by a king-size waterbed. The walls and furniture are white. There are books on shelves, plants, one piece of white sculpture. From under a thick white blanket come murmurs and grunts and sighs of sensual pleasure. They are suddenly interrupted by an alarm clock ringing musically.

SARAH (reaching out and shutting off alarm): Morning!

She kisses Stephen's bare shoulder, yawns, slips from the bed, stretches, and tiptoes into the adjoining bathroom. When she returns, she is fresh from a shower, a towel around her body, her long hair wet. In the half-light she dresses: underwear, a suit in a subtle shade of dusty pink, a soft blouse in a lighter shade, shoes. As she dresses she steals smiling looks at her watch and at Stephen, who is observing her from the bed. Her gestures are quick, hurried, absent-minded, though she touches her clothes, especially the silk blouse, with loving attention. She pulls a brush through her wet hair without glancing in the mirror. She applies no makeup. She opens a briefcase, checks its contents, and snaps it shut. For a moment she stands, holding the clasp, and goes through a mental checklist, then sets the briefcase by the bedroom door, puts on a heavy coat of white fleece, hoists up her shoulder bag, and approaches the bed. She sits down beside Stephen and opens her arms.

SARAH: Well?
STEPHEN (sitting up; he is a large, handsome shaggy man; he is wearing no clothes): You want some coffee? I could—
SARAH: I'll get some at the airport. (She starts to rise, but he pulls her down in an embrace more comradely than sexual; for a moment they rock back and forth; still embracing, she checks her watch, and this makes Stephen smile.)
STEPHEN: Time?
SARAH: Time.
STEPHEN: Good luck. With your speech.
SARAH (lazily): Not a speech, a paper.
STEPHEN: Good luck, anyway.
SARAH (pulling away): I'd better go. The cab should be here. You be shiftless and go back to sleep.
STEPHEN: It's still night! (He hoists himself out of bed, reaching for the white wool blanket, which he wraps around him Indian style; he puts an arm around her, and together they go down

a miniature staircase, so narrow they bump against the walls as they descend.) This is a crazy hour. You live a crazy life, you know.

Stephen opens the door to a city street; there is no front yard and it is only a few feet to the curb where a taxi waits, its light gleaming in the darkness.

STEPHEN: So long. (He hugs her.)

SARAH (peering at him critically): For a minute there I thought you were going to say "take care." Or "be good." (She is scornful of such phrases.)

STEPHEN: How about . . . (miming) . . . *ciao?*

SARAH (pulling away as she hears the taxi toot): All of a sudden I hate to go.

STEPHEN: Toronto in January. (He phrases this so that it sounds both a question and a declaration.)

SARAH: Not just that. I feel spooked for some reason.

STEPHEN: Four days. (He gives a clownish shrug.)

SARAH (stepping across the snowy sidewalk and getting into the cab): O'Hare. (She rolls down the window and looks at Stephen, who is shivering in the doorway, wrapped in his blanket. She waves slowly; he waves back. The taxi pulls away.)

TAXI DRIVER: Jesus, it's cold. (Good naturedly): Whyn'cha say goodbye to your boyfriend inside?

SARAH (with music-hall rhythm): That's not my boyfriend, that's my husband.

They both laugh. The cab proceeds slowly down the street. Sarah, still waving, rolls up the window. SOUND: a cheerful, piping woodwind.

SARAH (CAMERA close-up on her face): Lord! (Dissolve.)

Fade to: Interior, San Francisco Airport. Early morning.

MORTON JIMROY, a middle-aged man in a cheap light-coloured cotton suit, is waiting his turn in an immigration line. SOUND: the usual hubbub of a busy airport underlain by MUSIC: something symphonic and emotional.

LOUDSPEAKER: Flight 492 for Toronto now boarding. Flight 492 boarding now at Gate 77.

IMMIGRATION OFFICER (bored): How long do you intend to be in Canada, Mr. Jimroy?

JIMROY (testily): Four days. And I happen to be a Canadian citizen, and I am not obliged to stand—

IMMIGRATION OFFICER (mechanically): Business or pleasure, Mr. Jimroy?

JIMROY (annoyed; he is a man who takes all questions seriously): Business. Pleasure. Both. (He pauses; the immigration officer eyes him sharply.) A meeting. A symposium, to be precise. I will be attending a—

IMMIGRATION OFFICER: Nature of meeting? (He holds a rubber stamp in his hand.)

JIMROY: I resent this interrogation. As a Canadian citizen I am not required—

IMMIGRATION OFFICER: Meeting you say? Nature of which is? (He waves the stamp in the air.)

JIMROY (shrugging): Scholarly. Literary. (As though addressing an idiot): Poetry, if you must know. You know, as in "Jack and Jill went up the hill—"

IMMIGRATION OFFICER: Okay, okay. (He stamps the paper and hands it to Jimroy.) Next.

JIMROY (bitterly): Thank you. (CAMERA follows him as he disappears into the crowd. Dissolve.)

SOUND: noise of the airport crowd blends with the rushing sound of the train.

Fade to: Interior of the train. Daytime.

CAMERA focuses on Cruzzi and Rose who sit facing each other on the train. They are drinking coffee out of plastic cups, stirring it with plastic spoons, and behind them flash the snowy, rounded hills of eastern Ontario. The sky is grey and wintry, but the sun struggles through so that the top of the scene is pink with light. The ongoing rumble of the train blends gradually with the sound of Rose's voice.

ROSE: . . . well, you must of thought I was dippy, I mean, writing you a letter and suggesting we, you know, go to Toronto *together*, but, well, it's one thing to travel alone and another, well, I was saying to a friend of mine, *another* thing to have someone to chat with on the way, and, well, it was really Professor Lang . . . I suppose you know Professor Lang—

Cruzzi grunts and nods.

ROSE: Well, Professor Lang was in Nadeau, must of been three, four years back, you lose track of time, don't you, one year sort of blends in with the next one, doesn't it? And anyway, along he came one day, middle of the week I think it was . . . yes, because I remember I was sitting in the library surrounded by cataloguing. Even in a little library like our town has, you always seem to be cataloguing. It's suprising how much work, every time a new book comes in, you have to do. Of course it's different in the bigger towns what with computers and all, but I say it'll be a major miracle (laughs) if Nadeau ever gets a computer, not that I'm overly fond of mechanical things myself, but anyway, it's not very likely, financial restraint and what have you.

CAMERA close-up of Cruzzi's face; he is nodding, struggling to stay awake, yet something peaceful in his face shows that he finds the garrulous Rose more comforting than irritating. Rose, on her part, is blithely unaware of his inattention.

ROSE: . . . well, anyway, Professor Lang came along, just sort of dropped in, and he said he wanted to get a . . . feel . . . for where Mary Swann lived, her roots and all. You know what he said? He said we should have a sign at the edge of town, you know, like "Nadeau, Ontario, Home of Mary Swann, Distinguished Poet," and I said, Heavens, I didn't know she was *that* famous, and he said, Well, people were starting to take notice of her and in a few years . . . and I said lots of people right in this town maybe remember Mrs. Swann, at least the older ones, but hardly a one of them's ever read her book. Of course there's a copy in the library, at least there was up till recently, we're always losing books, people just walk off with them, kids! A real problem for librarians, the same everywhere I guess . . . Well, Professor Lang was so interested, had all kinds of questions and wanted to look around town real good, even drove out to see the old house where Mrs. Swann used to live before . . . well, you know . . . before! He even went out to the cemetery to see where she was buried, imagine, just a bitty little stone, and well, as I said, this was a few years back, she's a lot better known now, more famous, that is, and Professor Lang, I guess it was his idea, having a symposium about her, and you could of knocked me over with a feather when I got an invitation to come. I mean (laughs) well, this sounds crazy, but I've never been, well, to a symposium, I'm just a librarian, part-time. *And* town clerk, and I never . . . does that sound crazy to you? Me, never been to a symposium?

CRUZZI (jerking away and blinking once or twice, looks kindly at Rose and speaks gently): No, Miss Hindmarch, not crazy at all.

ROSE (pleased and relieved): Really?

CRUZZI: Not in the least.

ROSE: Whew! Well, I'm glad to hear that. Anyway, I got this letter from Professor Lang, the beginning of December, no, maybe it was the last week in November, I remember it was a Monday, blue Monday, ha, it always cheers me up, getting some mail on a Monday, I guess everyone feels that way, and, well, he said that Mr. Frederic Cruzzi, *you*, were planning to go to the symposium too, and you were going to give a talk and all, after all you were the one that published Mrs. Swann's book, it makes sense you'd be going, and he thought maybe I could give you a lift, but as I explained in my letter, I don't drive a car, just never learned, though a friend of mine, Daisy Hart her name is, says five lessons and I'd pass the test just like that, but I've never . . . anyway, I thought, it just struck me (laughs) that we could, you know, on the train, we could— (She falters at last.)

CRUZZI (waking up): . . . keep each other company.

ROSE (leaping in): Exactly, exactly. And then he also wrote to ask me if I'd mind bringing along the photograph of Mrs. Swann, which, well, you know it's the only one there is now. (She grimaces.) And he wanted—

CRUZZI (wide awake and interested): Ah, you have a photograph of Mrs. Swann?

ROSE: The only one! So they say, anyway. We keep it in the little museum we have in the old high school, just local history and so on, but . . . would you like to see it, Mr. Cruzzi? The picture?

CRUZZI: With pleasure.

ROSE: I'll just— (She stands and reaches for her overhead suitcase.) I've got it right here, I'll just— (She struggles, then takes off her shoes and stands on the seat; Cruzzi makes an attempt to help her, but she holds up a restraining hand.) Oh, no, Mr. Cruzzi, you mustn't strain . . . I'll just—

CRUZZI: If it's too much trouble, don't—

Rose stands on her toes in stocking feet to open her case. She fishes blindly for the photo.

ROSE: I put it in at the last minute, just slipped it in, didn't want the glass to break. (She continues to struggle, sweating slightly.) Not that it's the best likeness, blurred you know, just an old snapshot someone went and stuck in a frame. I'm sure— (She struggles, pulling the suitcase down; it opens, spilling clothes, a toilet case, a nightgown and, to her shame, a shower of underwear.) Oh! (Embarrassed, she gathers up the clothes and stuffs them back.) Oh, what a mess, oh, everything happens to—

CRUZZI: Can I help? (He says this doubtfully.)

ROSE (frantically stuffing clothes away): No! (She steals looks at Cruzzi and at the passengers at the far end of the car.) Here! Here it is. (She closes her case, unwinds the photo from its tea-towel wrapping and sits down again, this time beside Cruzzi on the double seat; she is breathing hard. The sun can be seen through the window, shining on the fields and lakes and woods.) Here! There she is. Mary Swann!

CRUZZI (taking the photo and regarding it quizzically, then discerningly, as though it were itself a work of art. He reaches in a breast pocket for spectacles so he may observe her even more closely, then says, with an air of pronouncement): Mrs. Swann.

ROSE (rattling on at full speed): As I say, not a good likeness. The sun's in her eyes, but, well, there she is! (She laughs nervously, still panting a little.)

CRUZZI: Of course I met her only once. My impression was— (he waves a hand) — fragmented.

CAMERA close-up of photo.

ROSE (looking on companionably, relaxed now): I'd say this was taken, well, around the mid-fifties, maybe earlier. She never seemed to age. What I mean is, she always, well, looked like *this*, sort of tired out. And old. Sort of sad and worried. But you know, she had, well, a kind of spirit about her, I guess it came out in her poems, like inside she was . . . like a young woman . . . not so, you know, down in the dumps, not so worn out. You can't tell from the outside what a person's really like, even when a person knows a person real well.

CAMERA side shot catches their two profiles side by side; Cruzzi's eyes are starting to close again; Rose, in a trance, talks on, her eyes straight ahead.

ROSE: It's funny. People always say I was the only one who knew Mrs. Swann, personally, but I didn't, not well. Well, no one really knows anyone *really* well, not the things they're worried about or scared to death of or what they're really thinking, people keep it all locked up like they're too shy or something. I don't know why that should be, do you?

There is no answer from the sleeping Cruzzi; Rose shifts her eyes, takes in his sleeping presence, and continues.

ROSE: Like all fall. (She glances at Cruzzi). With me, ever since, September, well, I've had these . . . health . . . problems and, you know, I kept putting off going to the doctor. Next week I kept saying to myself, and all the time I was, well, getting weaker and weaker, just not myself. "You're not yourself, Rose," people were saying, but I just said, "Who, me? I'm fine, just losing a little weight, that's all," and it . . . it kept getting worse and worse. (Rose steals another look at Cruzzi). You know how it is when you're going about your daily life, how you're always getting *ready* for something. Like, for example, a vacation coming up or Christmas or a bridal shower or something? Well, toward the end of November— (She pauses, looks again at Cruzzi; can she trust him?) I guess I got a bit . . . down, feeling so poorly and all, and one morning I woke up, it was after a real bad night, tossing and turning, and I said to myself—I live alone—I said, "Rose, kiddo, you're not waiting for a single thing, unless" . . . well, I'm not the morbid type, lucky for me, but I really did believe that I was going to, maybe . . . and so this dear old friend of mine took me in hand, insisted I got to a doctor, wouldn't take no. Which I did, and she, the doctor, it was a woman doctor,

said it was only *fibroids*! and all I needed was a simple little opera-
tion, routine, she said, it's a sort of woman thing, next month
they'll be doing it—I won't bother you with all the details, but
the thing is, just when I thought everything, *everything* had
stopped, it all of a sudden . . . just started up again. (She laughs.)
Oh, it was wonderful. I thought, so this is what flying is like,
when we were driving home from the doctor's in my friend's car,
my bones felt . . . so light, like a little kid's bones. I know it
sounds crazy, Mr. Cruzzi, but— (Rose turns her head to face him).
Mr Cruzzi! (Alarmed): Mr. Cruzzi!

For an instant Rose is certain he is dead; she half-rises, peers at
him, passes her hand in front of his eyes, but is reassured by a low
melodious snore. She sits down again beside him, puts back her
head, closes her eyes. CAMERA focuses on her face, on her lips, which
part in a smile, and on her closed eyes. She is still clutching the
photo of Mary Swann on her lap. Fields and small towns are seen
flashing by. SOUND: the rushing of the train fades into sprightly
organ music. Dissolve.

Fade to: Interior of an Air Canada jet. Daytime.
  SOUND: the music merges with the humming motor of an air-
craft. At the end of the aisle a flight attendant is demonstrating
emergency procedures; she is pretty, blonde, and possessed of a dead,
wooden face. Her monologue is indistinct; its rhythms are discern-
ible, but the words blend with the words of one of the male
passengers sitting in an aisle seat next to Jimroy. This man (about
sixty) is rangy in a Lincolnesque way with a thick thatch of white
hair. He wears horn-rimmed glasses, jeans, a neat silk cowboy shirt
with a string tie, and a casual outdoor jacket. His wife, a heavy
woman in a navy pantsuit with glasses on a chain and enormous
diamond earrings, is in the window seat, and Jimroy, squashed
between them and snapping his briefcase open on his lap, has the
look of a trapped, elderly child.

MAN (to Jimroy, speaking loudly): So! You're gettin' right down
  to work, eh?
WOMAN (wearing a headset, beating out music on her knees,
  and smiling loopily at Jimroy and at her husband): Da, da, da
  dee da.

JIMROY: Hmmm. (An affirmative grunt; he shuffles his papers and nods vaguely.)

MAN (clearly anxious to strike up a conversation): I expect you're involved in the world of commerce, right?

JIMROY (considering this for a moment): Yes. (He looks straight ahead, as though steeling himself, then returns to his papers, pencil in hand.)

MAN: I'm retired myself, the wife and myself. (He gestures to the woman, who continues to beat out music and smile.) Only my wife says I'll never *really* retire. (He chuckles.)

JIMROY: Hmmmm. (He writes something rapidly in the margin, not looking up.)

MAN (after a long pause): What kind of business you happen to be in?

JIMROY (again considering): Books.

MAN: Books, eh? You mean like to read?

Jimroy nods crisply and turns a page.

MAN: Interesting. (He pauses.) Books. (There is a longer pause.) Sales? You in sales? You in the book-selling business?

JIMROY (puzzled): Sales?

MAN: Your book business you're in. You sell 'em?

JIMROY: No. (He returns to work, making an elaborate correction on the corner of his paper.)

The man pauses, then folds his arm resolutely, determined to remain silent. But eventually curiosity wins.

MAN: Well . . . what *do* you do with them then?

Jimroy looks up, baffled. The wife is tipping her head back and forth to the music, her whole body bouncing and her earrings catching the light.

MAN (somewhat cross): Your book business you say you're into. What do you do with 'em? (Loudly): Your books.

JIMROY (calmly underlining a phrase in the text): I write them.

MAN (galvanized): Books? You write books?

JIMROY (affixing a note with paperclip, taking his time): Yes.

MAN (grinning): Whaddaya know. (He reaches across Jimroy to his wife and taps her knees.) Honey, this here's a book writer sitting beside you.

WOMAN (loudly): Huh?

MAN (to Jimroy): My wife here's the reader in the family. The books she puts away! (To his wife, who has now removed her headset): Honey, this here's a real author sitting here. Boy, oh boy!

WOMAN: Well, well, you never know who you're going to end up sitting next to. (She floats cheerfully into non sequiturs). You probably think it's pretty weird, us, sitting like this, me at the window like this and my hubby there, in the aisle seat. Well, the honest truth is, I'm not the best flyer in the world. Ron, he takes it in his stride, just like a Greyhound bus, he says, a Greyhound bus that—

MAN (emphatically, an old joke): A Greyhound bus with wings growing out the sides, I tell her.

WOMAN (chuckling): But me, I get queasy, you know? Not scared of crashing, not a bit, but the old stomach doing flip-flops, so it feels, you know, more safe like by the window, probably just psychological, but Ron, with his long legs, he's six-foot-six, he likes to have room—

MAN: Closer to the washroom too. (He winks at Jimroy, as though urination is a male conspiracy.)

WOMAN (confidingly): Oh, but we're forever flying here and there, on account of Ron's investments, he thinks it's only right, even if he's officially retired, to show an interest, and the branch offices just love when—

MAN (leaning over and reaching into his wife's bag): Got any gum, hon? My ears're poppin' again.

Jimroy looks straight ahead. He is unable to fit himself into the scene; his body is rigid and his face has become a stiff mask.

WOMAN (rummaging in large purse, chortling at the weakness of men and speaking with womanly authority): Coming right up. Dentyne? (To Jimroy): Go ahead, I've got lots. I never leave home without. Between Ron's ears popping and my stomach doing flip-flops—

FLIGHT ATTENDANT (in her deadly monotone): Anyone care for a sunrise surprise before breakfast? Champagne and orange—

MAN: Coke for me.

JIMROY: Milk. If you have it?

WOMAN: Glass of juice, please.

FLIGHT ATTENDANT (to woman): Orange, tomato, grapefruit, apple?

WOMAN (with maddening hesitation): Oh, tomato, I guess.

MAN: Oh boy, honey, you and your tomato juice! (He laughs uproariously at this, leaving Jimroy, milk to his lips, stunned, lonely, and lost. Jimroy does not "look down" on these people; he is puzzled by them, and in a curious way, deeply envious.)

WOMAN (sporting a tomato-juice moustache): So! Well! You really are a book writer?

MAN: A real one! What d'ya think of them apples.

WOMAN: That's the wonderful thing about travel, you meet people from all walks of life. Like once we—

MAN (interrupting his wife): Pretty good money in it? I've seen these authors on Johnny Carson, my wife and I—

WOMAN: Satin suits, covered with sparkles, just chatting away with Johnny, easy as you please—

MAN: I suppose you use a typewriter? When you're writing on your books?

JIMROY (looking wildly from one to the other): Well, I actually—

WOMAN: I expect you get used to it, being on the TV, talking away about—

MAN (as though struck with inspiration): Say, I guess it's pretty good publicity, pretty good market angle—creating the need, that's how the Japanese got us licked—

WOMAN: That's what that what's-his-name fellow said, wasn't it, hon? That real nice little man we met in Yokohama—

MAN: That's what the man said. Little fellow, but real smart; look to your markets, he said, keep an eye on your markets.

WOMAN: Only makes sense. (She laughs. To Jimroy): You use your own name?

MAN: On your books, she means. Or like a—?

WOMAN: Like a pen name? Made up?

MAN: You know something? When I saw you getting on this plane this morning, in the waiting room there, with your newspaper and all, I thought to myself: That fella looks, well, I've seen that fella before—

WOMAN: Ron always stays up for Johnny. Me, I need my beauty sleep. Ha!

MAN: But she's the reader in the family, always reading at something or other.

WOMAN (throwing up her hands, blushing, resisting this compliment with flustered modesty): Well, you see, Ron, he's so darn busy, the business, visiting the branch offices, his volunteer work, he works with the—

MAN: What kind of books you say you write?

JIMROY (determined): Well, my books are really—

MAN: I've thought of writing a book, but you know, I've never learned to use a typewriter and—

JIMROY (relentless): Biography's my field. I write biography.

MAN: Your life story, eh?

JIMROY: Not *my* life story. I'm writing the life of a poet. Her name is Mary Swann.

FLIGHT ATTENDANT: Breakfast! (She briskly hands out three trays.)

MAN: My favourite meal of the day, breakfast.

JIMROY (insistently, gesturing crisply): Actually, my books are about—

MAN: Hon? (He reaches across to take his wife's hand; their hands meet in the vicinity of Jimroy's lap; they bow their heads.)

WOMAN (urging): You.

MAN: No, hon, you.

WOMAN (capitulating): For what we are about to receive, for the blessings of warmth, love, fellowship, and heavenly guidance, we offer humble thanks and beg that—

Her voice fades. The CAMERA focuses on Jimroy, pinned between the praying couple, his mouth open as though he is about to speak. His eyes, bewildered, gaze at the joined hands on his lap. Dissolve.

Fade to: Exterior in front of Toronto Airport. Daytime.

CAMERA follows Sarah Maloney as she emerges from the airport door, her suitcase in tow. The wind is blowing and there is snow on the ground; she tugs her coat closer; then stops and addresses a redcap.

SARAH: The downtown bus? Over there?

She points; the redcap nods and points. Sarah walks over to the waiting bus, and the CAMERA follows her as she boards, pays, stows her case, and settles herself by a window. Other passengers are boarding, and the bus is crowded with luggage. Next to Sarah sits a woman of about forty, snuggled into a fur coat. The bus starts, and the CAMERA follows for a moment as the vehicle makes its way out of the airport area.

FUR COAT (darting looks at Sarah, who is staring out the window and shifting her purse and coat): Sorry. You have enough room?

SARAH: Fine, thanks. (She reaches for a paperback.)

FUR COAT (continuing to steal little glances at Sarah): Excuse me. I . . . I can't stand it any longer, but you look like . . . are you by any chance Sarah Maloney?

SARAH (smiling): Yes, I am.

FUR COAT: I knew it. I knew it. I've got your book at home and of course your picture's on the back—and I've seen you interviewed on TV. Twice, I think. This is surreal. Sarah Maloney. But I had an idea you'd be—

SARAH: Older. (She's heard this before). Everyone does. (She shrugs.)

FUR COAT: You sounded, in the book, I mean, so . . . (she searches for the word) so positive about everything.

SARAH: My wise days. (She smiles.) Actually I'm a little less positive now. About everything. A little more flexible, I've been told.

FUR COAT: You still feel the same way about female power? That a militant position offers our best—

SARAH: Yes. Absolutely. But with certain exceptions—

FUR COAT: What about men?

SARAH: Men?

FUR COAT: What I mean is, do you still feel the same about them? In your book, in the middle part, you talk about men as the masked enemy and—

SARAH (smiling, shrugging, acknowledging a joke on her younger self): I just got married. Last week.

FUR COAT: Ah! So you do believe in love.

SARAH: Love?

FUR COAT: Love and marriage. That they don't necessarily cancel each other out as you said in—

SARAH (with confusion): That's a tough one.

FUR COAT: And what about your idea that marriage is a series of compromises that necessitates—

SARAH: Actually, this is my second marriage. But this time it feels better. (She says this wistfully, her brightness clouded by a drop in pitch that suggests a fugitive sense of fear or uncertainty.)

FUR COAT: What about motherhood? How did you put it? "Motherhood is the only power conduit available to—"

SARAH (shrugging again, confidingly): I'm pregnant.

FUR COAT: Pregnant!

SARAH: Just a few weeks.

FUR COAT: Good God, you shouldn't be sitting in all this smoke. (She waves cigarette smoke away.) Even a small amount is damaging at—

SARAH: Lord! (She tries to open the window but it is stuck.)

FUR COAT: I tell all my patients—I'm an M.D.—that sidestream smoke is just as bad as—

SARAH (trying window again and succeeding): What else? Flying okay?

FUR COAT: As far as we know.

SARAH: I've got a conference here in Toronto. Four days. After that, though, I'm going to sit on my fanny and eat green vegetables and (putting her hand on her belly) feel it grow. You know something?—this is what I've always wanted only I didn't know it.

FUR COAT: But in your book, didn't you say something about childbearing being the— (Dissolve.)

Fade to: Interior of the bus, which is now in the city centre. Sarah and Fur Coat are talking with great concentration and energy and with the intimacy of old friends.

SARAH: Take Mary Swann, for instance. She's the reason I'm here, the one the symposium's all about. Okay, so she had zero power. This woman was a total victim—

FUR COAT: I'm not sure how you define a female victim, but don't you have to—

SARAH: Yeah, I think we over-simplify the whole thing. Victims get squeezed into corners and they either die or they invent a new strategy. I think that's why—

FUR COAT: And this woman? Mary . . .?

SARAH: Mary Swann. A classic case. She had a rotten life, dead end, lived on a marginal farm with a husband who wasn't even marginal—he was off the map, a bully, a pig. You know the type, doled out a few bucks every couple of weeks for groceries—

FUR COAT: And she survived?

SARAH: She wrote these poems. Not many, just over a hundred, but they're . . . there's nothing else like them.

FUR COAT: Is she still writing?

BUS DRIVER (calling out): Harbourview.

SARAH: Oh, I get off here. She's dead. Since 1965. Her husband finally—

FUR COAT: Her husband finally what?

Sarah hurriedly gathers her things together. The two women start to shake hands, then embrace quickly. Sarah gets off the bus, turns and waves.

FUR COAT (shouting through the open window): Her husband finally what?

SARAH (shouting from the pavement in front of the revolving doors): Shut her up.

FUR COAT: Did what?

SARAH (waving and shouting as the bus starts to pull away): He shut her up. For good. He—

She realizes her words can't be heard, turns and enters the hotel through the revolving doors. The CAMERA focuses on the large notice board. Between "IODE Annual Reunion" and "Dominion Leather Goods Sales Conference" there is a line that reads: "The Swann Symposium." The CAMERA lingers for a moment on the sign. MUSIC: fife and drums. Dissolve.

Director's Note: This scene marks the end of film SET UP. All major characters have been introduced and brought to their destination, the Swann symposium, at the Harbourview Hotel. Occasional motivational suggestions will be given to the actors, but it is hoped that directorial comment will remain non-specific.

Fade in: Interior, hotel reception room. Evening.

Overhead CAMERA, wide shot of about fifty heads moving about in the hotel reception room. The room is gracefully proportioned, designed to accommodate medium-sized gatherings. The look is opulent; updated traditional, but rather heavy with swagged velvet and ornate furniture. Waiters can be seen from above, moving among groups of people with trays of drinks and canapés. Lively background MUSIC mingles with the rich sound of conversation and the tinkling of glasses. CAMERA lingers for a minute or two on the assembly. The scene is that well-known cocktail reception that precedes most conferences and symposia. Very gradually the CAMERA lowers, coming closer and closer to the crowd, and the murmur of voices becomes, finally, audible. Random phrases rise and fall in the festive air.

. . . personally, I see Swann as being blinded by innocence, and by that I mean—

. . . no use pretending the woman's a feminist when she makes it perfectly clear she's accepted the values of—

. . . well, when you consider that Nadeau, Ontario, is not exactly the centre of the world—

. . . remarkable, yes, remarkable. I agree, yes, remarkable!

. . . Emily Dickinson never . . .

It's the love poems I'm waiting for.

. . . now this is only a suggestion, but if you look at what Swann does with the stanza and think of it as the microcosm . . .

. . . time for another edition. Past time, if you ask me.

. . . is it true old Cruzzi's here? My God, the man must be a hundred years old.

. . . It's a pleasure, an honour, as I was saying to Mick here—

And this, ahem, is Frederic Cruzzi.

. . . read your article on Swann in the October issue, or was it the September—?

. . . all these faces. Wouldn't our muse be amazed if she saw all these—

. . . giving the keynote address when it would have been more appropriate for—

. . . when, and if, Lang lets go of those love poems. What in Christ is he doing—
. . . wasn't quite what Sarah Maloney said—
. . . sweet as baby Jesus in velvet trousers!
. . . He's gone electronic, she's gone electronic, even the president has—
It's a good line, but it's not a great line.
Cosy.
. . . sibilance, don't you think?

The fragments of conversation intensify, grow louder, a roar, then once again becomes indistinct; the tinkling of glasses and shrieks of laughter begin to recede, replaced by the insistent sound of a spoon being struck against a glass. CAMERA close-up of a hand striking the glass with a spoon, and then the face of Willard Lang. His is a large, soft face masked with heavy naivety. Achieving silence, Lang raises his glass. He has the air of a man slyly keen to please.

LANG: Ladies and gentlemen. (He pauses for effect). My name is Willard Lang and it is my pleasure to welcome you (another dramatic pause) to the Swann symposium.
DRUNKEN VOICE: Hear, hear.
SOBER VOICE: Shhhhh.
LANG: I would like to extend a special welcome from the Steering Committee, which has worked long and hard to make this symposium possible, and to remind you that tomorrow morning, at nine o'clock sharp, we will be assembling in—

He is suddenly interrupted. The room is thrown into darkness. There is a great deal of evident confusion, and overlapping voices can be heard.

. . . the lights—
. . . power cut or, ahem, else—
. . . someone find the bloody switch . . .
Ladies and gentlemen—
Good heavens!
My God, talk about chaos—
. . . sure that if we remain calm the power will be restored.
Christ!

. . . so if you will be patient, ladies and gentlemen.
Ouch, that's my foot.
Sorry, I didn't mean—
If you think this is a nightmare, remember—

Someone in the crowd strikes a match; someone else lights a
lighter. Gradually the matches and lighters go on around the room,
revealing the assembled faces, buoyant only a moment ago, now
ghostly with shadow and looking surprisingly frail, a look of having
been caught doing something foolish. Very slowly the hubbub begins
to build again; there is even some laughter, though it is nervous
laughter, ignited perhaps by drink. An instant later the overhead
lights go on, blinding, brighter than before, so that people are caught
off guard, dazed.

. . . at last. I just about—
About time—
. . . talk about timing, I mean he just—
. . . miniature theatre of the absurd—
. . . major power cut, wouldn't be at all surprised—
. . . Mary Swann putting in an appearance—
Ha!
. . . as I was saying, ahem, Swann is a kind of symbolic
    orphan who voices the—
. . . wouldn't you think a hotel like this would have an
    emergency power source, or else—
(Remember that time at the St. Thomas in New York—
My briefcase!
It was right here.
. . . Oedipal darkness as a symbol of, but only a symbol,
    let me say—
. . . is going to publish those love poems. You know, the
    ones he found under the kitchen floor — the linoleum, actually.
It was a black leather briefcase, the standard size and shape—
. . . let's hope that tomorrow will—
It was sitting right here by this table leg before the lights
    went out, and—

CAMERA close-up: Jimroy is talking heatedly to two or three
waiters. As a crowd begins to gather around, him, CAMERA slowly

withdraws, rising to overhead position once again. We see the cluster of people around Jimroy increase, and over the murmuring crowd his voice rings out with extreme clarity.

JIMROY: My briefcase! All my notes for the symposium, my talk, the program, everything! I had them in my briefcase. My papers. And a fountain pen, a very valuable fountain pen. It was right here! Someone must have picked up—yes, of course, I'm sure. How could I possibly not know where my own briefcase was? It was right here beside me, you idiot, right here.

Jimroy has started to shout; his face, so smooth and amiable before, has grown red and has a furious boiled look; he is mortally offended, embarrassed, and angry; clearly he sees the blackout and the loss of his briefcase as damaging to his dignity. The CAMERA focuses on the image of his angry face and freezes.

Fade to: Interior of a meeting room. The next morning.

The frozen image of Jimroy's face slowly dissolves into Willard Lang's face, which is genial, smiling, perhaps a little ingratiating. He is eager, despite the catastrophe of the night before, to launch the symposium on the right note. People attending are seated in rows on folding chairs. Some of them have pens in hand, ready to take notes; others sit with books or papers on their laps; many are in conversation with one another. Lang is at the front of the room, standing at a small lectern equipped with a microphone. He clears his throat, but the buzz in the room persists.

LANG: Ladies and gentlemen, assembled scholars. (The voices die.) Good morning. Once again I welcome you to the first, but let us hope not the last, Mary Swann symposium. And let us also hope— (the microphone gives a jarring electronic squawk)—that the electricity will not fail us as it did last night. (Another squawk.)
MAN WITH OUTSIZE AFRO: Hear, hear.
LANG (slightly annoyed): Just two items before I introduce our keynote speaker. I wish to draw your attention to a display that has been set up in the corridor. Some off-prints of recent articles have been assembled, and also, you will be happy to hear, a

photograph of Mary Swann, which has been brought along by Miss Rose Hindmarch of Nadeau. Ah, is Miss Hindmarch with us this morning? (There is a brief stir: people turn their heads looking for Rose, who is seated in the last row.) Ah! Perhaps Miss Hindmarch would be good enough to stand and be recognized.

Rose, enormously embarrassed, rises slowly, her shy smile showing pleasure, awkwardness, confusion. She manages a gawky nod, a slight shake of her newly permed head, then sits down again to scattered, somewhat indifferent applause.

LANG: Thank you, thank you. And now for item two. A personal plea, if I may, concerning our mini-disaster (laughs dismissively) yesterday evening. If anyone should find himself, or herself, with an extra briefcase, black leather, initials M.J. on the clasp, Mr. Jimroy would appreciate its speedy return. And now, ladies and gentlemen, fellow Swannians, if I may address you in such a manner, it is my great pleasure to introduce our speaker. Not that Morton Jimroy, holder of two honorary degrees needs a—yes?

CAMERA picks up Jimroy sitting in a chair a little apart from the others. He is somewhat tense, a little strained. Almost bashfully apologetic, he lifts his arms in a shrug; he is holding up three fingers.

LANG (comprehending): Ah, excuse me, Morton. *Three* honorary degrees, of course! The most recent from Princeton University, I believe. Everyone in this room is familiar, I am sure, with Morton Jimroy's esteemed biography of Ezra Pound, *A Perverse Pilgrimage*, and his equally fine biography of the American poet John Starman, entitled *Verse, Voice and Vision* . . . (he becomes distracted). Yes? (He catches Jimroy's eyes once again.) Yes, Mr. Jimroy?

JIMROY (quietly, shyly, half-bobbing from his chair): That's *Voice, Vision and Verse*. Just a small correction. Sorry.

LANG (in tones of pompous injury): I stand corrected. *Voice, Vision and Verse*. As I was saying, Ezra Pound! John Starman! Giants of our literature. And now the question might be put— what is it about the obscure Canadian poet, because we must face the fact, ladies and gentlemen, that the seminal work of Mary

Swann is not as widely known as it deserves—what is it about this woman, this writer, that attracted the attention of the world-famous biographer of Ezra Starman and John— (A murmur from the audience tells him he has stumbled again, and he quickly corrects himself.) Ezra Pound and John Starman. A little early in the morning, I'm afraid. What was it that drew—but perhaps it would be best if I let our honoured guest tell you himself. (He gestures broadly). Mr. Morton Jimroy!

Jimroy rises and allows the applause to die as he stands at the lectern. He adjusts his papers, loosens his tie, lowers the microphone. He is a man who enjoys teasing his audience, believing it sharpens their attention. But he manages to appear more fussy than in command, and the audience responds with restlessness. At last he speaks.

JIMROY: Ladies and gentlemen, I must first ask your indulgence. Because of last night's mishap . . . my briefcase caper . . . I am forced today to speak from the scantiest of notes, and may be even more rambling than is my usual way. (He breathes deeply and plunges into his talk.) Why, our honoured chairman asks, have I devoted my attention for the last two years to the work and person of Mary Swann, a poet some have compared to Emily Dickinson, to Stevie Smith, and also, if it is not too extreme a comparison for so early in the morning (a sour glance at Lang) to the great romantic voice of the—

His voice fades to a murmur, rising and falling with a somewhat monotonous rhythm, but the words themselves are blurred. The CAMERA, as he speaks, wanders to various other faces in the audience, settles for a moment on Sarah Maloney, exceptionally alert and possessed of an expectant sparkle. She wears boots, pants, and a beautiful silk shirt, and is sitting boyishly with one leg drawn up, tuned to every word. Her look is one of critical appraisal. The CAMERA also falls on Rose Hindmarch sitting next to Sarah. Rose touches her hair repeatedly, scratches her neck, tries to remain alert, but is distracted by the excitement of the gathering. She looks to right and left, over her shoulder, etc. Jimroy's voice once again fades in.

JIMROY: . . . always referred to as "a Canadian poet," but I suggest the time has come to leave off this modifier and to spring her free of the bolted confines of regionalism. Hers is an international voice, which—

Jimroy's voice again blurs. The CAMERA falls on the bright, skeptical face of Frederic Cruzzi, octogenarian, dressed this morning in a grey suit with a red sweater beneath. He strokes his chin, a little bored, somewhat disapproving of the tack Jimroy is taking. An instant later his eyes begin to close; in recent days he has withdrawn more and more into his memories, a province he likens to a low, raftered attic with insufficient air.

JIMROY (voice fading in again): . . . and who would happily blow Mrs. Swann's past to ashes and make her a comely country matron cheerfully secreting bits of egg money, as well as those who want to force on her a myth she is too frail to support. She was a seer and a celebrant, and in her 125 poems, 129 when Professor Lang agrees to publish the love poems—
MAN WITH OUTSIZE AFRO: Hear, hear.
BLUE-SPOTTED TIE: But when, when?
JIMROY (turning to Lang): You see, Professor Lang, how eagerly we await publication. To continue, who really was Mary Swann?

His face dissolves again. The CAMERA travels across the faces of those in the audience; some take notes, some listen attentively, Cruzzi dozes, Rose fidgets.

JIMROY (again becoming audible): May I suggest further that the real reason we have come here is the wish to travel (pause) that short but difficult distance (pause) between appearance and reality. Who, given what we know, was Mary Swann? A woman. A wife. A mother. Perhaps a lover. (He eyes Lang, who looks away.) She was poor. Badly educated. A woman who travelled only a few miles from her home. She had no social security card, no medical records. Her only official papers, in fact, consisted (dramatic pause) of a library card from the Nadeau Public Library.

The CAMERA lights on Rose Hindmarch, who blushes appropriately and nods. CAMERA follows the faces in the audience; interest quickens and even Cruzzi jerks awake.

JIMROY: It is a mystery, just as our own lives are mysteries. Just as we don't ever really know that person sitting to our right or left. (Rose and Sarah exchange small smiles at this.) Appearance and reality.

Jimroy ends his talk with a flourish, a crisp nod to the audience. He bows stiffly, and walks back to his chair.

Director's Note: The repetition of the phrase "appearance and reality" must be framed with silence and intensity, since it can be said to define the submerged dichotomy of the film. The applause, when it comes, must be slightly delayed so that the words (and implications) will have time to register.

Lang steps to the microphone and leads the applause, gleeful as a cheerleader; after a moment he gestures Jimroy back to the lectern.

LANG: Our guest has kindly agreed to field a few questions. We have, I believe, just ten minutes before our coffee break. Questions? (Several hands go up at once. Lang, dancing like a marionette, pleased things are running smoothly, points to Dr. Buswell near the back of the room): Syd? You have a question for Mr. Jimroy?

Syd Buswell is a man of about forty, wearing blue jeans and a tweed jacket; he speaks with a nasal, aggrieved whine, employing truncated phrases that give the impression of self-importance.

BUSWELL: The question of influences! Very important as we all know. You mention, Professor Jimroy, that Mrs. Swann was an avid reader. A great borrower of books from the local library. Now I have *been* to the local library in Nadeau, Ontario. I have made a *point* of going there. I am sure you have as well. And I feel sure that you will agree with me that there isn't a great deal offered by the Nadeau Public Library. Pleasant it may be, but—

Director's Note: Another sort of director, distrustful of his or her audience, might employ a flashback at this point. Buswell, clad in a ratty leather jacket, prowling through the innocent shelves of the Nadeau library, or something along those lines.

JIMROY: Ah yes, but—

BUSWELL: For example. There is *no* T.S. Eliot in the Nadeau library. Just an example. Enough said? (He sits down, believing he has scored magnificently with this point.)

JIMROY (clearing his throat): Perhaps you're aware, Professor Buswell, that the librarian of the Nadeau Public Library, Rose Hindmarch, is in our midst today? (CAMERA close-up of Rose, who looks hideously alarmed.)

BUSWELL: I am perfectly aware that Miss Hindmarch is present. And she would no doubt agree. With me. That this particular library was in no particular position to offer. Much. Much substance that is. To someone like Mary Swann. Now it is all very well—

Rose has risen to her feet; there are tears in her eyes, and her face wears a mixed look of self-censure and wincing bewilderment; this is not what she expected.

ROSE (quavering): We have a budget. People don't always appreciate . . . a very small budget. Last year it got cut twice, the hockey arena got a hike, but we got—

BUSWELL (lazily): I'm sure you do the best you can, Miss Hindmarch. With a limited budget. I was not imputing (at this Rose blinks) that you run an establishment that is . . . less than—

JIMROY (icily): That is exactly what you did say, Professor Buswell, and—

BUSWELL (unperturbed): It is hardly an accusation to acknowledge that a particular rural library is . . . substandard. No Eliot. No Lowell. I ask you. (He sits down in triumph.)

ROSE (rising again): Every year I tell the council the same thing, we need money, the price of books—

JIMROY: Miss Hindmarch, there is no need for you to defend your—

BUSWELL (rising again): No one said anything about a need to defend. I am simply saying what we all know. That the Nadeau

Public Library cannot have provided serious nourishment to the mind of a poet like—

ROSE (on her feet, her terrible garrulousness shifting to its defensive mode): Oh, Mrs. Swann came every two weeks to the library. I don't think she ever missed, not for years and years, every two weeks, like clockwork —

BUSWELL: Miss Hindmarch. My interest is in addressing the question of influences. I assure you, I am not challenging you personally. It is Mr. Jimroy who makes claims for Mrs. Swann's familiarity with certain works in the modern trad—

JIMROY: I suggest only. I do *not* claim.

ROSE (not understanding the focus of the discussion): We *do* have a poetry section. We use the Library of Congress numbering system and you can find—

BUSWELL (to Jimroy, ignoring Rose): You point to parallels between Swann and Emily Dickinson and you suggest—

ROSE (still awkwardly standing): Mrs. Swann liked a good story. For example, Pearl Buck. I remember she liked Pearl Buck real well. And Edna Ferber—

Director's Note: Others in the audience watch the proceedings with distress, humour, annoyance, fascination. There must be a sense of order breaking down and a suggestion that an unwanted revelation threatens.

WOMAN IN GREEN TWEED SUIT: Is this really germane?

MAN WITH CRINKLED FOREHEAD: Of course it's germane. Everything that sheds light on—

WATTLED GENT: Why not let Mr. Jimroy reply? After all, he's the one who—

MERRY EYES: Order.

SARAH (rising, twisting her wedding ring as she speaks): Why can't we just say that Mary Swann was self-evolved and be done with it? Remember what Pound said about Eliot, that he made his own modernism—

GINGER PONYTAIL: And isn't it possible that her influences were general rather than specific—

WIMPY GRIN: The question of influence is oversimplified in most cases. For instance—

JIMROY (to all three comments): Yes. And furthermore—

BUSWELL: All I want to say, and then I promise to pipe down, is that the resources of the Nadeau Public Library *cannot* seriously be considered as an influence.

JIMROY (instinctively dealing in flattery, knowing how efficacious it can be in such a public situation): Professor Buswell, from previous discussions you and I have had, I know you to be a man of wide reading and sensitivity. Of course I understand that you are anxious to establish a link between Mrs. Swann's writing and her grasp on modern poetics—

BUSWELL: I only ask—

JIMROY: —and I can tell you that Mrs. Swann's daughter, whom I have interviewed in depth in recent months, has confided that her mother was familiar with that genre of verse commonly known as Mother Goose—

BUSWELL (with an appalled laugh): Nursery rhymes! Surely you're not serious—

JIMROY: I see no reason to dismiss—

MAN WITH OUTSIZE AFRO: Bloody rude son of a—

BIRDLADY: . . . snobbish approach to—

JIMROY (leaning on lectern beseechingly; he has clearly lost control, but will not admit to it): If you will allow me to enlarge—

LANG (stepping nimbly forward): Perhaps, ladies and gentlemen, it might be more profitable to continue this most interesting discussion over coffee, which I now believe— (he peers over the heads of the audience)—yes, I can see coffee is ready and . . .

Lang's voice fades; all around him people are rising to their feet and heading toward the coffee urns. They can be seen chatting, stretching, moving.

Rose rises hurriedly and heads for the door into the corridor. There are tears standing in her eyes, and her nose is red. She is a woman who can never speak coherently when her emotions are stirred, and for this reason she is anxious to escape.

SARAH (attempting to catch up with Rose): Rose, wait a minute. Excuse me, I want to—Rose! (She follows Rose into the corridor, looks right and left and sees nobody.) Rose! (She sees a door marked "Ladies," decides Rose is there, and enters. The CAMERA follows, focusing on three stalls, the door to one of them closed.)

Rose, you there? (Sarah leans on a washbasin and folds her arms, prepared to be patient.) Okay, Rose, I know you're in there. Now listen to me. You trust me, don't you? Buswell's a shit. Everyone in that room knows what he is. An asshole. Insecure. That's what the tenure system does to the insecure. The man's paranoid, Rose. Can you hear me? You can't stay in there all day, you know.

She continues talking while turning and glancing in the mirror; her face has the kind of seriousness that throws off energy. From her deep bag she takes a hairbrush and begins brushing her long hair, an act performed with a kind of distracted sensuality.

SARAH: I can tell you, Rose—I was on the Steering Commitee —that that twit, Buswell, is one hundred per cent on the defensive. He's running for the bushes. This is confidential, Rose, but I can tell you this much — he was supposed to be giving a paper himself, something idiotic and desperate on vowel sounds in *Swann's Songs*, and he's been working on it for two years (gives her hair a yank) and then he suddenly writes to the committee, this was in October, to say his notes had been stolen. Stolen! Everyone knows he's the most absent-minded nerd. (She puts the brush away, turns sideways, observes the curve of her abdomen and runs her hand over it.) He's the sort of crazy creep that loves to put the blame . . . well, they all are, the bunch of them, it makes me wonder if I want to spend my life hanging out with— Rose? (She sees that the collar of her pink shirt is standing prettily away from her neck, careless and controlled at the same time in a way that makes her happy.) Rose? Rose! (She pushes open the door, which swings in to reveal nothing but a solitary toilet.) Rose. (Softly, hands on hips): Rose?

Dissolve to: Interior, meeting room. Late morning.

Members of the symposium are enjoying a coffee break. People are milling about, relaxed, standing in groups of three or four, and there is a pleasing sense of animation. In one corner Jimroy, Buswell, and Cruzzi are conducting a cheerful but guarded discussion. CLOSE-UP on Lang, who scurries from group to group sociably, then joins Jimroy and the others; his look is amiable and conciliatory. A nearby group consists of Wattled Gent, Wimpy Grin, Ginger Ponytail, and

Sarah, who joins them belatedly and is handed a cup of coffee by Silver Cufflinks.

SILVER CUFFLINKS: Well, you might say Jimroy managed to capture the attention of—

GINGER PONYTAIL (earnestly): Threw some light on the early poems which you have to admit are . . . but it's the love poems we're all waiting for—

WIMPY GRIN (to Sarah): I suppose you must have met Morton Jimroy—

SARAH (distracted, looking over her shoulder for Rose): Met who?

WIMPY GRIN: Morton Jimroy—you must have met—

SARAH (focusing, but still distracted): No. I decided not to go to the reception last night. All that smoke—

GINGER PONYTAIL: So you don't know him at all?

SARAH: We've been corresponding. For about a year or so, but I haven't actually met—

LANG (approaching and taking Sarah by the elbow): Sarah, may I interrupt? I'd like very much to present you to Mr. Jimroy—

SARAH (detaching herself from the group and following Lang through the crowded, noise-filled room): Willard, have you seen Rose Hindmarch? She seems to have disappeared. I've looked in the—

LANG: Oh, she'll turn up. Probably in the loo. Unfortunate. Tactless bugger, Buswell. Utterly paranoid, still says his notes were stolen—

SARAH: Any news about Morton Jimroy's briefcase?

LANG (his face falling): Not yet. I can't understand who— (He steers Sarah over to where Jimroy is holding court.) Morton, sorry to interrupt, but you expressly asked earlier to meet Sarah, and I've managed to snatch her away from—Sarah Maloney, Morton Jimroy.

JIMROY (offering his hand and looking suddenly timid): How do you—?

SARAH (smiling broadly, unprepared for such formality): At last! (She embraces him warmly and plants a kiss on one cheek; she is a naturally demonstrative woman.) At last!

Jimroy, gratified but confused by so spontaneous an embrace, instantly draws back, squirming. CAMERA close-up of his face reveals a twisted scowl of mingled pain and desire.

JIMROY (muttering coldly under his breath): So good to meet you.

Sarah, interpreting Jimroy's cool behaviour as an act of rejection, steps back and attempts to explain to him, to the others, and to herself.

SARAH: After all the letters we've . . . I just felt, you know, that we were—
JIMROY (aloofly): I assume you've met Professor Buswell?
BUSWELL (carelessly): Old friends. We go way back.
JIMROY: I see.
SARAH (still puzzled by Jimroy's snub): I've been looking forward to—
LANG (recognizing an awkward situation and anxious to deflect it): And have you met Frederic Cruzzi? Mr. Cruzzi, Sarah Maloney.
CRUZZI (also trying to relieve the tension): We have met. By letter. A charming letter if I may say so.
JIMROY (blanching, pierced to the heart by this information): You must be very busy, Ms. Maloney, with all your letter writing.
LANG (rattling on expansively): It was Sarah who managed to persuade Mr. Cruzzi to attend our gathering.
CRUZZI: A most persuasive letter. How could I possibly refuse?
LANG: Actually we're very, very fortunate to have Sarah with us. Perhaps you know her happy good news?
JIMROY (icily): I'm afraid not.
LANG: Just newly married. Christmas Eve, wasn't it, Sarah?
BUSWELL (breezy, bored): Congrats.
JIMROY: Married. (There is more exclamation than query in this outburst.)
SARAH: To someone—(shrugs nervously)—someone I've known for some time.
JIMROY: My congratulations. Excuse me, won't you? I see someone I must have a word with. (He starts to leave.)

SARAH (perplexed): We *will* have a chance to talk later, won't we, Morton?

JIMROY (cringing at the sound of his name): I expect that *might* be possible—

SARAH: There are dozens of things I want to ask you about—

JIMROY (dismissively as he leaves): We must do that some time.

SARAH (to others): Did I by any chance say something wrong? Put my foot in it or what?

LANG (smoothly): I'm sure Mr. Jimroy is just tired, his long journey, and then speaking for—and without notes—

SARAH: No, not just that, Willard. I've been (she pauses) snubbed.

LANG (looking at his watch): Good god, we're running late. Completely lost track of time. You ready, Sarah? (To Cruzzi and Buswell): Sarah's on next.

SARAH (staring at Jimroy's back): I can't understand it. In his letters he was so—maybe he's brooding about his briefcase, or—

LANG: I'm afraid . . . mustn't fall behind, you know. (He firmly takes the coffee cup away from her and steers her to the front of the room.)

SARAH (still mulling over the snub): I must have done *something*. Or *said* something. Or—

WOMAN WITH TURBAN (grasping Lang's hand): Just want to let you know, Willard, that I'm looking forward to the love series. I've done some work—

LANG: Five minutes late! I don't know how we—

SARAH: Maybe I came on a bit strong. I do that sometimes.

WOMAN WITH TURBAN (clinging): I think all of us are—

LANG (at the lectern): Ladies and gentlemen. (People drift to their seats with looks of expectation.) Ladies and gentlemen. I am particularly happy to present our next speaker, Sarah Maloney, who is the person—and I think I can say this without exaggeration—the person most responsible for the rediscovery of Mary Swann, who, in her article a mere five years ago, pointed to Swann's unique genius and to—well, perhaps I should now turn the microphone over to Ms. Maloney herself. (Applause.)

Sarah squares her shoulders: whatever she says she knows it must be delivered with authority. Her eyes search the audience. She sees Morton Jimroy and sends him a tentative smile, then begins.

SARAH: Mr. Jimroy, in his keynote address this morning, raised a number of interesting points, particularly the notion we have of regarding Swann as a kind of curious cultural hiccup isolated from any sort of cultural tradition. It is a compelling belief, but shaky in my opinion, to think of Mary Swann's work as a miniaturized, spontaneous, virgin birth, but—

Her voice fades, becomes indistinct. The CAMERA pans the audience. Wattled Gent furiously scribbles notes; Rose, her nose red, listens dully from the back row; Jimroy sits with hooded eyes, looking trapped and betrayed, much as he looked on the airplane. Sarah continues, her voice very gradually becoming audible again.

SARAH: . . . And I'd like to state in conclusion that, like other self-generated artists, Mary Swann had the ability to state her truths with a sharpness and slant that lit up what had become stale by traditional use. It's this, more than anything else that gives her work its power. Ladies and gentlemen, thank you. (There is a pleasing roll of applause, and a number of hands immediately go up.)

LANG (stepping to microphone and holding up a hand): Just a few questions, I'm afraid. Lunch is ordered for 12:30 sharp. (He looks into the audience, spots Woman With Turban, and points.)

WOMAN WITH TURBAN: Dr. Maloney, I found your remarks about the resonance of the primitive imagination interesting—

SARAH: Actually, I didn't use . . . I deliberately avoided the word *primitive*.

WOMAN WITH TURBAN (waving this objection aside): Untutored then. Self-nurtured. Whatever. You seem to feel, if I understand you properly, that it is impossible for a twentieth-century being to escape the—what was the exact word—?

SARAH: Matrix.

WOMAN WITH TURBAN: Matrix, yes. That even at the edge of the social matrix, certain cultural ideas are absorbed. Even the social outcast—

SARAH: With respect, *outcast* is another term that I rather rigorously—

WOMAN WITH TURBAN (patiently): Even those at the *fringe* of the, shall we say, prevailing communal structure, are open to general patterns of cultural thought—have I quoted you correctly?

SARAH (recovering some of her combative sparkle, but fearful of where this line of questioning is leading): Yes and no. It is, of course, very difficult to pin down what Swann may have perceived about the direction and . . . (searches for word) *shape* of modern poetry—

WOMAN WITH TURBAN: But isn't that, in fact, exactly what we *must* do? Look beyond the work to some other form of documentation that reinforces—

SARAH: Ideally, yes, but we all know how rare the ideal situation is. In Mary Swann's case—

JIMROY (standing suddenly and interrupting; his tone is peculiarly aggressive): If I may interrupt our questioner—whose name I'm afraid I don't know—

WOMAN WITH TURBAN: Professor Croft. From Tulane.

JIMROY: Thank you, Ms. Croft. If I may interject . . . a special plea on my part, I'm afraid . . . that is to say, we are all anxious to discover *anything at all* that may illuminate the . . . character of Mary Swann's special muse. And we all lament, I am sure, that there is so little apparent light. Mrs. Swann, alas, left us no transcribed manifesto. She did *not* write scholarly articles or essays elucidating her poetic theories. She did not enjoy the pleasure of an extensive correspondence. But she did, and perhaps this is what my distinguished colleague . . . Ms. . . . sorry, I'm afraid—

WOMAN WITH TURBAN (crossly): Croft. From Tulane.

JIMROY: —what Ms. Croft (pause) of Tulane . . . was alluding to. The fact is, Mary Swann did keep a journal. I wonder, Dr. Maloney, if you, as the one person privy to the contents of this journal, might be persuaded to say a few words about it today? (He sits.)

SARAH: Well, I—

JIMROY (rising again): I am particularly interested, and I'm sure my colleagues at this symposium are equally interested—(he waves a hand airily)—in knowing when you intend to make Mrs. Swann's journal available to the public. (He sits.)

MAN WITH OUTSIZE AFRO: Hear, hear.

WOMAN WITH TURBAN (also rising): And while we're on the subject, maybe we should ask Professor Lang when he intends to publish Swann's love poems. We've waited for—

SARAH: I'm afraid—

LANG (half-rising): We seem to be straying from the original question—

JIMROY (rising): The question is really quite simple and can be answered in one word. When, Dr. Maloney, do you intend to publish Mary Swann's journal?

WOMAN WITH TURBAN: Surely the public, or at least those who have an academic investment, should be allowed access to the journal.

MAN WITH OUTSIZE AFRO: Hear, hear.

SARAH (nervously, rubbing her hair and taking a deep breath): The Swann journal . . . as you call it . . . which was given to me by Rose Hindmarch — (CAMERA close-up of Rose, who smiles in a vague and friendly way, apparently recovered from the earlier session)—given to me . . . precisely *because* there was so little of importance in it—

WATTLED GENT (rising): But there must be something. That is to say, the journal surely contains *words* and words contain *meaning* and so there must be, perforce, some . . . shall we say, value to even the most . . . cursory document. (He sits. There is an uneasy stirring in the room; people move in their chairs, murmur, clearly demanding an explanation.)

SARAH (at a loss): The journal . . . as you call it — and perhaps I should never have used that term in my original article — covered a period of just three months, the summer of 1950. This was, as you all know, before Mrs. Swann began to write her poems—

JIMROY (on his feet, jabbing the air): All the more reason, if I may say so, Ms. Maloney, that the journal holds interest for—

SARAH (regarding him directly; from this point the debate is between the two of them: the Woman With Turban and Wattled Gent fade away): But it is *not* of interest, Mr. Jimroy. I sincerely hoped, when I first looked at it, that it would be. But there is nothing—

JIMROY: Surely, Dr. Maloney, there is *something*.

SARAH (close to tears): There's nothing. Absolutely nothing that would interest—

JIMROY: Then why not demystify the document by allowing others to—

SARAH (exasperated): Shopping lists, Mr. Jimroy. That's what's in the journal. Comments about the weather. Once, once, she mentioned a door latch that was broken. Not a symbolic door latch, either. A real door latch. Anyone could have written the stuff on those pages. That's the tragedy of—

JIMROY (fiercely, but trying for control): Nevertheless, this material, marginal as it may be, and I suppose I must take your word for *that*, Dr. Maloney, this marginalia does offer a glimpse of that private person behind—

SARAH: But I am afraid it does *not*. Offer a glimpse, Mr. Jimroy. Otherwise I would have—

JIMROY (trying for a statesmanlike approach): I can't, of course, speak for my fellow scholars (he gestures broadly), but for the biographer (he claps a hand to his heart), for the biographer, that which *seems* trivial—

SARAH: This journal, Mr. Jimroy, is not even particularly legible—

JIMROY: Ah, that may be, but you see, even the illegible nature of the work offers a kind of comment on—

SARAH (flustered): It's really just . . . I can assure you . . . it is utterly lacking in meaningful—

JIMROY: Dr. Maloney, I am what you might call an old hand in this business of . . . shall we say, uncovering the core of personality. I know perfectly well what most journals are like. They are tentative documents at the most. Provisional. Rambling. Uncommitted to structure. I'm not, you know, such a novice as to presume exegesis. But the feebleness you suggest attached to Mrs. Swann's journal is surely balanced by the fact that it is, after all, a privileged communication and—

SARAH: I would agree with you in most cases, Mr. Jimroy. (She bears down on his name with bitterness.) But this is a special case—

LANG (stepping forward briskly, anxious to keep the proceedings genial): Awfully sorry, ladies and gentlemen, but the time—

JIMROY: One question, one question only. A simple yes or no will do. Do you intend, Dr. Maloney, do you intend, at any time in the future, to publish Mary Swann's private journal?

SARAH: Well, I—

LANG: I'm really terribly sorry, but time—

JIMROY: Yes or no?

SARAH (pausing, waving her hands weakly; her voice is unsteady, almost a whisper): No.

The announcement is greeted by an angry murmur; people turn in their seats and talk openly to their neighbours. In a moment the room is filled with an indignant uproar. Jimroy's voice booms from the back of the room.

JIMROY: And may I inquire (raising his voice in order to be heard)—may I inquire of our speaker why she has decided not to publish Mary Swann's private journal?

LANG: Lunch is now ready, ladies and gentlemen. If you will find your way to the LaSalle Room adjoining this room. I now declare this session adjourned—

JIMROY (over the uproar): —as to *why* Dr. Maloney has taken it on *herself* to withhold—

SARAH (whispering into microphone, the kind of whisper that brings instant silence): Because I can't. (She pauses.) Because . . . I am unable. The journal has been . . . I am sorry to have to say this . . . the journal has been . . . lost.

She holds out her hands in a gesture of helplessness and shakes her head. The audience stirs; people begin to speak from every corner of the room. SOUND is reinforced by the echo effects of the faulty microphone, so that the noise is crushing. Sarah can be seen mouthing the words again. "The journal has been lost."

Fade to: Interior, the LaSalle Room set up with tables for eight. Noon.

CAMERA focuses on buffet table where there is a large wet-looking salmon on a platter, several bowls of salad, an immense basket of rolls, plates of cheese and fruit, glasses of wine already poured. The members of the symposium are cheerfully filling their plates, then finding their way to the various tables. The room is loud with social chatter.

CRINKLED FOREHEAD: . . . seems damned unlikely in this day and age, what with storage systems—

WIMPY GRIN: . . . when you think of Willard Lang hoarding the treasure trove—

SILVER CUFFLINKS: . . . fresh salmon. I get so sick of looking at salmon, you'd think—

GREEN TWEED SUIT: . . . think Jimroy was a bit thrown off by the whole thing, first losing his briefcase and then—

ROSE: . . . was so embarrassed, I don't know when I've been so—

GINGER PONYTAIL: Frankly, the man is a tyrant, I don't care what you say, he's—

SILVER CUFFLINKS: How does that line go? From "Lilacs," starting with—

MERRY EYES: A terrible disappointment, and I'd been counting on—

BIRDLADY: I wonder if I could possibly have a glass of water?

WIMPY GRIN: . . . hair of the dog—

GREEN TWEED SUIT: . . . the way she just stood there and took—

WATTLED GENT: May I present Herbert Block.

BLUE-SPOTTED TIE: . . . delicious—

WIMPY GRIN: . . . all owe a great deal to the Peregrine Press, you know, and you have to give Mr. Cruzzi credit—

MAN WITH OUTSIZE AFRO: . . . mostly subsidized, of course, but without regional presses—

SILVER CUFFLINKS: . . . piece of fishbone in my throat—

GINGER PONYTAIL: . . . drenched with this rancid olive oil and then absolutely—

JIMROY: We are after all a community of scholars, and—

CRINKLED FOREHEAD: What the hell's wrong with the word *primitive*?

WATTLED GENT: . . . hasn't found it yet, his briefcase that is, but evidently he hopes—

BIRDLADY: . . . the giggle-and-tease school of criticism—

MERRY EYES: . . . spontaneity, always say spontaneity's just another name for shoddiness—

BIRDLADY: . . . was in Nadeau twice, I think, but there wasn't—

SILVER CUFFLINKS: . . . the way he had her pinned there, like a butterfly—

MAN WITH OUTSIZE AFRO: . . . bastard—

CRINKLED FOREHEAD: Would you mind if I join you?

WOMAN WITH TURBAN (turning her attention to Wimpy Grin, seated beside her): Well, of course I'm disappointed. Waiting two years for the love poems and now—

WIMPY GRIN: I'm more than disappointed. I'm thinking of—

WOMAN WITH TURBAN: I felt so sure the journal would serve as a kind of gloss, that is to say, enlarge the meaning of the Water Poems in particular.

WIMPY GRIN: Yes, the Water Poems. Especially those. Not that there's anything obscure about them.

WOMAN WITH TURBAN: Obscurity's not the point. Not at all. I'm talking about reference points. The journal would have expanded the number of reference points—and the love poems will—

WIMPY GRIN: But at least she—

WOMAN WITH TURBAN: Who? Maloney? Or Swann?

WIMPY GRIN: Sarah Maloney. She was very firm about that. That there was nothing in the journal of interest.

WOMAN WITH TURBAN: And you believe that! You honestly believe that? Maybe *she* was unable to see any connections, but—

WIMPY GRIN: Hmmmmmmmm.

The CAMERA moves to another table and focuses on Rose Hindmarch in conversation with Syd Buswell.

ROSE (daintily picking at her food): Well, as for myself, I was kind of disappointed. You see, I'd been thinking I might ask her if, well, if she'd care to donate the journal to our little museum, and maybe the rhyming dictionary, too, but I don't want to be an Indian giver—

BUSWELL (chewing and gesturing with his fork): Dictionary?

ROSE (rambling): Since you were in Nadeau we've got ourselves a new room in the museum, a real nice display of, well, you'll have to come and have yourself a look. It's up over the library—

BUSWELL: I'm sure you understand about my comments this morning. Just wanted to point out—

ROSE: Oh well, I'm pretty proud of our library. You see, in the old days, when it was in the post office, we didn't even have—

BUSWELL: . . . just wanted to make the point about the idiocy of influences. Jimroy did the same thing in his Starman book, said Starman's work had been influenced by *Moby Dick*. He exaggerates. Romances. The bugger should have been a novelist, not a bloody biographer—

ROSE (applying sauce to salmon): I haven't actually read—

BUSWELL (ramming a roll into his mouth): He's all talk. He talks documentation, but lives in fairyland—

ROSE: Oh, he's very famous. I looked him up in *Who's Who*—

BUSWELL: Inflated reputation. Happens too frequently. Conjecture. Ha! What about proof! The straight goods.

ROSE: Well, of course, Mrs. Swann and myself . . . we used to talk about . . . we were friends you know. We used to discuss this and that and sometimes we—

BUSWELL (bored): Yeah?

The CAMERA moves to another couple at another table: Merry Eyes and Blue-Spotted Tie.

MERRY EYES: . . . hard to understand how a thing like this can happen—

BLUE-SPOTTED TIE: . . . valuable documentation like that, well, should have been archived of course. I always make sure prime materials are duplicated and archived—

MERRY EYES: It's only common sense.

BLUE-SPOTTED TIE: Especially when you take the view, as I do, that this kind of documentation belongs to the whole scholarly—

MERRY EYES: . . . and not to any one individual. That's certainly the view I take. And as for Professor Lang sitting on the love poems—

BLUE-SPOTTED TIE: . . . really no excuse—

MERRY EYES: Even my working papers I keep in a little fireproof safe we have—

BLUE-SPOTTED TIE: Sense of responsibility.

MERRY EYES: Exactly!

Fade to: Interior, lecture room. Same time as above.

The CAMERA focuses on the empty lecture room. MUSIC: clarinet, a few repeated phrases. CLOSE-UP of Sarah, on the platform gathering together her lecture notes. Sadly, almost in a trance, she replaces a paperclip and puts the papers in her briefcase. Her air is one of defeat. In the empty room she appears suddenly small and vulnerable. She can hear the murmur of voices from the adjoining room, and this reinforces her feelings of abandonment. She pauses, looks out over the rows of empty chairs. "Well, that's that," her look says. Then her eyes (and the CAMERA) fall on Frederic Cruzzi, who has remained seated on the far side of the room, very nearly obscured by shadows.

CRUZZI (rising slowly with an old man's stiffness; his voice, too, creaks): Ms. Maloney?

SARAH: Mr. Cruzzi! I . . . didn't see you there. I thought you'd . . . you'd gone in with the others, for lunch.

CRUZZI (pulling himself erect): I was hoping to speak to you alone. If you can spare—

SARAH: Of course. (She descends the platform and, somewhat tentatively, approaches him.)

CRUZZI: May I suggest that, instead of joining the others, we escape for an hour. There's something I'd like to discuss with you, and—there's quite a good restaurant downstairs. Or perhaps the coffee shop might be quicker.

SARAH (pausing, smiling): Yes, let's. I'd like to get away for an hour. Especially after . . . (She gestures toward the platform.)

CRUZZI: Well, then. (He offers his arm in a rather old-world manner.) I don't move very quickly, I'm afraid.

SARAH: In that case (takes his arm), we can take our time.

The CAMERA follows them out of the room and into the corridor. Together they pause for a moment and regard the glass display unit in which can be seen a few off-prints and, in the centre, the photograph of Mary Swann.

CRUZZI (tapping the glass softly): Our woman of mystery.

SARAH: Yes. (She smiles at Cruzzi, and then the two of them proceed slowly down the corridor toward the elevator. MUSIC: organ, the upper ranges; dissolve.)

Cruzzi and Sarah are seated at a corner table. A waiter has just placed a large leafy salad before Sarah, a golden omelette in front of Cruzzi.

CRUZZI (relaxed and talkative, a man who expands in the company of women): This really is very pleasant—to escape. I'm not sure why it is, but I find that a roomful of "scholars" tends to bring on an attack of mental indigestion. That Delphic tone they love to take. And something chilly and unhelpful about them too. I'm speaking generally, of course.

SARAH (smiling; she too is beginning to relax): What I can't understand is Jimroy's attitude. To me, I mean. The antagonism.

CRUZZI (eyeing her keenly): Can't you?

SARAH: I've never met him before this morning. (She chews a piece of celery thoughtfully.) Not face to face. But we've been corresponding, writing back and forth . . . for more than a year now.

CRUZZI: I see.

SARAH: And (continuing to chew) to be truthful, he's a good letter writer. Very amusing, if you appreciate ironic edges—and I do. And surprisingly intimate at times. Open. He must have written me half a dozen times to say how much he looked forward to our meeting. (She puts down her celery branch.) But today—I can't figure it out. He was . . . baiting me. He was . . . today he was— (She stops herself, bites her lip.)

CRUZZI (patiently prompting): Today?

SARAH: Today—well you were there when Willard Lang introduced us. At first Jimroy seemed scared to death. Went all coldfish. And during the question time, after my presentation, I had the feeling that he—this may be putting it in a bit strongly, but I had the distinct feeling . . . he actually . . . hated me.

CRUZZI (calmly): Hmmmm.

SARAH: And . . . I don't know why. That's the scary part. The minute Willard Lang mentioned that I'd got married—did you see his face, Jimroy's? As though I'd smashed him in the stomach. I suppose, well, maybe I should have mentioned in my last letter that I was getting married, but . . . I didn't decide . . . the wedding was sort of a sudden decision. I'd been seeing someone else, another man, and that didn't work out and . . . Why am I blathering away like this?

CRUZZI: I wouldn't worry about Jimroy. Some men, you know—forgive me if I sound like a wizened sage—but some men only relate to women in the . . . abstract. And not in the actuality. A letter, even an intimate letter, is still somewhat of an abstraction.

SARAH: I hate to be hated. It's a failing of mine. Especially when I don't know what I've done to earn it.

CRUZZI: It's just a thought, but—(he pours mineral water into a glass, with deliberation)—could it be that you have something he wants?

SARAH (looking up abruptly from her salad): Like what?

CRUZZI: Perhaps—(he shrugs elegantly)—perhaps something he imagined to be in Mrs. Swann's notebook. Her journal.

SARAH: But I told him . . . you heard me . . . I told everyone in the room, and it's the truth, that there's nothing *in* the notebook. I know it sounds as though I'm making excuses. I did lose it. Okay. I'll never know how it happened, but I have to take responsibility for *that*. One day I had it, and the next day I didn't. *Mea culpa*. Eeehh! But I'm *not* concealing anything. There's nothing *in* the journal.

CRUZZI: Not what you hoped.

SARAH: I thought I was going to get a look right inside that woman's head. That she'd be saying the unsayable, a whole new level of revelation, you know what I mean. Instead I found "Tire on truck burst," "Rain on Tuesday," "Down with flu." Nothing.

CRUZZI: Yes, but—

SARAH: But?

CRUZZI (taking his time): As I understand it, you *did* have the notebook for some time. Three, four years? And you've steadfastly resisted the idea of publishing it.

SARAH (shrugging, regretful, but grinning): I know, I know. I kept reading it over and over. I kept thinking—there's just got to be *some*thing here. Like maybe she's got a symbol system going. Or maybe it's written in some elaborate, elegant cipher that . . . but (she shrugs again) in the end I had to conclude that there just wasn't anything! I hated like hell to admit she was so . . .

CRUZZI: Ordinary? (He swirls his drink and looks upward.)

SARAH (sending him a shrewd look): You know, Mr. Cruzzi, you are looking just the slightest bit doubtful. As though . . . you think I might be withholding something when I say there was nothing there.

CRUZZI: No. I believe you. Mrs. Swann, in my judgement, *was* an ordinary woman. Whatever that word means. Of course you were disappointed.

SARAH: And maybe, I have to admit it, a little protective. About her . . . ordinariness. Sometimes I've wondered if that's why Willard Lang hasn't published the love poems. He's had them long enough.

CRUZZI: You're suggesting they might be of doubtful quality?

SARAH (shrugging): Sentimental, maybe. Soft-centred. Valentine verse. You probably know how he found them? He bribed the real-estate agent at the Swann house, and then found these papers under a loose bit of linoleum.

CRUZZI: You may be right. Of course we have only his word that what he found were love poems.

SARAH: And *you* may be right, too, that Jimroy wants something.

CRUZZI (thoughtfully): Whatever I may think of Morton Jimroy personally, I am forced to admit he is a thorough biographer. You've read his books. I think he, quite simply, wants it all.

SARAH: All what?

CRUZZI: He wants Mrs. Swann's life. Every minute of it if he could have it. Every cup of tea that poor woman imbibed. Every thought in her tormented head. And what's more, he wants her death. Or some clue to it.

SARAH (looking puzzled): The notebook was written in 1950. And Mary Swann was murdered in 1965. Does he actually think he's going to find—

CRUZZI: . . . that there might be a hint? A portent? A scrap of prophecy? Yes, I *do* think so. I met the man—

SARAH: Jimroy?

CRUZZI: Yes. I met him only once. He paid me a brief visit in Kingston a year ago, and we spent some time talking. To be honest, I found him a dry stick, but I do recall some of our conversation. And I remember how hard he pressed me about Mrs. Swann's death. Did I have any "theories?" (Sardonically): He was, I thought, more than a little obsessive about the *cause* of Mrs. Swann's death.

SARAH: The cause?

CRUZZI: He feels . . . he made it quite clear that he'll never be able to understand Mrs. Swann's life until he understands her death.

SARAH: He actually said that?

CRUZZI: I find it a whimsical notion myself.

SARAH: Romantic.

CRUZZI: But then, he has a somewhat romantic view of a human life. Sees it as something with an . . . aesthetic shape. A wholeness. Whereas—whereas the lives of most people are pretty scrappy affairs. And full of secrets and concealments. As I'm almost sure you will agree.

Director's Note: The very long silence that follows Cruzzi's speech signals, to the audience, an abrupt shift of mood. LIGHTING also changes, and the CAMERA loses its sharpness of focus. A few bars of MUSIC (a single oboe) fill in the void. The gazes of the two characters, Sarah and Cruzzi, seem directed inward, rather than at each other.

SARAH (suddenly): I'm pregnant.

CRUZZI (smiling): Splendid.

SARAH: I just wanted you to know. What *I* was concealing. (She lifts a glass of milk to her lips, as though giving a toast.)

CRUZZI (also lifting his glass): And *I* am in love.

SARAH (pleased): Ahh.

CRUZZI: With a seventy-five-year-old widow. In love, but somewhat frightened of it.

SARAH: I *was* in love.

CRUZZI: And now?

SARAH: It didn't work out.

CRUZZI: Do you mind? Much?

SARAH: Terribly. I think he loved me too. But he loved a lot of other things more.

CRUZZI: Things?

SARAH: Money, chiefly. He never seemed to get enough. He didn't want to end up like his father, a working stiff.

CRUZZI: So you understand—*why*, I mean?

SARAH (pausing): Yes. And (patting stomach) this seems more important.

CRUZZI: Probably it is. In the long run.

SARAH: And what will you do? About your love? Your widow?

CRUZZI: Think about it a little. Try to get used to it. To be calm about it.

SARAH: Is that why you decided to come to the symposium? To give yourself time?

CRUZZI (nodding thoughtfully): Mrs. Swann *is* a puzzle, and puzzles are . . . (he shrugs) diverting.

SARAH: Her *death* is a puzzle? Is that what you mean?

Director's Note: The moment of intimacy has ended. MUSIC, LIGHTING and CAMERA focus and sharpen.

CRUZZI: Her *life* is a puzzle. Her death, as far as I'm concerned, is just one of those . . . random accidents.

SARAH: An accident! Mr. Cruzzi, you surprise me. (Her voice takes on heat.) That monster, her husband, shot her. Point blank. He hammered her face to mush—I've read all the newspaper reports. And cut her up into pieces and stuck her in a sack. That sounds pretty deliberate to me. And you call that an accident? Without any motive behind it?

CRUZZI (buttering a roll): And what would constitute a "motive"? Probably her "monster" of a husband was hungry and his supper was late. (Cruzzi is a man who speaks often with quotation marks around his words, a manifestation of his growing crustiness.)

SARAH (incredulous): You honestly think a man would hack his wife to death for *that*?

CRUZZI: He *was* a man of violent temper. That much came out in the inquest.

SARAH (gesturing wildly): So supper's a little late and he decides to shoot and dismember his lifelong mate. Show her who's boss.

CRUZZI: Or maybe she gave him a black look. Or talked back. Or burned the potatoes. Or ran out of salt. Or wasted three dollars on bus fare into Kingston. We'll probably never know.

SARAH (her face alight, one finger raised): But what if . . . what if she *did* have a lover . . . a secret . . . it's not impossible . . . and *he* found out about it somehow?

CRUZZI: Can you believe that? That exhausted woman? As you may know, I saw her the same day she was killed. She delivered the poems to my house.

SARAH: But there were the love poems. Under the linoleum. Maybe—

CRUZZI: In matters of love—(his face wears a self-mocking smile)— I have to admit that all things are possible. You've just told me about your own situation.

SARAH: I shouldn't have.

CRUZZI: Don't worry, please. I won't mention it again. But Mary Swann and a lover? Certainly it is what many would *want* to find. A thread of redeeming passion—

SARAH: —in a world that's mainly made up of compromise.

CRUZZI: I would imagine that even Jimroy yearns to discover it —a love affair for Mary Swann. It would provide specific motivation for the murder, and perhaps he hoped you'd be the one to give it to him.

SARAH (taking this in with a nod): If I ever do find the notebook—and I still haven't given up hope—*if* I ever find it, the first thing I'm going to do is send Jimroy a photocopy so he can see for himself that there's nothing, *nothing* that points to a love affair—

CRUZZI: I don't think, Sarah, that you are very likely to recover the journal.

SARAH (startled, especially by Cruzzi's ominous tone): And how can you be so sure?

CRUZZI: Because . . . well, one of the reasons I was anxious to talk to you was to discuss—but first, let me ask you something. How exactly did the loss of the journal occur?

SARAH (throwing up her hands, bewildered): Just what I said before—one day I had it, the next day I didn't.

CRUZZI: But where did you normally keep it?

SARAH: I've got a little shelf over my bed. What a perfect fool I was to trust—

CRUZZI: And one day you looked at this little shelf and the journal was gone?

SARAH: I must have picked it up by mistake, thrown it away. It wasn't very big, you know, and—

CRUZZI: Or perhaps someone *else* picked it up—

SARAH (stopped for a moment): No. No one else would have done that. (She shakes her head vigorously.) No!

CRUZZI: Why not?

SARAH: Because . . . who would want to?

CRUZZI (speculatively; it is his nature to be speculative): There are any number of reasons that . . . certain individuals might want access to Mary Swann's journal. Scholarly greed for one. Or the sheer monetary value of—

SARAH: Mr. Cruzzi. I don't know if I'm understanding you or not. Surely you're not saying that someone might have *stolen* the journal?

CRUZZI: Yes. That is what I am saying.

SARAH: That's— (she regards him closely, then laughs)—that's a little wild, if you'll excuse my saying so.

CRUZZI: Do I appear to you to be a crazy person?

SARAH (embarrassed): No. No, of course not, I—

CRUZZI: "Senile" perhaps? "Screw loose?" "Bats in the belfry"? Paranoid delusions?

SARAH: Mr. Cruzzi, I keep my doors locked. You know where I live? The south side of Chicago. I've got triple locks on my doors, back and front. On the ground-floor windows I've got iron bars, and I'm thinking of installing—

CRUZZI: Perhaps . . . perhaps someone you know. Someone who just happened to be in your house and saw—

SARAH (laughing, but only a little): Light-fingered friends I don't have. The people I know don't give two beans for Mary Swann. As a matter of fact, they're sick to death of hearing me talk about Mary Swann—they actually put their hands over their ears when I start to—

CRUZZI (interrupting, speaking with even-tempered deliberation; this is what he has been wanting to say to her all along): On Christmas Eve—are you listening, Sarah Maloney?—my house in Kingston was burgled. I was out for a few hours, and when I returned—I, too, lock my doors by the way, even in Kingston— and when I returned home I found certain items missing. I wonder if you can guess what they might be?

SARAH (alarmed by the gravity of his tone; she puts down her knife and fork quietly): What?

CRUZZI: For one thing, a file relating to the publication of Mrs. Swann's book, and . . .

SARAH: And?

CRUZZI: And four copies of *Swann's Songs*. The only copies I possess, by the way. We—my late wife and I—published only 250 copies of Mrs. Swann's book. That was the usual print run for a small press in those days—and I am told that only about twenty of those still exist.

SARAH: That's true. A friend of mine, well, more than a friend . . . the man I mentioned earlier—

CRUZZI: The man you loved?

SARAH (after a pause): Yes. He's in the rare book business and he says that's the norm, that books, especially paperbound books just . . . (gestures skyward) disappear.

CRUZZI: I'm sure you can imagine my distress when I discovered the books had been stolen.

SARAH: You're saying—?

CRUZZI: Nothing else in the house was touched.

SARAH (shaking her head in disbelief, unable to imagine what this means): But it must be a joke—maybe a practical joke.

CRUZZI (shaking his head): And naturally, with the thought of this symposium coming up, I was anxious to acquire a copy of *Swann's Songs*, simply to refresh my memory. With my own copies gone, I tried the Kingston Public Library. And then the university library. In both places the copies seem to have been, shall we say, "spirited away."

SARAH (first shocked, then solemn, then doubtful): But look, libraries are notorious for misplacing their holdings. Or else they've got lousy security systems and with all the petty vandals around—it happens all the time. Even in the university where I teach . . . (she pauses) . . . the university archives . . .

CRUZZI (sitting patiently with laced fingers; he senses what she is about to say): Go on.

SARAH: . . . even there . . . well, they've been known to . . . lose . . . quite valuable papers, whole collections even—

CRUZZI: The Mary Swann collection, for example?

SARAH: How did you know?

CRUZZI: I made a phone call. When I began to suspect that something was going on.

SARAH: Surely—

CRUZZI: I've also phoned the National Library in Ottawa, the University of Toronto library, the University of Manitoba—

SARAH (shaking her head over the absurdity of it all): And you began to suspect a worldwide conspiracy? Is that it?

CRUZZI: I can see . . . I can tell from your expression . . . that you believe me to be quite insane.

SARAH: I just—

CRUZZI: You have one of those transparent faces, I'm afraid, that gives you away. You observe this ancient gent before you. One eye asquint, the casualty of a recent stroke. Voice quavery. He has been babbling about love, of all things. Love! And now it is paranoid accusations. Academic piracy.

SARAH: But surely—

CRUZZI: I don't blame you for suspecting imbalance. I was of the same opinion. What kind of old goat was I getting to be?— that's what I asked myself. And then I talked to Buswell.

SARAH: Buswell! That self-pitying misogynist . . .

CRUZZI: Yes. Exactly. I do agree. But he has a similar story to tell. His notes for an article on Swann *and* his copy of *Swann's Songs*, he tells me, were removed from his desk. He had left the office for only a minute, he claims, and when he returned—

SARAH: It still seems a little—

CRUZZI: Fanciful? I agree with you there. As a matter of fact, it wasn't until this morning, when you yourself announced the loss of Mrs. Swann's notebook that I became persuaded that there was a rather remarkable, not to say alarming, pattern to all this. If you know anything about the laws of probability, you will quickly see—

SARAH: It's a little hard to see who would want . . . and for what reason? (The waiter puts the bill down on the table, and both Sarah and Cruzzi reach for it.) Please, Mr. Cruzzi, let me. Please. It's been my pleasure. (She places bills on the plate, and rises.)

CRUZZI (rising stiffly; his speech, too, is stiff, containing the awkwardness of translated words): I think, rather, that I have *not* given you pleasure. I have given you my own troubling concerns, and I am sorry for that. But I do feel . . . that this has gone far enough. And that something will have to be . . . (His voice fades and blends with the general noise.)

Sarah leaves the coffee shop, walking slowly by Cruzzi's side. CAMERA follows them into the hotel lobby; they can be observed talking, but what they say is drowned out by the general noise of passers-by and by MUSIC: a swirling organ tune that holds an element of agitation. They stand waiting before a bank of elevators, gesturing, conferring, questioning, shaking their heads; one of the elevators opens, and they step inside.

Cut to: Interior of an identical elevator. Same time as above.

Jimroy is alone in the elevator. The doors spring open, and he is joined by Rose Hindmarch who steps aboard in sprightly fashion.

JIMROY: Ah, Miss Hindmarch. Enjoying the symposium?

ROSE (laughing): Please, it's Rose. You remember—Rose!

JIMROY: Rose. Of course.

ROSE: Oh, I'm having the loveliest time. Everyone's so nice and friendly, well, almost everyone. (She makes a face, thinking of Buswell.)

JIMROY: I think you'll find the afternoon interesting. A number of papers on various—

ROSE (nervously): You don't think we'll be late, do you? I went up to my room for a little lie-down after lunch. I haven't been awfully well of late, and then all these new faces, well, it's tiring. And the trip down from Kingston, and the elevators—elevators always give me a funny feeling in the tummy. I'd of taken the stairs, but I didn't want to be late.

JIMROY: They can be tiring, meetings like this. (The elevator doors open. Politely he allows Rose to exit first, then he follows; they are about to pass the glass display case holding Mary Swann's photograph when Rose suddenly grasps Jimroy's arm.)

Director's Note: Jimroy must cringe at Rose's touch. It is important that the actor playing this role reveal, by facial expression and bodily contraction, that he finds Rose's touch repellent and that he regards the photograph of Mary Swann as vaguely threatening.

ROSE (girlish, garrulous): There she is! Don't you wonder what she'd think of all this fuss. I mean, she'd be just bowled over to think . . . (CAMERA focuses on Mary Swann's photo.)

JIMROY (speaking socially, composing himself): Good of you to bring the photograph along, Miss Hindmarch. Rose. Some people like to have a visual image to reinforce— (His manner implies he himself is not one of these people.)

ROSE: Oh, well, of course it's a terrible, terrible likeness. Out of focus, you know, and too much sun, that was the trouble with those old box cameras, you couldn't adjust for the light—

JIMROY (anything to shut her up): Well, as I say, it is most fortunate to have even a poor likeness. I don't suppose we can expect anything—

ROSE (suddenly courageous, seizing her opportunity): Mr. Jimroy. Morton. There's something—if you don't mind—something I'd like to ask you about.

JIMROY (gesturing at the open door of the meeting room where people are beginning to assemble for the afternoon session):

Perhaps we might converse a little later. I believe (he consults his watch) it's nearly time for the next—

ROSE (not about to let him escape): It's just, well, I don't want to seem impolite or anything, but, you see, there's something I've been wanting to mention to you. Ever since that time you visited Nadeau. I almost wrote you a letter once—

JIMROY (his expression is one of pain): I believe we *are* going to be late if we don't—

ROSE (pursuing): You remember when you came to Nadeau, that you wanted, you wanted to see everything, you were so interested in every last little thing?

JIMROY: A most pleasant visit as I remember. Most interesting. But really, we must—

ROSE: Oh, we talked and talked, I remember how you asked all about—

JIMROY: I believe, yes, we had a most interesting—

ROSE: You took me out for dinner. To the Elgin Hotel, remember? We had the double pork chop platter. With apple sauce. I'll never forget that. That evening. But do you remember the next day, I'm sure you do, visiting the museum, the Mary Swann Memorial Room, that's what I want to ask you about . . . Morton.

JIMROY (attempting once more to extricate himself): Most fascinating exhibition. A credit to your community, yes. Perhaps we can chat later, but now—

ROSE (doggedly): I showed you those two photographs of Mary Swann, the ones they found in a dresser drawer after she was . . . Do you remember that? There were—

The voice of Willard Lang can be heard from the meeting room.

LANG: Ladies and gentlemen, the afternoon session is now called to order and—

JIMROY: I really am awfully afraid—I don't want to miss . . . (He makes a helpless gesture toward the door.)

ROSE: There was *this* photograph *here* (points to display case) and then there was the *other* one. A much better likeness. Not so fuzzy. Her eyes, Mrs. Swann's eyes, were wide open, remember? You picked it up and said how her eyes showed feeling. Do you remember, Mr. Jimroy, how you picked up—

JIMROY: I'm afraid not. I don't really remember there being another—and I certainly never picked up—

ROSE: But it's true, I remember things like that. People are always saying what a memory I've got. Like a camera! You picked up the picture and—

JIMROY (attempting unsuccessfully to get around her): If you don't mind. This is really—

ROSE: —and afterwards, the very next day when I went into that room . . . I was showing a bunch of school kids around and—

JIMROY (dully, with desperation): Please!

ROSE: —and I was just about to show them the two photographs, and one of them was missing. The good one with the eyes open. It was gone, Mr. Jimroy. And now—I hate to say this, but facts are facts and you were the last person to . . . (gasps for breath) and I think it's only fair for you to—

JIMROY: This is outrageous! (He speaks loudly, not just to Rose, but to Merry Eyes and Wimpy Grin, who are arriving late, stepping arm-in-arm off an elevator, followed a second later by Sarah and Cruzzi.) I did not come all the way from California, Miss Hindmarch, to listen to . . . dim-witted *ravings*.

ROSE: Oh! (She covers her face with her hands.) Oh! (At the word *ravings*, she rushes in tears to the EXIT stairway, blindly pushing open the door and disappearing.)

JIMROY (shrugging to Merry Eyes, Wimpy Grin, Sarah, and Cruzzi, who stand in stunned bafflement before him): Poor soul. She's been ill apparently. Very ill. Under a strain. I'm not sure she's . . . (winces) . . . afraid she's not quite . . . (He taps his forehead meaningfully.)

Sarah's mouth drops. CAMERA close-up. She is taking in Jimroy's behaviour, which is close to hysterical. Her eyes move sideways and meet Cruzzi's.

Again the voice of Lang is heard from the meeting room.

LANG: And so if you will kindly take your places we will commence with—

Director's Note: The next few TAKES are fragmentary; their purpose is not to illuminate the film's theme or to advance the action, but to suggest the passing of time. The symposium has moved into its second stage; the atmosphere is calm, hard-working, serious, even somewhat plodding, and the faces of the actors must reflect this shift.

Fade to: Interior of the meeting room. Afternoon.

Blue-Spotted Tie is standing at the lectern, winding up a paper entitled "Regional Allusions in the Poetry of Mary Swann."

BLUE-SPOTTED TIE: And now, to sum up my main points of departure: the non-specific nature of the geo-sociological references in Mrs. Swann's universe, and the mythic and biblical implications of place names and allusions . . .

Cut to: Interior of small seminar room. Afternoon.

A workshop is in progress. Eight men and women are seated around a table. The discussion leader is Woman With Turban.

WOMAN WITH TURBAN: . . . would sincerely like to thank you all for your participation, especially Professor Herbert Block, who has been so kind as to give us his ideas concerning a post-modernist interpretation of Swann's Water Poems. (Polite applause.)

Cut to: Interior of meeting room. Late afternoon.

WATTLED GENT (at lectern): . . . and I do apologize for going overtime, but I want to express my thanks to you all for your enthusiastic reception of—but I see I'm getting a signal. Thank you. (Applause.)

Cut to: Interior of the LaSalle Room. Early evening.

The members of the symposium are mingling in a cocktail atmosphere. There is a sound of glasses, ice clinking, and blurred talk.

WISTFUL DEMEANOUR: . . . not a bad day, all in all—
WOMAN WITH TURBAN: . . . but it's the love poems we really came for—

MAN WITH OUTSIZE AFRO: The love poems, ha! I'll eat my necktie if Lang—

GINGER PONYTAIL: . . . splitting headache—

CRINKLED FOREHEAD: . . . was a trifle disturbed by his remarks regarding—

BIRDLADY: . . . blatantly sexist—

GREEN TWEED SUIT: Slash, slash—

GINGER PONYTAIL: Jesus, the smoke in here's thick enough to—

WOMAN IN PALE SUEDE BOOTS: . . . and the noise—

SILVER CUFFLINKS: . . . sorry, I didn't catch—

The noise escalates, loud, indistinct, overwhelming.

Cut to: Interior of the banquet room. Evening.

Dinner is over; coffee cups litter the long white tablecloths. Members of the symposium are relaxed at their places, some smoking, lolling in their chairs, only partly attentive to the speaker. Rose Hindmarch, dressed in a harsh red lace dress, sits between Cruzzi (in a dark suit) and Sarah (in dark green silk with a lace collar).

LANG (at head table): . . . has been a most profitable first day, ladies and gentlemen. Just a reminder before we adjourn—we will be meeting at nine-thirty sharp tomorrow for our session on Swann's love poems. Thank you.

People begin to rise from the tables. There is the sound of chairs being pushed back, spontaneous conversations springing up. The crowd begins to surge into the corridor and disperse. MUSIC: dense, lyrical.

Cut to: Interior of the hotel corridor, between the display case and the bank of elevators. Evening.

The crowd thins out; there is continuous chattering as people enter elevators, call good night and disappear. A small group stands in front of the display case.

ROSE: Well, I've had it for this day. I don't know when I've been so dog tired.

WOMAN WITH TURBAN: Gawd, morning's going to come early.

MERRY EYES: Anyone for a nightcap? I've some gin in my room and a little—

BLUE-SPOTTED TIE: Don't mind if I do. How 'bout you, Mr. Cruzzi?

CRUZZI: Ah, well, perhaps one—

WISTFUL DEMEANOUR: Why not?

CRINKLED FOREHEAD: Onward!

SARAH (to Merry Eyes, Blue-Spotted Tie, etc.): Good night.

CRUZZI (tapping on display case): Good night, Mrs. Swann.

SARAH (extending a hand to Cruzzi): Good night. I'm glad . . . very glad we've had a chance to talk. And you, too, Rose. (Her tone is weighted with meaning.)

Director's Note: There is a shaking of hands all around, a sense of people going off in their separate directions, and a sense, too, of a change in mood, a gathering of tension. MUSIC: begins slowly, a combination of strings and organ. Frederic Cruzzi, Rose, and the others enter the elevators and disappear, leaving Sarah alone in the corridor. Her hand moves to touch the elevator button, then hovers in the air uncertainly. Her face wears a look of intense concentration, and her wandering hand goes first to her mouth, then becomes part of a salute in the direction of the display case.

SARAH (softly, whispering): Good night, Mary Swann. Sleep . . . tight.

Fade to: Interior of the same corridor. It is approaching midnight, and the corridor is in total darkness.

MUSIC: alto clarinet, very soft. Complete darkness gives way to partial darkness. Light in the corridor is provided by the red EXIT sign over the stairs and by the illuminated panel above the bank of elevators. A portion of this dim light reaches the glass display unit and shines on its mitred eges. SOUND: clarinet diminishes until the silence is total; this lasts for a few beats; then the silence is broken by a small swishing sound. The door to the EXIT stairway opens, and the figure of a man slips quickly through. He is only faintly visible, but CAMERA picks him up in silhouette as, quickly and quietly, he approaches the display case, glancing catlike over his shoulder. From his pocket he takes two or three small keys and begins to tinker with the lock of the case. His first attempts fail; he then takes out a small knife and works it into the lock. There is a sharp sound as the locking mechanism breaks and the lid of the display case opens. At this moment, as he is about to reach for the photograph, a sudden beam of light falls on him, causing him to jerk with surprise.

SARAH (emerging from behind the coffee vending machine with a flashlight in her hand. The beam of light catches the man on his arm, which he quickly raises to cover his face. Sarah's voice is shaky but determined): Hello, Mr. Jimroy. I thought I might find you here.

The intruder jumps, letting the lid of the display case crash heavily. It breaks. He runs for the stair exit, pursued by Sarah, who has difficulty keeping the beam of light directed on him.

Sarah follows, but arrives at the stairwell in time to see only his fleeing back, in a maintenance man's uniform, disappearing down the stairs. She turns back to the display case and, as she does so, her light picks out the figure of Morton Jimroy, his back pressed to the wall at the doorway of the meeting room. The LIGHTING increases slightly, but only enough to suggest eyes growing gradually accustomed to the darkness. Seeing Jimroy, Sarah gasps.

JIMROY (sardonically, arms crossed on his chest): Well, well, Dr. Maloney. Prowling the corridors. And with a flashlight, I see. A regular Girl Guide on patrol.

SARAH (glancing back at door): And what are you doing here, Mr. Jimroy? If I may ask.

JIMROY: The same thing you're doing, I would guess. Guarding (gestures toward the display case) our high priestess from thieves and rogues.

SARAH: Who . . . ? (She is shaken and confused.) Who *was* that? (She gestures toward the exit.)

JIMROY: I'm afraid I didn't see *its* face. Not having equipped myself with a handy flashlight.

SARAH (holding up the flashlight): I borrowed it from the front desk. (She laughs nervously.) I told them I was . . . afraid of the dark. Who *was* that?

JIMROY: It looked like one of the maintenance men. At least he wore the garb. I gather from your . . . your outburst . . . that you thought it was *I* who was busying myself with the burglar tools.

SARAH: Do you think, Mr. Jimroy, that you might speak to me, just for once, in a normal voice. Not quite so loaded with venom.

JIMROY (continuing in sardonic tone): I was almost sure I heard my name ringing out in the darkness. Well, I don't have to ask you who planted the ugly seeds of suspicion in your head. I suppose our dear Miss Hindmarch has been spreading her libellous little tales. Which have no foundation, let me tell you.

SARAH: You *were* in Nadeau. She *did* show you the photo—she told me. And it disappeared the same day. I don't pretend to understand what you're up to, Mr. Jimroy, but—quite a number of things seem to be disappearing . . . as I think you know.

JIMROY: Including, if I may remind you, my own briefcase. During our little power break yesterday evening.

SARAH: Someone probably . . . in the confusion—

JIMROY (interrupting decisively): Do you know what was in that briefcase? Let me tell you. My notes for my lecture. All right, those notes are of little importance. I'm quite accustomed to speaking without notes. But I also had with me my copy of *Swann's Songs*. And need I tell you, it was my only copy. Can you imagine my . . . grief.

SARAH (softening): I'm sorry about that. Really. But about the photograph, the *other* photograph—

JIMROY: Would you kindly stop shining that light in my eyes? Your Miss Marple act is less polished if I may say so, than your . . . letters.

SARAH: And will you kindly stop addressing me with that accusing tone. Has anyone ever told you that continual sarcasm can be offensive?

JIMROY (always a man to take a question seriously): My wife.

SARAH: Your wife?

JIMROY: My ex-wife, I should say. Her daily complaint. Sarcasm.

Cut to: Interior of the stairwell. Same time as above.

The stairway is dimly lit and pin-droppingly quiet. Very gradually the sound of slow, trudging ascending footsteps is heard. CAMERA focuses on Rose Hindmarch, still in her red party dress, climbing the stairs. She is breathing with difficulty, clutching at the rail, resting occasionally. She is alerted suddenly by the sound of descending footsteps, rapidly approaching. Her look changes from exhaustion to fear, and she stops, listens, then flattens herself against the wall in the shadows. The footsteps continue to approach.

INTRUDER (coming into view, startled to see Rose crouched against the wall): What—?

ROSE (relieved somewhat at the sight of the maintenance uniform): I was just . . .

INTRUDER (attempting to get around her): Excuse me.

ROSE: Good heavens. Why—aren't you . . .?

INTRUDER (trying again to pass Rose): I'm in a hurry, sorry.

ROSE: But, don't I know you? You look so—I'm Rose. From the town clerk's office. In Nadeau. Wasn't it you—?

INTRUDER: Sorry, I don't know you.

ROSE (drawing back): Unless . . . maybe I've made a mistake.

INTRUDER: Must be. I've never—

ROSE: You could be his twin brother, do you know that? He just bought a farm in our area . . . A hobby farm, he calls it. He's the spitting image—

INTRUDER: Sorry. I've got work to do.

ROSE: I feel such a fool. Usually I remember faces. Names now, I have trouble with—

INTRUDER: I'm afraid I have to— (He succeeds in getting past Rose, and continues down the stairs, running, taking them two at a time.)

Rose shrugs, mystified, then continues puffing her way up the stairs. At the eighteenth floor she pushes open the door into a dark corridor and sees two shadowy figures, one of them holding a flashlight. She rubs her eyes with a bewildered hand, still panting from the exertion of the climb. Her voice shaking, she calls out.

ROSE: Who's there? Is someone there?

SARAH: It's me, Rose. Sarah. And Morton Jimroy.

ROSE: For heaven's sake. What are you doing—?

SARAH: It's all right, Rose.

ROSE (seeing the broken display case): I knew it! I knew it! I got back to my room and was about to get ready for bed, and I got to thinking—(she shoots Jimroy a baleful look)—that I didn't trust—

JIMROY: Good God, is she going to start up all that again!

ROSE: . . . so I said to myself, I'll just go see if everything's safe. I would of taken the elevator but my tummy always . . . so I walked all the way up to . . . and here he is. I knew I should have had it out with him right away when the other photograph—

SARAH: Now look, Rose–

JIMROY: There is such a thing as professional ethics, you know. (To Sarah): If you could please explain to Miss Hindmarch here that—

ROSE: . . . the very day it was gone I should have done something, maybe called the police, but I—

SARAH: Rose, he says he didn't—

ROSE: . . . and then to say I was ranting. *Ranting*, when all I wanted was to get the picture back. For the museum. That museum means an awful lot to me, you know.

JIMROY: Dear God, I've had about enough for one day.

SARAH: Rose, we've been talking, the two of us, and—

ROSE (snatching the photograph out of the broken case and tucking it under her arm): I'll just keep this in *my* room tonight.

SARAH: Rose, will you listen?

JIMROY: . . . ranting and raving—

SARAH: Rose, it was someone *else* who broke the case. M . . . Mr. Jimroy and I just happened . . . to be here when—

ROSE: I have to think about the museum. (She clutches the photograph.) I'm the one who's responsible—

SARAH: There was someone *else* here. Maybe you saw . . . on the stairs just now. Did you see someone? A man?

ROSE (calming down): One of the maintenance men. But it was so dark that . . . I couldn't see him real well. I thought—

SARAH: We saw him in the act of breaking into the case. Another minute and—

ROSE: A maintenance man at the Harbourview Hotel? What would he want with? . . . I still think— (She glares at Jimroy.)

JIMROY: I am not in the habit of—

SARAH: It's someone *else*, Rose. *Everyone*'s losing things all of a sudden. I've been talking to Frederic Cruzzi, and it seems all sorts of people have lost—

JIMROY: Including, if I may interrupt, myself. You will remember, I'm sure, that my own briefcase was stolen right here in the hotel. And there have been one or two other items as well.

ROSE: I thought—(puzzled)—naturally I thought—

SARAH: Frederic Cruzzi thinks—he and I had a long talk about it—he thinks all these disappearing objects are somehow connected. It sounds farfetched, but—

JIMROY: Too much for me, I'm afraid. I'm going to say good night. This day has been altogether too long. (He glares at Rose, then presses the button for the elevator.)

SARAH: Maybe we should all talk more tomorrow. See if we can resolve—

ROSE: I still don't understand why—

SARAH: None of us does, Rose.

JIMROY (as the elevator arrives): Until tomorrow.

Sarah shrugs and looks at Rose, who shrugs back.

Fade to: Interior of Sarah's hotel room. Midnight.

Sarah is in bed, propped up reading a paperback book. She holds a pencil in one hand and occasionally makes a mark in the margin. The small table lamp is her only light. Her concentration is interrupted by a knock on the door.

SARAH (getting out of bed and moving, with some hesitation, to the door): Who is it?

ROSE: Me. Rose. Rose Hindmarch.

SARAH: Rose? (She immediately undoes the triple lock and takes the chain off.) Rose!

ROSE: Can I come in? For just a minute? (She is wearing a robe belted over pyjamas, slippers, and is holding the photograph in her hands.)

SARAH: Come in, Rose. Sit down.

ROSE (entering and sitting gingerly on the unoccupied bed): I'm just . . . I don't know where to start . . . I got back to my room and I just . . . I just started to feel . . . scared to death. Just got a case of the shakes, you know. I don't know what I'm scared of. (She holds the photograph of Mary Swann at arm's length.) I looked at this, at her, and all of a sudden I just got scared to death. Of her. (Tears come into Rose's eyes.) And I'm so tired out I don't know what to do.

SARAH (reaching for photo): Would you like me to keep it here, Rose? For the night?

ROSE: Would you?

SARAH: I'll take good care of it. (She carries the photograph to the dresser and sets it up, leaning it against the wall.) Now look, Rose, why don't you stay here tonight. There's an extra bed, plenty of room, and you'll be asleep in two minutes. (She briskly turns down the bed for Rose.) Come on, now. You'll sleep better here. Okay? Why not?

ROSE: I couldn't— (She touches the belt of her robe.) Are you sure? Sure you don't mind? My nerves are so jangled up and—

SARAH: In you go. (She pulls up the covers.) There. Warm enough?

ROSE (relaxing): Fine. Better.

SARAH: Everything'll look better in the morning. (She gets into her own bed and reaches over to turn out the light.)

ROSE: My mother used to say that. It's one of the things mothers say, I guess.

SARAH (yawning): And it's usually true.

ROSE: I guess it's because—

SARAH (almost asleep): Because why, Rose?

ROSE: Well, at night we . . . (She yawns.) We feel the most . . . lonely. At least I do.

SARAH: I was feeling lonely just now. Just before you knocked on the door. (She breathes deeply, almost asleep.)

ROSE: I feel lonely . . . almost all the time. (Her voice blurs, and sleep comes.)

Fade to: Interior of Sarah's room. An hour later.

The two women are asleep. Rose's face wears a look of intense happiness. Sarah's face is more troubled, and she is curled into a tight knot. The sound of knocking at the door gradually causes her to stir and waken, while Rose sleeps on. Sarah rises, slips on a robe, and goes to the door.

SARAH (speaking through the door): Yes? Who is it? (Her voice is groggy with sleep.)

CRUZZI (softly): Frederic Cruzzi.

SARAH (undoing locks and chain): Hello. (She stares at him, puzzled.)

CRUZZI: I hope you weren't asleep. (He sees she *has* been sleeping, and glimpses the second bed, occupied.) I do apologize. I took a chance—

SARAH: It's all right. Come in. What time is it, anyway?

CRUZZI (looking at his watch): One A.M. Hardly an hour to come calling, but— (He stops and glances uneasily at the second bed.)

SARAH: It's Rose. She's . . . keeping me company.

ROSE (hearing her name and opening her eyes): Why, it's Mr. Cruzzi!

CRUZZI: I wanted to let you know—

SARAH: Here. (She offers him an easy chair.) Sit down. (She climbs back into bed and sits with the covers pulled up over her lap.)

CRUZZI: I suppose this could have waited until morning, but . . . I've been down the hall, talking to a few of the others. Professor Croft and that Kramer chap, and what's-his-name with the blue-spotted tie?

SARAH (all attention now): Yes?

CRUZZI: They got into a bit of a discussion—they were all pretty well into their cups by this time—over Block's interpretation of the Water Poems. I don't know if you were there—

SARAH: I heard about it—

ROSE (propping herself up on one elbow and reaching for her glasses): He thinks—

CRUZZI: I wasn't entirely clear about his theory. Thinks the poems are purely reactive rather than symbolic, something like that—(expresses impatience)—and then someone, the gentleman with the hair (holds up hands to describe Afro), suggested we settle the discussion by consulting the text itself.

SARAH: Yes?

CRUZZI: The long and the short of it was that nobody *had* a text. There were ten, twelve of us in the room, and no one had a copy of *Swann's Songs*. Professor Croft—from Tulane, you remember—went to her room to get her copy but came back a few minutes later to say she couldn't find it. She was rather . . .

rather frantic, as a matter of fact. Hysterical. Kramer and the gentleman in the blue-spotted tie and the other, with the hair, they all admitted they'd . . . that they'd recently *lost* their copies.

ROSE (fully awake now): Why, that's what happened to me. I had my copy, it was sort of falling apart, I had it in a magazine rack, in my suite, and when I looked for it—

SARAH (to Cruzzi): Then what?

CRUZZI: Well, the emotional temperature in the room began to rise. Of course, as I say, they were well down in the bottle, and at that point I thought I might see if you were still awake and what you made of all this.

SARAH: It certainly does seem as if— (She stops, hearing a knock at the door.) Who can—?

ROSE (cheery): Grand Central Station!

SARAH (again undoing the locks, but leaving the chain on. She opens the door an inch and peers out): Mr. Jimroy! Morton.

JIMROY: I was afraid you might have gone to bed. (He is wearing wrinkled pyjamas with a suit jacket over top.)

SARAH: As a matter of fact—

JIMROY: May I come in? For just two minutes.

SARAH (signalling him to enter with a sweeping gesture): Won't you join our late-night party?

CRUZZI (with coolness): Good evening, Jimroy.

ROSE (with gawky shrug): Hello again.

JIMROY (pained): I seem to be interrupting—

SARAH: Not at all. Do sit down. (She removes Rose's dressing gown from the desk chair to make a place.)

Director's note: This scene, in which the four main characters assemble their separate clues, may be played with a very slight parodic edge.

JIMROY: I've had a thought, something I thought might interest you. It was after we said good night. By the way (he looks around), this is entirely confidential.

CRUZZI: Of course.

ROSE: Naturally.

SARAH: After we said good night? (prompting).

JIMROY: I returned to my room and got, as you see, ready for bed. But for some reason I was unable to sleep.

ROSE: Exactly the way I felt! Full of the jitters.

CRUZZI: We've all had a long day.

JIMROY (annoyed at the interruptions): *At any rate*, I started to turn over the events of the day, and quite a few things began to fall into place.

CRUZZI: A "pattern" more or less.

JIMROY: More or less. And I began to wonder if—now this may surprise you, Sarah (he says her name with a break in his voice, as though testing it for substance), but I began to wonder (pauses) if the notebook, Mary Swann's notebook that is, the one you *say* you lost—

SARAH: Yes?

JIMROY: Well, at the risk of sounding . . . ludicrous . . . I wonder if it ever occurred to you that the notebook might have been—

ROSE (pouncing): Stolen!

JIMROY: That was my thought.

SARAH (smiling toward Cruzzi): What a coincidence! Mr. Cruzzi had the same idea.

JIMROY (deflated): Oh.

CRUZZI: It does seem to fit the—

ROSE: The pattern!

JIMROY: Mary Swann is in a most peculiar position. As a literary figure, I mean. She has only been recently discovered, and her star . . . as they say, has risen very quickly. Too soon, for example, for her book to have been reprinted. Too soon for those who admire her work to be sufficiently protective about those artefacts that attach—

CRUZZI: What you're saying is, the situation may have attracted an unscrupulous—

ROSE: You know what I think? (She is terribly excited.) I think it's an inside job. (She looks eagerly at the others.)

CRUZZI: I agree.

SARAH: Someone here? Attending the symposium?

JIMROY: Yes. Most certainly possible.

SARAH: But why would anyone—?

JIMROY: Someone who wants to corner the available material. Cut us out, all of us, as Swann scholars.

CRUZZI (musing): I'm not sure scholarly acquisitiveness ever goes to quite such extremes. I think it's more likely to be—

ROSE (waving an arm in the air): Money!

JIMROY: Money?

CRUZZI: Yes, I would agree, money.

JIMROY: I still don't see how—

SARAH: I don't either. Whoever is cornering the market won't have any market to sell to. I mean, there's no Swann industry if there are no Swann texts.

JIMROY: I couldn't have said it better.

ROSE: Blackmail! (She speaks with wonderful deliberation.)

CRUZZI: I beg your pardon.

ROSE: Not really blackmail. What's the word! (She attempts, and fails, to snap her fingers.) Like when someone has something you want—like hostage taking!

SARAH: You mean ransom? Extortion?

JIMROY: We don't want to get *too* fanciful about this.

CRUZZI (mulling): And do you think that—

ROSE: It happens all the time. In books. I read quite a lot of books—mysteries, espionage, that sort of thing. You see, Nadeau isn't a big place and there's not a lot going on—

SARAH: So what do you think will happen, Rose?

ROSE: I think whoever it is, well, will try to contact us. Sell us back what . . . used to belong to *us*.

CRUZZI: For an inflated price, of course.

SARAH: Of course.

JIMROY (addressing Rose, now, with respect): And you think it's someone here? One of us? In this hotel?

SARAH: What we could do is go through the symposium list—

JIMROY: Precisely my idea. As a matter of fact, I've brought along the registration list, and, well, if it's not too late—

SARAH: We're all awake now anyway.

ROSE: I'm wide awake.

CRUZZI: What are there—sixty names?

SARAH: Sixty-seven. Take away the four of us, *and I think we might safely do that,* that's sixty-three.

JIMROY: Shall we begin? (He waves the sheets.)

ROSE (thrilled): Yes. Begin.

CRUZZI: Might as well.

JIMROY (reading in alphabetical order): Aldington, Michael J.

CRUZZI: Afraid I can't quite place—

ROSE (without a moment's hesitation): The one with the pink shirt. Lovely silver cufflinks and the—

SARAH: From Alberta. Michael's straight as an arrow, can't be Michael.

JIMROY: Cross off Aldington. (He gropes for a pencil, then remembers he is in pyjamas.)

SARAH: Here. (She holds out a pencil.)

JIMROY: Thank you.

Director's Note: The handing over of the pencil must be done so that the audience understands that Sarah and Jimroy have broken through to some sort of understanding. Jimroy's voice has lost its hostility; he has surrendered his privately held fantasy of Sarah, as well as his perverse anger at the loss of his fantasy. His hand, grasping the pencil, trembles; Sarah's smile, at first provisional, indicates a measure, at least, of this transformation.

SARAH (meaningfully): You're welcome.

ROSE: Who's next?

JIMROY: Anders, Peter. He's the one with the jowly face. A bit of a schemer.

CRUZZI: Anders. I think he was one of the ones involved in the discussion tonight. He seemed most indignant, and that might indicate—

SARAH: I guess we can cross him off then.

ROSE: Of course, you can't be absolutely sure, just because he was a little—

CRUZZI: What do we know about him?

SARAH: Not much.

JIMROY: I'll put a question mark for Anders. Barcross? Susan Barcross.

ROSE: She's the one with the suede boots.

JIMROY: Feisty.

CRUZZI: Pleasant woman.

SARAH: Bright.

JIMROY: Cross her off?

SARAH: Might as well.

JIMROY: Herb Block. I suppose he's safe. He's only been working on Swann since last summer.

SARAH: You can cross him off.

JIMROY: Sydney Buswell?

SARAH: Buswell! That paranoid—

CRUZZI: Nevertheless it would be ludicrous—

ROSE: True.

JIMROY: Cross him off?

SARAH: Yes.

JIMROY: Off. Butler? Jane Butler?

SARAH: Jane Butler. Isn't she the one—

ROSE: Green tweed suit. Little orange scarf. Lots of blush.

CRUZZI: The one who asked about semi-colons?

JIMROY: Right. From Montreal.

SARAH: She'd never—

JIMROY: Off?

ROSE: *Maybe* a question mark. Sometimes the most innocent—

JIMROY: Question mark? All right, question mark. Byford.

SARAH: Tony Byford. With the hair. (She holds up her hands to suggest an outsize Afro.)

CRUZZI: Charming man. Not the sort at all.

ROSE: Awfully polite. He complimented me on—

SARAH: Cross off Tony. Who next?

JIMROY: Carrington, Richard. Isn't he from—?

SARAH: I vaguely remember. In my workshop—

CRUZZI: Moustache? I can't quite place—

JIMROY: Question mark? We can always go back . . .

Director's Note: The voices become indistinguishable, but the scene continues a few seconds longer. The late hour and the curious impromptu nature of this mini-symposium demand a surreal treatment. MUSIC overrides the voices, almost drowning them out. A burst of laughter comes through, indicating the charged air. Jimroy is seen, stroking off names, his mouth curved into a smile. Rose, cross-legged on her bed, is slicing the air and expressing reservation. Sarah gestures, makes a point, laughs. Cruzzi, his legs elegantly crossed, shrugs, speaks, smiles ruefully, signals to Jimroy to continue. VOICES grow increasingly indistinct, then fade completely. Dissolve.

Fade to: Interior of Sarah's room. Early morning.

A few bars of light enter the bedroom. Sarah is seen sleeping on her side. Rose is sprawled on her back, asleep, her mouth wide open. Cruzzi sleeps in the armchair, his collar unbuttoned, his tie loose, one foot on the end of a bed. Jimroy is curled on the floor with Rose's dressing-gown pulled over him. The registration list, covered with pencil markings, is spread on the floor beside him. SOUND: a telephone ringing.

SARAH (jerking awake, she gropes blindly for the telephone and croaks into the receiver): Hello. Hello. Yes this is . . . Stephen! . . . Yes. . . . No . . . Fine, honestly . . . Yes. (She slides languorously down under the covers with the phone cradled next to her face.) Of course! . . . No, she's fine, just fine. (She pats her stomach, smiling.) Not complaining one bit. She loves travelling. No . . . no . . . yes, it's . . . lonely here, too. I know. (She looks around the room, takes in Cruzzi, Rose, Jimroy.) No, really . . . Yes . . . Me too, you know I do. (She laughs.) . . . What can I say? I know . . . me too . . . I promise, yes . . . Bye. (She replaces the phone. Across the room Cruzzi is seen smiling with his eyes closed; Rose is attentive, at attention, but pretending to sleep; Jimroy shuts his eyes grimly.)

CRUZZI (rising from his chair, almost crippled with stiffness, and stepping across Jimroy on his way to the bathroom): Good morning, comrades.

ROSE (singing out): Good morning.

JIMROY: It's morning. (He regards the sun coming through the window with pleasure.)

SARAH: Anyone for breakfast? (She reaches for the phone.)

ROSE: I could eat a horse.

SARAH (into phone): Three full breakfasts. The Bay Street Specials, orange juice, bacon, eggs, toast, coffee. One wheat cereal with double milk, also double orange juice. (She sits up and stretches.)

Cut to: Interior of Sarah's room. Breakfast time.

Sarah and Rose sit on the edge of the bed with the breakfast table in front of them. Across from them, seated on the other bed, are Jimroy and Cruzzi. Jimroy, with a smudge of egg adhering to his chin, is rechecking his list.

JIMROY (businesslike): A quick rundown then. With single question marks we've got Anders, Carrington, Gorham, Loftus, Norchuk, Oldfield, Skelton, and Tolliver.

ROSE: Urbanski? What happened to Urbanski?

JIMROY: Who?

SARAH: The one from Los Angeles. With the short socks. I think we decided he was okay.

CRUZZI: I must have drifted off at that point.

JIMROY: And—with *double* question marks we have—Crozier, Hall, and Webborn.

SARAH: And?

JIMROY: *Triple* question mark—Lang.

CRUZZI: Willard Lang. I *did* drift off.

JIMROY: I've never trusted the man. One of us—today—should ask him if he still has *his* copy of *Swann's Songs.*

SARAH: I'll volunteer.

ROSE: Wouldn't it be funny if—

SARAH: If what, Rose?

ROSE: Well, if here we were, all sixty-seven of us. All of us here to talk about Mary Swann's poems, and what if—what if not a single one of us has a copy of her book?

SARAH: That would be strange all right.

JIMROY: Statistically speaking . . .

CRUZZI: It's possible, I suppose.

JIMROY (bitterly): Of course some of us *came* here with a copy and—

CRUZZI: Well, my four copies are certainly gone. All four.

ROSE: And mine. I don't know how I could have—

SARAH (spooning up cereal): Luckily I've got mine.

CRUZZI (delighted): You do! I hadn't realized that you—

SARAH: Well, not with me. I didn't bring it, as a matter of fact. I've lent it to a friend, and he hasn't returned it yet.

Director's Note: Sarah's face—and her voice—must convey the warmth of affection. She stretches, smiles, bites her lower lip on the word *friend*.

CRUZZI: You're sure he *will* return it—your friend?

SARAH: Oh, Brownie would never lose a book. He's in the business, rare books. Books—(she stops to think)—books to Brownie are holy. Other things he's careless about, but books, well, with book's he's—

JIMROY: Where is it? The copy he borrowed? (He asks this in an abrupt, almost rude tone.)

SARAH: Where?

JIMROY: What I mean is, can you get your hands on it? Today?

SARAH (doubtfully): He works out of Chicago, my friend. Well, more than just a friend, actually . . .

JIMROY: I wonder if you should warn him. Make sure it's safe with him. It may be the last copy we have.

CRUZZI: A good idea.

SARAH: I suppose I *could* phone him. (She smiles at the thought.) Just to make sure. I could phone him at work. (She looks at her watch.) He's always there by eight o'clock, a real workaholic, that was part of the . . . he was always working.

ROSE (handing Sarah the phone): Here.

SARAH (looking around at the others): Maybe . . . maybe I should . . . make it a private call. He's sort of . . .

ROSE: I'm going back to my room anyway to get dressed. It's getting late.

CRUZZI (tactfully): I should be going too. (He rubs his chin.) A shave, perhaps, is in order.

JIMROY (gathering up papers): I'm going to have to duck my way back. (He gestures at his pyjamas.)

ROSE: Me too. (She laughs. Jimroy flinches, then follows her out.)

The instant they are gone Sarah takes up the telephone. She makes an effort to compose herself, strokes back her hair, breathes deeply, then dials with almost childish deliberation.

SARAH: Hello. Hello, it's Sarah Maloney. May I speak to Brownie please. Mr. Brown. Yes . . . Oh . . . (Disappointed): Well, what time will he be in? . . . Are you sure? . . . Well, do you know when he's expected back? I was anxious to get hold of him today. Something's come up, business . . . No, I don't think so, I have to speak to him confidentially, because . . . You don't happen to know where he is at the moment? . . . No, I'll be happy to hold on . . . (She hums while she waits, taps her fingers on the table, smiles.) Yes. But *someone* there must know where he is. I mean, hasn't he left some kind of . . . I see. Yes. But he must have something written on his appointment calendar . . . Yes, I'll hold . . . (She rubs nervously at her hair, twirling a strand around a finger.) Yes. Is that all? . . . Just that one word . . . I see. Symposium. (She puts down the phone and for a minute sits on the edge of the bed, unable to move.) Symposium.

Fade to: Interior of the meeting room. Morning.

Members of the symposium are taking their seats. The mood is congenial and relaxed, with a distinct sense of anticipation.

BUTTER MOUTH: . . . running a bit late this morning—

MERRY EYES: . . . not like Lang to be—

TOP KNOT: What a night! I'm so goddamn hungover—

SILVER CUFFLINKS: This is what I've really been waiting for—

CLIPBOARD: . . . and this is why I came, if you want to know the truth—

CRUZZI (to Jimroy who is sitting next to him): Well, do you think it's really going to happen?

JIMROY (deeply sceptical): He's promised to *talk* about the love poems, but as far as actually *giving up* the poems themselves—

ROSE (sitting beside them): There's Sarah now. (Calls): Over here. I've saved you a seat.

SARAH (dazed): It's a quarter to ten. I thought I'd be late.

ROSE (conspiratorially): Did you get through? To your . . . friend?

SARAH: No. (Her face is stiff with incomprehension, and she speaks as though in a trance.) He's . . . out of town.

ROSE: You can always try later.

SARAH: No. (She pauses, gives a violent shake of her head.) I don't think so.

SILVER CUFFLINKS (loudly): Hey, what's up? I thought Willard was supposed to start at 9:30.

CRINKLED FOREHEAD (at lectern): Ladies and gentlemen, fellow scholars. Professor Lang appears to have been delayed. If you'll just be patient, I'm sure he'll be along in a minute or two.

WATTLED GENT: . . . bugger slept in—
GINGER PONYTAIL: . . . not Lang, he's always right on the button—
GREEN TWEED SUIT: Personally, I can't sit too long in these chairs—
WISTFUL DEMEANOUR: What's a love poem to one ear is just a—
WIMPY GRIN: . . . bird calls and mating dances—
CLIPBOARD: . . . a tad elitist, but he's managed to trash those elements most cherished—
GREEN TWEED SUIT: Almost time for the coffee break—
CRINKLED FOREHEAD (stepping up to lectern again): We've just telephoned up to Professor Lang's room, and since there's no answer, we assume he's on his way. Please bear with us for a few minutes longer.

As though a signal has been given, the meeting room falls silent. All eyes are fixed on the empty lectern and on the clock behind it. The only sounds are throat clearing, coughing, sighing, and shuffling of feet. It is now 10:00 A.M. There is some rustling of papers, an air of expectancy. The clock does not actually tick, but there is a distinct *sense* of a clock ticking. The seconds pass, then the minutes. It is now 10:02. Crinkled Forehead once again approaches the lectern.

CRINKLED FOREHEAD: I'm sure any minute now—
WOMAN WITH TURBAN: Has anyone looked in the coffee shop?
CRINKLED FOREHEAD: He's not there. We checked.
SARAH (rising): Perhaps one of us should go to see if—
JIMROY (on his feet): I'll gladly volunteer. I think we've been sitting quite long enough. (He heads for the doorway.)
ROSE: I'll go along with you, Mr. Jimroy. Keep you company.
SARAH: Maybe I will too. Might as well.
CRUZZI: I'll just—
CRINKLED FOREHEAD: Well, I'll just tag along too, perhaps.
WOMAN WITH TURBAN: Might as well join in—
BLUE-SPOTTED TIE: Why don't I come along—?
CRINKLED FOREHEAD: He may be ill.

A group of ten or twelve rapidly assembles and walks along in lock step toward the bank of elevators. MUSIC: a skirling tune, strings mainly, with some bagpipes. The small, silent swarm squeezes through the corridor. An elevator arrives, and the group, acting almost as a single being, pours itself inside. CAMERA then picks up the group inside the elevator, where there is total silence except for:

JIMROY (in vice-admiral's voice): Twenty-fourth floor, I believe. Right down the hall from my room.
CRUZZI: Right. (He presses the button, and the elevator swiftly rises.)
ROSE (gasping): We're here.

The group exits, with Sarah in the lead. Long CAMERA shot of the silent march down the corridor.

SARAH (stopping before the door): This is it. (She knocks. There is no response.)
WOMAN WITH TURBAN: Try again.
SARAH (knocking again): Nothing. (She puts her ear against the door, listening and knocking again. She motions to Cruzzi to listen too.)

Cruzzi presses his ear to the door, listens, and nods, then steps aside for Crinkled Forehead who repeats the procedure.

ROSE (pushing forward, placing her ear to the door): I hear something. (She holds up a finger for silence.)

Director's Note: From the distance comes the strangled sound of Lang beating on the wall and calling out. His cries gradually grow louder and more wild, but they are also faintly theatrical and subtly exaggerated.

LANG: Help! Help!
ROSE (to others): Did you hear that? Someone said help. (She tries the door.)
LANG: Help! Get me out of here!
ROSE: It's Professor Lang.

Cut to: Interior of Lang's hotel room. Same time as above.
    CAMERA close-up of the bathroom door, which is tied with a curtain cord, the doorknob looped and secured to the knob of the clothes closet next to it.

LANG (from inside the bathroom): Get me out of here!

Director's Note: Because the employment of the curtain cord, a staple in crime films, is intended here to be an ironic, self-referential nod in the direction of the genre, the CAMERA lingers on the subject for several seconds before moving into the room and focusing on the intruder in his maintenance uniform. He is a short man, agile, with curly hair, busily stuffing papers into a pillowcase, the same man Rose Hindmarch encountered on the stairway the evening before.

Cut to: The corridor. Same time as above.

ROSE: I think we should force the door.
CRUZZI (in reasonable tones): I'm sure we can get a key from the desk—
CRINKLED FOREHEAD: Someone telephone down. I'll just—
WOMAN WITH TURBAN: What's he saying in there?
JIMROY (always a man to honour questions): He's still saying "Help," I believe.
ROSE: The only thing to do is break the door down.
SARAH: Rose has a point—
BLUE-SPOTTED TIE: If we all leaned together—
JIMROY (vice-admirally): One, two, three, push. (Though they all push at once, it is a poorly executed move, almost comically clumsy, and the door fails to give way.)
LANG (muffled): Help! Help!
ROSE: One more try. One and a two and a three—

Crinkled Forehead returns with three bellhops, one of them carrying a key. MUSIC: a loud orchestral crash, the sort of music that, in western films, traditionally accompanies the arrival of the posse.

Cut to: Interior of Lang's room. Same time as above.
CAMERA close-up of intruder who hurries with papers, hearing the commotion in the corridor. He looks to left and right, goes to the window and wedges it open. For an instant he regards the street twenty-four storeys below. He pushes the bag through the window

and reluctantly lets it drop just as Jimroy, Cruzzi, Sarah, and the others crowd into the room. The intruder ducks neatly behind the curtain, the same curtain from which the cord has been taken.

LANG: Help! I'm in the bathroom!
ROSE: He's in the bathroom. Look, a curtain cord!
LANG: Get me out of here.

Director's Note: The excitement as the members of the symposium cluster around the bathroom door is intense, and not one of them notices the faintly stagy sound of Lang's voice. Everyone is talking at once, and Jimroy is tugging at the curtain cord.

Cut to: Exterior of building. The CAMERA picks up the pillow case as it falls through the air; some of its contents fly out as it descends, mixing with the snow and carried by the wind into the street.

Cut to: Interior of Lang's room. Same time as above.

LANG (staggering from bathroom; he is wearing undershorts and a towel and appears agitated): I was just having a bath and . . .
CRUZZI (looking around): Looks like a burglary.
ROSE: Check the closets. Under the bed—
LANG (growing hysterical). For God's sake, never mind that! My papers . . .
SARAH: What exactly's been taken?
LANG (wildly histrionic): My papers! My years of work!
JIMROY: . . . got everything I suppose.
ROSE: The pillow case . . . a pillow case is missing!
CRUZZI: . . . made the most of his moment—
LANG: The love poems. Don't tell me the love poems—(He is waving his arms extravagantly and wailing, but his face is watchful.) I had the love poems over there, on the dresser. The originals!
GINGER PONYTAIL: Take it easy, fellow, take it easy.
BLUE-SPOTTED TIE: Give the man breathing room.
MAN WITH OUTSIZE AFRO: Jesus, he's in shock, we'd better get a medic up here.

ROSE: *And* the hotel detective.

CRINKLED FOREHEAD: Water! Get him some water.

WOMAN WITH TURBAN (to Lang): Here. Take my raincoat. I insist.

Director's Note: It is important that the confusion in this scene (which lasts less than a minute) be palpable; it must obscure and animate at the same time, filling the room like a blizzard and numbing the perceptions of those who are acting and reacting. The Swannians have gathered around Lang, and they are all talking at once. Not one of them observes the intruder as he slips from behind the curtain and walks nonchalantly past them, into the corridor, glancing back over his shoulder just before he disappears. Only Willard Lang, struggling into the raincoat and babbling incoherently, catches, and holds, the intruder's gaze for the briefest of moments. The look between them is shrewd and culpable—and ambiguous enough to puzzle the sort of reflective movie-goers who like to dissect the variables of a story over a cup of coffee on their way home from their local cinemas.

Cut to: Corridor. Same time. Long shot of intruder running toward exit stairs. CAMERA close-up on Sarah, stepping into corridor, regarding running figure.

SARAH: Brownie? (She whispers his name, and then repeats it more loudly, even recklessly.) Brownie.

Director's Note: The intruder—it is uncertain whether or not he hears his name—dives through the exit door, leaving CAMERA on Sarah's face. She looks first puzzled, then wistful, then knowing. Her mouth opens a final time, mouthing the word "Brownie," then closes abruptly. She closes her eyes, sways slightly, then opens her eyes widely. One hand goes to her mouth, rests there.

Fade to: Interior of meeting room. Later in the day.

A meeting is in session, but there is no one at the lectern and no one, seemingly, in charge. People are seated in a sort of circle, speaking out, offering up remembered lines of poetry, laboriously reassembling one of Mary Swann's poems. Sarah is writing, a clipboard on her knee.

Director's Final Note: The faces of the actors have been subtly transformed. They are seen joined in a ceremonial act of reconstruction, perhaps even an act of creation. There need be no suggestion that any one of them will become less selfish in the future, less cranky, less consumed with thoughts of tenure and academic glory, but each of them has, for the moment at least, transcended personal concerns.

BUSWELL: We all agree, then, on the first line.

WATTLED GENT (quoting): "It sometimes happens when looking for"

MERRY EYES: Yes, that's it. Did you get that down?

SARAH (writing in notebook): "It sometimes happens when looking for." Are you sure?

MAN WITH OUTSIZE AFRO: Second line?

WISTFUL DEMEANOUR: It's a run-on line, I'm almost sure. "It sometimes happens when looking for/ Lost objects, a book, a picture or"

CRINKLED FOREHEAD: That's it, I'm positive.

SARAH: Close, anyway. What comes next?

WOMAN WITH TURBAN: "a book, a picture or/A coin or spoon."

GREEN TWEED SUIT: Wait! Is that "spoon or coin" or "coin or spoon"?

BUTTER MOUTH: "Coin or spoon" I think. Yes.

JIMROY (quoting): "That something falls across the mind—"

CRUZZI: "Not quite a shadow but what a shadow would be."

SARAH (looking up): "In a place that lacked light."

MUSIC: an organ, dense, heavy. The words of the poem grow indistinct; only the rhythm remains strong.

BUSWELL: "As though the lost things have withdrawn/ Into themselves—"

PALE SUEDE BOOTS: "books returned—"

JIMROY: "To paper or wood or thought"

CRINKLED FOREHEAD: "Coins and spoons to simple ores"

WOMAN WITH TURBAN: "Lustreless and without history"

BLUE-SPOTTED TIE: "Waiting out of sight."

MUSIC continues; CAMERA shot of photograph of Mary Swann; CREDITS roll across the photo as the voices continue.

SARAH: "And becoming part of a larger loss"
CRUZZI: "Without a name"
WOMAN WITH TURBAN: "Or definition or form"
JIMROY: "Not unlike what touches us"
CRUZZI: "In moments of shame."

LOST THINGS
By Mary Swann

It sometimes happens when looking for
Lost objects, a book, a picture or
A coin or spoon,
That something falls across the mind—
Not quite a shadow but what a shadow would be
In a place that lacked light.

As though the lost things have withdrawn
Into themselves, books returned
To paper or wood or thought,
Coins and spoons to simple ores,
Lustreless and without history,
Waiting out of sight

And becoming part of a larger loss
Without a name
Or definition or form
Not unlike what touches us
In moments of shame.

Carol Shields

The Republic of Love

'Mythical and modern, ironic and moving, exhilarating and melancholy. A love-surveying love story that is enticingly seductive.'
Times Literary Supplement

Fay is a folklorist whose passion for mermaids provides her with a sense of continuity with the past. But is Fay in danger of using the past to escape the present? Of forsaking spontaneity for security? Tom, the host of a late-night radio show, is certainly spontaneous. If Fay is in danger of loving too little, Tom may have loved too well. Married and divorced three times before his fortieth birthday, he hopes desperately that next time around he will at last make the right choice. For both Fay and Tom, falling in love at first sight is at once an immense surprise and the cause of not a little trepidation.

'Carol Shields's novel is a hymn to the transformative power of romantic love. First *Mary Swann* and then *Happenstance* revealed her to be a writer of huge talent. *The Republic of Love* suggests that she is simply getting better. No longer can our perception of contemporary Canadian fiction begin and end with Margaret Atwood.'
Literary Review

'A novel that's so engrossing it makes you want to retire to a squashy sofa until you reach the end. Vividly fresh . . . glittering and spangled with fabulous surprises.'
Sunday Times

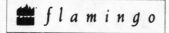 *flamingo*

Carol Shields

Happenstance

'The biggest pleasure remains Shields' prose, at once dense and delicate. Her great strength is her ability to capture small moments and make them important . . . Shields displays in her careful delineation of her characters a tenderness for the ordinary which shines through the sheer cleverness of her work.'   *Literary Review*

'A celebration of marriage as historical accident, *Happenstance* makes a delightful portrait of a partnership, full of quirky humour.'   *The Times*

'The beautiful irony of *Happenstance* is that its novels are both bound together and held apart by the strength of the marriage they describe.'   *Harpers & Queen*

'I highly recommend *Happenstance*. Both stories are funny – but compassionately so. Crucially, Carol Shields allows all the characters dignity. This is a tender, lovely book, about people who need each other. It is also superbly told.'   *Marie Claire*

'With dazzling deftness Shields demonstrates the alienation innate in the most loving relationships . . . *Happenstance* is a remarkable, perceptive and painfully accurate work that yields more with each reading.'   *Sunday Times*

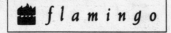